James Girls

F.J. Stevens

JAMES GIRLS

Dedication

To my angels: My parents, Richard and Elnora showed me what love looks like and taught me to believe in myself; my brilliant grandmother Joanna inspired me to always aspire to new things; my beautiful baby sister Jessica taught me to be fearless and push forward no matter what's in front of me.

You are my inspiration. Shining examples of intelligence, grace, courage and strength. I have learned so much from each of you and I can only hope to take a fraction of what you are to make a better me.

Until we meet in heaven, I'll be down here doing my best to make you all proud.

Acknowledgements

I owe a tremendous debt of gratitude to my good friend Lisa Wright, my sounding board and cheerleader. You kept me encouraged through every step of my insane writing process and I'm truly grateful for your support.

To my editor, Rob Bignell; my cover artist, web designer and creative partner Thomas Holmes, Joy Bhattachrjee, Kariz Marcel, you are exceptional at what you do and you've made this process so much easier for me.

Claude, Dana, Ladonya, Lauren, Mela and Olivia, I thank you for your time and your invaluable feedback on the story. You kept me in line.

To my family: My son, my gift and my very best friend Steven. You truly make me a better person and I love you with everything I have. Dana, my sister and my biggest supporter I thank you for keeping my back. Richie my little bro I thank you for always being there whenever for whatever I need and Aunt Joann you keep me encouraged, grounded and thankful. You remind me of my purpose and that means everything.

Many, many thanks to you all.

Prologue

I remember, I was still trembling when I walked into the doctor's office that day. Unannounced and seriously on the verge of a nervous breakdown. Although I'd never been to a shrink, if there was ever a day for some psychological intercession that was definitely the day.

I hadn't slept in over 24 hours. Too scared to close my eyes I guess. Didn't want to replay what I'd seen. But I couldn't get the horrific scene out of my head no matter how desperately I wanted to.

Shaken to the core, I had absolutely no clue what to do or where to go, but I needed to get things off my chest before I blurted them out to the wrong person and had my life played out in a tabloid.

Fishing through my wallet on the red eye flight from hell that morning, I ran across Dr. Cartwright's business card. She was - and still is – my best friend Carmen's psychologist. Carmen had been bothering me to sit on this woman's couch for *at least* a year, but I wasn't into it. I didn't need it. And I was convinced she was only going because counseling was the new it thing for us rich black folks to do.

And Dr. Cartwright was the new go to counselor for those dreadfully messy socialites on the DC Housewives reality tv show; something that I'm sure influenced Carmen's decision to seek help for her yet to be disclosed "disorder".

Anyway, I was desperate that day. I needed to download on someone and the situation at hand was way too sensitive to share with anyone, without assurance of the strictest confidentiality. So, several frantic phone calls later I had an appointment with the celebrity it doctor and I was ready to spill.

My appointment was her last of the day. After business hours and at double her already ridiculous hourly rate, considering she had to cancel a business dinner to accommodate me. But it didn't matter. I would have paid a mint to make some sense out of the foolishness they burned into my brain.

I walked right past the receptionist desk toward the doctor's office. The skinny blonde receptionist followed me with her clipboard in tow, yelling for me to wait, but by the time she finished instructing me on what I needed to do before I could see the doctor, I'd already gone in to see the doctor. And closed the door behind me.

Dr. Cartwright noticed me and stood, extending her hand and a plastic, albeit friendly smile.

"Hello, Mrs. Coleman?"

I shook her hand, trying to hide my nerves. "Yes Dr. Cartwright. Thank you so much for taking this appointment. I understand your schedule is tight and I really appreciate you accommodating me after business hours."

"Well, after my assistant told me how many times you called, insisting to be seen, I figured this was an appointment I should take."

"Yes, I'm so, so sorry about that. It's just...I really needed to see someone."

She noticed my trembling hands and offered some aid. "Please, have a seat. Can I get you a drink of water?"

"No. No thank you, I'm fine."

"Alright, so tell me, what brings you so urgently to my office?"

"Honestly, I'm not even sure where to start."

"Well, let's make it easy. How about we start at the beginning."

"Um. Yeah, ok. Well..."

I can laugh about it now, but my initial response was pretty embarrassing. I started off by telling her when and where I was born. To which she replied, "Ok, well maybe not that far back."

We giggled but my ignorance of proper counseling protocol actually broke the ice a little. After that, I unbuttoned my blazer, unclenched my Birkin and got a little more comfortable.

There was much to discuss. Abandonment issues, emotional detachments, inferiority complexes, depression. Plenty of billable hours to accrue. I, Melissa Delores James-Coleman am the product of a torrid affair that my mother had with her very married and very white boss who I'm told, denied me from birth, as if my honey blonde hair and ice blue eyes were some sort of mystic occurrence.

I never really fit in, anywhere, so I was often left out. Too white for these and too black for them. So I built up a wall, worked my *ass* off and designed a perfect life for myself. A high life that I deserve.

I scratched and clawed my way from one of the worst housing projects in DC to one the wealthiest suburbs in America and along that journey I experienced extremes to the likes most could only imagine.

The highs were amazing, monumental even, but the lows were so deeply wretched that at times, I questioned my very existence.

Less than 24 hours before I sat in the good Dr.'s comfy brown leather chair, I was right there, at my lowest. I uncovered a secret that would send my entire world into a tailspin. And it was a good thing Dr. Cartwright was bound by confidentiality because my revelation was truly the stuff the $2.99 tabloids in the grocery stores were made for.

Void of the energy to exorcise *all* of my demons, I hit the fast forward on my life story and came a little closer to the problem at hand, my loving husband.

I started at the beginning. Gave her the whole sordid history from the cold winter afternoon we met through to the present day, where my nerves were so shot I could barely keep my lunch down.

When I got to the tragic end, all the good doctor could say to me was, "I see." Then she cleared her schedule for the next day and a half. Suddenly I was patient priority number one.

*****

Today is the day I bury my best friend, the love of my life. I still can't believe this is really happening. Even with all the shit Melvin was doing in the streets, I just didn't see this coming. He was nobody's angel. I know that. But he was a good man, and I loved him with my whole heart.

People never saw the Melvin I saw. The kind and sweet, generous man I loved. The man that helped his kids with their homework every evening and put his baby girl in the bathtub every night.

No matter where he was and what was going on in the hood, he came in every night at 7:00 sharp, bathed and tucked her in. That's the man I loved, and that's the man they took from me. My best friend. My family.

The day he died, I was busy packing suitcases, preparing for our vacation. This year it was the beautiful island of Turks and Caicos. You know, the island where Lisa Raye's husband was the king or bishop or whatever he was. It was our annual family trip. We'd already done Disney, Great Wolf, Vegas; we had the New York City experience, historical Atlanta, all the best beaches, and a few other American tourist traps on the east coast, but this would be our first time leaving U.S. territory.

Melvin was afraid to fly, so every year we saddled up the kids and hit the road. We'd drive for hours with the kids screaming in the backseat, filthy gas station bathrooms and greasy fast food. But not this year. I fought long and hard for this trip. I had a couple valium and a few miniature bottles of cognac tucked away in my suitcase, so he'd be good. And even if he wasn't he'd just have to suck it up and deal with it.

Myrtle Beach was a beautiful place for a family vacation, and strolling Miami Beach with my girl Tina was always a good time, however, I was ready for whiter sands and bluer waters. It was going down.

We had just gotten our passports rushed in the mail and were supposed to leave the next day. The kids were beyond excited because this was their first time flying. MJ and Brandy were bragging to their friends and Mandy was just excited to get on an airplane with her daddy. Fast forward to today, I'm struggling to get them dressed so they can go and say good bye to their daddy for the last time.

Looking out the window I see all his stupid ass boys, poppin bottles and building a memorial amidst all the other trash on the ground. Champagne bottles and packs of cigarettes. Melvin didn't smoke *or* drink. Everybody walkin around with my husband's face plastered on their chests, all puffed up like they gon do something. Please.

What's really a trip, is that with all the bullshit mourning they're standin out there doing, not one of them really liked Melvin. They envied him, most were afraid of him, and they all respected him, but I can't say that I knew one guy out there that really, truly liked him.

They were all there for the money. For what he could do for them. And that was especially true for his right hand man, Daye. *That* bitch. I swear my eye twitches every time I hear his name.

Fridaye Mbulango, a.k.a. Daye, was Melvin's best friend and they'd known each other since they were kids. He was the only person in the world – other than myself – that Melvin really trusted, which *killed* me because as far as I was concerned Daye was the last person Melvin should have ever put his trust in.

I'd heard so many stories about him over the years. Stories that if true, would make this man one of the most conniving, jealous, cowardly snakes you would ever meet. There were no bodies on him. He wasn't a killer, but he was dangerous just the same.

I saw how he looked at Melvin sometimes, and the look in his eyes had nothing to do with love or loyalty. There was something dark behind his beady eyes. They were too close together or something. Shifty. The way he talked to Melvin was crazy, too. The smart ass remarks, the sarcastic undertone. I shut his ass down every chance I got, and Melvin hated it, but he knew better than to check me on it.

I saw Daye's ambition even if Melvin chose to ignore it, and I knew it was only a matter of time before they'd part ways. Until that day, my antenna was up, my eyes and ears were wide the hell open on Fridaye Mbulango.

Today, my sixth sense is on fire. The streets are already talkin, and the word is some Jamaicans from Silver Spring killed my husband. I'm sure it's no coincidence that Daye has a sudden affinity for yellow sports cars and beef patties.

His new "piece", as he calls her, is a tall Jamaican amazon named Jenny, with dirty blonde dreads and a whole wardrobe full of colorful spandex. Oh, and neon pumps. How could I forget those lime green pumps? Ugh.

He brought her to the house a couple times. We chatted. Once. I didn't like her. She looked shifty, too. And oily.

The real issue, the one that gives me the most pause, is Melvin's been gone almost three weeks now and I've only seen Daye once. In passing. He hasn't called or stopped by to check on me and the kids. His God-kids. I'm still mad I let Melvin talk me into that bullshit. Anyway, the one time I saw Daye he couldn't even look me in the eye. I know something's up.

Everybody says he's just hurting and doesn't know how to deal with what happened. But that ain't it. It's something more. I feel it in my bones. I know he's involved in my husband's death somehow, someway and I'm damned sure gon get to the bottom of it. But first thing's first. I gotta go bury my husband. Lord give me strength…

Love at First Sight

Football Sundays in January were especially frigid. During the way too long walk from her car to the side entrance of Skins Stadium Missy could see her breath in front of her face as she cursed at Carmen for dragging her out of her warm bed on her only day of rest.

At the time Carmen was dating Roman Elliott, a first-string kicker for the Skins that she was crushing on real hard. It was the biggest game of the year against Dallas and the game had been sold out for months, but as Roman's new main squeeze Carmen had just been granted the privilege of enjoying the games from the sky box with the player's wives. That was the detail that got Missy up and out of the house.

Missy entered the suite, and as usual all eyes were on her. Hands down she was the most stunning woman in the place. Dressed casually in Second Skin denim, the latest Louboutin spiked tennis shoes, and an oversized red leather Chloe bag, she was football stadium chic. Her long blonde hair was pulled back into a neat ponytail, and her makeup was subtle but flawless.

The only jewelry she wore was a pair of small diamond studs – very modest for Missy, but she knew she couldn't over do it for the athletes. They'd take anything to bed, but the girls they *kept* were the natural beauties that were somewhat stylish but didn't look *too* into the bling. She knew the game. Missy had been courted by enough athletes to have learned all the do's and don'ts of dating them and she conducted herself accordingly.

The accommodations in the sky box were fabulous. Gourmet foods and desserts were catered, and the champagne was flowing. There was, however, a lot of tension in the room. So much so, that very little attention was actually being paid to the game.

There was a mix of NFL wives, girlfriends and several soon-to-be baby mamas. You know, the ones that would never get the ring, just child support and bragging rights. Silly groupies. They got it all wrong. But to each girl her skanky own, she thought.

There were cliques in every corner. Plenty of side eyes being given, snarky remarks, and mean girl giggles echoed throughout the room; messiness that Missy wanted no parts of.

One of the impregnated groupies looked a lot like her little sister's former bff, Cheryl. Cheryl was relegated to former friend because she'd tried to sleep with Brenda's boyfriend Melvin back in high school. Missy remembered her little sister being put on a year of probation when she took hold of Cheryl after that info was leaked.

Missy suddenly realized she'd stared a little too long. She'd been spotted. "Dammit!" she thought.

"Missy! Missy is that you?!"

Cheryl was coming her way and there was no escaping. So she sucked it up. "Heeey! Cheryl right? How are you?"

"Oh I'm excellent boo boo." Cheryl smiled wide as she rubbed her several days' overdue baby bump. "Due any day now, but you know I couldn't miss my baby daddy's first game against them boys."

"Oh, ok. Who is your *baby daddy*?" Missy immediately regretted the question. One, because it was crass, and two because she really didn't care to keep the conversation going. "I'm sorry, that was so rude of me."

"Girl please. I ain't trippin off that. Trey my baby daddy!"

"Trey Simmons?"

"Yeah, that's my *boo thang*. You know he ain't want me comin out the house today, but I told him I was *not* gon miss this game. Okay!" She sucked her tongue hard, letting out that loud pop that turned heads and made Missy cringe.

Missy thought, now who does girl think she's fooling? Trey Simmons was a third-string running back with bad knees and a reputation for being one of the biggest man whores on the DC social scene. Though he was engaged to the daughter of a very prominent DC politician, he'd seemingly fathered children with every woman in DC *but* his lovely fiancé of six years.

Trey had a penchant for unprotected groupie sex, which was the reason Cheryl was in the building, standing there rubbing her belly and cutting her eyes at Trey's fiancé who was sitting with his parents on the other side of the room. It was all so messy. Missy was ready to step off.

"Oh, ok. Gotta support your *baby daddy*. Well it was good seeing you sweetie." Missy grabbed her drink from the bar and started to walk over to the other side of the room but Cheryl followed close behind.

"So what you doin up in here girl? Who you fuckin wit?"

"Excuse me? I'm not seeing anyone on the team. I'm here with my girlfriend Carmen, just watching the game."

"Girl please, don't nobody watch the game."

"*I* watch the game."

Cheryl looked up quizzically at the ceiling. "Carmen...Carmen? ...Oh you mean Carmen that went to McKinley Tech? You still hangin wit *her freak ass?*"

Missy scowled at her. Cheryl was the biggest freak in the neighborhood and had earned a reputation all over the city for trickin. She claimed she had "white liver," which was just a whore's medical excuse to keep her legs open.

Cheryl was into girls, threesomes, white guys, whatever paid. Way back in the day the word was for a hundred dollars you could run a train, i.e. gangbang with your homies. And the worst part is she had no shame about it. There was video proof of it. Missy thought, *the nerve.* She needed to be checked.

"Yes, Carmen went to McKinley Tech, and you know you are *real* wrong for that, Cheryl. I *know* you don't want to go *there*...Miss *Choo Choo Train...*"

Cheryl let out the loudest shriek of a laugh, causing the room to turn around and stare. "Uh uh! No you didn't! But it's cool. I'm a freak, but I gits that paper tho." She put her hand up for a high five. Missy disregarded it. Cheryl sighed loudly, slightly embarrassed by the diss but grateful to be in conversation with someone in the suite. She kept talking.

"So where Carmen at? I wanna say hi."

Missy scanned the room desperately hoping to see Carmen, somewhere...anywhere. "I don't know. I thought she was going to the bathroom, but she must have left the suite."

Missy was visibly annoyed that she was stuck talking to this girl. It was clear that none of the other girlfriends or player wives would entertain her, and she had no intention of allowing Cheryl to annoy her for the rest of the game. She looked at her and shook her head, thinking it was amazing what 24 inches of weave, a set of double D implants and a series of ass shots would get you in DC. Apparently knocked up by a baller and chillin in a suite at Skins stadium. Missy made a mental note to curse Carmen's ass *out* for leaving her alone.

As usual, the Washington/Dallas game was tight and came down to the last play. Tied at 24, the game went into overtime, and for the second week in a row Roman kicked the game-winning field goal. He was on a streak. At 38 consecutive field goals he was chasing the all-time NFL record and he reminded everyone, daily.

As the rowdy fans made their exit, Carmen convinced Missy to go down to the player's lounge so she could congratulate Roman on winning another game for the team. Of course, Missy never missed an opportunity to put herself in a position to expand her social circle, so she was all in.

They were sitting at the bar chatting with a couple of the wives when Roman and Ray walked in. The guys were being bombarded with congratulatory greetings when Carmen ran over to Roman, wrapped her arms around his neck and planted a big wet kiss on his lips, purposely interrupting an extra special congrats he was getting from one of the cheerleaders.

"Congratulations baby! You are *so* amazing. And I have something amazing for you too…as soon as I get your fine ass home." She shot the cheerleader a get-the-fuck-away-from-my-man gaze before she rolled her eyes and pulled him away. "Roman, this is my friend Missy I was telling you about. Missy, this is the love of my life, Roman Elliott."

Missy couldn't remember the last time she saw Carmen so giddy. It was kinda nauseating. She extended her hand. "Pleased to meet you, Roman. That was a great game you guys played. You really did your thing out there."

"Well thanks, it's kinda my job." They all laughed at his uncharacteristically modest but slightly snarky remark.

Then Carmen chimed in, giving her very best Marilyn Monroe impression. "And you do your job *so well* Mr. Elliot." She pinned him against the bar and planted another sloppy wet kiss on him. Another exhibition for the salty cheerleader staring at them from the other side of the bar.

Missy and Ray stood by smiling awkwardly and waiting for them to loosen their lip lock. Ray cleared his throat loudly, and Roman pulled himself away, only slightly embarrassed by Carmen's carrying on.

"I'm sorry Missy. This is my buddy Ray."

Before the intro was fully out of Roman's mouth Ray reached for Missy's hand and brought it to his lips for a gentle kiss. "I really can't remember the last time I've seen a woman *so* beautiful."

Missy blushed and batted her eyes, as Ray stood there staring in awe of her. After a brief pause, she said, "Pleased to meet you, Mr. Coleman."

Ray turned back to his friends. "I'm sorry, Carmen, Ro. Will you excuse us?" He took Missy's hand and led her to a corner table on the far side the room.

She followed willingly, but not before turning around and extending a half-hearted apology to Carmen and Roman. "Yes, please excuse us." When they reached Ray's table he summoned a waitress. She walked over with an ice bucket chilling a bottle of Krug and a couple of champagne flutes. Missy smirked as she knew he was about to try to put on the moves. "Ok, Mr. Coleman."

"Ray."

"Ok *Ray*, is there any particular reason why we need privacy right now?"

"Yes. I need to have you to myself right now. I'm sorry, was that rude of me?"

"No, it's fine. I'm just teasing."

Ray stared into her eyes smiling to himself. "Hmm."

"Hmm, what? Why are you staring at me like that?"

"Don't do that."

"Don't do what?"

"Fish for compliments. It's unnecessary."

Missy laughed. "What!"

"You asked me why I'm staring."

"Yes. And?"

"You know that if I answer that question, I'd be forced to compliment you again."

"Ok, *that* is ridiculous."

"Is it? Tell me. How many times a day are you paid a compliment, Miss Missy?"

She blushed. "What? Oh my goodness. What kind of crazy question is that?"

Ray playfully checked his watch. "Go ahead. I'll wait."

She laughed. "I'm not even going to dignify that with an ans—"

Before she could finish her sentence, Ray leaned over and kissed her on the lips. Softly and gently. He pulled away, staring into her sparkling blue eyes with the adoration of a schoolboy.

"Damn, you fine."

Missy gave him a coy smile. "You know; I should slap your face for that."

Ray smiled wide. "But you won't."

He was pouring on the charm and though she tried to keep up a somewhat hard to get posture, Missy didn't mind it at all. The man was fine. She crossed her legs, seductively toward him and ran her fingers through her long ponytail, pulling it to one side. Then she took a dainty sip of her water.

Ray was already smitten. Watching her every move. She was beautiful and graceful. Perfect.

He mumbled, "Umh hmm. You know what you're doing."

"Excuse me?"

"Seriously, I bet you have to beat em off you like fleas, huh?"

Missy smiled. "I do ok."

"You do ok?"

"Yes, I do ok."

"Yeah I bet you do. Mrs. Coleman." He poured their flutes half full and handed her a glass.

"I'm sorry, what was that you just called me?"

Ignoring the question, he leaned over and whispered to her. "You know I'm gonna have you right?"

She leaned in closer to him. So close their noses nearly touched.

"Is that right?"

"That is exactly right." Ray raised his glass. She grabbed hers.

"So what are we toasting to Mr. Coleman?"

"To life. To me getting what I want. Always. Cheers."

He touched her glass with his, leaned back onto the sofa and took a sip; confident and satisfied that he'd just clued her in on the way things worked in Ray Coleman's world.

Thoroughly amused by his brazen cockiness, Missy hesitated for a second, as if to challenge the bold assertion.

Then she tilted her head to the side, batted her heavily mascara'd lashes and smiled. "Cheers."

As she sipped the sweet champagne from her glass she thought, *let the games begin.*

A Guilty Conscience

The morning of Melvin's funeral, Daye was in a pretty bad headspace. Even though he felt justified in doing what he did, seeing what they did to his man took his mind on a serious trip.

He didn't know people could really be that cruel, inhumane. He thought that kinda shit was just in the movies or maybe in one of those hungry third world countries. But it wasn't. It was real. It happened and he set it in motion.

For the life of him, he couldn't get the image of Melvin's mutilated body out of his mind. The nightmares were vivid, and he hadn't gotten more than a couple hours sleep in two weeks. Every time he closed his eyes, he saw his friend. He just wanted to forget.

Burned, stabbed and slashed to the bone. They even threw some kinda acid in his face. Melvin was barely recognizable lying on the cold concrete floor of the empty warehouse. He laid there writhing in pain; moaning and oozing blood and puss. A horrendous sight.

Daye's eyes welled as he reached behind him and pulled out his nine. He stood there holding the gun in his hand, so long it got heavy. He listened to the moaning for as long as he could. Then he closed his eyes and squeezed the trigger. The moaning stopped, and his friend let out one last gasp. It was the right thing to do.

The next morning the headline in the Washington Post read:

Unidentified black male found dead in Northeast DC

The article went on to say:

> *After being brutally beaten and tortured, victim succumbed to a single gunshot wound to the head. There are no suspects at this time.*

It was the hardest thing he'd ever had to read. And today would be the hardest thing he'd ever have to face.

He had managed to avoid Brenda since it happened, but today he'd have to face her. Look into the faces of Melvin's children. The thought of it made him nauseous.

The crew pulled up in front of his house and blew the horn. Daye laid across the bed, still in his underwear, staring out the window. Watching as people piled up in their cars getting ready to take that long drive to Frederick Maryland for the funeral.

He was almost alright, until the hearse rolled by. It was too much. He began to feel nauseous again, so he just laid back on the bed staring at the ceiling. He needed something to get his mind off everything. Maybe a jay would help. No, a jay would only make him think. He needed something stronger than that. Something to make him forget.

As he was spacing out his buddy Kevin walked in.

"What up Daye? I know you heard us out there blowin the horn. You going to the funeral or what?"

"Nah man. Y'all go head."

"What?"

"I don't do no fuckin funerals. No jails, no hospitals, no funerals. Y'all go head. I'll see y'all niggas later."

"What? Nigga, you a pallbearer! How the fuck you not gon go?"

"Whatever man. Just go head."

Sensing that he just needed a little encouragement, Kevin sat down on the bed next to him. "Come on man this is Melvin. This is your man. Trust me, don't nobody wanna be going to that church today. But you know, it is what it is. It's part of the game. Come on and roll with us, man. Pay the nigga some respect."

Daye threw his pillow hard Kevin's head. "Look man, I said I'm not going. So go ahead!"

Kevin shook his head. "Aaight but you know people gon be looking for you. That's all I'm sayin. I'll holla at you later on my nigga." He extended his fist. An official goodbye. Daye gave him a weak dap and Kevin left the house.

Daye laid there a while longer. Thinking. The phone rang.

"Hey my lucca American gang-stah. What na up to dis evenin eh?"

It was his Jamaican princess, Jenny. Just the diversion he needed. "Aye wassup. I'm tryna see you. You comin over here today?"

"Ahh! He wantin a lucca ja makin jerk off? Yeah I'll be dare. Roll me up a fat one eh?"

"Oh I got a fat one for you aight."

"Sound like music to my ears, papa. Be a good boy an ave it ready for me when I get dare."

"You know I gotchu."

Daye had already smoked two packs of cigarettes, and it was barely 10 a.m. His nerves were shot. He was out of weed, and the only thing to get high on in the house was a few loose vials of coke that must have fallen out of a package. He wanted to get high, but not *that* high.

A while back, he let a young broad from New York with a long tongue and a real big ass talk him into snortin some coke. The sex, he said, was on one thousand, but after staying up for two days straight and experiencing what he thought was a heart attack, he vowed never fuck with coke again. The herb was good enough. Until then anyway.

His connect was out of town, so he'd have to go out on the block to find something. A couple bags of that good shit, cause Jenny smoked joints like cigarettes, and when she was real faded she was real freaky. Some good weed and some good head was just what he needed to get his mind right. And maybe even a few shots of Patron. Jenny liked Patron. So he headed out to the liquor store, and then over to 6th Street to see Calvin, the weed man.

Calvin was sittin in the usual spot. On the trunk of his car, slingin and talkin his usual shit to anybody that would listen. Daye walked over to the car and extended his hand.

"Waddup Calvin!" They dapped and hugged. His last customer walked away.

"Daye! My muthafuckin man! Aye man I'm sorry to hear about your boy. Melvin was a good dude."

"Yeah, yeah. Thanks. I need some smoke. I mean good shit. Not no bush. A nigga tryna get nice right about now. I got this Jamaican bitch comin over this morning, and she won't suck my dick unless I get her blazed first, so you know, I need that right shit."

"Yeah, yeah dats wassup. So you ain't go to the funeral, man? I heard that joint was way out Frederick. That's a nice lil ride. Niggas rolled out early as hell this mornin to get out there."

Daye ignored the question. Calvin got the hint. "So what you got? Hydro? Oh, oh nah, let me get some of that sour diesel shit they be talkin bout. Kevin said that shit had his head *right* the other night, for real."

"Nah, man. Niggas came through this morning and bought up errything. You know they was tryna get high before the funeral. All I got is water right now. I'll give you that shit cheap, though. I'll prolly have some dro for you by tomorrow."

Daye laughed. "Water? Oh nah man. I ain't fuckin wit no boat."

"What! Nigga you scared? That shit is *nothin*. Dog. I'm bout to hit me a cigarette right now, go back in the house and fuck the shit out my baby muvva." They both laughed and dapped again. Calvin could be really animated. "Seriously, Daye, the shit don't do nothin for me but make my dick extra hard. What them Jamaican bammas be sayin? Hard like Rott-weiler?"

Laughing, Daye pushed Calvin back away from him. Calvin was a funny dude, but a man jumping out at you with his hand on his crotch, even as a joke, is a bit too much. "Man, get the fuck outta here! I saw that nigga Derek get but ass nekkid outside in front of his own mother the other day. He even waved his dick at her. I ain't fuckin wit nuttin that'll make me do no wild ass shit like dat."

Calvin shook his head and proceeded to make a sales pitch for his good product. "Nah, that's cause that nigga is *weak*. Derek be smokin wooties and doing all type of stupid shit, so it ain't no tellin what he was trippin off for real. Aaight how bout this…" Calvin pulled out a pack of cigarettes from his jacket and took out a single. He reached into his pants pocket and pulled out a small glass vial, opened it and dipped his cigarette into the liquid. "Hit this one with me right quick, and if you like it I'll give it to you. Then if you want some more, I'll look out for you."

Daye watched, amazed and a little aggravated as Calvin lit the end. He felt like a mark. Thinking to himself, *I know dis nigga ain't tryna get me to smoke no dipper out here*. So he declined. "Nah, go head man."

Not one to take an easy no, Calvin decided to go the psychological route on him. "Fuck you scared of?"

Daye nodded at the drug. "*THAT* shit."

They both laughed. Calvin decided to take another approach. "Aight, aight, you got me. I'm just tryna get rid of this shit for real. To tell the truth, it's weak. I think the nigga I got it from be puttin some extra shit in it. Like some fuckin tap water or some shit. Derek had some yesterday and he said it ain't even get him high."

"Aaight then what the fuck you tryna sell it to me for."

"Cause you a beginner muufucka. I know you can't handle the

real shit, but this right here? This shit'll put you right where you wanna be. Straight up."

Daye had never smoked boat in his life. He'd never even been tempted. But with everything going on his head... "Yeah I *hear* you."

"Don't hear me my nigga. Feel me." Calvin took a pull of the cigarette and started dancing to the go-go music that was blasting from his car stereo.

Daye smiled as he shook his head no, but Calvin could see he was breaking down. Just a little bit.

"Look man I swear on my kids, ain't nothin gon happen to you," Calvin said. "I smoke one of these joints like erryday. The real shit. And you ain't never heard bout me doin no crazy shit, right? Look. All this shit right here does is get ya head right man. If you got somethin on your mind that's stressin you out – bills, bitches, whateva – that shit is gone like immediately after you hit it. Trust me."

Daye shook his head again. His nervous smile had turned into a slight giggle, which only encouraged the sales pitch but he held his ground. "Nah man. Go head with that shit. I'm good."

"Yeah aight then nigga. Take yo azz back up the street and stay stressed out. I know you fucked up right now. And that Patron you got in that bag ain't gon do shit for you. I'm tellin you." Calvin laughed and waved Daye off. "Just come back and holla at me tomorrow. I *might* have somethin for you."

They shook on it, and Daye turned to walk away.

Not one to give up, Calvin made one last ditch effort. He leaned back on the car and called out. "Aye. They say that nigga Melvin was fucked up. Closed casket type shit. They say it was them Jamaicans. But ion know. Jamaican's don't usually rock like that. That medieval torture type shit."

Daye had only gotten a few steps away before stopping. The memories came rushing back to him. The smell of burnt flesh. The gurgling sound Melvin made as he choked on his own blood. His eyes staring up through swollen, bloody lids.

As Daye stood there frozen in his thoughts, Calvin knew he had him. So he walked over and tapped him on the shoulder. "You gon hit this shit with me or what?" Daye turned around. Calvin took another pull, inhaling the chemicals from the thick smoke. He closed his eyes and took in the euphoric wave. Then he grabbed his crotch again. "See, my dick hard already."

Daye laughed as he pushed Calvin back again. The gay shit was to get on his nerves, but he was grateful to be pulled away from his dark thoughts. Despite the chilled morning air, he was sweating profusely and his hands were trembling, slightly as he held the heavy plastic bag filled with Jenny's junk food groceries and a gallon of premium tequila.

Daye wiped the sweat from his brow and took a deep breath. Fuck it, he was goin in. "Aaight, aight. You can kill the sales pitch nigga. Imma hit that shit. But I bet not lunch out!"

Calvin passed him the damp cigarette, with a devilish grin. Daye took a long pull and coughed the thick white smoke through his nose and mouth. Calvin rubbed him on his back. "You aight man?"

Daye pushed him off again, but hard. "Yeah, nigga. I'm good! And don't say nothin else to me bout your dick!"

Calvin got the message. Daye got his mind off his troubles. For the moment. It was the beginning of the end.

The Courtship

Ray Coleman was a dream come true, and Missy had truly been swept off her feet. They'd been dating three months and for the first time she didn't feel the need to have a couple guys in reserve. Missy James was in love and officially off the market. She was in a relationship. A real relationship, and for the first time in her life, she was truly happy.

Ray was the first guy she had ever made wait. Much to her amazement, he didn't mind. He was extremely patient and told her that she was worth every minute of the wait. So for months they kissed and caressed but never went past a dry hump. Kinda like in junior high.

Missy knew full well that a man of his considerable wealth, fame and stature, not to mention his general gorgeousness may be getting it elsewhere, but it didn't matter. She really wanted to keep up the chase so she put that out of her mind. Once she *really* had him she planned on keeping him. And have him she would.

Three months to the day of their meeting Ray planned a special semi-surprise anniversary date. It was semi-surprise because she had less than a day's notice.

He called her on a Thursday night after practice and asked if she could get off work early the next day. When she asked why, he reminded her that it was the three-month anniversary of the day they first met.

Missy was really taken aback by that because although she was used to her men being thoughtful, what guy celebrates a three-month anniversary? Most men have trouble remembering their own wedding anniversaries, she thought. But far be it from her to deny a man the pleasure of honoring her, so she was game.

She decided to break out the first white outfit of the spring season. A perfect one shoulder, white silk jersey jumpsuit from Saks. It was from Donna Karan's latest spring collection, and it was five shades of fabulous.

The jumper hit every curve of her body perfectly, and the white really popped on her newly tanned skin. The tan was courtesy of a weekend business trip to Puerto Rico, as was the beautiful turquoise and gold statement necklace she planned to wear with it.

The showstoppers, however would be her new Jimmy Choos. 5 inches, liquid gold, sexy ankle strapped stilettos with gold leaf and flower embellishments. She thought, *these babies could walk in ahead of me and work the room before I even get there.*

She finished the look with a gold Fendi clutch and there it was. Perfection! Just as she was finishing the dress rehearsal, her cell phone rang.

"MISSSSAAAAYYYY!!!!!!"

Missy laughed. "Hey Carmen. What's all the screaming about?"

"Because it's-a-bout-ta-go-down! You ain't ready for this."

"Ready for what?"

"To become the new and *improved* Mrs. Ray Coleman, of course."

"Girl, what are you talking about? We're not *there* yet."

"Oh…I think you are."

"Carmen…"

"A little birdie told *me* that a certain handsome football hero is ready to propose to a certain lady friend of his…who shall remain nameless."

"What?!"

"Yes girl! Yes!"

Missy was smiling ear to ear. It was hard not to get sucked into Carmen's excitement. But she had to be tripping with this one. "Ok please tell me what's happening and start from the beginning."

"Ok, ok. Last night, Roman came home *completely* wasted, but strangely agitated. When I asked what was wrong with him, he said, *Ray is not ready for this man. He's not ready. It's not time for this yet.*

"When I asked him what wasn't Ray ready for he said *to get married.* I started asking more questions and I think he realized he was saying too much, so he completely shut down on me."

"Then what?!"

"Then he said he was tired and needed a shower."

"Damn! That's it?"

"That was all I could get out of him. I brought it up again this morning at breakfast and he tried to play dumb. But I know it's going down. Roman has said that Ray can be really impulsive. He asked his first wife to marry him after only a few months."

"Well I don't know if that's a good thing or not."

"Nooooo. Don't take it like that. Ray loves you. He just wants to lock you down, girl. You better get with the program. You told me you loved him."

"I do. I guess. But this is like really fast, Carmen."

"You guess? Are you serious? Ok, Missy you need to stop it. You got the perfect man that meets every one of your insane standards, you love him, he obviously loves you and he wants to give you his name. Where's the conflict? Isn't this what you've been working for all these years? Correct me if I'm wrong, but isn't this what that whole crazy 3-step program for getting a good man was for?"

"Yeah—"

"Ok, so w*hat* is the problem?"

"There's no *problem*. I'd just like to get to know him a little better. That's all."

"Ok. Fair enough. But don't come crying to me if you fuck this up. This man can have any woman he wants and he has chosen *you*. Shit if you don't want him pass his fine ass over here."

"Shut up, Carmen. Before I tell Roman."

"Roman is a kicker. Tell him." They both laughed.

"I'm going to act like I didn't even hear that. Can I ask you something?"

"Sure."

"Does Roman like me?"

"Of course. He loves you, why do you ask?"

"Well from what you just told me, he obviously doesn't think Ray should marry me."

"No girl. Roman is just afraid to lose his best friend. He just doesn't want things to change again. He's told me many times that Ray's ex-wife was a nightmare and she drove a wedge between them. I think he's just leery of that happening again. That's all it is."

"Hmm."

"Whatever the case, Roman is not the man you need to be worrying about right now. Ray Coleman is ready to make you his wife, darling. So what you need to focus on right now is what you gon wear to your engagement!" Carmen screamed out. "Aaahhh!! I'm so excited for you, girl!"

Missy was starting to get sucked in. She hadn't expected a

proposal so soon, but maybe Carmen was right. She loved Ray. She wanted to be his wife someday. What difference would it make if they got engaged now? They could have a long engagement. They didn't have to get married right away. She shook off the trepidation and imagined the possibilities.

"Carmen! Is this really happening? I mean really? Am I about to be a football wife?"

"Girl. It is hap-pen-ing!" Carmen heard the front door slam shut. "Damn, Roman just came in the door. I gotta go." She whispered into the receiver. "Get yourself together tonight and make SURE you call me! I want *all* the dirty details! Love you boo!"

"Love you too, girl. Bye."

After talking to Carmen, Missy's head was spinning. She expected Ray to propose at some point but definitely not that soon. A year would have made more sense. Three months was crazy!

They'd been spending a lot of time together and were definitely getting closer, but they hadn't even said the L word yet. They hadn't even had sex yet! She giggled to herself and thought, *I know my man-bait is proper, but is my game that good?*

As she laid down on the bed fantasizing about the beautifully lavish, celebrity-studded, multi-million dollar wedding she'd be having sometime next summer in the Hamptons, a sudden wave of panic rushed over her. *Wait, I'm getting married?*

The Funeral

Standing at the gravesite, Brenda's cell vibrated in her purse. She ignored it the first two times but when she pulled it out to turn it completely off she noticed the missed calls were from her mother, Betty's dialysis center. The text from the nurse said that Betty was rushed to the emergency room. Brenda thought, *could this day get any fuckin worse.*

The service concluded and as they lowered Melvin's coffin into the ground all Brenda could think of was getting back to DC to check on her mother. So as not to cause a panic she whispered the situation to her cousin Rita and asked to use her car. Rita agreed to ride with the kids in the family car to the repast while Brenda went to the hospital.

Brenda was grateful for the alone time. She needed a second to clear her head. To cry without anyone trying to hold her hand or wipe her tears. To scream out loud. To talk to God and give Him a piece of her mind. Her life was about to change in more ways than even she could know.

The funeral service and burial was held in Frederick where Melvin's family was from, so she had a bit of a drive to get back to the hospital in DC. Plenty of time to reflect.

Through her tears, she saw Melvin's face. Replayed their last conversation in her mind. She heard his last words: "Baby, I can't wait to see you on the beach in that sexy bathing suit. You know I love you, right?" And then he growled at her like a tiger and kissed her goodnight. She smiled, thinking how corny her husband could be sometimes. She'd always loved that about him. He may have been a big man in the streets but when it came to his family, especially Brenda he was as soft as a teddy bear. And he didn't care who knew it.

She thought about how preoccupied he'd been in the days before he died. He'd been getting home later and later, and the night before he died he barely beat the sun up. That was a first and completely out of character but Brenda knew that if it kept him from his family it had to be important.

The night before he died Melvin mentioned he had some important business to handle before their vacation. He said it was long overdue but he didn't go into any more detail. Which was fine. Brenda knew exactly how Melvin made his money, but they had a deal. They would only discuss his business when his business was legit. He said he was working on it, and that was good enough for her.

They'd made many big plans for the future. When the time was right they were going to open their own businesses. Something to be passed down to their children so they wouldn't have to live and eat by the streets. A tow truck company for Melvin and maybe a little soul food restaurant for Brenda.

They'd both go back to school. Get small business loans. Work hard and pay taxes like normal folk. Really do things legit. It would all come together in time.

As she sat at the intersection, deep in her thoughts, holding up traffic behind her she began to cry. It was almost impossible for her to fathom. There was no more time.

Betty came to mind. She drove on. Wiping the tears from her eyes. The windshield wipers were on full blast as the rain fell hard, making it even more difficult for her to see the road in front of her. The valium Rita gave her before the service had kicked in. She was loopy.

Her mind drifted to the day's events. The service was beautiful. The singing was great and the preacher spoke so highly of Melvin, as if he was some kind of saint. That was far from the truth but despite what he did in the streets, he really was a good person and he touched a whole lot of people. Most of them stood and expressed just that, despite the minister's plea for them to keep their comments to a minimum.

Melvin paid phone bills and utility bills and peoples past due rent. He stopped car repos on the spot, sponsored block parties and trips to amusement parks for the entire neighborhood.

Hearing all the kind words made her feel good. It brought her a measure of peace knowing that her husband was regarded as something more than just a thug and a drug dealer.

Most people didn't know he'd been the man of his house since he was eleven years old. His father was killed, his mother was on crack cocaine and his baby sister Angel was born addicted. Until the day child services came in and took them away he was the sole caregiver and provider for the both of them, doing whatever he had to do to put food on the table.

Two years of being shifted to different foster homes and his aunt Regina, his father's sister came to claim him. His other aunt Evelyn took Angel in. Shortly afterward, Regina and Melvin moved to DC.

Midway through the 8th grade school year in a crowded cafeteria, a cute, cuddly baby Huey kinda boy they affectionately called "Heavy" bumped into a smart, sassy and way too mature for her age – and her own good - Brenda James and the rest as they say was history.

First came love, then came a carriage, a couple more carriages and eventually a marriage. With little help from their respective guardians, and Melvin's refusal to have anything to do with the government, it was the first carriage that spurred everything; a life in the underworld that eventually grew into one of the most lucrative and well organized drug enterprises the city had seen since the Rayful Edmond era.

Melvin made money. What they called "trash bag" money. So much that it had to be stored in hefty bags until it was put to use.

Brenda lived lavishly off of Melvin's money and the kids never heard the word no. Luxury cars, designer clothes, expensive vacations. Jewels and furs. Melvin spread the wealth around the neighborhood too and a few mishaps aside, life was damn good in the hood. Until it wasn't.

Brenda thought about the luxuries. Was it even worth it? She'd give anything to have her husband back. To hear the jangle of his keys in the front door. To have him hug her from behind as she hovered over a hot stove making his favorite dinner. To fuss at him for letting Mandy splash water all over the bathroom rug during her bath time.

Eighteen years of loving him and all that was left of him was memories. Memories and questions. Unanswered questions that were gnawing at her every minute of the day.

Brenda neared the hospital parking garage an uneasy feeling came over her. A nagging feeling that she couldn't shake. It wasn't Betty. In her grey goose and valium induced fog, it had just dawned on her that Daye wasn't at the funeral. She thought, how could she have missed that. Daye should have been the first person up there speaking on Melvin's behalf. Shit he was supposed to be a pallbearer!

Against her better judgment and her own personal feelings about him, she listed him as a pallbearer in the funeral program. Considering he and Melvin were so close, giving him that duty was the natural thing to do. But the motherfucker didn't even show up.

The more she thought about him the more upset it made her. Her head heated up and started pounding. Tears welled in her eyes. She thought, *so that's it*. As far as she was concerned, his little disappearing act was all the confirmation she needed. He was involved in her husband's murder and he couldn't come to the funeral because he couldn't face her. He couldn't face the kids after what he'd done. She felt it in her gut.

Brenda parked the car and pulled herself together. Betty was calling. But as soon as everything and everyone was settled, she planned on paying Daye a visit. Standing before him and looking him straight in the eye. She wanted answers, and he was going to give them to her, one way or another.

True Romance

Knowing this was the day Ray would propose, Missy couldn't concentrate on anything anyone said in her early morning meeting. She woke up an hour earlier to finish her hair and nails. She stocked her smallest makeup case with all the essentials and packed two outfits to bring with her to work.

She brought her nude colored Herve Leger bandage dress and a black and gold jersey knit, strapless party dress she got from a vintage boutique in Soho. Both options were simple but sexy. She brought gold and diamond accessories, her favorite red bottomed stilettos and the gold Jimmy Choo sandals. She just couldn't leave them in the box. The Fendi clutch went with everything and everything else she packed was interchangeably fabulous. She was all set.

The plan was to sneak off to the gym around one to get ready. Ray was picking her up at 2 p.m., and she planned to make his mouth water at the sight of her. Her assistant buzzed her.

"Missy, you have a call on line 2."

"Thanks Tracey. I got it. This is Melissa James."

A deep, sultry baritone voice came over her line. "Why yes you are."

She smiled at the sound of her man's sexy voice. "And how may I help you, Mr. Coleman?"

"You can help me by being ready on time this afternoon, Ms. James."

"Ha ha. Very funny. Don't worry, I'll be ready."

"Good. There's been a change of plans."

"Change?"

"I won't be picking you up. I'm sending a car for you. I still need you to be ready to leave at two o'clock, though. I have a lot planned for the evening and we really need to stay on schedule."

"Ray, please stop it with the suspense. You know it's kill-ing me! Where are we going?!"

"Baby, I got this. You just get ready to have the best night of your life."

"Ooh. The best night of my life? That's a pretty bold statement, Mr. Coleman. You sure you up to that challenge? I mean you better be prepared to bring it if you talking to *me* like that."

"Ms. James, you have *no idea.*"

"Do tell?"

"No. But nice try."

She laughed. "Dammit! Come on Ray. Pleeeease. Just a little hint. Something?"

Ray let out a heavy sigh. "You know you're impossible right?"

"And don't forget irresistible."

"Yes, that you are. Ok I will give you one hint. One. But you have to promise me something in return."

"Ok, yes. Anything!"

"Ooh, anything? Now *that's* a bold statement." They both laughed.

"Ok, Ray I'm serious now. Come on!"

"All right, but if I tell you this one thing, you have to promise me that after that you'll just go with the flow."

"Are you kidding me? Done!"

"I'm serious, Missy. That means no more questions. No input or suggestions. Just gooooo with the flooooowww. Do you think you can handle that?"

"Yessss I caannnnn. Now tell me something!"

"Ok. I really do have to go but I'll leave you with this. It's a beautiful thing, when history repeats itself."

"Wait. Wha…"

"I'll see you soon, beautiful." He hung up the phone.

After talking to Ray, she was more anxious than ever. And confused. What the hell did he have planned? The suspense was killing her! She smiled to herself as she repeated over and over in her head, "It's a beautiful thing, when history repeats itself." What did that mean?

She tried her best to get some work done, but it was hopeless. Trying to guess what the evening held was a way better use of her time. Again. *It's a beautiful thing, when history repeats itself. Hmm.*

The next hour went by at a complete snail's pace, and at one o'clock she shut down her computer, wished everyone a lovely weekend, and headed for the gym.

After hours of thoughtful consideration, she decided on the

Herve and the Choo's. With carefully orchestrated, *effortless* waves in her long blonde highlighted hair, dark smoky shadows accentuating her eyes, golds and bronzes highlighting her high cheekbones, and a subtle pink gloss over her full pouty lips, Missy was official Hollywood glam for her anniversary.

As she checked the front, side and rear views in the full length mirror, the one word that came to mind was *Flawless*! Ray's jaw would definitely hit the ground upon site! And she couldn't wait. She gave one last glance before she folded the expensive clutch under her arm and set off for the evening.

The town car was waiting downstairs for her at two o'clock sharp, but there was a ton of traffic. The 295 interstate on a Friday afternoon was always a nightmare. She used the extra time to primp…and ponder.

Missy couldn't help thinking this Friday night would change her life. She was *this close* to an engagement to Washington's number one defensive end, a legend, one of the greatest to take the field since the days of Dexter Manley and Reggie White. Soon her wildest dreams would come true. And she was ready.

There was a good hour of stop and go traffic before the driver took the exit off the interstate to the National Harbor. The car pulled into the driveway of the Gaylord Hotel and Damon (pronounced De'mone), Ray's new personal assistant was waiting at the entrance to take her up to her room.

He handed her a glass of champagne and they proceeded to walk through the swanky chic lobby to the private elevator, up to the penthouse suite. When Damon flung the double doors open she could not believe her eyes.

There stood a full on entourage of the most fabulous glam squad any woman could have asked for. There was also a personal chef and wait staff. All there to pamper her and make her ready for her special evening. She knew that Ray spent some serious money and pulled some very serious strings to make this night happen.

Missy stood there in amazement as Damon began introducing folks, most of whom needed no introduction.

"On behalf of Mr. Ray Coleman, I present to you, hairstylist extraordinaire, Ms. Kim Kimble." Kim was in the middle of taping the second season of her reality show surrounding the goings on in her hip Hollywood beauty salon.

Kim leaned in for a hug and touched her hair. "Ok, girl you are working that blonde hair, but you know I can make that better. Beyoncé won't have nothin on you tonight, boo."

"Next, we have fashion stylist to the stars, Ms. June Ambrose." June was fresh off her own reality show where she styled B-list celebrities in hopes of reviving their careers. She was one of the most fashionable women in the business and very highly coveted.

June leaned in for a double air kiss. "Muah. Muah. Darling, I am feeling those Jimmy Choo's, but the Herve is so last year. So cliche. So…real housewives. Let's take a look through my racks and see what fabulousness June can create for you this evening. The fashion blogs will be going crazy for you by tomorrow morning, my dear, so do prepare yourself."

"Next, we have up and coming makeup artist and businesswoman Portia Breeden of Breed Beauty Cosmetics."

Portia had just patented and sold her organic skin care line to Sephora and was recently hired as the lead makeup artist on the hottest new modeling competition on television. She extended her hand. "Wonderful to meet you Ms. James. I'm so anxious to put a brush to that beautiful face. You will be beat to the gods tonight, hunny. Trust"

As Missy walked around the suite to take in the rest of the magnificence, she felt drunk with euphoria. There were gorgeous views of the Potomac River from every room, the fragrance of dozens upon dozens of calla lilies was intoxicating. Calla lilies were her favorite flower and she wondered how Ray knew. She didn't remember telling him.

Standing ice buckets with chilled Perignon were scattered about the suite for all to enjoy. In the kitchen, her favorite chef Waynette Garcia was plating all of her favorite hors d'oeuvres – shrimp and avocado ceviche, succulent jumbo sea scallops seared and wrapped in Applewood bacon. For desserts, there were her favorite salted caramel cupcakes, dark chocolate truffles and assorted fruits for fondue. It was heavenly.

After greeting Way with a hug, Missy grabbed a truffle and a second glass of champagne before she set off to explore the rest of the enormous suite. Fittingly, Maxwell's "Urban Hang Suite" album played in the background and everyone was really vibing. The champagne was beginning to take effect. Missy was overwhelmed.

The thought that someone would go to so much trouble and expense just for her was utterly awesome. It's not that she didn't believe she was deserving of the very best that life had to offer, but what was happening around her was beyond anything she could have imagined from Ray.

And the best part was this was just the beginning. It was not only the prelude to a wonderful evening to come but it was the start of what she knew would be a wonderful life with a man she adored. The life she always wanted. Missy felt like the luckiest woman alive.

As the entourage scurried about setting up their respective stations, she slid into the massive massage chair to relax and enjoy a mani pedi. Not that she needed one. But when in Rome.

She sat the champagne glass down and summoned one of the servers for an energy drink. Something told her that she had a very long evening ahead of her and she certainly didn't want to be too tired for it. God only knew where they were going and what he had planned. If the preparation was any indication, it had to be something big. Much bigger than him getting down on one knee in the middle of a nice restaurant.

She allowed her mind to wander for a bit before she relaxed into the promise she made to Ray. It was time for her to just goooo with the flooooow.

*****

Exactly two hours and fifty minutes after her arrival at the hotel, Missy was ready for her evening. As she stood in the full length mirror she couldn't believe how good she looked. Her glam squad worked a special kind of magic that she hadn't expected.

She was stunning in an ice blue Eli Saab haute couture gown with strategic illusion mesh and silvery gold floral applique that perfectly complimented the gold petals on her Choos. The look June said she was going for was "ethereal ice princess" and she captured it perfectly.

Kim insisted that she wear her hair simple, pulled back into a long, almost waist-length ponytail to showcase her high cheekbones.

Her makeup was sultry but tasteful. Portia blended a medley of gold, bronze and blue smoky shadows to compliment Missy's piercing arctic blue eyes. She gave her a sheer nude lip to accentuate her plump pout and her face was contoured to perfection. She was impossibly gorgeous and couldn't wait to find out what Ray had planned for the evening.

Whatever he had on the agenda was obviously a black tie affair.

She knew that as soon as she saw June's clothing rack laden with more than a dozen floor-length gowns. All of the accessories were of diamonds and various elaborate jewels, so if nothing else, Missy knew she was in for something fancy.

Ray said the car would be waiting downstairs at six o'clock sharp. Thankfully she was on time, so she didn't have to hear his mouth about staying on schedule.

When she walked through the lobby of the hotel, every eye in the place was on her. She could hear the comments, the compliments and even a little hate. One of the hotel clerks snapped his finger up to the sky and down to the ground before he yelled, "Beat to the GODS, hunty!"

That was all the validation she needed. She smiled graciously at her admirer and flipped her 28-inch ponytail one time for the haters to her left. A group of women standing and staring with sour looks on their faces. Have *that*, she thought.

The limo was waiting at the entrance with a police escort to help navigate through the rush hour traffic. As the car sped down the shoulder lane behind its escort, Missy tried her best to figure out where it was headed. She just couldn't help herself. It seemed they were headed to Virginia, but where would they be going in Virginia that was formal? A party at the governor's mansion?

The driver pulled onto the George Washington Parkway and took the exit to Reagan National Airport. That immediately upped the excitement ante. She was positively beaming as the town car pulled into the private hangar.

They passed a half-dozen planes before stopping at the tail of a G6 where Ray stood handsomely in a very well-fitted tuxedo, holding a glass of champagne and grinning like a Cheshire Cat. Clearly he'd already had a couple.

She thought, *God, he looks good.* He walked over to her as the driver opened her door, and she stepped out of the car onto the tarmac. The bottom jaw moment.

"Baby, baby, ba-BY." His hand grazed her cheek. "I never thought you could look more beautiful than you did the first time I laid eyes on you. But I was so wrong. You've really outdone yourself tonight."

"No, your glam squad outdid themselves. Ray, how in the world did you get all those people to come to DC? I can't even imagine what June Ambrose cost you."

"Well, let's just say I'll spare no expense for the love of my life."

It was the first time she'd heard him use the L word. "Wow. You love me, Ray?"

He took a step closer and leaned down so that they were eye to eye. "With everything in me."

Then he took her face in his hands and they shared a long and very passionate kiss. Missy felt her eyes begin to well and fought hard to hold back her tears. Couldn't ruin Portia's creation before the main event.

They boarded the jet and got ready for their flight. Missy settled into the plush white leather chair and buckled in as instructed. "So baby where are we going?"

"What happened to going with the flow?"

"I know, but I'm already so overwhelmed by all your amazing hard work. I just don't think I could handle many more surprises. You really are a wonderful man. You know that?"

He laughed, clearly satisfied with how things were going. "Sweet talker."

"I'm serious. If we ended the night right here, right now, it would qualify as the best night of my life. Just sitting here with you, right here. Right in this moment is more than enough for me."

"So I'm doing good so far, huh?"

"You're doing excellent, sweetheart." She unbuckled the seatbelt and moved closer to him. She kissed him on the neck and rubbed his knee. Her hand traveled slowly up his trouser and just before she reached that particular spot he grabbed her gently by the wrist and whispered seductively in her ear.

"Missy."

She knew she had him right where she wanted him. "Yes sweetheart."

"I'm still not telling you where we're going." Then he reached over her and slammed the shutters down on the window.

Mildly disappointed but slightly amused she fell back into her chair and re-buckled. "Fine." They both laughed.

Defeated, Missy took another sip of champagne, reclined the comfy seat and prepared to enjoy the ride.

After what seemed like only 15 minutes in the air, the pilot announced that they needed to prepare for descent. He said they would reach their destination in approximately 15 minutes. Since she wasn't allowed to raise the shutters on the windows she had no idea where they were headed. Wherever it was it was definitely close. Philly, New York, Atlanta, Charlotte? She really had no idea.

When they landed it was drizzling a bit so they were literally rushed from the plane to the car. A black S550 Mercedes Benz with shutters on the windows that were of course closed shut, per Ray's instruction.

So Missy was riding again with no idea where she was or where she was going. It was beginning to get a little nerve racking but she knew she had to be a good sport about it.

What was really annoying is that after all the fuss those damned Choo's were starting to hurt her feet. She hadn't been on her feet for more than 20 minutes in total and she was already starting to get that familiar burn on the balls of her feet. It was definitely going to be one of *those* nights.

The car finally came to a complete stop and when she stepped out onto the sidewalk she immediately recognized the area. They were in Manhattan. Greenwich Village to be exact. Ray led her up a staircase to a beautiful five-story walk up where there was some very official looking security on the porch. She thought, *Bodyguards? Secret service? It's definitely a wealthy neighborhood. Maybe the mayor would be there or something.*

Once they checked in with the hostess on the first floor and made their way to the stairway they started seeing celebrities all over. Of the A-list variety. De Niro and his beautiful chocolate wife Grace were standing arm in arm right in front of them, and in front of *them* was Will and Jada Smith. Jada was doting and straightening Will's bowtie as he brushed back a wisp of hair from her face. Missy smiled. Black love.

Once inside Missy's mind was reeling. Wall to wall heavy hitters. You could smell the money in the room. Hollywood power couples, billionaire businessmen and political elites. Fame, power and prestige.

In one corner of the room there was Kerry Washington, channeling Olivia Pope in an all-white ensemble and elegant diamonds. Standing at her side laughing cheerily was Ellen DeGeneres and Michael Kors. The Clintons were seated at a table with the Bloomberg's who were sitting next to Salma Hayek and her new billionaire husband of the infamous Louis Vuitton Moet Hennessy fashion house and winery in Paris. Missy was positively salivating over that fact.

The celebrity sightings went on and on. Her head was spinning just trying to take it all in. She could not believe she was standing there breathing the same dehumidified air as Oprah Winfrey. It was too much!

Just when she thought things could not get more amazing, the infamous Prada wearing devil from Vogue magazine, Anna Wintour and Missy's favorite white sister from another mother, Sarah Jessica Parker, of Sex and the City fame called the room to attention.

By that time Missy was really beginning to feel her fourth glass of champagne kicking in, but she managed to hear Sarah Jessica say, "Welcome to my home."

The next thing that happened completely blew her mind. Sarah Jessica proceeded to introduce the President of *"OUR"* Unites States, Mr. sexy swagger himself, Barack Obama. She nearly fainted.

As they joined the crowd in a thunderous round of applause, Missy suddenly remembered hearing about the president having his campaign fundraiser at Sarah Jessica's house. It had been all over the news for weeks. It was the hottest ticket in America at $40,000 a plate, and Ray had gotten her in. Talk about *pull*.

When President Obama appeared, Missy squeezed Ray's hands so hard she nearly broke a nail. She could NOT BELIEVE they were there, hobnobbing with such an amazing group of people. Ray had certainly outdone himself for their anniversary.

As the evening went on, they dined on the finest foods served on the finest china, sipped the finest champagne from the finest crystal. They rubbed elbows with some of the wealthiest and most influential people in the free world. It really didn't get any better.

Just when she thought they were leaving and the perfect night was over, Ray took her hand and led her over to a corner of the room where Obama and his beautiful brown wife Michelle were holding court. Much to Missy's delight, President Obama immediately recognized and acknowledged Ray, giving him a pound no less. Missy thought he was every bit cool as he seemed in the press. Smiling bright and full of charisma. He was personable and approachable, even to the common man. You couldn't help but to be drawn in by him.

The introductions were made and eventually they were engaged in conversation about life in the District. The only DC native in the bunch, Missy represented very well for herself and as she stared at Ray's beautiful mouth in motion, speaking comfortably with the most powerful man in the land as if they were equals, Missy was as impressed as she was turned on. She couldn't wait to get him alone.

Ray mentioned that it was their anniversary and after the well wishes President Obama suggested that they take a photo together. He motioned to a photographer and assembled the small group which also included Oprah and Stedman.

Though she played it cool Missy was jumping out of her skin with excitement. She brushed a hand across her head to tame any fly-aways, put on a most dignified smile and thought, *so this is what it feels like to be a star.*

I Wish You Would

Daye's habit had gotten worse. He was completely off of weed, and dippers were his new drug of choice. It was the only thing that took him where he needed to be – *elsewhere*. He loved everything about it, too. The pungent smell, the bitter chemical taste, and best of all that high. It was like taking flight. Mind elevation.

Half a cigarette in, he was ten times smarter and his dick ten was times bigger than all them niggas on the block. After a good hit, every girl 'round the way had their eyes on him, too. They wanted him bad. And he could have his pick if he wanted. But he played it cool. Always cool.

In reality, when he smoked that shit his eyes were red and glassy, he was sweating the stinkin embalming fluid from his pours, and people just wanted him to walk the fuck away.

In his head, though, he was throwing out that good knowledge to the hood; puttin em on to some game. Daye was once the man in the hood. No doubt. He had the cars, the clothes, the girls. The life. Now he was pitied by most. Even the yougins, because they could see how far gone he was. Yet he had no idea.

They'd seen it a thousand times before. The graduation. From weed to dippers, dippers to coke and coke to crack or heroin. It was the trap. Some escaped it, but for the ones who didn't, it was tragic. He was well on his way.

Dippers were the new thing. One of the hottest go-go bands in the city, had just released a song named for the drug and every time he smoked one he played it. Every time he played it he lost a little more of his mind.

At that point, he was a bona fide "dipperhead," and as negative a connotation as that title carried in the hood, Daye was completely unbothered by it. He thought, if muthafuckas knew what *he* knew, they'd smoke them a dipper, too. He was gone on it.

73 degrees and sunny on a Saturday afternoon was a day in hood heaven. Everybody was out. The birds chirped, the kids played

out on the sidewalk, the usual suspects were gathered outside talkin shit and Daye was holed up in his room fittin ta light one up. Calvin had just dropped off a couple vials of water and he had a half pack of cigarettes lying in wait. The thought of it excited him.

After he smoked his special cigarette, his head was right where he wanted it. He laid down on his bed and closed his eyes. Suddenly he jumped up and got dressed. He needed to get some air. He wanted to go for a ride. Maybe get over to his girl Kim's house and break her off some good dick then get him something to eat from the carry out.

He paced the floor, contemplating. He laid back down several times before he remembered he had some place to be. He looked for his keys then he found them, then he lost them and looked for them again. He was tired so he laid down again. He was hot, so he took his clothes off again. What happened to his wallet? Somebody probably stole it again. He laid down again. Somewhere in the distance, a phone was ringing.

His buddy Terrence yelled upstairs from the basement. "Aye Daye! Daye!"

Daye sat on the edge of the bed. He was feeling a little stuck. Sitting there for like, ten minutes trying to get one sock on. Terrence popped in the doorway. It startled him, but he was too stuck to react.

"Daye!"

The trance was suddenly broken. He yelled back, "What nigga?"

"Fuck you hollerin at like dat? Telephone man!"

"Who is it?"

"I think it's Brenda again."

"What she want?!"

"Ion no. I ain't your fuckin secretary. Ask her yourself." Terrence tossed him the phone and walked off.

"Hello?"

"Hello!"

"Oh hey Brenda. Wassup."

"Where the fuck is my money."

"What?" Daye started to laugh. "Damn. When we get *there*, Brenda?"

"Oh you think it's funny. We got *there* when you started playin with my money. My husband's money. Daye, you know you still owed him, and I told you we need it, so stop fuckin DUCKIN me and get me my muthufuckin money."

"Come on Bren head. You know I..."

"FUCK THAT! I'm getting tired of remindin your ass what the fuck you owe me. Every week the same muthafuckin shit! You know how many times I been past your house?"

"Ok, ok. Calm down girl. How much you say I owe you again?" Daye started to laugh again.

"Seventeen thousand, five hundred and fifty muthafuckin dollars!"

"Aight. Aight, umma get you your money, but you know it's hot out here on these streets since that shit happened, Brenda. A nigga can't really get no money on the block right now. You know I got you tho. "

Brenda laughed, frustrated. "See, this is the shit I'm talkin 'bout. I'm not PLAYING wit you Daye. You think this shit a game. But it's not. I'm not *knockin* on your door no more. I'm not *callin* your phone no more. Best believe, this the LAST muthafuckin time I'm gon ask you bout *my* money."

Daye looked at the receiver with a frown on his face, thinking, *is this bitch crazy?* He put it back to his ear. "Then what the fuck you gon do Brenda?!"

"I already told your ass! This the last muthafuckin time..."

"Aye! Come on, Joe. Stop talkin to me like you fuckin crazy. For real. I told you imma get that to you so imma get it to you."

"Yeah, then get it, nigga. Get it. And if I have to..."

"Bitch! Who da fuck you think you talkin to?" She was bringing his high back down.

Brenda replied, "Bitch? *Bitch?*"

"You heard what the fuck I said. I ain't your son, and I ain't your nigga. So watch how the fuck you talk to me. And stay in your lane, before you fuck up."

"Before I fuck up?" She laughed. "So you threatenin me now, Daye? It's like that?"

"Exactly like that. Matter fact..."

Daye paced the floor and spoke with his hands, as if Brenda could see him and somehow understand just who the fuck she was talking to. Clearly she had forgotten. She must have lost her muthafuckin mind talking to him like he was one of Melvin's young flunkies.

"You know what, I was about to run you that paper, but since you wanna play big, since you wanna be on some ole gangsta bitch type shit, I ain't givin you SHIT! Fuck you *and* nem kids. Starve! Beggin ass bitch! Don't get mad at me cause that nigga left y'all broke. Sell your car. Sell some ass. Matter fact, don't nobody want your old ass any muufuckin way. Sell Brandy ass. It's gettin a lil fat. I'll buy that shit. For seventeen thousand, fie hunnid and fiddy dollaz."

He held the phone quiet for a second, smiling to himself, waiting for a response. Daye never minded a good argument, and he knew he hit a nerve with that last one.

Brenda was so heated at that point she couldn't think of what next to say. Her eyes welled up and her throat was beginning to burn. And when that happened it usually meant it was about to go down.

Daye killed her husband. She knew it. Even if he didn't pull the trigger he was responsible. And he continued to disrespect her family. Over and over. It made her sick. The next thing that came out of her mouth turned the whole situation on a dime. "You gon be home for a minute?"

"What? Yeah bitch. I'm home and umma be home. You called me, so you know where da fuck I'm at."

"Yeah I know where you at." As Brenda hung up the phone, she could hear Daye yell into the phone. "Dumb ass bitch!" Her head got even hotter, and her left eye started to twitch. She knew things were going to the point of no return, so she got on her hands and knees…then she reached under the bed for her lockbox.

She sat it down on the bed beside her and took another swallow of liquid courage. It was time to put an end to the bullshit. She flipped the latch. The gun was gone.

A Thank You Piece

In back of the sedan, they kissed and caressed like two teenagers in love. The driver took the scenic route. Few words were spoken. Just very comfortable silences.

Missy didn't inquire any further about anything, she just laid there on Ray's chest gazing out of the window and enjoying the warmth of his strong arms as the driver navigated his way through east Manhattan in the rain. It was peace.

Overcome with love and gratitude she desperately wanted to show him some appreciation. So she reached down and slid her hand inside his trouser. Before she made contact, he reached down and pulled it back out. He gently kissed the palm of her hand as the car pulled into a cobblestoned driveway and he said, "We're here."

They were parked at the entrance of the Waldorf Astoria Hotel. Once again Ray reserved the most beautiful penthouse suite the hotel had to offer – 3,300 square feet of sheer opulence. Plush mauve carpeting and crystal chandeliers. Famous prints from some of the world's greatest artists adorned the walls. The finest linens and draperies. It pleased her very much because she had shared with Ray that she'd always wanted to stay there.

Sure she enjoyed the modern vibe of hotels like the Delano and the Gansevoort, but Missy was much more into old Hollywood glamour. Character. Charm.

She walked into the marble tiled bath with the gold fixtures. Ray had brought in all of her favorite toiletries and had them neatly arranged on the shelves. She couldn't wait to take a soak in the enormous claw footed tub.

When she opened the closet doors, she saw that he had done some shopping. He'd covered all bases. Everything from a Chanel tracksuit with matching sneakers to a beaded Valentino gown with coordinating accessories.

The antique dresser was laden with the most exquisite undergarments from La Perla. She figured Carmen must have helped.

It was amazingly thoughtful. Ray definitely played the game to win.

As she explored the suite, Ray was in the foyer taking a call from his agent, Matt and making himself a drink. He had a tendency to be a little long winded on his calls with Matt so she took that opportunity to freshen up a bit.

After taking a quick tee bath – the kind where you wash from head to crotch and armpit to armpit – she pulled on a pair of black silk and pearl G-string panties and slipped into a long black silk night gown with sheer panels along the sides, designed to accentuate her hourglass frame. Then she pulled her hair down from the ponytail and gave it a quick tease.

Since Ray preferred a natural looking woman, she removed the heavy makeup. Everything except the lashes. Then she dusted on a little pink blush for color and a pale pink gloss to highlight her lips.

The pièce de résistance was a little man getting concoction she carried in her purse for emergencies. A pheromone enhancing body oil with a slight hint of musk and vanilla. It drove men crazy! She knew because she'd put it to the test on more than a few occasions.

When she emerged from the powder room, Ray sat on a bar stool next to the kitchen counter. He was still on the phone, but when he saw her walking toward him, he lit up like a holiday tree.

She stopped just a few feet in front of him, then slowly removed the silk gown, allowing it to fall to the floor. She stepped out of the gown and walked toward him wearing only the pearl thong, her stilettos and a smile.

Missy instructed him to keep talking as she pulled him to his feet and began to undress him. She kissed and caressed him as she slowly removed each item of clothing. First, unbuttoning his shirt and pulling it down over his strong arms. She unbuckled his belt, unfastened his trousers and let them fall to the floor, exposing second skin designer boxer briefs that barely contained his excitement.

Ray continued to talk on the phone as she led him over to the sofa. She smiled seductively, and he braced himself when she reached inside his briefs with both hands and pulled them down, revealing the most beautiful erection she'd ever seen.

She bent down in front of him, balancing herself expertly on her stilettos and took him in her hands. Both hands which still failed to cover his full erection. It was as magnificent as she'd imagined.

Ray stood looking down at her, throbbing in anticipation of the treat he was about to receive. He held the phone in one hand and ran his fingers through her soft blonde hair with the other. He savored the sight of her kneeling down in front of him; her bare back leading down to a perfectly round ass that nearly swallowed the pearl thong she was wearing. And her scent was so intoxicating. Ray was near peak arousal.

Staring up and into his eyes she started at the head of his penis, kissing and licking it gently, flickering the tip of her wet tongue up and down his long hard, warm shaft. Then she began to tongue kiss it, as if she were kissing his mouth.

Sensing that he'd be unable to maintain his composure through the wondrous blow job he was getting, he started to interrupt Matt and end the call, but again Missy instructed him not to hang up the phone. "No, no baby, keep talking."

He grew harder in her mouth, which only made her mouth wetter. As she stroked the base with her hands she sucked on the head of his penis letting it go further into her mouth until it hit the back of her throat. The wetness from her tongue ran down to the base of his manhood, making it wetter, and her wetter, and him harder.

She continued to stroke it, and lick it, and kiss it, and suck it as his eyes rolled back into his head. Soon she started to feel his veins pulsate in her mouth. He was getting ready to release.

Missy let go of him for a moment, to allow him to compose himself, then she pulled him down to the sofa and returned to her fellatio.

She started sucking him again, but this time with her hands at his waist. She made long intense strokes letting him pass through her full lips through to the back of her throat, using the flicker of her tongue and the tension of her lips at random.

Ray's hips moved rhythmically with her as he grabbed a handful of her hair with one hand and thrust slowly in an out of her mouth. The strokes were longer and deeper until she started to gag on him again, which caused her mouth and then him to get even wetter.

By that time, Missy was smiling because she knew he'd never had head like *this*. Not many men had. Ray whimpered, as he neared his climax. All phone etiquette was lost, as he pressed a button abruptly ending the call.

Then he pulled her by the hair and pushed her to the floor. He grabbed two fistfuls of her hair and drove himself into her mouth until she gagged. Missy thought she'd throw up.

Being the freak that she was, this was only turning her on more, and she was dripping wet, throbbing for him now. He shoved himself in and out, letting her up periodically for air and pulling her hair tighter as he gripped it in both hands. Things seemed to be getting kinkier, and Missy was totally into it, just wishing he would hurry up and mount her before he came.

Ray pulled out of her mouth and bent down to kiss her. He kissed her hard on the lips, smearing the wetness all over her face and in her hair. He moaned loudly as he kissed on her face and neck. Missy was so hot and wet and ready to feel him she was near tears.

When she started to speak, "Oh baby...", he screamed out, "Shut the fuck up!" And then things really got weird.

*****

"You're a nasty little girl huh? You want me to fuck you don't you?"

At that point, Missy wasn't sure if she should speak or not. He loomed over her, rubbing his hardness on her, up and down her stomach, attempting to tease, but it was beginning to turn her off. All the way off.

Missy jumped when he screamed. "Answer me!"

She responded. "Y..yes baby."

"Yes *what*?"

"Yes. I...I want you to fuck me?"

He looked down at her with a devilish grin and pulled a leg over her, resting on his knees, straddling her with his penis sitting on her stomach. "Yeah. I know. I knew you wanted this dick. Playing hard to get. Making me wait like I'm a fuckin nobody. Three months? Do you know who the fuck I am? I'm Ray muthafuckin Coleman, and I can have any bitch I want. Including a freak ass little hoodrat like you. Can't I?"

"Ok. Baby. This is getting a little..." She attempted to get up, but he grabbed her by the hair and shoved her back down to the floor.

His eyes went dark. Vacant. "Don't. Fuckin. Move."

Missy began to panic inside. She wasn't sure what she should do. What to think. Was he serious? Was he in character or what? Was she safe? He kept talking.

"Look at you. So pretty. You're my pretty baby, aren't you? But you like to play games. All pretty girls like to play games, huh?

Yeeeesss. Yes, they do. Can I have a kiss, pretty girl? Can I kiss those pretty lips?"

"Yes."

"Yes *who*?"

She wasn't sure what to say. "Um, yes *sir*?"

"Yeah. Sir. I like that."

He stroked her hair, leaned down and kissed her softly on the lips. Missy laid there stiff and unsure. He gently bit her lower lip, trailed the top with his tongue before parting them and shoving his tongue deep into her mouth. Just then a surge of energy went through her, and it rested between her thighs. Her body was aching for attention. Ray's hardness rested on her stomach as he thrust his tongue hungrily inside her mouth. She received his sweet tongue and returned his passionate kiss as she held his face in her hands.

Missy moaned as the anticipation mounted. She wanted him inside of her. He rolled off of her and flipped her onto her stomach, then he crawled back up to her and began kissing her on the nape of her neck. Soft, erotic kisses that had the hair standing on the back of her neck. For a moment, she'd forgotten how creepy he'd been and allowed herself to fall into all the sensations going on within her.

He continued kissing her down her back and when he got to her ample ass he pulled her G-string to the side, opened her wide and stuck his tongue deep inside her. In and out, up and down, licking and sucking her sweetest spots. At this point her body was responding to him but her mind started to race again. In her head she heard that loud booming voice tell her to *shut the fuck up*. Then she thought, *did he call me a hoodrat?*

She wondered if it was just innocent role play or if the dude was a little disturbed. Should she be worried about him or what? He had her mind going in five different directions, but he had her body writhing with pleasure she hadn't known. His tongue was incredible.

Missy really didn't want him to stop, but she was still kind of nervous about where he was going. It was exciting, in a mildly perverse way. She thought, *this is SO not what I expected when I set out to give him a thank you piece.*

As he worked her ass over with his fingers and his hot tongue, he reached under her with his free hand and started working her clit with his forefinger and thumb. With all the mixed emotions she had going on, her nerves were on end and that only made the feelings more intense.

Suddenly she felt that familiar wave closing in on her. She was beginning to climax but was almost afraid to make a sound. She tried hard to hold it in, but when the orgasm came over her she let out a scream, releasing so hard she wet herself, him and the carpet beneath them. It was like someone had breached a dam inside her.

Still squirming around on the floor, Ray pulled her by her hips onto her knees. At that point, she was spent, and her body was nearly limp. He pulled her panties hard, breaking the pearl strand and scattering the beautiful iridescent beads about. And then he shoved himself in her ass. Hard.

The pain was jolting, and she screamed aloud. He started pumping harder and harder. Missy reached back behind her to push him away, but he grabbed her hand and squeezed it tight, as he plunged harder and deeper inside her body. Her screams were louder. She pleaded with him to stop, "Baby! No, wait!", but her pleas went unanswered. In fact, they seemed to turn him on more. He moaned, "Your ass...your ass is so tight, baby. It's so fuckin tight."

He thrust in and out of her, harder and faster. The pain was excruciating. He pushed her head to the floor and went even deeper inside her. She screamed again, "Ray! Stop! Please..."

"SHUT THE FUCK UP!"

He pumped away, tearing into her flesh, pressing her face so hard into the carpet she could feel it starting to burn her cheek. His moans began to get louder and higher in pitch, and she desperately hoped he was near climax. She needed the nightmare to end.

He pulled her up by the hair and put his other arm around her neck, causing them both to fall back to the floor. Then he leaned in and bit down hard on her ear lobe. He squealed like a wild boar being freed from its pen. Finally, he released deep inside and fell on top of her.

As she lay there under his massive body, in so much pain, she wondered what the hell had just taken place. Her ass was aching like she'd just given birth from it. Her head throbbed and the back of her throat burned from trying to hold in her tears.

Ray jumped up, slapped her hard on the ass and shouted, "Whoo! That was good. Let's go to bed baby." He never even looked back at her when he walked away.

Missy laid still on the floor for a while, just trying to digest. She could hear him in the bathroom shuffling around. The water ran for a while and then all the lights shut off in the bedroom. She thought,

This motherfucker is going to bed? Really? Missy was fully expecting him to come back out and at least check on her. Apologize. Acknowledge. Rub her ass. Something! He'd just torn her body apart and left her lying on the floor like an old rag doll.

About an hour later, she was finally able to pull herself up from the floor. She went into the bathroom to clean up. Unable to sit in a tub, she made her way into the shower and tried her best to clear away the filth from her body.

Missy stood in the mirror, trying to assess the damage. He'd broken the skin on her earlobe when he bit her, and there was the slightest strawberry on her left cheek from the carpet. He'd pulled her hair so hard her scalp was red and sore to the touch. Missy felt like she was in a bad dream.

She could hear Ray in bed snoring loudly, sleeping peacefully as if nothing happened. She walked out into the bedroom and stood over him, angry and confused. As she watched him rest without a care in the world, so much was going through her head.

Ray treated her like a groupie. A jump off. He abused her. She felt like...almost like she'd been raped. She thought, how could he go from 0 to 100 like that? This was their first time being intimate. How could he just assume that she was ok with anal sex? How could he handle her that way?

Now, Missy was a pretty kinky girl, so rough sex had never been a problem for her, but this just seemed so...wrong.

Part of her wanted to pack her bags and leave him without a word. Another part of her wanted to go in there and punch his ass awake. Maybe shove her curlers up his ass and let him see how it felt. But the rational side of her thought, maybe this wasn't enough to end a relationship with "the man of her dreams."

She had always wanted a man that was comfortable enough to have wild sex with her, respect and love her just the same. It had been her experience that once a guy was ready to wife you, he suddenly wanted you *out* of freak mode. She hated that. She thought, *maybe this is a good thing?*

The rational side of her started to reflect on the night's events, before the weird sex. This man was clearly in love with her, and she loved him back. If they could come to an agreement that he would never "butt rape" her like that again, maybe it would be the best sex she ever had.

Ray had everything she wanted and needed in a man, and any

woman would be crazy to walk away from him. Wouldn't they? And when would she meet another man of his caliber? One that wanted to love her, shower her and give her the world? Maybe never. At 33 years, Missy wasn't exactly an old hag, but she was no spring chicken either. Maybe this was it.

The rational side of her won, hands down. She slid into bed next to him and snuggled up onto his back. *Fuck it,* she told herself, then fell into a deep, satisfying sleep.

Brenda's Haze

Missy's phone was ringing off the hook. It was her mother. And for the umpteenth time. She hadn't spoken with her in a couple months, not since Betty had come home from the hospital.

She arranged to have a nurse come to Betty's house to care for her, since Brenda wasn't up to it. It was the least she could do, since she didn't really have time to deal with her.

Brenda was a complete mess, in mourning over her husband. The nurse called a couple times earlier in the week to tell Missy that the kids were running amuck all over the house, and it wasn't good for Betty's recovery.

The last thing Missy felt like doing was driving into DC to deal with Brenda's nonsense, but she had to go into Georgetown for a nail appointment anyway. So after her mani-pedi…and a peppermint facial, she took the dreadful drive back down Rhode Island Avenue, to the inner city.

Riding through, she could see nothing had changed. The same ol niggas standing on the corner and sittin on the stoop. Only they were older now. She hit the alarm button on her Bentley and made her way through the crowd to Brenda's building.

Everyone recognized her, but no one spoke. It was of no consequence to her. She wanted to get in and get out as quickly as possible. The quicker the better.

Several minutes passed before Brenda answered the door. Missy banged like the police. She had no intention of coming back anytime soon so Brenda would have to open the door. Brenda finally appeared and as soon as she opened the door Missy could smell the liquor as it wafted out into the hall.

They didn't speak. Brenda turned and walked back inside. She didn't offer Missy a seat, which was fine because Missy had no intention of taking one.

"So what brings *you* to the hood?" Brenda stumbled back over to the sofa, next to her half empty bottle of Stoli. She poured herself a refill. Neat.

Missy glared at her, annoyed. "It is eleven o'clock in the morning. Are you *serious* right now?"

Brenda rolled her eyes and swallowed the entire drink down. She wiped the drip page from her mouth with her sleeve. Missy was disgusted. "Brenda please. Get up and get in the shower right now. I swear I can't even talk to you like this. And what is that smell?"

The comment was ignored and there was a good couple minutes of awkward silence before Missy decided to take a seat. She stared over at her little sister, just lying there smelling of cheap alcohol and stale sweat. Hair all over her head. Wearing dirty socks and what had to be one of her husband's old sweatshirts because it was about seven sizes too big for her.

She looked around the filthy room. There were empty takeout boxes and half-empty soda cans everywhere. The sink was filled with dirty dishes, and trash fell out of overflowing cans. The bare floors were sticky, and the carpet soiled.

Brenda and Missy hadn't been close since they were kids, but Missy thought *this* didn't seem like any Brenda she ever knew. She felt a little sad for her. But then again, she needed to hurry up and get back home.

"Sweetie you have got to snap out of this. I mean really. It's not healthy. What are you *doing* to yourself?"

"Missy, leave me alone. Please." She laid back down on the sofa and closed her eyes. "Who asked you to come over here anyway? I didn't ask you to come over here fuckin with me. Just go home. I'm good."

"Well, you're a lot of things but good certainly isn't one of them. Look. I can't say that I know what you're going through right now, but I know you've got to snap out of this right now Brenda. I'm sorry to say it, but Melvin is gone, hunny. And there's nothing we can do about that. But right now, your children need you, and mother can't do it anymore. She can't."

Brenda replied, rhetorically, "What do *you* know about what mama can handle."

"Well, the nurse called today and said the kids are running wild over there. It's not good for mother's recovery. Now I know she's helped you with them in the past, but she can't handle them anymore. Maybe I can help you out with some childcare or something. But you've got to go and get them Brenda. So come on, get dressed." Missy clapped her hands loudly. "I've got to be out of here by twelve."

Brenda rolled her eyes and turned on her side.

There was another brief silence before Missy kicked the sofa. "Get your ass up!"

Brenda angrily jumped up off the sofa. "You know what? You right. You DON'T know what I'm going through. So don't bring your ass up in here tryna tell me what the fuck I need to do. Just go home! Go back to Potomac. Go back to your perfect little life with your football player and your perfect little kids. Just go home and mind your fuckin business...like you been doing all these years."

She sat back down and started ranting under her breath. "Tryna come up in here and tell me what the fuck is goin on. You don't know nuttin bout my fuckin life. *Or* mama's." She grabbed her blanket and laid back down on the sofa. "Bye Missy. And lock my door on your way out."

Missy was getting frustrated. The clock was ticking and she really didn't have time to deal with Brenda's foolishness. So she tried a different approach. "Brenda. Sweetie. I'm worried about you."

If looks could kill, Missy would have fallen dead right there on the floor. Her comment only added to Brenda's growing aggravation. "Yeah well you don't need to worry about me. You don't need to worry about me, my family, what's going on back in the hood. None of that. We good over here Missy! I'm good, mama good and all my kids are GOOD!"

"Ok, YOU are NOT GOOD. And I'm not gonna let you kill my mother!"

Brenda jumped back off the sofa. "What?! You not gon let me kill *your* mother? Who the fuck you think you talkin to, Missy?" Brenda moved to within an inch of Missy's face. "You come to my fuckin house acting like you runnin somethin? Talking about you not gon LET me kill *your* mother. Really? You don't even *see* your mother."

Missy realized the comment may have sounded a little out of place. "No...well what I really meant to say was..."

"No. Uh uh. Let's put it on out there. You so worried about your mother, where were you last year when she had the triple bypass surgery? I know where I was. I was at the Washington Hospital Center. All night. Slept in a chair outside the operating room. I didn't see *you*. Where are you three times a week when your mother needs a ride to dialysis or to the doctor or the grocery store? Where the FUCK ARE YOU when she has a bill that needs to be paid, Missy? You da one with all the money. You think *mother* can survive on that bullshit Social Security check?"

Missy stood silently.

"Nothing to say? No? Exactly. With your SELFish ass." Brenda took a step closer. So close their lips nearly touched. She spoke slowly, just above a whisper. "And don't you *ever* talk about my kids. You don't even KNOW my kids. So how about you get back on that bullshit white horse you rode over here on and go back to wherever the fuck you came from this morning. Before I put my *hands* on your ass. Now get outta my house, Missy."

Brenda walked back over to the couch, laid down and closed her eyes. Satisfied that she had finally said what she needed to say to Missy for so many years now, she just wanted her sister to leave. She didn't care about hurt feelings, and for the first time she really didn't care what her mother would say about it.

Her head was pounding, her mouth was dry and at that moment, all she wanted was a Goody Powder, a strong cold Sprite and to be left the hell alone.

As for Missy, she was done. If Brenda didn't want her help, oh well. She grabbed her purse from the table and turned to leave, but before she reached the door she heard a sniffle.

She turned and surveyed the room once more. It broke her heart.

Her baby sister was lying there helpless and lost, clutching a bottle of vodka to her chest. So far outside of herself she was hardly recognizable. Trying desperately to maintain her strength but clearly breaking inside.

Missy thought back to the days when they were close. They fought like cats and dogs as kids but there was no doubt how much they loved each other. Brenda was a little terror. A busy body that was always into something. But Missy would never let anything happen to her. And no matter how many bougie wannabe snobs Brenda called her, Missy knew she would fight to the death for her big sister.

So much had changed since then. Their lives had gone in such different directions that they didn't even know each other anymore. But that wasn't really Brenda's fault.

An overwhelming sense of guilt fell upon her. Why had *they* fallen apart? Missy's issues were with Betty, not Brenda. It wasn't fair to punish Brenda for Betty's crimes. But it was more complicated than that. Still there was no reason for things to stay the way they were. Whether Brenda realized it or not, she needed her. And they had to start somewhere.

So she decided to try once more, at least. "Look Brenda, I didn't come here to argue or to fight with you. I know I've made mistakes. I'm not perfect, and I don't always do the right thing, but we're talking about you. We're talking about you being there for your children and being here for our mother."

Brenda was near the end of her rope. She thought, *this bitch is determined to get her ass whooped in here today.* She fought the urge to get up from the couch again.

"I been here, Missy! Where were you?!? Where the fuck you been!" Though her eyes were still closed, tears formed and soon streamed down the sides of her face. "I swear to God; I just can't deal with this right now. I'm tired, I have a headache, and I just want to go to sleep. I'm not gon keep asking you, Missy. Go home PLEASE."

"Brenda get up! I'm not leaving here until you—"

"Bitch! I already told you..." Brenda raised up and lunged at Missy, who stood on the other side of the coffee table. She tripped over the coffee table, shattering the glass and cutting her leg. Then she fell to the ground crying hysterically.

Instinctively, Missy ran to the kitchen to grab a towel to stop the bleeding. She placed the towel over the wound and applied pressure until the bleeding slowed. She held Brenda tightly in her arms until she calmed down. Just like she used to when they were kids. Missy wondered how could she have let things get this far.

"Brenda. I'm sorry. Please don't cry. I know you're going through it. It's ok. I'm here for you, baby. And I hear you, but trust me, my life ain't no *crystal stair.*" She brushed away Brenda's tears and kissed her on the cheek. "Come on, let's get you cleaned up. I think it's about time we have a talk."

The Proposal

After one of the strangest, and most exhilarating nights of her life, Missy woke up to the aroma of her favorite Jamaican Blue Mountain coffee. Ray walked in pushing a server's cart with several covered trays.

He wore a towel around his waist, his upper body still wet from his morning shower. Missy thought, "Damn my baby is fine." And that he was.

Ray had the height and beautiful deep brown complexion of Idris Elba, a body chiseled from stone not unlike The Rock, Denzel's sexy swagger, and the deep velvety voice of Barry White. All kinds of sexy.

He was well-educated, well-spoken, well-traveled and outgoing. So charming. She could sit and talk to him for hours. And that package. Length, width and girth. Enough said. She wanted to unwrap that towel and make love to him right then and there. The proper way.

She couldn't take her eyes off him. He kissed her on the forehead and broke her trance.

"So how'd you sleep princess?"

"Oh, I slept ok."

"I think you slept better than ok. You ran me out to the sofa with your snoring!" He laughed. "I couldn't even wake you to answer your phone. You got a call around 6 a.m."

Thinking nothing of the comment, Missy grabbed the carafe and poured her coffee into the fancy gold rimmed china. "Oh, I did? Ok."

There were a few seconds of silence before Ray cleared his throat. "Well?"

Missy looked up from her plate. Ray had a serious look on his face. "Well what?"

"Well, aren't you going to check your phone?"

"Oh. Yeah. Let me grab it." She walked over to the credenza

where it was plugged in and brought it back to the table. When she sat down, she clicked the message and tried to stifle a giggle but nearly spit coffee on the table. She put the phone back down, quietly. "So what's for breakfast, baby? Everything smells so good!"

Ray feigned a smile. "I'll tell you what's for breakfast if you tell me who that was on the phone. *Someone* had you smiling just now. "

He was looking intently into her eyes waiting for an answer. His smile was gone, as was his pleasant demeanor of just a moment before. Missy instinctively knew it wouldn't be wise to tell him it was her ex, Chucky the comedian, who always made her laugh.

"It was just my sister, Brenda."

"Oh yeah? Brenda? And what was so funny?"

"Oh my God, Ray! What's with the third degree?" Missy laughed, attempting to diffuse the situation *and* to let him know it was definitely not ok to question her like that. He was throwing out some serious red flags this trip.

He smiled. "I just want to be the only one to make my baby smile like that. That's all. Have some breakfast before it gets cold. I wasn't sure what you wanted so I just told them to bring you everything on the menu."

With each cover he pulled away, there lay a more delectable plate in front of her. Eggs benedict with lemon truffle hollandaise and smoked salmon; buckwheat pancakes with fresh berries and whipped cream; shrimp Provençale with Israeli couscous; chicken apple sausage with their famous hammered potatoes.

There was an assortment of pastries, a fresh fruit and cheese platter, fresh squeezed juices. Enough food for a small village. Wasteful, but wonderful.

"Ray this is perfect. You really know how to treat a lady don't you?"

"Correction, I really know how to treat *my* lady." With that he stood and kissed her ever so gently on the lips. He took a sip of orange juice and grabbed a pastry. "Enjoy your breakfast, baby. I have a meeting with Matt in 30 minutes, so I've gotta get outta here. I'll be back in a couple hours."

"Noooo." Missy pouted. "You're really not having breakfast with me?"

"I'm sorry, baby, I really have to make this meeting. But you go and relax. Have a nice bubble bath in that big fancy tub you like. Drink a mimosa. Enjoy yourself. Just be ready to hit the streets when

I get back." And he was off.

After Ray left, she finished her breakfast, popped the cork on a bottle of Cliquot and made herself a nice healthy water goblet full of mimosa. She ran a hot bubble bath and put her iPod on the dock. The Neo Soul station on Pandora was rockin as she sang every song, slightly off key, "Is it the the waaaay, you loooove, me baaaabaaayyy…" She was in heaven.

The hour long bubble bath and breakfast cocktail had Missy feeling pretty loose for an early morning. She thought. *What the hell. I am on vacation.* She walked out onto the terrace to take in the amazing view of the New York skyline.

The morning air was crisp and there was the slightest fog obstructing the view, but the sun shone brightly through it, radiating enough warmth to make it cozy for lounging. As she sat out on the terrace, luxuriating in the plush white monogrammed robe and savoring her second cup of Jamaican Blue, she couldn't help but smile. For once in her life, everything felt perfect. Really right. Outside of a little carnal confusion, she was on top of the world.

Her thoughts drifted back to her anniversary. The anticipation. All the wonderful surprises. The party of the decade. She was still reeling from it all. It suddenly dawned on her that an event that big *had* to be in the paper so she ran out and grabbed the Post from outside the door and perched herself back out on the chaise.

When she reached the infamous page six Missy nearly choked on her brew. "Oh my Gooood!" she screamed aloud. She was staring herself square in the face.

Gracing the same pages as so many of her favorite celebrities was the picture of Missy and Ray with the first couple. The caption read "A Lister's Come Out in Packs for Barack Obama's $40K Per Plate Fundraiser". She squealed with excitement as she thought, *Damn I looked good! I gotta get more papers!*

She couldn't think of a better way to start the day. Making page six of the New York Post, being photographed with the Potus *and* the Flotus, being referred to as an "A lister".

The rest of the day was nothing to sneeze at either. Ray arranged for a carriage ride through Central Park, a private tour at the Metropolitan Museum of Art and finally some power shopping on Fifth Avenue. Missy lived for Bergdorf's shoe department and Ray looked on lovingly as the personal shoppers served up champagne and catered to her every whim. He'd instructed them to give her the royal treatment and they did just that.

After several hours of shopping they headed back to the hotel to relax a bit before their night out. Exhausted, Missy fell asleep as soon as she sat down on the sofa. When she awoke Ray emerged from the bathroom looking more delicious than she'd ever seen him.

He wore a pair of distressed Seven jeans, a crisp white button down shirt and a cranberry colored single breasted Versace blazer. He finished the ensemble with gold embellished Versace loafers and a matching Rolex timepiece. He looked good and he knew it.

"Come on sleeping beauty. We have a schedule to keep."

She yawned and grinned. "Umh. Don't *you* look handsome. And you smell good too." She walked over to him and reached into his jacket. "You make me wanna throw you down and undress you again."

Ray backed away from her, dismissing her advance. "Missy we don't have time for that. Come on let's go!" He clapped his hands at her loudly before he took a phone call.

Missy was slightly put off by his abruptness. But she let it go. Apparently they had a schedule to keep. So she proceeded to the bedroom to get herself in costume for the evening. There was an outfit laid out on the bed. A complete ensemble down to the accessories. She thought, *Oh no he didn't.* So she went back to the living area and grabbed her shopping bags to find something more to *her* liking.

Thirty minutes later she sauntered out into the living room wearing a white sheer chiffon pirate sleeved Valentino blouse and a pair of high-waist denim jeans. The boots were thigh high suede and she had a matching suede chain linked Chanel bag. Her hair and makeup was on point as always. Sexy. She felt fabulous. "So…baby. You like?"

Ray was still on a call. He looked over at her and put the phone to his chest. "No. Go back and put on the outfit I picked. The Michael Kors dress. And hurry up!" He placed the phone back to his ear and resumed his conversation.

She stood for a moment, a little disappointed. But ultimately she decided it was a small thing, so she hurried back to the bedroom and changed.

His outfit was nice enough. Chic but modest. It matched his, which was kinda corny, but again, when in Rome. She switched up some of her accessories and came back out to make sure everything was good. "You like?"

He smiled wide. "Beautiful baby. Now let's hit it. We're already late!"

First, they went for cocktails at Missy's favorite Asian fusion spot, Tao NY. Then Ray whisked her away to dinner at Le Cirque, his favorite. Missy wasn't a big fan of French food, but he was being romantical, so she went with the flow. They ended the evening cruising the Hudson River.

The weather was so perfect that night – clear skies and a bright full moon, a warm gentle breeze out on the water. As they sailed further across the river, the view of the city in the distance was absolutely breathtaking.

Ray held her closely from behind, and she melted into his strong arms as they sailed along. One of her favorite tunes from the Whispers began to play. "I'm gonna make you my wiiife, you're the air I breathe…" Ray sang softly in her ear. Every word deliberate and with conviction, as if he'd written the song just for her. "I'm gonna buy you some riiings…" She felt especially loved and at that moment Missy couldn't help thinking, *this would be the perfect time for him to propose.*

She turned to face him, to look into his eyes while he sang to her. As soon as she did he took a few steps back so he could comfortably kneel. Missy thought, *Oh my God! It's happening! It's happening!* Indeed, it was. Ray pulled that familiar little red box with the gold detail from his jacket pocket and opened it slowly, for a dramatic effect.

She tried to hold it in, but it was impossible. Her heart pounded and tears flowed in a steady stream meeting at her chin. As if it were a foregone conclusion, Ray reached for her left hand and placed the ring on her finger. He stared into her eyes as he sang each soulful word with purpose. When he stood back up, he kissed her gently on the lips and wiped her tears away.

It was a most spectacular gesture and the other passengers ate it up completely. They burst into applause, when the lead singer of the cover band announced, "Ladies and gentlemen, she said yes! I present to you the future Mr. and Mrs. Ray Coleman!"

Not 24 hours before Missy was hobnobbing with the most elite group of people she ever imagined in one room, thinking it was best night of her life. But once again Ray had outdone himself. She held her hand up to view the beautiful gem in the moonlight and thought, *it just doesn't get any better than this.* It's funny how quickly things can change.

The Revelation

After a hot shower, a few aspirin and a mug full of strong black Folgers, Brenda's head was near clear.

Missy had relaxed the grip on her Birkin bag and loosened up a bit. She was ready to talk. "You got anymore vodka left in here?"

Brenda exaggerated an eye roll. "Uh, no. It's too early to be drinking, remember?" They laughed.

"Forget you. I figure I may as well have something to take the edge off before we get into it."

"Wow. It's that bad?"

"Pretty much."

"You sure you wanna talk right now? We don't have to if you're not ready. Missy, I'm sorry for what I said. It's just…"

Missy waved her hand. "Brenda, please. Stop it. You don't have to apologize. I know I deserved it. There's just so much you don't understand. Do you mind if I open this?" Brenda signaled no as Missy cracked the seal on the oversized bottle of Patron that was sitting on the makeshift bar.

She poured a half glassful and sighed before she made herself comfortable in Melvin's old leather lounger. "Everyone thinks I'm living this great life of luxury. Everything looks so great from the outside looking in, but it's so fucking far from that, little sis." She took a healthy swallow of the tequila and grimaced as it burned the back of her throat. "To tell the truth. I'm miserable. I'm miserable every day."

Brenda laughed. "Ok, let me stop you for a second. You carrying a twelve-thousand-dollar bag and driving a Bentley Coupe. You're living in a six-million-dollar home with an Olympic-size swimming pool, a basketball court, tennis court…"

"Brenda, Brenda, Brenda. You keep naming all of this material crap. Cars, clothes, a house. They're just things. I don't care about any of that!"

"Well then give them to me."

They both laughed. "Seriously, that stuff is not even important to me."

Brenda leaned back into the sofa, a look of disbelief on her face. "What? Since when? Now if we gon talk, we gon have to keep it all the way real, Missy. This is *me* you talkin to. Since when do *you* not care about things?' That's all you've ever cared about. That's all you ever talked about."

"Yeah, well 'things' change, ok." She took another gulp of her drink. The second swallow went down a little easier. "Things change."

"Yeah, well you need to tell me what's changed that much in the last two years."

"You know what, just drop it. I don't want to talk about it. You couldn't possibly understand."

Brenda laughed, sarcastically. "Ex-actly."

Missy sighed. "Exactly what?"

"That is exactly the shit that has you so disconnected from us Missy. Your dumb uneducated, GED havin, hoodrat little sister couldn't *possibly* understand anything going on in your world, huh?"

"Don't put words in my mouth. I never said that."

"You never had to. Tell me something. Are you really that ashamed of us, Missy? Really? Let's put it all out on the table. Since I've got you here and I seem to have your attention for once, let's put it all out there."

"Go ahead."

"You sure?"

"Yeah. Go ahead and say what you gotta say, Brenda."

"Ok, none of us were invited to your wedding. Not even mama. We've only seen your house in Ebony magazine and that's only because we heard about it from Aunt Wanda, who just happened to pick up the magazine at a nail salon. Me and mama only met Ray once and that was just recently. Because she was in the hospital damn near on her death bed. Even then you acted like you didn't wanna be there. He was clearly uncomfortable being there. My children don't even *know* you. You don't see nothin wrong with that, Missy?"

Missy looked away. Unable to form any sort of reasonable response to the truth, she was forced to hear her sister out. So Brenda continued.

"As close as we were growing up, you live an hour away, and I can count on one hand how many times I've seen you in the past two years. Mama makes excuses for you, but I know it hurts her. Hearin about what y'all doing from random people in the neighborhood. Seeing y'all on tv. Knowing she can't share in any part of your life. And what's a trip, is that through everything she never says a negative word about you. She never allows anyone else to either. All I hear is how smart you are, and how beautiful you are, and how successful you are. How you've 'made it.' She's so proud of you, and it eats me alive knowing that she can't spend time with the one person she'd probably give her life for."

Brenda could feel the emotions beginning to swell inside her. She swallowed it down, cleared her throat and continued. "As much as I do for her and as hard as I try, in her eyes I'll never be you. I'm just the dumb one that had a baby in high school and married a drug dealer. I'm the baby maker of the family. I would *like* to think she compared me to you, but in her eyes there was never any real comparison. Real talk, I've resented you for so long because of that, Missy. I mean borderline hated you. But now that I've gotten it off my chest…I guess I can finally let it go. I'm happy with me and what I've been to my family."

Missy was halfway through the bottle of tequila at that point and staring at the ceiling. They sat quietly for a few minutes until Brenda broke the silence.

"Still nothing to say. After all that."

Missy screamed. "WHAT THE FUCK DO YOU WANT FROM ME?!"

Brenda sat for a second, staring Missy down with a most disgusted look. "You know what, big sis? I want from you exactly what you have given this family. Nothing." She stood up, walked into the kitchen and threw her glass into the sink so hard it broke. "And you can lock the door on your way out. I'm going back to bed." She walked back into her room and slammed the door shut.

Missy sat there nursing the bottle and crying to herself. After a while, she was completely wasted and drained from the emotional ride. She wanted to tell her secrets so badly, but it was just too much. Too much for her to put out there.

Missy had worked so hard to maintain the image of perfection and if she ever let out the truth everyone would know it was all a lie. The happy family. The successful wife, mother, businesswoman, philanthropist, socialite, was all an elaborate lie built by Ray's PR machine. All of it orchestrated to serve him and to keep her quietly in her place.

So she sat and drank, and sat and drank until the bottle was empty and all she could do was curl up in the lounger and close her eyes.

Several hours later, Brenda emerged from the bedroom, dressed, refreshed and ready to go pick up her babies. She was proud that she had finally dealt with the bullshit and now she was ready to move on. She noticed Missy still asleep in the chair and a wave a fury came over her. She kicked the chair hard. "MISSY! Get UP! Come one now, you gotta go!"

Missy opened her eyes, still in a haze. "I...I'm sorry. I'm going. Where...where are my keys?"

"They right here." Brenda snatched her purse and keys and threw them hard in her lap. "Your purse, your keys, now come on let's go."

Missy tried to get up but halfway to her feet she got dizzy. She fell backward into the chair and curled up into a ball. Then she started to sob. Weird, loud cries like some kind of wounded animal. "Ahhhhhhhh. Ahhhhhhhhhh."

Brenda kicked the chair again. "Oh no! I don't *even* have time for this bullshit. I really need to go pick up MY kids so I don't kill YOUR mother, remember? So imma need you to get your ass up off my chair, grab your keys, and keep it movin."

"No. I can't. I can't. Please just let me sleep. I'll go in a little while, Brenda."

"No sweetie. You got a life to get back to. You can't be slummin down here with us po folk. My house probably not clean enough for you anyway. Maybe you should get your nice white pants off this chair. Mandy peed on it last night. Wouldn't want you to sit down in your Bentley with pee on your pants now, would we? As a matter of fact, we might need to go check on your car. You know how niggas is around the hood. They not used to nothin nice. We wouldn't want that thing to get scratched."

Missy was getting tired of the mocking. She'd had just about enough of Brenda and her self-righteous bullshit for one day. But Brenda kept at her.

"Oh and wait, your husband probably put an APB out on you by now. We *definitely* don't want him upset. Good ole Ray Coleman. He sho do love his wife don't he. Yes, ma'am. He loves his Queen. Look how pretty that ride is sittin out there. What's that a couple hundred thousand? Damn and look at that rock?" Brenda picked up Missy's hand to examine her ring. "That gotta be what, 6 carats? Uhm hmm. 6 carats, perfect yellow diamond. Makes my little 2 carats look like a bubble gum machine ring don't it? Oh how I wish I had a husband like him. Ray Coleman. A good strong man. A man to come sweep me up off my feet and take me up out this hood. You so lucky, big sis. How'd you get that man anyway? Girl tell me what did you do! You got Ray Coleman. Uhm um mm. With his fine football playing ass. A dream man. He's rich. He's famous. He's smart. He's handsome. He's–"

Missy leaped to her feet, snatched up her keys and purse and screamed to the very top of her lungs, "HE'S GAAAAYYYYYYYYY!"

Kim Davis

Melvin's gun was never found, so outside of the baseball bat in the coat closet and the mini pepper spray on Brenda's keychain there was no protection in the house. DC had just passed a law making it legal to own a gun in your home, but Brenda was ineligible for a license due to her criminal past; which wasn't an extensive past, she'd just roughed up a couple girls, on a couple different occasions for coming at Melvin. Wifely stuff, but those "incidents" made it impossible for her to legally own a gun.

There was a wilderness and hobby shop in Adams Morgan, one of the more affluent neighborhoods in the city, that sold guns. Mostly rifles, but there was a small selection of handguns that were available to view by request. Most people didn't know they could request them. Brenda did.

The store was sometimes run by the owner's daughter Kim Lee Davis. A half black, half Korean girl from around the way, sort of. She and Melvin had an "understanding" – i.e. she sold him guns out of the back door.

Kim ran the store on Thursdays, so Brenda made her way to Adams Morgan early enough to be the first customer. When she got there, the store already had a few customers, so she decided to peruse until they left.

An hour, and about a half dozen customers later, Kim walked over to her to offer some assistance, and to find out why this young black woman was walking in circles, going between fishing rods and fencing gear. Either she was up to something or she needed some help. "Good morning ma'am. Can I help you with something here?"

"Um, hi. I mean good morning," Brenda whispered. "I'd like to see your selection of handguns."

"I'm sorry ma'am, we actually don't carry handguns in this store. Just these hunting rifles you see here. But I'm happy to show you our catalog. Maybe you'll find something there to your liking."

Kim gave Brenda a knowing look. Brenda wasn't exactly sure what the look was about, but she hoped they were on the same page.

"Okay."

"Please, follow me. So how are you this beautiful Thursday morning?"

"I'm fine, thanks."

"Here is our catalog. Take a look at pages twelve through sixteen here, and let me know if you see anything you like. I need to take care of these customers, and I'll be right back with you." Another curious glance from the young Asian lady.

"Ok, thanks."

Kim rang up her last customer and sent him on his way. She walked back to the counter where Brenda was still sifting through the catalog. "Waddup Brenda! Long time no see!"

Brenda looked puzzled. "What? You know me?"

Kim laughed. "Girl you so craaazy. You seriously don't remember me?"

"No. I mean I know *of* you–"

"It's KIM! Kim Davis? We went to elementary school together. Noyes Elementary? Sixth grade. Mrs. Strong's class? Y'all used to call me *Egg Roll*."

Brenda suddenly remembered. "Oh my God, Kim! You know I didn't even recognize you. You look so different now!"

"Yeah, I have my orthodontist and my Lasik eye surgeon to thank for that."

"Oh no hunny." Brenda gave her body a once over. "I think you got a couple more people to thank for all *that*."

Kim laughed. "Well…yes. I did have my boobs done, a little lipo, an eye lift, my nose was a little crooked before…and I got a little extra junk stashed in my trunk." She turned and ran a slow hand over her new booty. "A girl gotta eat, right?"

Brenda laughed. "I know that's right. It looks good on you though. I mean I really did not recognize you at all."

"I'll take that as a compliment from you. Miss new booty."

Brenda smiled modestly. Somehow reference to her body always made her uncomfortable. "So aside from the extreme makeover, how are things with you?"

"Girl I'm hanging in. I been running this store since my father got sick a few months back. He's in a nursing home now, and I been trying to get my mother to sell it but she's not having it. We ain't really making no money, and I'm tired of sitting here all day every day just passing time, you know."

"Wow. I'm sorry to hear about your father. I remember Mr. Davis. Military guy. He used to drop you and pick you up from school every day right?"

"Yes girl. I couldn't walk nowhere, couldn't do nothin. I guess that's why I started hoe 'in early. O-Kay!" Kim broke out in hysterical laughter.

Brenda remembered the rumors about the little Korean girl. Somebody got her pregnant in junior high, and right after that she disappeared. She came back the next school year. Nobody ever heard what happened to the baby. "You a mess. I wasn't even gon touch that one. Does your family still have that convenient store, over by the school?"

"Yeah, my brother Hung is running it now."

"Oh yeah. I remember your little brother. So cute. How is he?"

"Fine I guess. Making babies left and right. Don't want nothing but a hoodrat. We don't really talk like that. Anyway, what are you buying a gun for? Gettin one for your man?"

"No, I just been thinking about gettin one for a while, and now they're legal but you know." She lowered her voice a bit. "I had a little *trouble* in the past."

"Oh, ok. Well, you know I gotchu. Do you know how to use one?"

"Yeah my husband showed me how. I'm actually pretty good with it. I gets my Charlie's Angels on at the range."

"Ok good. I see that rock. Damn girl! So how long you been married?"

"Well I was married to Melvin for twelve years but we'd been together since high school."

"Melvin? Melvin Johnson?"

"Yeah, you know Melvin. He told me you did business together. That's why I came in here to see you."

"Girl yes. That's my boo!" Kim noticed Brenda's expression change. "Oh no, not like that. I used to mess with his friend Daye. I just meant that Melvin was cool as shit. We did business here and there."

Brenda relaxed her face again. "Right."

"So how is Melvin doing? I haven't heard from him in a minute."

There was a long pause. Brenda began to tear up before she muttered. "Melvin was killed a few weeks ago."

"WHAT!? Killed! Oh my God! I'm so sorry, Brenda. What happened?"

"Girl, it's just so much. I can't even go into it." Brenda started to cry. "I don't know what, I don't know where, I don't know who. I just got a call from Daye at three in the morning telling me to come up to the Hospital Center. When I got there, Melvin was already gone. Shot at point blank range in the head. His throat was slit from ear to ear. He was beaten and tortured. They threw acid in his face Kim. I barely recognized him." Brenda buried her head in her hands and cried so hard her body shuddered.

Kim grabbed some tissues from behind the counter and handed them to her. She rubbed her back and listened.

"And when they found him he didn't have anything on him. His gun, phone, wallet and his house keys. Everything, gone."

"Oh yeah Brenda, you definitely need a gun in the house."

Brenda sighed and wiped her face. "Yeah, I don't feel safe in my own house anymore. I changed all the locks, switched security systems. I'm even thinkin about gettin a dog. I just feel like nothing is enough. I'm constantly on edge. Every little noise I hear. I feel like I can't even function. But girl, I swear to God if my alarm ever goes off a muthafucka *will* be gettin shot. That's on my life. I ain't here to be nobody's victim and I ain't letting nobody fuck with my kids."

"I hear that." Kim took a thoughtful pause. Unsure if she should proceed. "Brenda I know we haven't kicked it in a long time, and I'm not tryna be all up in your business, but I think we should talk."

"Ain't that what we doing right now?"

"I mean really *talk*. Are you in a rush right now?"

Brenda grabbed more tissue from her purse and composed herself. "No. Well not really. I was just about to go and pick up my daughter from my mom's house, but I have a little time."

"Good. I just got a case of champagne in last night. I'm thinking we could use a cocktail right about now. Relieve a little bit of stress."

"That's so sweet. Thank you Kim. I could really use a break."

"Ok, just give me a minute to shut the shop down and I'll meet you in the back. Go on back there and make yourself comfortable. We got a whole lot to catch up on girlfriend. Starting with your boy Daye."

"Daye?"

"Yeah. Just give me one second."

The Countdown

72 hours until the big day. It was supposed to be the happiest time of her life but instead Missy was filled with dread and anxiety. As she sat in the sauna trying to sweat off those last centimeters for her wedding dress, her mind raced back to the day that she and Ray met. The butterflies she felt in the pit of her stomach the first time he called her Mrs. Coleman.

She went back to the day he whisked her away to New York City on a private jet for her Cinderella moment with the President and First Lady; the night he proposed to her under the stars aboard a mega yacht, cruising the Hudson River. It was all so exciting then.

Then her mind went to their first sexual encounter. The first time he lost his temper with her. The cavalier way he confirmed that he had children. Two of them with two different women. And the way she found out...from Carmen. Ridiculous.

The day they returned from New York Missy shared the news of the engagement with Carmen over lunch. Carmen gloated over breaking the proposal news first and gushed over all the juicy details. After telling Missy for a third time how lucky she was, she casually asked if "the kids" would be in the wedding. Missy's response was, "What kids?"

Missy dropped a hundred-dollar bill on the table and went immediately to Ray's house to confront him. When she asked him outright, he blew it off. Said he thought she already knew and intimated that she should have known. "Missy, everyone knows I have children. Don't you read?" She was speechless.

Once she gathered her thoughts they had their first big fight. She called him a liar. He accused her of being petty, of all things. He said that if she couldn't accept his children the wedding was off.

Missy explained her position. It wasn't about the kids. He was a 38-year-old professional athlete with two ex-wives, why wouldn't he have kids. It was the fact that he hadn't mentioned them the whole time they were together. She screamed, "Three months and no mention of a five and two-year old? What kind of man does that?"

He twisted it around on her. Said she insulted his character and his love for his children. So he was done with her. She was done with him. It was over.

Several hours, and earth shattering orgasms later, they'd reached a happy medium. She would meet the kids the following weekend and he would never keep anything from her again. Everything was cool.

Many times since that day Missy wished she would have just walked away when Ray gave her that out. Often, he'd act like a jerk, but then he'd do something sweet. Charm her in some way. Ray knew exactly how to push her buttons and every time he did something to drive her away, he'd reel her right back in. Usually a declaration of his love followed by an expensive gift and a really good romp on his satin sheets. She'd bask in the afterglow and remember why she loved him *so*. It worked every time. It was very clear who was in control.

From the very start, the wedding drove a wedge between them. Not 24 hours after the proposal, Ray and his agent had already hired premier event planner to the stars, Preston Bailey. He said it was his gift to her, but Missy knew that it was just Ray's way of maintaining control of the wedding, of having everything his way.

What woman wouldn't want to plan her own wedding? Missy had been planning her wedding in her head since she was 10 years old, and now he was taking that away from her. He had pretty much taken all the joy out of the event for her.

With every meeting and every idea that was thrown out, her wedding was becoming less and less about her. She had not been able to digest the engagement before Ray had the wedding date set.

They were to be married three months to the day of their engagement, and when Missy said that she couldn't plan a wedding in three months, his response was "That's what Preston is for." When she complained, he called her ungrateful. She was beyond frustrated with the whole situation.

No one could see her point of view, not even her best friend, Carmen. She kept warning Missy not to blow the best thing that ever happened to her. Everyone and their mama thought she should just be grateful that out of all the women he could have had, Ray Coleman chose her. But she didn't feel that way. Not exactly.

She was having major reservations and after the last meeting with the pastry chef for the cake tasting went awry, Missy knew she had to say something.

About six weeks prior to the wedding, Missy and Ray were lying in bed, and she summoned the nerve to have "the talk." Her intentions were good but she had no idea he would react the way he did. She definitely didn't expect a blow up.

She snuggled in next to him, laying her head against his chest. "Baby?"

"Yes my love?" He kissed her on the forehead and pulled her in a little tighter.

"I need to talk to you about something."

"Anything."

"Do you think we're rushing into this?"

"Rushing into what? Marriage?"

"Well I've been thinking a lot about it. It's my wedding and I'm not even involved. I know you said you wanted to take the stress off of me with the planning and everything…but…"

He pulled away from her, moving his arm from behind her head. "But what?"

She sat up in the bed and faced him, determined to get everything out despite his attitude. "Well, can I be honest?"

"Please do."

"Well it…it just doesn't feel right, Ray. Maybe we should take a step back. Postpone it for a while. I mean…it's not like we're pregnant. There's no shotgun. There's no rush, right?"

"Right." Ray turned over and turned off the light on the bedside table.

Missy turned the lights back on. "Baby please, don't shut down on me. I just thought I should be honest with you about my feelings. It's not something I'm set on. I just wanted you to know how I felt. I mean…I want to get married and everything…but…"

Ray jumped up out of the bed and threw his clothes on. "I'm going to sleep at my place tonight."

"No! Why?"

"I have an early flight tomorrow."

"A flight? To where?"

"Atlanta."

"You didn't tell me anything about a trip. When did–"

"Missy! I forgot okay. I need to go home and pack anyway." He grabbed his jacket and headed for the door. Missy was close at his heels.

"Well when are you coming back?"

"In a few days. I'll call you when I land."

"Ray. Please don't be angry."

He slammed the door behind him. Missy stood there wondering if she had made a huge mistake. She loved Ray and she thought she wanted to marry him but everything was happening way too fast. She wanted to take some more time to get to know him, to explore those red flags of his.

Marriage was too important to her to just try it out. She wanted to make sure this man was indeed her happily *forever* after and since he'd been married twice before he wasn't exactly an authority on it.

Missy knew she wasn't overreacting; she just hoped that Ray could see her point of view. He could have the night to cool off and think about it and she'd call him in the morning. Maybe by then he will have come to his senses. Or at least be ready to have a conversation.

The next morning, she called and got no answer. That was the first time it had ever happened. Ray kept his phone on his person at all times, even in the bathroom and it was always charged so he always answered by the second ring. She thought maybe he was in the airport or in flight. He never did mention what time his flight was. She decided she'd just wait until he called.

At eight o'clock that night, she still hadn't heard from him so she called again. There was no answer. She left a message. An apology of sorts. She asked if he would call her just to let her know he was ok.

By midnight, she still hadn't heard from him and he was still not answering his phone. She was getting angry but also a little worried. Five more calls. Five more messages. Still, no response.

Three days came and went with no word from Ray. She decided to call one more time before she'd go out to his house. The phone rang twice and was picked up, but there was no one on the line. She heard a female voice call Ray's name and then the phone went dead.

She looked down at the receiver in disbelief. She thought, *Oh hell no! I know he's not over there with some bitch!* Missy jumped in her car headed straight to his house. She didn't even know if he was back in town for sure, but she decided to take her chances.

She parked right in front, beside Ray's car. *So he is home*, she thought. Missy banged on the door like SWAT and he answered in short order.

Dressed in just his briefs and holding a brandy sniffer filled with cognac, he opened up the door, turned and walked away from her.

"Ray! What the hell is going on here!" She slammed the door behind her and followed him into the family room.

He responded, very nonchalantly. About two swigs shy of being completely drunk on his ass. "You tell me."

"Who's here with you?" She attempted to walk past him and look through the house. He grabbed her by the arm.

"Where the hell are you going?"

"Is there a woman here, Ray?"

"What? No."

"I haven't heard from you in three days! When did you get home?! Why haven't you been answering your phone?! Why haven't you called me back?!"

"Call you. For what?"

"Are you fucking kidding me?! We're supposed to be married in five weeks! Who does this?!"

"Oh so we're getting married again?"

"Don't fuck with me right now Ray. Please."

"No! YOU don't fuck with me. One minute you accept my proposal and act like you're happy to be my wife and the next you wanna 'take a step back' so we can get to know each other? Who does THAT?!"

"Listen—"

"No, YOU listen. I love you. I want to make you my wife. I've asked you. I've shown you. Hell, I even sang it to you! I don't know what else I can do to show you how much you mean to me. Baby I want to spend my life with you."

Missy stood quietly. A mess of mixed emotions. She didn't know what to say. Her silence infuriated him.

"You know what? If that's not what you want, Missy, then so be it. I won't beg you, and I'm not about to let you dictate MY fuckin life. That's for damn sure. If you're not ready, then you're not ready. It's fine. Just leave the ring on the table on your way out."

She let out a sigh of exasperation but didn't respond.

Ray turned his back to her and walked away, yelling behind him. "Get out!"

She followed him into the living room. "Ray! I love you!" She grabbed him by the arm and pulled him to her so she could look him in the eye. "You hear me? I love you. Baby I just want to make sure we're *sure*."

"Is that right? Well let me tell you something, Missy. *I* was *sure* when I proposed to you. I was *sure* when I walked into Cartier and picked out that ring you have sittin' on your finger." His tone softened and he looked directly into her eyes. "I was *sure* the night I saw you standing next to the First Lady, looking so gorgeous and confident in your skin. I thought to myself, me and Barack picked us some winners." Missy smiled wide at the compliment. "Hell, I was *sure* the day I met you. When I laid eyes on you I knew I needed you in my life right then." He caressed her cheek. "You looked *so* beautiful to me. With your hair slicked back in a ponytail like a little cheerleader. Your sneakers and lip gloss and your 'round the way girl' outfit. You remember that day?"

Missy was melting right in front of him. Ray really had a way with words. A real charmer he was and he looked so incredibly sexy standing there bare-chested and semi-erect, pouring out his feelings. She answered. "I do."

"You remember I had to steal you away from your friend so I could have you to myself? I couldn't keep my eyes off you the entire night. I told you right then and there that you were gonna be mine. Mrs. Coleman. You remember that?"

"I do."

Ray moved closer to her. "Yeahhh, that's right. Go ahead and practice those words for me baby. Say it again for me.

The sexual tension was intense. She pulled off her jacket and moved closer to him. "I do."

"Say it one more time for me."

"I—"

Ray grabbed the back of her head and stuck his tongue down her throat in a deep passionate kiss that instantly made her wet. That move got her every time. He led her over to the chaise and laid her down.

Missy wore her favorite bead and sequined tank top. He grabbed it at the neckline with both hands and ripped it slowly down the middle, exposing her bare breasts and spilling the beautiful beadwork on the floor. He stared at them for a few seconds before he started to caress them.

Gently he traced her left nipple with his forefinger. It stood erect, eager for more of his attention. He leaned in and gave it a brush with his tongue. Then he pushed both breasts together and began licking and sucking each nipple.

His tongue trailed slowly up from her breasts to her chin, which he kissed softly before moving over to the left side of her neck. He knew that was her spot, the one that made her wet her panties if she let you linger there too long. He lingered, and she released.

She could smell the liquor on his breath, and it was strangely intoxicating. Maybe because she knew it was contributing to his emotional and animalistic behavior.

As he slid his hand into her panties and began to push all the right buttons inside her, Missy's mind went back to the night they first made love. She couldn't help thinking how tender he was with her this time. Passionate and intense, but very thoughtful and careful in his touch. This was exactly what was missing the first time they were together.

They'd only had sex twice since he proposed, and both of those times it came and went so quickly she barely got to enjoy. But not this night. Something had awakened in him. Maybe it was the thought of losing her? Or maybe it was the idea that she'd stood up to him. She didn't know and she didn't care. She just wanted more of him, in this way.

His kisses went from long and deep to soft and titillating. His breathing was heavy. As if he was trying to breathe her in. His tongue found its way back to her spot, and the hairs on the back of her neck began to stand on end. He pushed another button and Missy released again, this time letting out a scream. He hushed her with a kiss.

They continued to kiss slowly as he pulled off his briefs and exposed the longest, hardest penis that had ever been so close to her inner thigh. He worked off her skirt, and soon nothing lay between them but a lace and satin thong.

Missy ran her hands over his strong chest, up and down his back and down to his perfectly round, perfectly toned ass. And what a beautiful ass it was. Feeling his warm naked skin on hers and his erection so close to where she needed it was driving her crazy with anticipation. Missy felt like she was going to explode from the inside out. Her feelings were intensifying with every second of every touch.

Ray whispered, "Do you love me?"

"Yes."

"Will you marry me?"

"Yes baby."

As if in reaction to her response, he slid off of her and pushed her legs far above her head. Then he pulled her thong to the side and proceeded to give her more of his tongue. His glorious tongue. Her eyes rolled to the back of her head as she relaxed into the best head she'd ever had.

Just after her third orgasm, he crawled back up to her for a kiss, while he slowly pulled her leg onto his shoulder and slid inside her. Ray was a big guy in every sense of the word, but taking him in was easy, as her juices flowed steady and her body opened to him completely.

They made love for hours – lying on the chaise lounge in the family room, standing up against the bannister on the staircase, sprawled out on the soft black satin sheets on Ray's custom king bed. She fell in love with him right then and there, and HELL YES they were getting married.

She laid there next to her sleeping giant; naked and basking in the afterglow of the best sex she'd had in years, thinking, *Why in the world didn't he do all this shit before? Sex is a beautiful thing. Yesss, a beautiful thing indeed.*

Fast forward to 72 hours pre-wedding, and she was no longer what Jilly from Philly likes to call "dickmatized." Reality had set in and she was consumed with anxiety.

Ray was drinking more every day, his temper getting worse. There wasn't a day that went by that she didn't think of calling it off, but with each passing day and each dollar spent, that decision became more difficult.

She loved Ray, but she worried what kind of life they would have after the pomp and circumstance of the wedding was over.

Everything was about the wedding, nothing about their life after. She was becoming unhinged.

The final rsvp's were in, wedding announcements had been printed in all the major publications and hundreds of thousands of dollars had already been spent. People had already made their travel plans and her girlfriends were all abuzz about the spectacular bachelorette party they had planned.

Everyone was excited but the bride. And that was a huge problem. Huge.

To Know The Truth

Kim walked Brenda to a small room at the back of the store where there was an old futon, a few chairs, and refrigerator. She grabbed a bottle of chilled sparkling wine from the fridge and a couple of Styrofoam coffee cups from a desk drawer.

Brenda walked across the room and over to the desk chair. She was not about to expose herself to whatever nastiness Kim was probably getting into on that futon. When Kim noticed her glaring at the futon she commented, "You don't wanna sit on my futon huh?"

"Uh, no thank you."

They both got a good laugh before Kim popped the cork off the champagne and poured two rim grazing cups full of bubbly. She raised her cup. "So, first of all cheers to reconnecting. May this friendship be blessed with love, harmony and true sisterhood."

"Cheers." They bumped cups.

Brenda was immediately relaxed. She needed a break and was actually glad to have stumbled upon someone she could sip with and talk to. "Ok so please tell me what you know about Daye."

"Right. Well I wanna start by saying Melvin was good people. I didn't know him that well but you just know good people when you meet em."

"Thanks for saying that, Kim."

"Absolutely. Ok, so I met Daye when I was working in the liquor store. One day he came in lookin cute, flirtin heavy, and of course I reciprocated. I mean he *is* fine; you know what I'm saying." Kim raised her hand for a high five, but Brenda wasn't about to cosign that. Kim realized she got carried away. "Oh, my bad."

"Girl, please. Continue."

"Well, you know he runs his mouth real crazy. So one day I overheard him talking to a youngin about some guns. He was going off on the young dude because he got pulled over and the police took a gun he had loaned him. Me, trying to get some business on the side, I wrote down my number and slid it to him. I told him to call me that night and said I had something he needed. Of course, he was thinking I wanted to hook up, but when he called I quickly corrected him and told him what I was really offering. We started doing business right away and it was good, money was flowing, but eventually we started fuckin. And of course that fucked things up."

Brenda shook her head. "Kim. How you get caught up with him like that? You know you don't shit where you eat."

"Girl, he caught me one night after the go-go when I was nice, and trust me when I say I wasn't thinking about shittin or eatin. I was thinkin bout the licky and the sticky, bitch!" She laughed aloud then abruptly stopped herself from going for another unwelcomed high five. "Anyway, I was going to my car when he walked up and hugged me from behind. Gurrrrl. I was like nigga, is that a flash light in yo pocket or is you just happy to *see me*! O-kay!"

Brenda couldn't help laughing at Kim's overly animated ass. She couldn't even believe how ghetto this little Korean girl was. "Girl, you are stuuupid! Ok, go head."

"Well after a while the dick got good, and I started giving him big discounts. Then the dick got better, and I started wholesaling. Not just to him but to his man and then his other man, and his man's man, and so on, and so on. Chile, it was getting way outta control."

"Wait, did your father ever find out? How did you hide that?"

"Yeah, he found out. He started noticing the guns missing, and I stopped as soon as he said something. The money was real good and I wasn't about to give it up, so eventually I figured out how to start buying the guns myself using his dealers' license. After that, I didn't need to mess with the store's inventory anymore. I just ordered them and had them delivered to the store on his days off and sold them the same day. Things ran pretty smoothly for a good while."

"Sounds like you had everything worked out."

"Yeah girl, I was making money hand over fist for almost a year when things got crazy. One of Daye's trap houses got raided, and they confiscated around 50 guns that were all traced back to my dad. Several of them had bodies on them at that point. It was a complete nightmare. We're still dealing with it. I kinda feel like it contributed to him getting sick. He already had a bad heart. That shit really fucks with me sometimes. It's hard, you know."

"Wow. So you fessed up?"

"Fuck no! He doesn't know if it's me or my brother. I think he suspects me more, though. I'm the one who's been in trouble before.

He's never asked me directly, so I just played stupid and hoped it would all go away, eventually."

"So Kim, you really let him think your brother had something to do with it?"

"No, not really. Well, I guess you could look at it that way."

"Wow."

"Ok, well back to the subject at hand. During the time Daye and I were dating–"

"Fuckin."

"DA-ting."

"Daye dates?"

"Ok! Ok! During the time we were MESSING with each other, I heard a lot of conversations. I saw a lot of shit go down and when he got high he bragged about a lot of foul shit he did."

"Like?"

"Girl, if you don't stop interrupting me! I'm trying to paint a picture here."

"I'm sorry. Go ahead. But I gotta pick Mandy up in like 30 minutes, and I'm starting to get really buzzed, so give me the short version, Kim."

"Well the short of it is Daye is a very cruddy dude and can't be trusted. He set a lot of dudes up to get robbed or killed when he owed them money. A lot of them were his friends, too. He always bragged about being the next Rayful Edmond."

"None of that surprises me. I never trusted his ass. Melvin loved him like a brother, so I never really spoke out about it, but I saw the way Daye looked at him. I'm not saying he didn't fuck with him at all, but a cruddy nigga ain't got no loyalty for real. I heard that he talked a lot of shit about my husband in the streets, too. Told some people he was soft and they could get at him if they wanted to. Daye is very quick to smile in your face and talk about you as soon as you walk away. He's known for that shit."

"Yeah that's him. Um hmm. Muthafucka. Ok Brenda. I have one more thing to tell you, but I gotta know it stays in this room."

"Of course."

"I mean no matter what happens, no matter what you do or how you handle it, this cannot be repeated. I'm sticking my neck out for you with this, Brenda."

"Kim, I promise you. It stays here."

"Ok, a couple of months ago, Daye got really mad that he

wasn't in on some big coke deal with this new dude they called Spider."

"Yeah, the Jamaican dude. The one with the yellow Acura, right?"

"Yeah, that's him. One Saturday night after the club, we were going to his house to chill when he got a call and told me to go ahead and wait for him at his house. I was there for about an hour or so when he comes back in rantin and ravin about niggas taking him for a joke. Wherever he went after he left me he got high. Not a weed high either."

"What? Like coke?"

"Yes. I know a coke high when I see one. Trust me. He was real amped up, sweatin and talking real reckless, waving his gun around. In hindsight, I should have gotten the hell outta there but I decided to pry. My nosiness is gon get me killed one of these days I swear. I let him go on for a while before I started my little inquisition.

I said, 'Hey baby, what took you so long?'

The he said, 'Man fuck dat! This nigga gotsta go. That's all it is to it. He gotta go man.'

Then I said, 'Who? Who you talkin bout, Daye?'

He ignored my question and then he started laughing. One of them weird crazy ass laughs, too. He noticed my phone sitting on the table and asked to use it. I was like *ok*, so he picked up the phone and dialed a number. Whoever he was calling didn't answer right off, and Daye was pissed. When they finally answered he was *really* mad.

'Damn nigga. So I gotta call you from another number to get a answer from you? It's like that now? So you don't fuck with me for real, huh? I been your man for 15 muthafuckin years and you bring Pernell in on that money? *Pernell?*'

He was holding the phone quietly so the other person must have been talking for a minute. Then he started up again.

'So I'm not supposed to eat? And you wasn't even gon tell a nigga about it. That's the shit that fucks me up. After all the shit I done for you?'

There was another long pause, then Daye said, 'Nah it's cool man. You gotta do what you gotta do. I understand. Now I gotta do what I gotta do. I'll holla.'

So he hangs up the phone and makes another call.

'Wassup my nigga? Yeah, his bitch ass tried to cop a plea. He said he wasn't sure he was doin business with y'all yet so that's why he didn't tell me. I ain't tryna hear dat bullshit. It's aaight though. This shit is long overdue anyway, dog. I been runnin this whole shit since day one any muufuckin way. All that nigga been doin is sitting back gettin paid while I'm puttin in work. This nigga got time to chill and take vacations, worry free with his family while I'm holdin the block down. I might as well go ahead and do this shit dolo, you feel me? Yeah that playin the background shit is dead. It's bout time for Daye to break on em son.' He laughed. Then he said. 'Bottom line: That nigga gotta go.' And he hung up the phone."

Brenda felt uneasy. Butterflies in her stomach. It was pretty clear where Kim was going. But she sat and listened anyway. She needed to hear it all.

"Now you know me with my nosey self. All I wanted to do was get to my phone to see who he called, but as soon as he hung up the phone he came right at me pushing me back into the bedroom. I couldn't even enjoy the sex cause all I was thinking about was that damned phone call. Meanwhile, he's totally hyped up on that coke, so I thought he would never finish fuckin me. I swear I never wanted a nigga to cum so bad in all my life."

"Kim! Come on girl, I ain't come here to hear that. Move on!"

"Ok, Ok. After he fell asleep I waited a few minutes to make sure he was really out and I went out into the kitchen to grab my phone. I was praying he didn't somehow erase the last couple of calls. But as soon as I fuckin unlock my phone, what happens?"

"What!"

"It shut down. The fuckin battery was dead! Girl, I wanted to throw that bitch! Of course, I didn't have a charger with me, so guess who was gonna have to wait until the next damn morning to charge up her phone."

Brenda rolled her eyes. She was ready for Kim's overly dramatic ass to get to the end of it.

"Exactly. Girl, I was so pissed off I went back to bed and laid back down. It was pretty much impossible for me to sleep at that point, so I decided to get my ass up and go home. I eased out of the house and when I got to the car, what did I see? The car charger hanging from my cigarette lighter. I was like 'Oh yeeeaah! I don't know *why* I didn't think of that in the beginning? Anyway, I plugged the phone in and headed home. As soon as I pulled into my driveway, I grabbed my phone and unlocked it. So the last call he made was to a New York City area code. No way to figure out who that was without calling it and faking a wrong number. I figured I'd do that first thing in the morning. Maybe get my girl over at the phone company to look the number up for me and get me a name. But it was the *first* number that tripped me out tho, girl. It was already programmed in my contacts…Heavy."

Brenda sat there, very nearly in shock. She whispered. "Melvin".

Kim hollered, "Yes! Melvin! And girl when I heard he got killed I was like oh my mufuckin God! I knew exactly who it was and…"

Kim went on and on as Brenda sat there, entranced. Trying to digest what she'd just heard. Kim's voice trailed off as Brenda got lost in her thoughts. She pictured Daye on the phone ordering her husband's murder with a shifty, evil smirk on his face. She could hear the echoes of her footsteps as she walked the long, white, sterile hallway to the hospital morgue. Images flooded her mind. Melvin's mutilated body through the top half of a body bag. The casket being lowered into the ground. She could hear her children's screams as she told them their father was gone.

Without saying a word, she picked up her purse and walked out of the store. Kim followed behind.

"Brenda! Brenda! You ok girl. Say something!"

She kept walking. Down the hill. Past her car. Not really sure where she was going. She just needed some air. Shit just got real.

Brenda went to that gun store to get a piece, and she left a complete mess. But she had answers. She thought, it was funny how things get revealed when you ain't even lookin for em.

So it was official. Daye killed her husband. Maybe he didn't pull the trigger, but he killed him just the same.

There were still so many unanswered questions. So many unknowns. Brenda wanted answers and she was gonna get em, one way or another. And she knew exactly where to go.

Where My Girls At

Forty-eight hours before the wedding, and Missy was in rare form. She had long surpassed her usual three cocktail limit and felt absolutely no pain as she clumsily straddled a stripper pole.

The bachelorette party was in full swing as 12 of her wildest and craziest sorority sisters dirty danced to the latest Beyoncé and threw back glittery sugar-rimmed vodka shots one after the other. At this juncture of the evening, the girls were a little more than inebriated and a little less than inhibited. And the night was still very young.

Carmen really outdid herself. Everything was meticulously planned and arranged to appease all of Missy's guests. Earlier in the afternoon there was a beautiful bridal shower held in a reception hall at one of DC's most luxurious new hotels on the National Harbor.

There were fresh flower arrangements, white tulle and satin decorations all about. Fancy hors d'oeuvres were served, and fine champagne flowed plentiful. A carefully selected playlist of easy listening, jazz and old school R&B music played softly in the background as the ladies chatted away. It was very classy, very elegant, tasteful, and pain-full-y bor-ing.

Missy couldn't wait for her shower to be over. She'd had enough of the lame shower games, enough wedding talk and more than enough of the unsolicited marital advice. She was ready to get rid of all the player's wives she never cared for, her co-workers that were just there to be nosey and her country ass soon to be in-laws. Ready to round up her sorority sisters and get the *real* festivities underway.

When the night fell and the last of the saditty committee left the reception hall, the sisters of Delta Theta Ro made a beeline for Missy's suite so they could gloss their lips up and slink into their freak em dresses. It was about to be, as they say, "on and poppin."

Blocking the entrance to the hotel was a 22-passenger luxury limousine party bus that was stocked with premium liquor and equipped with a lighted stripper pole. Everything was perfectly planned and by the next day it was a given that everyone would be buzzing about Missy's fabulous pre-wedding festivities.

The first stop for the evening was Luv nightclub in the northeast quadrant of DC. Carmen knew the owner, so she had several tables reserved in his VIP section on the rooftop.

The weather was beautiful as were the Deltas clad in their sexiest LBDs and stilettos, the uniform for the evening. Missy was the standout dressed appropriately in a white mini dress that highlighted every curve and sky high strappy heels. After a few drinks Carmen had even convinced her to wear the corny faux wedding veil. But only on the party bus.

One of the hottest male R&B acts in the country was performing that night, so the club was jam-packed and there were more than a few celebrities in attendance. The owner brought Mr. R&B over to meet the ladies and to personally wish Missy well. After a cocktail and a few photos, Carmen rounded the ladies up to head back out to the limo.

The second stop was at H20 nightclub. It was another DC hotspot that was located at the southwest waterfront overlooking the Potomac River. The ladies filed out of the limo looking fabulous and knowing it. They walked in front of the hundred or so frustrated partygoers waiting in line and ignored a few insults from the haters. That just went along with the territory.

The owner, Abdul Ramir, a tall dark haired and very handsome Arab guy, waited to greet them and show them to their reserved area. Before they could get comfortable in the booth, Beyoncé's newest dance song began to play. The music was pumping and Missy was ready to dance.

As she and several of her most intoxicated sisters did their best Beyoncé impressions on the dance floor, a guy slid behind Missy and began to hump. She turned around and pushed him back almost causing him to fall.

"Chucky!"

"Yeah it's me! In the muthafuckin flesh, baby! Stop actin like you 'on know me, girl. Back that ass up on me."

Missy laughed so hard she spilled some of her drink. Sean Paul's new reggae song started to play, and she suddenly felt the need to oblige him, so she handed Carmen her drink and backed it up on him as instructed.

They danced for two more songs, and she was having a great time. She and Chucky always had the best time together. He was a character and sometimes got carried away with the jokes but he kept her laughing and smiling. When the music slowed down he led her out to the terrace for some air.

"Whoo! It's hot as hell in there girl. Got a nigga sweatin like a pimp in church."

"Yes." She pulled a handkerchief from her purse and dabbed the sweat from her forehead and nose. Careful not to muss her perfectly painted face. "Dammit I need a mirror. I know my makeup is a hot mess by now."

"No, your makeup is perfect. As always." He touched her cheek. "Just like you. You know I miss you girl."

His touch was warm and his hands were so soft. Just like she remembered. She missed it. "Stop it, Chucky."

He pulled back. "I'm sorry. You know I can't help myself when I'm around you."

"Well try."

"Ok, ok. So I heard you were getting married. *Congratulations.*" He gave her an exaggerated roll of his eyes and turned his head to the side.

Missy laughed. "Yes I am. In fact, you're interrupting my bachelorette party right now."

"For real?"

"For real."

"Wow. My Missy is gettin married. And *not* to me. You know you breakin my heart, right?"

"How am I breaking *your* heart?"

"Come on. You know I wanted to marry you. You were supposed to be *my* wife."

"Well you never asked."

"So that's all I had to do, was ask?"

"I'm not saying that, but if that's what you wanted, you should have let me know that. If you would have given me a *ring* instead of a key to your condo, maybe we wouldn't be right here right now." She couldn't believe the words that had just come out of her mouth.

"Well damn. Is it too late?"

"Chucky. Please."

"OK! So how is life with Mr. Perfect anyway?"

"It's good."

"Wow. That was dry."

"What?"

84

"I'm just sayin. That's not how you s'posed to sound when you gettin married in a couple days." He pushed up on her. "He must not be hittin that thing right."

Missy pushed him back. "Shut up, Chucky." Carmen came out onto the terrace and interrupted. As far as Missy was concerned it was just in time.

"Missy, we gotta head out. The limo's waiting. Hey Chucky."

"Wassup Carmen?" Chucky said. "How you been?"

"I'm good. How bout yourself?"

"Suicidal. Probly gon kill myself later on. Carmen, why y'all lettin her marry this nigga?"

"Chucky, you are stupid. We really gotta go though." She grabbed Missy's hand. "Come on Mrs. Coleman."

Missy turned to Chucky. "Goodnight."

He pulled her arm. "Wait. Missy you know I was just playing around right? I'm happy for you baby girl. I mean…I'm happy if you are. *Are* you happy?"

"Goodbye Chucky." She turned and walked back into the club.

Shortly afterward the girls head back to the limo for the third and final stop for the evening.

Carmen's brother, Santino, owned a little hole in the wall club called Bella's. It was in Waldorf, Maryland, which was about an hour away from DC but 20 minutes from their hotel at the Harbor. In Southern Maryland, it was far enough from the city that they'd never see anyone they knew and close enough for them to get back to the hotel at a reasonable hour.

The distinguished ladies of Delta Theta Ro were alumni of some of the finest universities in the country and wives of some of the most successful men in the country. But you wouldn't have guessed it that night. On the long ride to Bella's, they were hiking up their dresses and meowing like kittens as they showcased their skills on the stripper pole, one by one.

The pearls were definitely "unclutched," as they waited for the opportunity to see the dancing penises Carmen promised them before the end of the night. After all, what was a bachelorette party without a few well-built and well-equipped young men to straddle you in front of your best girlfriends.

Santino greeted the girls at the door and escorted them to Bella's' VIP section – a long booth with badly worn red leather cushions set aside a ragged wooden stage that was barely a foot off the ground.

The patrons were as ragged as the seat cushions and the makeshift stage. They were like a bad bag of mixed nuts; country bumpkins and local yokels wearing entirely too much makeup and $10 store fashions.

Under normal circumstances, the ladies would not have set their expensively heeled feet in such a tacky, seedy spot, but the shots and the promise of swinging ding-a-lings gave them all a good case of tunnel vision.

Their table was anchored by a giant Mylar balloon in the shape of a champagne glass and in the center of the table was a sheet cake in the shape of male genitalia, complete with chocolate shavings for pubes. It was positively disgusting, and the ladies loved every single second of it.

At exactly midnight, the club lights dimmed, and they cranked up the smoke machine on the side of the stage. As if on cue, the ladies began their cat calls and left their seats headed for the front of the stage.

A woman with a heavy voice greeted the ladies over a loudspeaker and introduced one by one some of the tastiest looking men they'd ever seen. All shades of beautiful masculinity they were: strong arms, chiseled backs, and 12 packs; spandex, tassels and specially made thongs that held their manhood at attention. The ladies were pleased to say the least.

After the finale, all of the men came over to the girl's table and pulled the guest of honor on stage. They were instructed to give her a proper send off, no holds barred. Missy was having the time of her life. It was definitely a night to remember.

Small Favors

The District of Columbia Correctional Treatment Facility (CTF), a medium security privatized penal institution

"Good morning ma'am. Who are you here to see?"

"Patricia James, please."

The guard checked the list and buzzed her back to the visiting area. She sat there at the booth waiting for Aunt Pat to come out. Pat was Betty's younger sister. She was doing her last six months of a 23-year sentence for killing her second husband, Tim, who was also the second husband Pat had killed.

As James' legend tells, Aunt Pat and her first husband, Willie Earl, were high school sweethearts that married the day after graduation. When they married, Pat was already two months pregnant and Willie Earl had just gotten the notice that he'd been drafted. He was headed to Vietnam in a week.

He was high-strung and on edge because he was nervous about going off to war. The night before he was supposed to ship off, he stayed out half the night drinking with his buddies. When he got home, he burst in the bedroom door cursing her and calling her every kind of whore in the book. Apparently one of his friends had told him that he'd seen Aunt Pat's old boyfriend Rudy's car sitting in front of their house the day before.

Willie Earl snatched her out of bed and beat her mercilessly. When he was done, she had a blackened eye, a split lip, four of her front teeth smashed in, and a couple of cracked ribs.

As soon as she was able to break free from him, Aunt Pat ran out of the house. He didn't give chase. He stopped at the door cursing her and telling her never to come back to his house. She ran almost eight miles down the road to Mama Joe's house.

Pat didn't wake anyone in the house, she just went into the closet and got Mama Joe's shotgun. She walked back home exhausted and in excruciating pain but determined to make Willie Earl pay for what he had done to her.

When she walked through the door, he was passed out on the living room sofa. She fired a shot into the ceiling, and he jumped up. There was some conversation that no one is really sure about, but the second shot left part of Willie Earl's skull on the wall and seven years of Pat's life with a Carolina State correctional facility.

After the beating she'd taken and considering she was with child, the prosecutor took mercy and offered her a plea of voluntary manslaughter with the lowest sentence. She agreed.

By the time she was released from jail, she had developed a fetish for pretty girls and a pretty mean heroin addiction. That brings us to Uncle Tim. Her second husband. That she killed.

No one but Pat had the whole story, but the long and short of it is that Tim was her pimp before she married him. He fell in love with her, but she loved women, and she loved smack. She took his women and she took his business and she left him.

They went back and forth with each other for a few years. He beat her pretty badly one night, and afterward she shot him in the chest.

Brenda was a little girl at the time, so she wasn't exactly in the loop on grown folks' business but after Aunt Pat went to jail no one ever really talked about her. She was just another bad ass James girl bringing shame to the family. Probably the baddest.

Betty never let her girls visit any of their relatives that were in jail, but Brenda had an impromptu visit with Aunt Pat one summer when she was about seven months pregnant with MJ. She was 15, and Melvin was serving a six-month sentence in the youth center of the Lorton Virginia correctional facility, on a weed charge.

There was a family day fair for all of the inmates and their families, and while Brenda was sitting at a picnic table with Melvin and his aunt Regina, she noticed a woman staring at her from a few picnic tables down.

By the time the woman walked over to Brenda, the fair was almost over. Visitors were heading back to their buses and before they reached the gate, Aunt Pat stopped her and hugged her tight. Then she whispered in her ear, "Little girl. You know you ruining your life right? What you doin down here with this nigga? I know my sister raised you better than this. And you pregnant? You think that shit is cute? You think that shit make you grown? Make this the last time I see you down here. You hear me? Don't let me catch your muthafuckin ass down here again."

Brenda's fifteen-going-on-thirty-year-old mind couldn't comprehend how a jailbird crack-ho that had never done anything for her could fix her mouth to judge. She thought, who the fuck was *she* to say *anything*? And so Brenda cussed her ass out like the stranger her Aunt Pat really was. It got so bad that the guards had to pull Brenda off her aunt and escort her off the premises. They didn't arrest her because she was pregnant, but after the melee Brenda was banned from the prison.

Pat never admitted it, but she provoked Brenda on purpose. She just didn't want to see her niece back at that prison again.

So now, the reason Brenda was at another correctional facility, some 17 years later was that she needed Aunt Pat's help. The woman still had a reputation on the street after all those years and Brenda knew that if anyone could find out what happened to her husband it was her.

Putting her pride aside, she was prepared to suck it up and eat some major humble pie to get what she needed. She'd apologize, beg, plead. Whatever it took.

When Aunt Pat walked out into the visiting hall, again, Brenda hardly recognized her. She was at least 60 pounds heavier than she was the last time they saw each other and now she was rocking a Caesar haircut and jail tats across her neck. Aunt Pat's arms were huge and she had a thick neck like a football player. She really looked like a dude. That wasn't surprising for a woman in jail, but going from a tall frail long-haired prostitute to a big burly man was a little unsettling for Brenda.

She wanted to ask who Consuela was since the name was emblazoned across the side of her aunt's neck, but she figured that was a question for some time later. Maybe when they got to know each other better. That's *if* they got to know each other better.

After all the dirty crackhead muthafuckas Brenda called her that family day, she really wouldn't have blamed Aunt Pat if she had told her to go fuck herself. But she didn't. She seemed genuinely happy to see Brenda.

"Baby girl!"

"Hey Aunt Pat. How you been?"

"Ah you know. I'm hangin in. On some short time now. 6 months. Can't wait to get up outta here. How you doing baby?"

"I'm good."

"Oh, you good?"

"Yeah I'm ok."

"Well I'm having a hard time believing you good or ok when you up here. What brings you to see *me* after all these years? Last time I saw you, you told me to go kill myself." She laughed.

"Aunt Pat. I'm so sorry I said that to you. You know how it is when you young and you think you know."

"Yeah I'm just messin with you girl. It's all good. I never even took that shit personal. So, I know it's been rough for you lately. How you holding up?"

"Rough, for *me*?"

"Yeah, rough. Melvin gettin killed, the kids cuttin up, Betty in the hospice. I tell you, I'm prayin my sister can hold on til I get outta here. I really need to see her face. I got so much to say to her. I need to make some shit right, you know."

"So you know about Melvin? My kids?"

"Come on Brenda. I keep up with my peoples. It ain't much I *don't* know. Just cause I'm locked up don't mean I'm out the loop."

"Wow. Actually, that's kinda why I came up here."

"Tell me something I *don't* know." Aunt Pat smiled. "So what you need from me?"

"I need to know who killed my fuckin husband."

"Whoa. Come on girl." Aunt Pat shook her head no and looked down at the phone. "Do I look like a detective to you? Just keep checkin in with the police. I'm sure they on it. They'll find out what happened and bring whoever killed your husband to justice. Just be patient. It'll all come together soon enough." Pat nodded again. "So tell me, what's going on in the hood?"

Brenda realized that Aunt Pat knew something, but she couldn't talk about it over the phone. So they changed lanes and kept the conversation light. Caught up on family events. Brenda was floored to find out just how much in the loop Aunt Pat was on everything and everyone. She thought, *who the hell is she talking to?*

They really bonded that day. Not only did Brenda have a new source for all the hood gossip, she had her family back. It felt good.

Three days after their visit, Brenda received a four-page letter in the mail from Aunt Pat. It was confirmed. The who, the what, the where and the how. It was all right there in black and white, and it was so far beyond gruesome she had to read and reread it again.

What those animals had done to her husband was inhumane and

for what they had done they would all have to pay. She wanted instant revenge. Not tomorrow, not next week or next month but that night.

After she read the letter for the third time, Brenda cried herself to a migraine, went to the metal box under her bed, and pulled out her fresh new Glock 9mm with the pearl pink handle – a gift from Kim. She held it in her hand, tracing the beautiful detail on the handle with her fingertips. She raised it up and pointed it at the mirror, practicing her shooting stance. Feet shoulder width apart, knees slightly bent. Shoulder squared with your target. Just like Melvin taught her.

She went to the kitchen and grabbed a fifth of Grey Goose vodka, cracked the seal, and drank it straight from the bottle, warm, no chaser. About halfway through and half out of her mind she grabbed her keys and purse. She was almost out of the door when the house phone rang. Something told her to go back and answer. A familiar robotic voice began to speak.

"You have a collect call, from a District of Columbia Correctional Facility…"

Will You Still?

Twenty-four hours until the wedding. It was a long and painful flight to St. Maarten. Dark sunglasses, Evian and Advil were the essentials for the day. The bachelorette party was as crazy as Carmen planned for it to be and the ladies were all paying for it.

Missy protested initially but on this day she was thankful that Ray planned the ceremony for Sunday. It gave her an extra day to recuperate. And she needed it.

The flight was smooth, as was the landing. St. Maarten was absolutely beautiful with white, sandy beaches and turquoise-colored water. She couldn't wait to get out to the beach to soak up some rays and get a little more color for the wedding photos.

When they reached the hotel, Missy bid her girls adieu so that she could get in a quick nap before lunch. She was beginning to feel good about things. Her wedding anxiety was being overshadowed by the magnificence of the island and the thought of getting married in paradise. For the first time in a while, she started to fantasize again.

She had her doubts about marrying so quickly, but there was no doubting that she loved Ray. He really was a good man, and he loved her, in his own way. Yes, he was controlling, stubborn, a bit of a chauvinist with a wee bit of a temper, but that was her man, and it was about to be she and he for better or worse.

Missy had weighed all the pros and the cons and at the end of her list one thing stuck out: She may never do any better than Ray, but she could damned sure do a lot worse. So…she was about to become Mrs. Ray Coleman. And that was that.

She opened the door to her suite and heard the TV playing loudly. When she walked into the bedroom, Ray was sitting on the bed.

"Hey you! How's my husband to be?" She leaned down to kiss him, and he turned his head. Missy sat down next to him. "Babe what's wrong?"

Ray unfolded his laptop and sat it in front of her. Then he

pressed play. Missy was like a deer in headlights. She tried to fold the computer back down, but Ray held it open. "No, you're gonna watch this."

It was a video of the strippers' grand finale at Bella's. Missy stared down at the image of herself on stage, lying back in a chair as several oily, sweaty and completely naked men took turns simulating sex with her. One was on his knees with his head in her lap and her legs wrapped around his neck. At the same time, two other dancers held her head and pumped away at her face.

Next they removed the chair from the stage and laid her on the dirty floor while they played out what looked to be a scene from one of those old Taboo films. The crowd screamed with excitement, and Missy appeared to be loving every minute of her special attention.

"Ray, I can explain."

"That's just one of the videos posted to YouTube this morning. If you search 'Missy's Bachelorette Party,' there's plenty more. And plenty worse." Ray pulled out his phone and handed it to her. "These were sent to me this morning."

Missy took the phone reluctantly. She already knew what it would be. There was photo after photo of her and her girls in very compromising positions throughout the evening. On the stripper pole on the party bus, suggestively eating the penis shaped party cake, measuring strippers' penises with their straws. One of her sisters ended up ended up with a lil sumthin...well...a big sumthin in her mouth.

It seemed each photo was worse than the last, and most of them were of her. She was mortified. "Ray. I don't even know what to say. I'm so sorry. We were drinking and–"

"Did you have sex, of *any* kind, with any one of those men last night?"

"What? No! Hell no!"

"Then I'll see you at lunch." He grabbed his phone and walked out, slamming the door hard behind him.

Missy suddenly felt sick with worry. What did this mean? Why the hell was Ray so calm? Was he playing nice and planning to embarrass her later or something? She was in a total panic. She needed some help. She picked up the phone.

"Hello?"

"Carmen."

"Missy? Are you crying?"

"Can you please come to my suite? Right now."

"I'm on my way."

When Carmen got there, the door was open. Missy was crying and pacing the floor with a mini bottle of vodka from the mini bar in her hand.

"Hey what's going on?" Carmen said.

Missy hit the play button.

Carmen yelled, "Oh my God! Where did that come from?"

"Fuckin YouTube! Ray was waiting to show me this when I got here. Who took this fuckin video, Carmen? I didn't see anyone with a camera!"

"Damn, I'm sorry babe. I have no idea. I didn't see a camera either. It was probably done with a cell phone. YouTube actually shows who posts the videos. Look here. One was posted by a richbitch1980. It looks like all the rest were posted by a 2cute4ubitches. Either one of them sound familiar?"

"No! I wouldn't know anybody that would go by those stupid ass names!"

"Well damn. Don't yell at *me*."

"I know. I'm sorry. You know he has pictures, too. Somebody sent them to his phone this morning. I can't believe this shit is happening to me right now."

"Dammit. What are you gonna do?"

"What *can* I do?"

"Well, what did he say?"

"That's just it. Nothing. He didn't freak out. He didn't yell or scream. He just gave me a really disappointed look and told me he'd see me at lunch. Then he slammed the door behind him. That was it. I was expecting to get slapped or cursed out or *something*."

"Well maybe he'll just get over it. I mean come on. It *was* a bachelorette party. Yes, you were off the chain, but so was everyone else. It's not like it was just you. Shit happens."

"Carmen, please shut up. That is absolutely no help to me. This is a mess."

"No, seriously. Maybe he didn't freak because of what *he* did at *his* bachelor party. Ever think about that? All those football players at a bachelor party in the Caribbean? No telling how many island groupie whores they had running around this hotel last night. Think about it."

"I don't know girl. I'm like waiting for the other shoe to drop. Is he gonna embarrass me in front of his friends or leave me at the altar or w

hat?"

"No. Ray loves you, and he wants to marry you. Besides, it's not like you fucked somebody. Just go in there, get dressed, and make yourself so damn beautiful that he and everyone else will know why he's marrying you tomorrow."

Missy did just that. She pulled on a sexy long strapless maxi dress and barely-there strappy sandals. Her hair was pulled back in a long slick ponytail, just the way Ray liked it. She wore minimal makeup, just as Ray liked. A little moisturizer, mascara, and lip gloss. Bronzer for a perfectly sun kissed effect. Then she dabbled a little of the pheromone oil on her pulse points and behind her ears.

Satisfied with her sexy island ensemble and faux natural face, she headed down to the hotel restaurant to get her man.

Lunch was perfect. The food was great, and Ray was as loving and attentive as he was the night he proposed. He seemed genuinely happy, and it put Missy at ease. She thought Carmen was right. It was just a bachelorette party. Besides, who could stay mad in paradise? Still, she made a mental note to have the videos taken off the site as soon as they got home.

After lunch, she changed into her bikini and went down to the beach to soak up the last of the day's rays. Everything was alright.

As she lay there sunbathing with her wide floppy hat and dark shades she listened to the sweet sounds of Sade on her iPod. The weather was perfect and Missy thought how wonderful it was that her life was finally falling into place. Yes, there were a few bumps in the road; Ray wasn't perfect, but then again neither was she. It was clear that he loved her. And that was good enough. She was getting married.

Missy reached over to grab her bottled water and felt a presence. When she pulled off her shades and lifted her hat, Ray was standing in front of her.

"Oh, hey baby! What are you doing down–"

He interrupted her in mid-sentence "Are we doin this?"

"What? Yes, of course."

"Do you really want to marry me, Missy?"

"Ray, of course I do. Please don't let what happened–"

As she started to make her plea he raised his hand to quiet her. "It's fine. I just wanted to confirm. I'll see you at the rehearsal dinner then."

He turned and walked away as quietly as he came. Missy was nervous again. He was acting weird. Obviously he wasn't ok with what happened. She knew she was going to have to talk to him again. Before something crazy happened.

P. J.

Patrick James, aka Miss P, aka PJ, was the son/daughter of soon to be ex-con Patricia James. Raised by his paternal grandmother after his father was killed, PJ was a 29-year-old flaming pre-op transsexual that was hopelessly addicted to ecstasy pills and living life in the fastest lane he could.

He was known in the hood as Roller. The name was actually given to him by his best friend, Sheena. He took a roll, i.e. a bad trip on some ex one night and Sheena never let him live it down, but everybody in the hood assumed it was because he lived like a high roller. Which he did.

PJ lived quite large on the income from his various, mostly white collar crimes – bank fraud, credit card fraud, securities fraud, fraud fraud. Everything about him was a fraud except his labels and his beautiful jet black locks that he'd been nurturing since he was sixteen. His crown and glory.

PJ drove the finest cars, wore the finest clothes, jewelry, furs and had more passport stamps than you would ever imagine for someone that had dropped out of high school to turn tricks.

After the life he had to live with his grandmother, Miss P was gonna get his by any means necessary and he didn't give a fat fuck what anybody had to say about it. That included his grandmother and it especially went for his good-for-nothin-but-doin-time mother. He thought, *Fuck family. Where are they when you need them? Nowhere.*

Miss P was exactly 6 feet tall (6'5" in heels) with hazel eyes and curves for days, thanks to several years of hormone injections at Dr. Bill's office, and perfect size C implants, which were a gift from his first wealthy beau.

If you didn't know him personally, there was no way you would be able to tell he wasn't a natural born woman. He was stunning and turned heads everywhere he went. He lived in a beautiful 5,000-square-foot home with his latest boyfriend Ahmed in Accokeek, Maryland, but his everyday hang out was Sheena's little apartment in the Ridgewood Terrace projects.

There he had a whole entourage of flaming young queens willing to do anything for him, to be like him; to partake in the ex-tra-va-gan-za he referred to as Miss P's World.

From the outside looking in, he had it all. Everything he'd ever wanted. But life wasn't always so good.

*****

PJ was 5 years old when his mother was convicted and sent off to prison. The day she was sentenced, he sat in the courtroom with his grandmother, Janice and the rest of his father's family.

They gave her a life sentence, like it was nothing. She'd be eligible for parole in 23 years but as far as everyone was concerned, it was life.

PJ was dressed in the same little blue suit and matching neck tie that he wore to his father's funeral. When the verdict was read, the room was in total chaos. His father's side of the family cheered, as his mother's family screamed the things he wasn't allowed to repeat.

The judge banged on his tall desk over and over again. PJ yelled for his mother as they hauled her away in handcuffs. Tears streamed down her face as she cried out, "It's ok PJ. Don't cry baby. You be a big boy for mama, ok? Mama loves you. Don't cry now." She yelled at Janice to get him out of there.

When Janice grabbed his hand he snatched it away from her and ran out into the aisle toward his mother. He yelled for her as he attempted to climb over the wooden partition. Janice caught up to him and snatched him by the collar of his jacket, pulling him out of the courtroom as the volume on his little voice seemed to escalate. It would be 23 years before he'd see his mother again.

Living with Janice was a nightmare. The worst place he could have gone. She was a raging alcoholic, mentally and physically abusive, and didn't seem to care about him at all.

In fact, her reason for taking him in was to collect the social security benefits that PJ was entitled to when Tim died. She told him as much.

In less than three months she and her druggie boyfriend Ronnie had gone through every dime from the life insurance policy she had on Tim. $50,000 gone. Just like that. By the time she was granted custody of PJ, all that was left was the money in PJ's trust and if it weren't for the strict provision that the money couldn't be drawn until he turned 18, he would have surely ended up with nothing.

Janice and Ronnie spent years trying to devise ways to get his money. Letters of hardship to the trustee, even bribery. But nothing worked and PJ was thankful because by the time he was old enough to understand what he had coming, he planned to use that money to get as far away from his family as possible.

Every day he felt like he was being punished for something. Punished for what his mother had done or because they couldn't access his trust. Because his skin was too dark or he grew out of his clothes too fast. It was misery that no kid should have to endure.

Janice didn't cook, she didn't clean, she didn't bathe him or wipe his nose when he had a cold, which was more often than not because she made him stay in the cold wet basement of the raggedy house they lived in.

There was never a kind word. Not even on the third of the month when she cashed his social security check. Not even when he brought home straight A's on his report cards. He couldn't do anything right, and she reminded him of that every day.

When he was eleven he was accepted into a private school that one of his teachers recommended him for. The teacher took the liberty of submitting an application for a scholarship and it was accepted. PJ would be bussed to one of the best preparatory schools in the country, tuition free. He ran all the way home holding the acceptance letter in his hand. So happy he could burst.

Janice didn't waste any time bursting his bubble. She told him he couldn't go. Accused him of thinking he was too good for his neighborhood school and trying to be "smarter than errybody else". It was the first time PJ spoke up for himself and it would be the last. She beat him mercilessly and kept him home from school until the visible bruises healed.

They lived on Taylor Street in Northeast, a block over from the Ridgewood Terrace projects. It was a raggedy three-bedroom townhouse that Janice's father left her when he died. It was paid for when he left it to her but thanks to her good for nothing boyfriend, there were two mortgages on it.

He convinced her to refinance it and take out the equity her father spent his whole life building. Between the weekly trips to the Charlestown racetrack and their various *other* habits, they blew through that money in about a year. Shortly after that, he had her put the house up as collateral for his bail. When he didn't show up for court, she put a second mortgage on it and took out the last bit of cash. It was shameful.

Mortgages came due and since neither of them worked or planned to work, she started taking in foster kids to pay the bills.

So not only did PJ have to take care of himself, at 12 years old he was taking care of a gang of other dysfunctional kids that they didn't need or want.

Despite everything going on at home, PJ excelled in school. It was a welcomed diversion from his home life. He tested well above grade level in the seventh grade, and since he was denied the opportunity to go to private school his teachers rallied to get him skipped a couple grades ahead and admitted to the high school AP class.

He didn't bother to tell Janice, just forged her signature and started his new school. She never came to his school so she'd never know anyway.

All of his teachers loved him, but some were really concerned. It was for good reason. He was unkempt, and his hygiene was bad. He was always hungry, and never had anything he needed – school supplies, a good winter coat. He was never able to participate in any school activities or go on any outings because he never had the money to do it.

Only one teacher had the courage to address it. Mr. Bell. Toby Bell. He taught physical education, and after smelling PJ's armpits a few too many times in gym class he decided to take matters into his own hands. He brought PJ a backpack full of toiletries and school supplies. They discussed hygiene, and he taught PJ how to properly care for himself.

Over time, they developed a very strong bond. He even tried to visit the house once, but that ended badly. Janice and Ronnie cursed him out and ran him off. Calling him all kinds of perverts and pedophiles.

When PJ was comfortable enough he confided in Toby. He told him everything that was going on at home. The beatings, the neglect, the caring for all the foster kids in the house. Toby wanted to intervene but PJ begged him not to. Pleaded with him to let it go. He couldn't imagine what would happen to him if Mr. Bell sent the welfare people to his house. Janice and Ronnie would probably kill him. Or they'd put him in some horrible foster home where he'd be molested, beaten and starved to death. That's what Janice always told him would happen if he ran away. He'd threatened to do that once.

Eventually Mr. Bell let it go. They just began to spend more time together to keep him away from the house. After a while Janice didn't care. An anonymous letter, and subsequent pop up visit from social services revealed that she had a convicted felon living in the home. The foster kids were promptly removed and there was no need for PJ to be there. As long as she was still getting his check every month Janice couldn't care less where PJ was.

So he was finally free. Free to have a life and some happiness of his own. School was great, he'd made a bunch of new friends and thanks to Mr. Bell he was participating in the extracurricular activities he couldn't afford before. He felt really good about himself.

Mr. Bell was like a big brother to him. His savior. Just what he needed in his life at that time. That is…until he wasn't.

On his thirteenth birthday, Mr. Bell took his virginity and his innocence. It would change the course of his life.

Enough Is Enough

Brenda pulled up to the house, grabbed two cans from the trunk and started pouring gasoline all around. She made a trail from the front yard, over and through the tall dry grass to the back of the house. She ran back out to the front, lit a match and waited for him.

Within seconds, there was a ring of fire around the house. Something exploded in the back, and Daye came running from the front door. Before he could get to the lawn Brenda raised her gun and let off three shots, hitting him twice in the chest and once in the stomach.

She stood and watched his body fall to the ground disappearing behind the growing flames. It was done.

She ran back to the car ready to hop in and speed off but noticed her friend Tina was gone. Just as she started to get out to find her, Tina came running from the side of the house, back out to the car carrying a duffle bag.

Tina yelled, "Get back in the car, let's go! I got it!"

Brenda hollered back, confused, "You got what?!"

"Your money, bitch! Let's go!"

Brenda jumped back into the car. Her hands were shaking uncontrollably as she tried desperately to get the keys into the ignition. The gravity of what was happening set in. Panicked, she dropped the keys to the floor and her gun, pretty, pink and still warm from its first discharge fell from her lap. "Oh God! Oh my God! Tina what did I just do! What did I just DO!

Tina glared at her wide eyed, in disbelief. "Bitch is you serious!" She hopped out and ran over to the driver's side. Brenda was too stuck to even move, so Tina shoved her over to the passenger side and got in. She put the key in the ignition and turned it over. Nothing. The engine stalled and then there was a loud pop.

Gunfire shattered the rear windshield. Tina ducked down but Brenda sat there entranced, in some sort of shock. Tina reached for Brenda's gun which had managed to get lodged underneath the front seat. She pulled it free, jumped back out and returned fire on a tall dark haired woman that was running down the street, firing shots in their direction. Tina ducked back down and yelled at Brenda, "Start the car! Start the fuckin caarrr!"

Brenda jumped to attention. She pushed her left leg over the console and as soon as she raised up another bullet hit what was left of the rear windshield. Another hit the front. Tina raised up and let off her last two shots as the woman took cover behind a car parked across the way. Brenda turned the key again. It started. She yelled, "Come on! Tee! Let's go!"

Tina hopped back inside and put the car in drive. Barely in control of the wheel and with the door still slightly ajar she floored it and peeled away from the curb, with Daye's house blazing and the faint sound of a fire engine in the distance. Before she could get to the end of the block, a black cat ran out into the street, and she swerved to miss it. The car slammed head on into a city metro bus.

Brenda shook herself awake. She was soaked with sweat and could hear the sound of a fire truck in the distance. A metro bus pulled away from the stop outside her window.

The dream was so vivid, so real. Her heart was still pounding. It was a recurring dream with her confronting and killing this man she hated. Each dream was more vivid than the last.

Brenda sat at the edge of bed, still breathing heavily. She knew she had to deal with Daye, and do it soon. So she could finally get some rest.

Lights, Camera, Action

The day had finally come. Missy's wedding day. The day that almost every girl dreams about from the age of six. The day that most every woman pre-plans in her mind until meeting Mr. Right and finally having a chance to put those plans into effect. It was supposed to be the happiest day of her life, but Ray had done his damnedest to make it the most worrisome.

Carmen was a gem. She'd handled her maid of honor duties to a tee. The shower, bachelorette party, and all other pre-wedding drama was in the books. Missy had the old pearl and diamond earrings that her mother passed down to her on the night of her senior prom; her new diamond-encrusted hairpins that had been so carefully placed into her bridal coif and a diamond tennis bracelet that she borrowed from Carmen's mom.

Last, but certainly not least, were the Manolo Blahnik "Something Blue" wedding shoes, just like the ones Carrie wore when she married Mr. Big in the Sex and the City movie. She'd been looking for them for months and Carmen found a woman willing to part with them for triple the retail price. They were the only thing in the whole wedding Missy was excited about. All that was left to do was get married.

As the makeup artist applied moisturizer to her face, Missy sat there reflecting on the previous day's events. After Ray walked away from her on the beach, she was a ball of nerves. She felt she needed to talk to him again, find out where his head was.

She went to his room, and he wasn't there. He wasn't answering his cell, and no one else had seen him. Three hours later, he showed up at the rehearsal dinner, and he was back to being the model fiancé, gazing at her lovingly, feeding her from his fork, which was a new one. At the end of dinner, he toasted his bride to be and gave the most heartfelt soliloquy on finding true love. He even seemed to get a little emotional at the altar as the minister walked them briefly through their vows. It was strange, and unnerving.

The Dr. Jekyll/Mr. Hyde routine had Missy completely thrown.

Especially since right after the rehearsal Ray disappeared again.

Though they had agreed not to see each other again until the wedding, Missy wanted to have one last reassuring kiss from him before she went to sleep. So she went to his room and once again he was nowhere to be found. No one, not even his best man Roman had seen him. And when she went to his room that morning she found that his bed hadn't been slept in.

Now she was expected to put on a smile and pretend nothing was wrong. Everything was wrong. The whole damned scene was wrong.

Ray had orchestrated this whole shotgun situation, and there was something so very unsettling about it. She had no input and no family there to support her. Everything was done his way, on his time, and on his terms – always. She wasn't sure she could live with that for the rest of her life.

Staring out the window onto the ocean, she fantasized. Not about the fabulous, star-studded, over-the-top extravaganza everyone was preparing for, but getting onto one of the boats at the dock and sailing the hell away from that island. Drifting off into the sunset with Ray and *his* million-dollar wedding fading away in the distance.

She thought about Chucky, and the last thing he said to her. How good he looked. How he smelled. She missed him. She wished he would come and take her away from there, rescue her from the madness.

Carmen interrupted her thoughts. "Missy! Omg you look so gorge. So you decided to go with red lipstick. Very nice. Very SJP."

"Thanks."

"Damn. Thanks. What's eatin you?"

"Hmm. My wedding."

"Come on, Missy. Don't start that shit again."

"Why? Why not start? Why can't I tell you how I feel? Why is it that every time I start telling people how I'm feeling they quickly remind me that my feelings don't matter?"

"I didn't mean it like that. Of course your feelings matter."

"No, actually they don't."

"So what are you saying, Missy?"

"Nothing."

"No, not nothing. Talk to me."

"Ray didn't sleep in his room last night. He was acting all weird yesterday."

"Weird? Are you serious? After that toast, you can still sit here and tell me that you're not sure about him? He loves you, Missy."

"Will you just listen to me! Please! Carmen, Ray is really good at making appearances. You guys don't see what I see. It's like…it's like this doesn't add up or something."

"What doesn't add up?"

"Us! This whole thing! The way he rushed me into this wedding. His temper. Our sex life, or the lack thereof. We're not having sex Carmen and when I bring it up there's always a new excuse. He has a headache; he doesn't want to tire himself out before practice or he's too tired after practice. I've literally tried everything. Now he's saying it's because he wants to wait until we're married but that's just more bullshit. Literally the only time he touches me is if I threaten to leave. Then he fucks me into submission."

"So you think he's messin around?"

"Probably. Maybe. I don't know what the hell is going on with him. And the worst part is I don't know if I really care. Now he's acting flaky, and I can't tell what he's thinking. Ever since I got here it's like I'm playing a sick game of 'He loves me…he loves me not.' A part of me wishes he'd just call it off. Let me off the hook. I swear I wouldn't even mind. Why the hell are you looking at me like that?"

"Like what?"

"Like *that*."

"Because I know you don't really want to hear my opinion. So I'm just listening. Letting you know that your feelings matter."

"You are of absolutely no help to me." Missy's eyes started to well.

Carmen grabbed a tissue and handed it to her. "Ok, before you completely ruin your makeup, let me just say that I'm here for whatever you want. You wanna call this shit off, so be it. We can get out of here right now. Leave everything behind and get a taxi to the airport. Hell, we can hop on one of those sailboats out there if you want. It's up to you. I won't say a word either, I'll just move."

Missy dabbed her eyes with a tissue. "Thank you for saying that, Carmen. I'm not calling anything off, but thank you for saying that. Believe me, I've been eyeballing those sailboats all morning…but I guess I'll say a little prayer and get this show on the road."

"You sure?" Carmen sucked her tongue and put on her best sister girl impression. "Cause you jus say the muufuckin word, boo boo, and we can definitely blow dis joint. Sheeeeeit. You know I got yo front and yo back. We ain't even gotta do dis shit, o-KAY?"

Missy laughed aloud. Just getting her feelings out made a difference. "Girl, shut up and help me get into this dress."

The unrehearsed alternate wedding plan was about to get underway. The ceremony had to be brought indoors because of the hard rain, so it was almost an hour late. Still, Missy had to admit, Preston had done an amazing job with the ballroom. He brought the outside décor inside and it was just as beautiful as he described in the consultation.

The illumination from hundreds of candles placed throughout the room and the sound of the rain falling against the picture windows was intoxicating. Romantic. The sparkle from the crystal chandeliers, all of the crystals that adorned the tables and the enormous exotic floral arrangements lent to the room's opulence. As Wendy Williams would say, it was *everything*.

The bridal party was finally in place and Missy stood waiting for the bride's song to play. She was already tearing under her veil. It was really happening. She didn't have the guts to stop it, so it was really happening. She swallowed down the bile that had risen from her queasy stomach and took the first step toward the isle.

As a wedding surprise from Ray, her favorite singer Johnny Gill stood and began to sing his own rendition of "You Are So Beautiful to Me." She was completely unfazed by the gesture. Preston smiled gleefully and informed her that it was time for her to walk. "Darling, they are playing your song," Preston said. "You must walk now!" So she kicked the dress forward and began to walk.

The room let out a collective gasp at the full view of her beautifully embroidered strapless gown with the sweetheart neckline and mermaid silhouette. She decided to shelve the over the top Princess Di ball gown and cathedral veil that Preston and Ray approved. Instead, she had her good friend Mark Badgley of Badgley Mischka custom make a gown more to her liking. Something a little sexier. Something more her.

Her hair was pulled back into a sophisticated chignon, and she wore a simple veil off her face to showcase the masterpiece the makeup artist created. Her wedding look was everything she had always envisioned, and it was the one thing she was actually happy about that day – it was the one decision she'd made on her own.

Ray smiled wide as he waited for his beautiful bride-to-be to join him at the altar. Missy sauntered down the aisle with the poise and grace of a princess. She was the envy of every woman and the fantasy of every warm-blooded heterosexual man in the room.

Ray was also a vision in his impeccably tailored custom-made tuxedo from Hugo Boss. Even the pastor couldn't resist making reference to the bride and groom's beauty. There was no denying that Missy and Ray were one of the most handsome couples many had ever laid eyes on, and in an incredibly superficial way that lent to the day's ambiance. People really do love beautiful people.

The wedding went off without a hitch. The vows were short and sweet but seemingly heartfelt. The bride and the groom shed tears along with many of their guests, but God only knew what emotions truly lay behind the waterworks.

The minister pronounced their marriage and presented the newlyweds to thunderous applause. As they walked down the aisle hand in hand, she looked around and could see the love in everyone's faces —friends, colleagues, family. *His* family. They were all so happy. She wanted to scream. She wanted the day to be over.

She could give a shit about the magnificence of the reception room. The hundreds of thousands of dollars spent on orchids flown in from Japan, Wedgewood china, Waterford stemware and free flowing Krug Grand Cuvee champagne. All she could think of was that she wished to God she was just a guest at this magnificent wedding. Maybe then she could actually enjoy it.

When the DJ announced that it was time for the wedding dance, Missy felt like somebody had glued her to her seat. She couldn't get up. Ray held out his hand for her and walking out to the dance floor - that was so elegantly designed with their special monogrammed letters- felt more like walking a plank. Hearing the Whispers sing her *former* favorite song, just took her back to the night he proposed. The night she wished she would have told this motherfucker the truth.

She tried so hard to be a good sport and let everyone else enjoy *her* wedding day. There were several different photographers and videographers. Capturing every angle of her secret agony. Ray was playing the part. Loving and doting all over her. They looked like the perfect couple, but with every click of a shutter Missy felt like she died a little inside.

After a dramatic dip he brought her close to him and whispered in her ear, "What happened to the dress we picked out for you?"

Missy kept smiling as she looked him into his eyes. "You mean the dress that you and the wedding coordinator picked out for me? I changed my mind. I wanted to pick my own dress for *my* wedding. You picked everything else. I thought it was fair. I actually thought you'd like it."

Ray twirled his bride around the dance floor and pulled her back in close to him. Then he whispered, "But that's not what we agreed on, sweetheart."

"Ok, so I guess that means you don't like my dress."

"That's putting it mildly. The dress is way too sexy, Missy. And what's with all the makeup? Red lipstick?"

She wanted to slap his face so badly, but instead she leaned back and gazed lovingly into his eyes for the spectators. "What's wrong with my makeup, Ray?"

He returned her gaze and pulled her in closer. "If I wanted a whore for a bride, I would have found one in Bangladesh. Now please do yourself a favor and go change into the next outfit. And do us both a favor and wipe off that red lipstick so we'll have *some* decent pictures for the wedding album."

Missy was speechless. She felt a lump forming in her throat. Holding the tears back was impossible, but somehow she was able to contain her sobs. She laid her head on Ray's chest and just let the tears flow.

The guests were touched by the display of unbridled emotion, which was magnified on the giant screen above the dance floor. When the song ended, Ray took Missy's face in his hands and kissed her softly on the lips. Then he wiped the tears from her face. The DJ shouted, "Let's have a round of applause for the happy couple – Mr. and Mrs. Ray Coleman, y'all!" It was officially the worst day of her life.

Love On The Run

Three years into what had turned into a full-fledged romance, an arrest warrant was issued for one Tobias Antonio Bell. 39-year-old African American male, approximately 5'10", medium build, short black hair, brown eyes, tattoo of a small spiral shaped triangle on the back of his neck. He was wanted for first degree sexual assault. At the time the warrant was issued there were four victims of record, including PJ.

Toby's first victim – PJ was calling him Toby at that point - came forward a month earlier. Jefferson High suspended him with pay pending an investigation. That investigation yielded concrete photographic evidence that he committed sexual acts with at least four boys between the ages of eleven and sixteen years old. Two of those boys, including PJ were his students. Every news outlet in the area reported it on the hour.

Prior to the news reports Toby received a call from his mother informing him that the police had just kicked in her door with the warrant. He and PJ were holed up in a fleabag motel two states away. He'd grabbed his computer, packed a bag and left his apartment the day his suspension came down. He knew things were about to get crazy.

After the phone call he knew it was only a matter of time before the police would catch up to him. He logged onto his computer and checked the news outlets. Sure enough, he was mentioned on every one. And of course there was a picture. He thought, they managed to find the one picture that made him look like a devious perv.

It was late and PJ was hungry so Toby sent him out to get food. He couldn't risk being recognized. So PJ left for the grocery store. Toby gave him a long list. He wanted enough food so that they wouldn't have to go out for a while. He needed some time to figure out his next move.

The trunk was loaded with goodies. Lots of microwavables and sweet treats they could share. As he drove along, cautiously and unlicensed, PJ was all smiles. He was completely unbothered by the rumors. He knew Toby better than that. Those boys were just mad because Toby didn't want to be with them. Just like he said. He was just trying to help them and they turned on him. Toby promised he would take care of everything so they could be together. But for now they needed to get away. Let everything die down. PJ was happy to be along for the ride.

When he pulled back into the motel parking lot there were police cars everywhere. Two officers were escorting Toby out of their room in handcuffs. They met eyes just before Toby was shoved into the back of the police car. PJ backed out of the lot and drove away.

When he got home he turned on the television and sure enough, Toby's arrest was breaking news. There was footage of his arrest and PJ even caught a glimpse of himself pulling away from the scene. He was devastated. The streets were talking. People were coming at him left and right with questions. It had gotten so crazy he didn't want to leave the house.

Janice and Ronnie confronted him, wanting to know if he was sleeping with Toby too. Not because they were concerned, they just wanted to hear the gossip first hand. And they wanted to gloat. Janice burst into his room after the news broadcast. "Didn't I tell you! I told you that muthafucka liked little boys. Fuckin pedophile!" Ronnie just looked him up and down, disgusted. Then he shook his head and walked out.

PJ was humiliated and worse, he had no way of contacting Toby. He was underage so he couldn't visit the jail without an adult. He planned to write him as soon as he could. But he'd never get the chance.

A week later, more breaking news on Tobias Bell. He committed suicide. Death by asphyxiation. Somehow he managed to get a belt inside of his cell and beat *himself* nearly unconscious just before he strung *himself* up on the bars of the cell door. No witnesses. The case was quickly closed as was the investigation into his sexual misconduct. It was for the best.

Toby's death sent PJ spiraling into deep dark depression. Food had no taste; life made no sense. After a failed suicide attempt, he spent a few months recuperating in St. Elizabeth's Mental Hospital on the Southside of DC.

Janice had him committed after she found him in the bathtub, half-conscious and bleeding from his wrists. He didn't care. He wanted to get away from her house anyway. Enough had happened there that if he never went back it would be too soon.

The night he tried to take his life he'd truly reached his bottom. For months he'd relegated himself to the depths of the musty basement. No school. No friends. Except for the old floor model television and the few pictures of Toby that he had tucked away, he was completely alone. Left to himself, with his thoughts, which were getting darker by the day. This night he was feeling especially hopeless. After staring at Toby's picture and crying himself to sleep he awoke with a new purpose. To see Toby again.

He went into the bathroom and turned on the shower. Opened the cabinet and emptied every one of Janice's old prescription bottles. There were a few Xanax pills, some blood pressure medication, a few extra strength Tylenol and about a third of a bottle of Nyquil. He figured if he took it all he'd drift off, quietly and painlessly into the next life, where Toby would be waiting. Just like in his dreams.

So he took every pill and drank down all of the Nyquil. Then he undressed and sat in the tub to wait for the medicine to take effect. The shower rained on him and after a while he felt relaxed. It was a good feeling. He reflected on his life. The little good, the constant bad and the unendingly ugly.

He thought, in all his years on earth, the only good he could reflect on were the few memories he had of his mother in the park and the time he spent with Toby. The two most important people in his life were gone and all that was left was this misery. Nothing about his life was fair and what could he possibly have done to deserve it?

He shifted his focus to Toby. The way he smelled. His touch. The way he looked into his soul. PJ wanted desperately to be with him again. More than life. So he closed his eyes, ready to drift away. From everything. He thought, *goodbye Janice, you greedy, filthy, slovenly, flat footed, bad wig wearin, sorry ass excuse for a woman. Goodbye Ronnie, you lazy, shiftless, musty, dirty clothes hamper diggin in, crack smokin piece of shit. Goodbye world. And fuck you very much.* He was going to sleep.

In the distance, he could hear knocking. The knocking turned to a heavy banging and he could hear someone yelling. "Boy! What the fuck you doin in there? You better open up this goddamn door with your lil punk ass! I know you hear me out here!" The bathroom door swung open, crashing into the wall so hard it punched a hole in the drywall behind it.

When Ronnie walked in and saw him in the tub he cursed. "Lil stupid muthafucka in here takin a bath. Got me standin out here bout to piss on myself. I know you heard me calling you, boy!" As he relieved himself, he looked around and noticed the empty pill bottles on the floor. He zipped up his dingy khakis and grabbed one of the bottles from the floor. "What the fuck you in here doin?"

He picked up the other pill bottles and the empty Nyquil bottle. "You took all this shit? Stupid muthafucka. You gon have the police all up and through this house. Get your faggot ass out that goddamn tub! You hear me, boy?!"

PJ heard him, but at that point he could barely move. All he could manage was a smile. The drugs had taken affect, and it was the best feeling he'd ever felt. Ronnie snatched the curtain back and turned off the shower. He stood there staring at PJ's naked body for a moment and then he reached down and grabbed his penis, squeezing it hard. "Little faggot. I always knew you was a faggot. Lettin that teacher fuck you. GIT yo muthafuckin ass out that tub."

He dragged PJ out of the tub by his arm and dropped him on the floor. PJ's body was all but limp at this point. His back was leaning against the tub, when Ronnie reached down and grabbed his penis again. This time he was gentle. PJ's body responded. Involuntarily.

He couldn't believe what was happening to him, and he was powerless to stop it. Ronnie kept stroking him and talking to him. But he wasn't yelling anymore.

"Yeah you like that shit, don't you? Faggot muthufucka. This what you let that nigga do to you? You suck his dick, too?"

Ronnie unzipped his pants and pulled them down to his ankles. Then he knelt in front of PJ and tried to open his mouth. PJ would never forget the stink. A sour, sweaty, musky stench that made him gag. When he couldn't get PJ's mouth open he yelled at him, and when PJ didn't respond he punched him hard in the face.

"Open your fuckin mouth!" *Whap!* Another hard punch to the jaw. "Open your fuckin mouth!" *Whap!*

PJ was groggy and weak but refused to open his mouth. He half hoped that Ronnie would just knock him out so it would all be over. When Ronnie tired of trying to get his mouth open he lifted PJ up and threw him over the side of the tub. Then he showed him just what kind of man he was.

When he was done, Ronnie stood, zipped his pants and walked out. But not before spitting on PJ and whispering, "Now go ahead faggot, kill yourself."

PJ laid there on the floor, exposed. Feeling at his lowest. He couldn't even die right. But he was about to fix that.

Between the punches and the violation, the effects of the drugs had all but worn off. He was awake and painfully aware of everything around him. The exact opposite of what he was trying to achieve.

Desperate to make it all go away; he went back to the medicine cabinet. Ideally, he wanted to drift off into the darkness, but there was no chance of that happening. And now ending the pain was more urgent than it had ever been before. He didn't want another minute to think of what had just happened to him. Another second to contemplate the how's, the why's and what to do next. So he grabbed one of Ronnie's old shavers and twisted the knob until a razor, rusted at the edges fell out into the sink.

He grabbed the razor, climbed back inside the tub, turned on the faucet and wept as the tub slowly filled with tepid water. With his left hand, his strong hand, he raked the dulled razor across his right wrist, digging in deep. He had every intention of making the first cut the last. When it was done, he closed his eyes and waited for a darkness that would never come.

Just Say The Words

"Well I can certainly see why your marriage isn't working. Your husband is in control of everything. It seems, from the moment you met him he's been running things. He pulled you away from your friends, informed you that you were going to be his wife. He decided when you'd marry, how you'd marry and everything in between. Mrs. Coleman you've given him all of your power. You do realize that he put an engagement ring on your finger without you officially accepting his proposal."

"I know."

"Tell me. How does that make you feel?"

"I dunno. Powerless."

"I'm sure it does. Now we have to figure out how we take that power back. How to give you a voice in this marriage."

"That's just it. I don't need a voice anymore."

"Ok. Why is that? Why wouldn't you want to have some control of your own life? Why wouldn't you want to…"

"Because I'm done, Dr. Cartwright. I'm done."

"I see. When I asked what you hoped to accomplish in therapy you said you just wanted to figure out how you ended up where you are. I didn't realize you wanted to end your marriage. Quite frankly I thought you were here to save it."

"No that's not at all why I came here. And I'm sorry I've wasted so much of your time."

"You don't have to apologize for my time. You take as long as you need. I'm not here to push you. That's not what therapy is about."

"Thank you. And I do appreciate that. But this is our third session and I haven't even gotten to the reason I came here in the first place. I dunno. It's…it's like I can't say the words out of my mouth or something." Missy sighed. "Maybe this isn't gonna work."

"Ok, let's try this. Let's take a break. Call it a day. You go home, sleep on it. Take some time to think about what you need to say and we can reconvene first thing in the morning."

"No...sleeping on it won't help." Missy sighed. "I need to just come out and say it."

"Then just say it Mrs. Coleman. You're safe here. We can discuss anything you want."

"OK...ok, you're right. I can tell you anything. Missy took a deep breath. And then another. And then one more. After the fourth or fifth breath she no longer had control of them. She was beginning to hyperventilate. She held on to the arm of the sofa with one hand and clutched her chest with the other. Her chest tightened and then her heart began to race.

Dr. Cartwright grabbed a bottle of water from the small refrigerator behind her desk and raced over to Missy's aid. "Mrs. Coleman, here, put your head down, between your legs. Now breathe in. Slooowly. Inhale through your nose. Yes, good now exhale out of your mouth. Again, inhale..."

After a few breathing exercises Missy calmed down and took a sip of water. "Thank you Dr. Cartwright. I'm so sorry about that."

"Please don't apologize. Tell me. Has this ever happened before?"

"Yes, just once. The night it happened."

"It. Ok, well I don't think we're ready to discuss *it* today. Not until we figure out how to deal with your anxiety." She pulled a prescription pad from her desk drawer. "I'm going to prescribe you..."

Missy yelled. "No! No I don't need any medication. No medication. I'm stronger than that."

"Mrs. Coleman, with all due respect, I understand that you may feel..."

"No, no, that's just it. You don't understand how I feel. No one understands. I don't need any medicine. I...I just need to get it out. I feel like if I can just say the damn words...I can get over it. Or something. Shit." Missy glanced at the clock on the wall behind her. "I have twenty-three minutes left in this session. I am not leaving this office until I get this out."

Dr. Cartwright leaned back in her chair and clasped her hands in front of her. Missy inhaled deeply through her nose and exhaled out of her mouth. She shook her hands back and forth in front of her and then had another sip from her water bottle. "Whew. Ok. I got it. Ok. Well, a few days before Valentine's Day..."

Saving Grace

"Heeey, Auntie Pat." Brenda slurred the few words she spoke. "How you doin?"

"Hey Brenda. What's up? You alright? You been drinking?"

"Umm. A lil bit." Brenda laughed at the lie and then she hiccupped.

"Yeah, you might need to ease up on the sauce a lil bit baby. I been hearin some things about you."

"About me? Me? What you heard about me?"

"Yeah about you. Just take it easy on that shit. For me, alright?"

"Who…who talkin shit about me Auntie? Huh?" She hiccupped again. "I'm good."

"Come on, Brenda. You got too much going on for that. Those kids need you, and that's the only thing that's important right now. You hear what I'm sayin?"

"Umh hmm."

"You get my letter?"

"Um…yeah. I just read it. Good stuff."

"You ok?"

"Fuck no. I'm pretty fuckin…" She hiccupped. "… fuckin far from ok. As a matter ooof FACT, you caught ME on my way out this muthafucka."

"On your way out? To where?"

"Out to see the muthafucka that killed my boyfriend. I mean my um…my fuckin husband. That's where."

"Oh so you gon go take care of it, huh?"

"Got damn…muthafuckin right. Umma take care of the shit myself."

"Brenda, go sit your ass down."

"No! No! I'm sick…I'm sick and muthafuckin tied of playin with these muthafuckas out here. I ain't nothing to be played with, Auntie Pat. My muvva ain't raise no bitches up in here. Ain't noooo bitches ova here. I'm a muthafuckin James girl. We don't play that muthafuckin shit. Do we, Auntie Pat?"

"No baby, we don't. Can you do somethin for me?"

"Yeah."

"I want you to go get yourself some aspirin."

"Huh?"

"Yeah, do it while I'm on the phone. You got some aspirin?"

"Yeah."

"Then go get it."

"Now?"

"Yeah. Right now." A few seconds passed, and there was a crashing noise in the background. "Brenda? You ok?"

She fumbled with the phone for a second. "Um...yeah. I'm ok."

"You got the aspirin?"

"Yeah."

"Now go get some water."

"Now?"

"Yes, now." A few seconds passed. She could hear Brenda stumbling around in the kitchen. "Brenda?"

"Huh?"

"You got it?"

"Yeah."

"Ok, now take three right now. While I'm on the phone." A few seconds pass. "Did you take it?"

"Yeah."

"Ok now go in your bedroom."

"What?"

"Go into your bedroom. While I'm on the phone, Brenda. And hurry up. I gotta go in a minute. Go ahead in your bedroom. You there?"

"Yeah."

"Ok, now one more thing."

"What?"

"Lay your motherfuckin ass down and go to sleep. Don't you leave that house, Brenda. I'm not playing wit u."

"Auntie—"

"Auntie my ass. Lay your ass down and go to sleep! I mean it! Do NOT leave that house, Brenda. You know I'll be home in a few weeks. If I find out you left and did some stupid shit, Brenda, I swear you gon have me to deal with. And trust me when I tell you, you DON'T want that. You hear what I'm sayin to you?"

"Yeah I hear you."

"I said do you HEAR me?!"

"Yes! I HEAR YOU!"

"Good. I'll call you back in the mornin to check up on you. Good NIGHT, Brenda!"

"Goodnight."

Brenda hung up the phone irritated…and queasy. She hadn't eaten anything since breakfast and when the cold water hit her empty stomach, she knew what little was left in there was coming back up. She ran to the bathroom and after hugging the commode for a few minutes made her way back to the bed and passed out.

*****

Brenda's Aunt Carolyn banged on the door for a while before she decided to use the spare key. When she walked inside, she saw an empty bottle of vodka sitting on the coffee table. The house was a complete mess, which was very unusual for Brenda, the neat freak.

She walked back to the bedroom and could hear the faint but familiar sound of vomiting in the distance. She took Mandy to her room and closed the door. When she walked into the bedroom, she found Brenda hanging on the side of the toilet.

The vanity mirror was broken and glass was all over the floor. The stench of alcohol seeped from Brenda's pores. So she helped her up and over to the bed. She undressed her and put the covers over her, then she went out to the kitchen and put on a pot of coffee. When it started to brew she walked back into the room and shook Brenda awake.

"Brenda. I'm taking Mandy back to my house, and I'll be back in a little while to check on you. When I get back, me and you gon have us a talk. You hear me?"

Brenda pulled the covers up over her head. "Yeah."

A couple of hours later, Brenda pulled herself out of bed to go to the bathroom. Her head was pounding, and she walked down the long hall using the walls to hold her steady. She found Aunt Carolyn in the kitchen making hangover food – fried potatoes, eggs and toast.

"Come on in here and sit down. Here take this." She handed Brenda a Goody Powder and an ice cold Pepsi. "Eat some of this food. I want you to get some strength. Get ya mind right so we can talk."

"Aunt Carolyn, I'm so not in the mood for this."

"Girl do I look like I care what you in the mood for? I wasn't in the mood to have Mandy for another day, but you didn't leave me no choice now did you?"

"Then just bring her home."

"Bring her home? To this? I don't think so. Brenda, do you know where your kids at right now?"

"Of course I know where my kids are. MJ is at mama's house and Brandy is over Keisha's."

"No, MJ is not at yo mama's house. He's stayin over in southeast with Monte. He been there a week and you know what they be doin over there. And Brandy ain't got no business stayin with that little girl. Her mama on that crack, and she already strollin a baby around. You wanna be a grandma?"

"Brandy is a good girl, Aunt Carolyn. She knows better."

"Oh she know better? Like you did?"

Brenda ignored the comment. It was a particularly low blow, but she didn't have the strength to retort.

"You sho ain't settin no kinda example for her. Layin around here drunk every day. You lookin crazy, your house is nasty. Can't even get up and care for your baby. Girl, what are you doin?"

"What do you mean what am I doing? I'm survivin! I'm doin the best I can by myself. Ain't nobody helpin me and my kids. You wouldn't understand."

"So *this* is yo best? Look Brenda, I know you hurtin and everything, but sweetie you ain't the only woman out here that lost her husband, and you damn sure ain't the only single mother out here strugglin. Now I ain't got to go into my life story for you to understand that. You gotta do better than this here, baby."

"I'm try-ing! You know I'm gon have to leave here soon. I can't afford to stay here. Melvin didn't leave me no money, and what I had saved is almost gone. God. What the hell did I do with my life?"

"You spent it here. Holed up wit a street nigga. That's what you did."

"Damn Aunt Carolyn. Tell me how you *really* feel."

"Well. You know I gotta call a spade a spade. That's the whole problem. Don't nobody tell your ass the truth. You laid up, had babies, and married a drug dealer. You and nem kids lived good off that dope money for all dem years, and now you ain't got nothin to show for it. Nothin."

Brenda began to cry. The truth was pretty hard to hear, especially from Aunt Carolyn, who had a special nack for twisting the knife after she stuck it in. She knew the twist was coming.

"Ion know why you cryin now. You thought ya life was different from all these other dumb ass little girls out here cause that nigga put a ring on yo finger. Cause he was takin care of y'all. But you ain't no different then they is. Yeah, you was good to your mother, and yeah y'all helped a few people out here with Melvin's dirty money, but you didn't do shit for yo self and you didn't set no kinda example for dem kids. How da hell you gon tell dem kids to do right when you and Melvin ain't never done right? Who dey s'posed to follow?"

Brenda laid her head down on her arms and sobbed.

Aunt Carolyn walked over and gave her a hug. "Go'on baby. Get it out. You probly needed a good cry anyway. I know you not used to nobody tellin you the truth. Hell, I probly wouldn't a told you if you didn't ask me. But you gotsta face it. That's the onliest way you gon be able to deal with it."

"I know. But I'm scared."

"Well you should be. All these years living high on the hog, and you ain't got shit to show for it but two cars you can't pay for and a house you gotta pack up and move out of. That boy ain't leave you no insurance. You can't get no social security off no drug dealer. Ya kids runnin wild in the streets, and you in here drunk on your ass. What kinda shit is that, Brenda? You know better than this."

"I know. You right."

"You goddamn right I'm right. Dem kids got everything they ever wanted. Walked around with a pocket full of money. New tennis shoes on they feet, jewelry all down they necks, thinkin they better than errybody. Better than the rest of the kids who parents got out here and worked hard for a living. Y'all fucked them kids up good. I blame Betty, too."

"No, it's not her fault."

"I ain't say it was her fault. But she was spendin on Melvin's money, too. She know dat shit wuddn't right. I tried to tell her that too. But she lissen bout as much as you do."

"No. This is all on me. I shoulda done better by my kids. Done more for myself. I shoulda made Melvin stop. I really wanted him to. I swear I did. You don't know how many times I asked him to stop, to just do something else."

"Well coulda woulda shoulda. Don't much matter now do it? Besides, it ain't what you say you want, it's what you do. It's how you live, Brenda. That's what people respond to. You can't tell a man you want him to stop makin a livin doin what he doin and you ain't got no better way for him to live. You mightta told him that, but you was still spendin on the money you say you don't want him to make. How much sense that make? It don't work like that. You gotta do yo part if you expectin him to do his baby."

Brenda sighed. "Well I don't know what umma do now."

"Yeah you do. Betty's house is just about paid fo. Move ya asses back there and start over. Sell off summa dis shit you got layin 'round here so you can put some money in yo pocket. Me and ya Uncle Edward ain't got much money to give you, but you know we'll help where we can. Now go'on wipe your face off and eat some of this food before it get too cold. Umma get out of here and go get that baby. You know she don't like Edward so she probably hollerin right now. I don't know why y'all got that girl spoiled like that. Can't nobody keep her."

Brenda laughed. "Thanks Auntie. You know I appreciate you."

"You ain't gotta thank me. You just get some rest cause I'm bringin Mandy cryin ass back here early in the mornin. And clean up this nasty ass house, Brenda. This is filthy. And you looking bad, too. Girl, I ain't never seen you like this. And I really wish you would just—"

"Aunt Carolyn!" Brenda yelled as she held her head in her hands. "Please. Enough with the truth. I get it, ok. You called it. I'm a spade."

Carolyn smiled. "Well, long as you get it. I'll see you in the mornin. *Early* in the mornin!" She kissed her niece on the forehead and left.

Brenda finished her food and went back to bed. As she swallowed the strong cold Pepsi she laid there thinking about everything that Aunt Carolyn said. She knew it was right. Things had gotten way out of hand and it was time for her to get things back in order.

Her life had changed and she had to find a way to deal with it. A way that didn't involve a fifth of vodka and a pity party. A way that kept her family together and strong. She thought, she would sleep this off and wake up renewed. Ready for the world. If only it were that easy.

My Funny Valentine

On his last game of the post season, Ray suffered a career ending injury to his knee and was forced to retire a year earlier than he planned. It was a heartbreaking season and an agonizing defeat, where the 'Skins lost the NFC championship game in overtime, to Dallas no less.

Ray was more depressed than Missy had ever seen him. He was drinking day and night and despite her best efforts to cheer him up he had become ten times as nasty as he'd ever been. He'd even started being mean to the kids, which was way out of character for him.

In an attempt to lift his spirits, she suggested they take a weekend trip for Valentine's Day to reconnect. From his reaction, you would have thought she asked him to buy her a new house. She got a long profanity-laced lecture about how he didn't have any money to waste on a bullshit holiday or on her.

Then he proceeded to tell her things were about to be different since he was retired, so she'd better start scaling back.

Missy wanted to say, *Negro, I have my own money*, but of course she didn't. What was between her and her account manager was between them.

That same day Ray got a call from Matt, telling him that HBC Sports wanted him to co-host a documentary series on football's greatest heroes. The show was being taped down in Atlanta on Valentine's Day, and of course he accepted.

Missy was sick of all the fighting and just wanted to do something to let Ray know she loved him, so she decided to fly in and surprise him. He hated surprises but she planned on giving him a Valentine's night that was so special and so fantastic that he'd have no choice but to love it and her. The reward was totally worth the risk.

Ray flew down on the 13th, and the network put him up in a really fancy corporate apartment at the Ritz Carlton on Peachtree Street downtown. She peeked at his itinerary and found out that he'd be at the studio taping his show until 6 p.m. on Valentine's Day. He had dinner reservations at Avanze, a restaurant near the hotel. The reservation was at seven, so she guessed he'd be back at the apartment somewhere around nine.

Her plane landed at one o'clock, so she had plenty of time to do a little shopping, pamper herself a bit and get the apartment set up before Ray returned. She arrived at the apartment at six o'clock and the concierge, a very animated little gay guy named Wendell, let her in. When she told him what she had planned he squealed with excitement and offered to help.

They set up candles and rose petals making a path from the front door, up the staircase and into the bedroom. Then Wendell retreated to his post with instructions to ring her cell the minute Ray walked into the lobby.

She stocked the bar with his favorite Louis XIII cognac and poured a healthy dose in his favorite oversized monogrammed brandy snifter. She left that on the living room table so he'd grab it before he came up to the bedroom to find her. She figured he'd naturally follow the lighted path up the stairs and when he opened the door he'd find her sprawled out on red silk sheets wearing nothing but body shimmer and his Super Bowl ring, which she had just added more diamonds to as a Valentine's Day gift.

Beside the bed, were all of his favorite toys and treats and a bottle of Kristal chilling on the bedside table with their wedding flutes. She'd even bought a tube of numbing cream so that she could at least *pretend* to enjoy his brand of lovemaking. Missy was definitely ready for action. She was getting her husband back.

By nine, she had the candles lit, the cognac poured, and the scene set. All she had to do was freshen up. As she brushed her teeth, she heard the door slam shut downstairs. She thought, *dammit Wendell!* Her first instinct was to run to the bedroom and hurry up to get into character, but she heard voices. She listened a little closer. Ray was with another woman.

She tip toed out to the hall, peeked down over the railing and saw them kissing. Ray had the woman pinned up against the front door, and they were really going at it. She wanted to go down and make a scene, but something stopped her. She didn't know if it was the curiosity of how far he would actually go with the woman or the fear of Ray's wrath when he found that she'd followed him to Atlanta and snuck into his hotel. Probably a little of both, but whatever it was, she stood still and watched silently as her husband made mad passionate love to another woman. A very beautiful woman. A very beautiful Latino woman with a thick accent and an even thicker everything else.

With every moment that passed, Missy's anger heightened. Her heart sank to the pit of her stomach as she watched him ravishing this woman in a way that he hadn't done her since before they married. In fact, their marriage was virtually sexless, but Ray was clearly getting his in.

He and the Spanish lady kissed for a couple minutes, and then he tore her blouse open exposing her bare breasts. He sucked and licked her and kissed her until she began to get impatient, so she shoved him down on the sofa and started pulling away at his pants. He noticed the snifter on the table and drank it down completely, obviously eager to get back to his business. She pulled him out of his pants and before her head disappeared from view Missy heard her say, "Happy Valentine's Day, Papi." He returned the sentiment right before he laid back and closed his eyes.

Missy stood there with tears streaming down her face, unsure what she should do, and too scared to move. She literally had to cover her mouth with her hands to keep herself quiet. She thought, *should I confront them? What will happen if I do? He'll probably throw ME out and continue his night with this woman just out of spite.*

Honestly, she knew Ray cheated. Ray knew that she knew he cheated. They just never spoke of it. They weren't having sex, he didn't come home most nights and when he did he slept in the basement, as far away from her as he could be. That said, if she'd confronted him at that moment he'd hardly respond like the typical cheating husband caught red-handed. So she decided to keep quiet. For the moment.

After a couple more minutes, he pulled his lady up, gave her a very passionate kiss on the mouth and suggested they "take it to the bedroom."

By that time, he was completely naked, and she wore only her skirt and heels. He took her hand and when they got up from the sofa, headed toward the stairs, Missy hurried into the bathroom hoping not to be caught. She stayed there listening to them kissing and moaning, oohing and ahhing. Then his moans stopped and hers began.

She heard the strangest muffled noises, and then the lady started speaking in Spanish. It was the one time Missy regretted taking up French. The muffled noises went on and on. She couldn't really figure out what was happening, and the curiosity was eating her alive, so she decided to sneak out of the bathroom to take a peek.

The master bedroom was huge, and the bed was far enough from the doorway that she could peek in and not be seen.

Ray and his lady were at the far end of the room on the other side of the bed. The woman stood with her back to the door. She was tall and at that point naked except for a red lace garter belt attached to matching red stockings. Her long black hair fell down to her tiny waist, and she had an extremely big ass. An abnormally, disproportionately big ass. That only made Missy angrier because Ray had always told her that her ass was *way* too big. He said she had a "ghetto booty" and he didn't mean it as a compliment. This lady's ass was at least twice her size. *Motherfucker.*

She kept watching. She didn't see Ray at first, but just as things were starting to really come into focus Ray stood up and pushed the lady backward down onto the bed. Missy was not at all prepared for what she was about to witness.

When the lady's back hit the sheets, there it stood at full attention and in its full glory. About seven and a half inches, give or take a half inch, of rock hard penis standing like a joystick on an Atari game.

Before Missy could get her mind wrapped around what she was seeing, her husband, Ray "Mr. All American. Mr. Macho Homophobe" Coleman climbed up on top of her, kissed a trail up her thigh and then he commenced to giving this "she thing" the best fellatio Missy had ever seen in her life.

She simply could not believe her eyes. Her jaw dropped, and she covered her mouth tight with both hands to make sure her thoughts remained in her head. *What the FUCK!* It felt like she was in a really bad dream. The kind where you can't seem to move even when you try your hardest. She was paralyzed in shock and disbelief. And it was impossible to look away.

When Ray was done with his dirty foreplay he turned the lady over and mounted her from behind. She screamed something in her native tongue as he grabbed her by both shoulders and ravaged her backside, taking Missy's mind back to her first disturbing sexual encounter with the man.

A few thrusts in, and Missy was able to shake herself out of her stooper. She backed away, grabbed her bags from the spare bedroom and left as quietly as she came, with the sounds of their moaning trailing off behind her.

She barely made it to her car before she broke down. Crying hysterically and cursing herself for being so stupid. *Of course he's gay!* Then she panicked. Her health! She thought, *oh my God I have to get tested!*

Her emotions ran the gamut. Hurt, shame, fear and anger. And she was so full of questions. She had no idea what to do or where to begin. But one thing was for sure, after that Valentine's Day, her life would never be the same.

Back to Life

Five months after laying Melvin to rest, Brenda was desperately trying to get her life back on track. Back to normal, so to speak, but it was hard to even know where to begin.

She sat at the kitchen table sifting through a stack of past due bills, and freaking out. Second and third notices. She had no idea how she was going to pay them all.

Rent was due, it was almost time for the kids to go back to school and there was no money for clothes or school supplies. Betty's co-pay for the hospice was more than her social security check would cover and the bills at her house needed payin too.

Melvin's funeral was more expensive than she imagined and she had absolutely no help. With all of their input and unsolicited opinions, his family never offered her a penny toward the funeral costs. She got plenty of advice and plenty of compliments on how things were handled, but not one dime from any of them.

Everyone assumed she had some big insurance policy on Melvin. A reasonable enough assumption, but there was no policy. Too embarrassed to admit that to anyone, she never asked for help, just hoped someone would be kind enough to offer.

She and Melvin talked about getting insurance for the family but they never got around to actually doing it. Over the years they'd filled out dozens of those mail inserts for cheap term coverage but never took the time to complete the process. Just figuring there would be time. She felt foolish.

Even though Brenda knew she didn't have the means, Melvin Johnson deserved the very best, and she was going to give him exactly that. That was her thought five months ago, but as she rifled through the mountain of collection notices she could see things much more clearly. She fucked up.

Going over the receipts from the funeral she thought, *Why didn't anyone stop me?* The sales people at the funeral home went to work on her right away. Taking full advantage of the young widow in her time of bereavement. Convincing her that the more expensive the funeral, the more she loved her husband. All the while they were just lining their pockets, selling her all the dumb shit that no one else ever bought.

24K gold "remembrance ornaments" and keychains. A custom website for friends and family to make their own personal tributes. $9,000 to be in a vault at Lincoln cemetery, $6,000 for a custom tombstone with his picture laser drawn on it. Brenda maxed out her only credit card at Neiman's buying him a $700 Prada suit; it was a closed casket service. And he didn't even like suits.

She booked three Humvee limousines for family cars and had the repast at a banquet hall, catered by Melvin's favorite soul food restaurant. Madness.

Everything was completely over the top and she thought how the hood would be bragging on her husband's home-going for months but it would probably take her years to pay for it all.

All of his *so called* friends said they would take up a collection for the kids, but after the funeral she never heard from any of them. Some of them spoke when they saw her on the street but she could tell they were hoping she wouldn't stop to talk.

Then there was Daye. He owed thousands but after their last heated argument, he definitely wasn't giving up anything.

Ever since the whole down-low revelation Missy had pretty much fallen off the face of the earth. Brenda decided to let her have her time. She'd come back around when she was ready. Besides her drama wasn't exactly something that could be fixed with a glass of wine and dose of sisterly love. *Her* shit was next level.

So, with Missy out of the equation and Daye unwilling to repay his debt Brenda needed to figure something out, fast. All that was left was a few thousand dollars from Melvin's stash and that would be gone in a couple months. The kids probably had money stashed somewhere, but she couldn't think of asking them. Or could she? No.

She would have to find a job, and soon, but what could she do for immediate cash? Pawn her jewelry? Sell her shoes and handbags? That would keep them afloat for a little while, but what was the long term plan? And the embarrassment. Lawd the embarrassment. Being forced to sell her belongings to feed her children. Watching the bank come and haul away their cars. She could just imagine the snickering and the gossip.

Brenda poured up a healthy vodka-cranberry, drank it down completely, like warm fruit punch and flipped the table with all of its worrisome contents on its side.

At that point, there was only one decision left to make. One that should have been made months ago. She grabbed her keys and headed out the door. To the Uhaul store. It was time to pack it up. Time to move.

Angry as Usual

Missy made the long drive back to Potomac. Still reeling from the revelation she'd just made to her little sister. She was half-relieved but still full of anxiety, wondering if her secret would be repeated. Some secrets were just too big for a person to keep.

Up until then the only person she'd told was Jesus, and Dr. Cartwright. In the four months since V-Day she'd logged many hours on the good head doctor's soft leather sofa and still had no idea what to do with her life. She thought her life would have been fixed by now, with all the money spent. But then again she hadn't followed any of Dr. Cartwright's advice.

Confronting Ray with his truth was job one and that was supposed to have happened already. But Missy didn't have the nerve to open that can of snakes. Not at all. Plus, she neglected to tell the Dr. that Ray's abuse had long gone past the point of emotional.

Oversized diva shades, long sleeves and designer ascots kept her closeted abuse within the confines of their home and that's where it would stay, until she was ready to deal with it, and she would, in her own time. A time when Ray wasn't so testy. When he found steady work or "figured things out" - in is words.

Since he was forced to retire Ray was always on edge. And he claimed money was suddenly tight, which was confusing and when she'd asked for more information on their financial status he slapped her so hard across the face with the back of his hand that he broke the skin in the corner of her mouth with his ring. Afterward he warned her never to ask him about his money again. And she didn't.

So the thought of confronting him with something as heavy as his sexuality, and the circumstance that led to her discovery made her tremble. Living a lie was killing her, but telling the truth would probably get her killed. She tried to put it out of her mind. Her mind needed a break. And maybe another drink.

When she got home the house was dark. She flipped the lights on and nearly jumped out of her skin. Ray was sitting in the family room on the sofa.

"Ray! I…I didn't know you were back in town."

"Yeah well you never know where I'm gon be do you. Where the fuck was you, and why does Maria have the kids? You went somewhere they couldn't go?"

"I…I went to see Brenda, and I know you don't like them going into Ridgewood, so I took them over to Maria's. I was only gone a few hours."

"Really. Maria said you dropped them off this morning."

"Well, yeah I had and appointment at Red Door and then went straight to Brenda's. I wasn't planning on staying long but…she's not doing well at all. Her husband was killed."

"Head or chest."

"Huh?"

"Where'd he get shot, in the head or in his chest? He got shot right?"

"Uh, yeah I think he did."

"Yeah. What a shock. I swear those motherfuckers will never learn. So what's your little hoodrat sister gonna do now? Probably go on welfare. You didn't give her any of my money did you?"

"No, Ray. She never asked me for any money."

"Um hmm. Well see that you don't." Ray swallowed the rest of his drink and poured himself another highball full. "I'm not taking care of her babies. Well. I guess I will after she goes on welfare. And why am I just finding out about this anyway?"

"You were away. And I didn't think you'd care."

"You thought right. I don't. But when you start dropping my kids off with random fucking strangers, I think I should know what's going on, don't you?"

"Ray they've been to Maria's a thousand times. She watches them whenever we go out. You know I'd never abandon our kids."

He took a gulp of his drink. "*My* kids."

Missy ignored the hurtful comment.

"Just don't leave them again."

"Ok."

"So. You see any of your old boyfriends when you went to see your 'sister?'"

She hopped up off the sofa. "What? Who? I…I mean no!"

He sat his drink down on the bar and walked over to her. Missy sank back down into the sofa, realizing she should have just let him talk. He stood in front of her staring down at her. At this point, she knew what was coming, and the tears begin to form in her eyes. She pleaded with him.

"Please Ray. I just went to make sure my sister was ok. That's all. You know I don't even like being in Ridgewood."

Ray grabbed her face with one hand, pulling her back to her feet and squeezing hard into her cheeks until she tasted blood inside her mouth. He stared into her eyes for a few moments, and then he threw her back down to the couch hard. He smiled wickedly and walked back over to the bar for his drink. "Let me tell you something I learned pretty early on in life. What people do in the dark eventually comes to light." He headed toward the foyer and started up the stairs. "Be careful not to let that light shine on you Mrs. Coleman." When he got to the top of the staircase, he yelled down, "Now GO get my fuckin kids!"

Still lying half off the sofa, Missy wiped the tears from her eyes and breathed a sigh of relief. The kids were coming home, so she knew the worst was over; for tonight. She thought, I have to find a way out of this mess

Resentment Issues

Brenda and Missy were getting along wonderfully. Ray had been traveling a lot so Missy had a lot of time to spend reconnecting with her family. In the course of a month, the sisters had spent more time together – at spa days, brunches, shopping trips – than they had in the last ten years. Uncle Edward had even dragged them to a noon day church service. And it was actually ok.

They sat up late nights just catching up on all the family drama. Since they'd pretty much lost touch since Missy left for college, there was much to discuss, including the events leading up to and through Missy's wedding. Missy gave a full account. Every juicy detail. The good, bad and especially the ugly.

They were having a ball together. Finally bonding like real sisters. After service, they went back to Betty's house for lunch. Brenda made them a superbly delicious and extremely unhealthy Cobb salad before she started preparing dinner for the kids.

"Wow, that chicken smells so good, Brenda," Missy said. "I wish I would have learned how to cook like that."

"You could have. Why didn't you?"

"I don't know. I guess I was brainwashed. Thought it was better to know how to order a meal than to cook one."

"Well I do like to eat out sometimes, but it ain't nothing like a home-cooked meal. And I love my own cooking so I don't mind. Melvin always loved my cooking. He said it was the second thing he fell in love with." Brenda winked and pooched her butt up in the air. "*If* you know what I mean."

"Yeah I'll bet. Nasty." Missy took a bite of a freshly fried piece of chicken. It was so good it practically melted in her mouth. Steaming hot, perfectly seasoned salty, crunchy goodness. She closed her eyes to really savor it. "Seriously Brenda. You really have to teach me sometime. Ray would die for this chicken. How much would you charge me for lessons?"

"No charge. All you gotta do is come by more often."

"Don't worry. I'll come by. Do you have something to drink?

"Like what, liquor?"

"No, a plain ole beverage. Tea? Lemonade? I don't drink *every day*."

"Well *I* do. I think I may have developed a lil problem."

"So I've noticed."

"Whatever. I can stop an-ty-time I want to. But I don't want to."

"Spoken like a true alchie."

"Shut up." Brenda reached into the fridge and grabbed a pitcher of something purple with sliced lemon on top."

Missy shrieked. "Ooh! Is that what I think it is?"

"Yes ma'am. We still drink Kool Aid 'round these parts."

Missy took a sip, closed her eyes and smacked her tongue. "Oh my goodness. I haven't had Kool Aid since I left this house. And you still make it so good. The lemon just makes it so much better."

"Yes it does."

Missy danced in her seat. "Girl. Between the chicken and the Kool Aid I may never go home."

Brenda smiled. It was really nice to get a compliment from her big sister. She couldn't remember the last time she'd gotten one from her.

"So. How are you doing?" Missy said.

"What do you mean?"

"With everything. Melvin being gone. I know we've been hitting the town pretty hard lately and you've been keeping pretty busy with the kids. But how are you dealing with everything?"

"Ok, I guess. Just keeping busy. Mandy is a handful, so the only time I really get alone is during the day when she's at daycare. At first, I felt guilty putting her in a center, but I'm so glad I did. Melvin was always against the kids being in daycare. He said he didn't trust anyone but family with his children. But when he died, I needed a break. Ma got sick right away and there was so much going on. Now those six hours she's at the center are my me time. And she seems to be adjusting pretty well, so it's fine."

"That's good. How are the kids coping?"

"The girls seem to be doin ok. Mandy randomly asks if her daddy is in heaven. It makes me tear up every time. Brandy is actually handling it really well. Almost too well, which worries me a little bit, but she's always the strong girl. I haven't seen her cry once. She just acts like everything is ok."

"That doesn't seem normal. Considering how close you say they were. It may not be a bad idea to go to therapy. Grief counseling can be very effective."

"What, a shrink?" Brenda waved it off. "Girl please. I don't need no white man on no white couch that don't know me or my problems, telling me what he *thinks* is wrong with me. No thank you."

"You do realize that we have black therapists. They come in all colors you know."

"Whatever. I'll pass."

"I'm just saying. Don't knock it until you try it."

"So you've tried it?"

"Every Wednesday at three o'clock."

"You got way too much time on your hands."

"Whatever you say. But I'm alright."

"Is that so? Well, what does the shrink have to say about you letting your husband beat you upside your head?"

"Ok, time out. How did we get on this subject anyway? I just asked you about the kids."

"You started it."

"Yeah I guess I did. How's MJ doing?"

"Girl MJ is the one that's giving me the blues. When he's not angry he's distant and withdrawn. I know he's smokin weed again. He's says he's not but you know I can tell."

"Well that's not good. What are you gonna do about it?"

"He's too old for me to beat on or punish. I talk to him but he doesn't hear me. He acts like he hates me sometimes."

"I'm sure he doesn't."

"I know he doesn't *hate* me, but I'm sure he has his issues with me. He definitely has some resentment issues."

"Resentment? For what?"

"About the way we live. A few months ago, Melvin came down on him really hard about him trying to sell weed. It got physical. Before he ran out the door, he called us hypocrites and said he should turn both of us in to the police."

"Oh wow. How are you handling that?"

"It's hard. He doesn't want to be here, and I'm trying to give him some space without totally letting him go. He's splitting his time between our house and here with Uncle Larry. I come here every day to cook and clean and make sure he's ok."

"I'm telling you, you should really think about counseling. You never know. It could help."

"I dunno. Maybe. I'll think about it. I guess it couldn't hurt."

"I worry about you, Brenda."

"Yeah, well I worry about me, too. It's been months, but I still feel like I'm in a dream sometimes. Like Melvin's gon walk through that door at any moment. I dream about him almost every night. Either we're in bed or at the dinner table. The last dream I had, we were in Turks on the beach. He was sittin back on a lounger showing his sexy man boobs while he watched me model the bathing suit he bought me. You know the last thing he said to me before he left the night he died?"

"What was that?"

"That I looked beautiful in my bathing suit and he couldn't wait to get me on the beach. I was trying it on in the mirror when he walked out the door. It was the last time I would ever see his face."

"Melvin really loved you, Brenda. Even when you two were young. It was so serious. It was crazy."

"Yeah." Brenda smiled. "That was my baby. Tell me somethin. Why didn't you and Chucky ever get together? You were on and off for a while, and I know he was into you. What happened with that?"

"I thought about it. I actually might have considered it if he would have asked, but instead of popping the question, he decided to offer me a key and invite me to shack up with him out in LA. You know that wasn't happening"

"Oh, he's in LA now?"

"No he's back in the DMV but a few years ago, right when he got the tv show I started seeing him again. Things were going pretty well, but it was moving slow, and I just don't think he was ready. Oh and I was also dating Kevin Clark at the time so..."

"Kevin Clark the mayor? Ain't he married? Oh, you a lil hoe."

"No, I am not a whore, Brenda, I just don't like to put all my eggs in one basket. And he wasn't married at the time. Nor was he the mayor, he was on the city council back then."

"Umh hmm. Well what happened with him?"

"Ooh girl." Missy frowned. "He was a gherkin."

"A what?"

"A gherkin. You know those little cocktail pickles."

"Ohhhh, he had little dick."

"Bingo."

They slapped high fives and laughed so hard they could barely breathe.

Missy replenished her drink. Brenda took a long thoughtful pause. "Can I ask you something?"

"Sure."

"Anything?"

"Anything at all. Wait, hand me another piece of that chicken first."

Brenda laughed and dropped another fresh piece on her greedy sister's plate. "What was your issue with ma? The *real* issue."

Missy was taken aback by the question. She picked at the skin on her chicken for a second, trying to formulate a response that would somehow stave off Brenda's curiosity and shut down the conversation at the same time. "Where'd that come from?" *A fail.*

"You just sad I could ask anything."

Missy sighed. "Brenda, it's complicated."

Brenda rolled her eyes and went back to cooking. "Never mind then. Forget I asked."

"No, don't be like that. It's just really hard for me to talk about."

"And you think sittin here discussin my dead husband was easy for me to talk about just now?"

"No. I'm sorry."

"Don't be *sorry*. You asked because you care. The same reason I'm asking you. Missy, I really need to understand it. I think if I can understand you a little, maybe that'll help me with the resentment that I've had for you all these years."

"Wow. You're really throwing that word around today. You just learn it?"

"Forget you!" They both laughed.

"You resent me, Brenda?"

"Well...I mean I have. And I think if I knew what it was and what you were thinking, maybe I could begin to understand how you could walk away from us and not look back. I ask mama but she don't say much. I'm like, what is up with y'all? Me and you can sit here laughin and shootin the shit, but you haven't called her or stopped past the house one time since she left the rehab. What is up with that?"

Missy let out a heavy sigh, knowing things were about to get very, very heavy. "Can I at least have a glass of wine first?"

Brenda perked up. Anticipating some long awaited answers to the family drama. "Ok, I'll get the glasses."

It took Missy quite some time and quite a few cocktails to come up with a convincing enough story. One that would reasonably justify her disdain without completely obliterating her little sister's image of her mother. It had to be done. The truth was way too painful and it was a whole other can of snakes Missy was not ready to open. Not yet anyway.

Puppy Love

The phone rang.

"Hi Ms. Brenda. Is Brandy home?"

"Yeah, who's calling?"

"It's Keisha."

Brenda paused. She really didn't like Brandy hanging out with Keisha. The little girl barely went to school, already had a baby, and from what she heard was well on her way to getting another one. Brenda had enough on her plate without having to worry about her daughter being influenced by this fast ass little girl. "Hold on a minute." She yelled upstairs. "Brandy! Telephone!"

Brandy hollered back. "I got it, ma! Hey girl what's up?"

"Nothin. Wassup with your muvva?"

"Whatchu mean what's up with my muvva?"

"She don't never speak when I call your house."

"I don't know. She been actin strange lately. She got a lot going on, I guess. Don't worry about it. So what's goin on?"

"Nuttin. You wanna go for a walk?"

"Not really."

"Why not?! Girl, you a hermit. You need to get out and get some fresh air sometimes."

"Whatever."

"Well you wanna come over here?"

"I can do that."

"Ok, come on."

"I'm on my way."

Brandy grabbed her purse and jacket and headed for the door.

Brenda peered out of the kitchen. "Brandy? Where you going?"

"Over Keisha's house, ma."

"For what?"

"Huh? Just to chill. Why?"

"Because I don't like that little girl, Brandy."

"Why not? You don't even know her."

"I don't need to know her. She too damn grown, and you don't need to be hanging around her. Ain't she pregnant again?"

"No ma. Stop acting like that. Keisha is not too grown, and she's not pregnant again. I don't understand how you can act like that when you were pregnant at the same age she was."

"Don't get cute with me. I'm just saying she's not the best influence. Don't you have any other friends?"

"Yeah but you don't like them either."

"Oh yeah." They both laughed.

"Ma, please stop worrying about me. I got my own mind. Can't nobody influence me to do nothin I don't wanna do. Trust me. I'm good."

"Well I hope not."

"No need to hope. I'll be back in a little while."

With that, Brandy slammed the door behind her. She walked out of her gate and there were several guys playing craps and smoking weed on the sidewalk, something they didn't dare do when her dad was around.

Things in the neighborhood had changed so much since he died. Guys that never looked at her before were now asking for her phone number. One even had the nerve to touch her on the ass. She pushed him in the bushes and told him what she'd do to him the next time he touched her. Problem solved.

She considered telling her mother but knew that would bring on a whole new set of unneeded problems, including not being able to go outside alone anymore. It just wasn't worth it. Besides, she could handle it herself. No sooner than the thought came into her head, the same stupid boy spotted her walking toward the alley and ran to catch up to her.

"Hey! Wassup Brandy. Where you on your way to?"

"Boy, get the fuck outta my face before I throw your dumb ass in that trash can. And how you know my name?"

"Cause I know everything."

"Hmm."

"So you gon throw me in the trash, Brandy?" He smiled and brought his face in close to hers. She pushed him back, hard. He got the message. "Ok, ok. I'm sorry. I'll stop. Where you goin?"

"None of your business. Boy go somewhere and stop fuckin followin me."

"I'm not following you. I'm on my way home."

"You live around here?"

"I just moved around here to stay with my older brother."

"Good for you."

"So can I walk with you?"

"You already walkin with me."

"Girl, why you gotta be so mean?"

"I'm not mean. I just don't like niggas puttin they hands on me."

"I know. I swear I didn't mean to do that. I was reaching for your hand, you turned and it just happened. You didn't have to push me in the bushes like that, though. That was mean. Look at my arm." He pulled off his jacket and showed her two long deep scratches he got from the sharp branches in the bush.

"Umh. Well I didn't mean to hurt you. Just don't put your hands on me again and you won't get hurt."

"Stop tryin to act like you so hard, girl. You *know* you like me."

"Boy please. I *am* hard and don't nobody like you." She smiled inside at the sound of the lie she had just told. "Don't even flatter yourself."

She looked away and picked up her pace, walking up ahead of him so he couldn't see her blush. The truth was she did like him. He was the most handsome chocolate thing she had ever seen, and he had the biggest, brightest white teeth. He was a little shorter than she liked, but he had a nice build and a very handsome face.

She could tell he was much different from any of the boys she had gone out with. He was trying to fit in with the boys in the hood, but she could tell there was nothing hood about him. She wanted to know more about him but didn't want to seem too pressed, so she let him talk. Boys like the chase, so she thought she'd let him do just that. Chase her.

"...And stop calling me boy. Ain't no boy round here. I'm a man, baby."

"And I ain't your baby. You know my name."

"Yes Brandy. And do you know my name?"

"Nope."

"Do you *want* to know my name?"

"Nope."

"It's Tay. Short for Talib."

"What kind of name is Talib?"

"I thought you weren't interested?"

"I'm not."

"Talib is West African. It means 'seeker.' I *seeks* things." They both laughed.

"So you're African?"

"Yup."

"You don't look African."

"Well, what does an African look like?"

"You know. They wear those funny dresses and Jesus sandals. Plus, they stink."

"Aww now that's messed up."

"I'm just playin. But you really don't look African."

"My parents are from Nigeria. I was born and raised here. In Frederick. My mom went back to Nigeria to take care of my grandmother so I'm staying with my brother until she comes back."

Brandy slowed down at Keisha's gate. "Oh. Ok, well I'm here now."

"Me too. I live right down the street. Thanks for letting me walk with you, Miss Brandy." He smiled a wide toothy smile."

"No problem. See you later." Brandy started walking up the stairs to Keisha's porch.

Tay yelled. "Wait! Can…can I call you?"

"No."

"No?"

"No! You think I'm gon give you my number just cause you told me some of your business?"

"Well…"

"You can give me *your* number. Maybe I'll call you."

"Damn." Tay rattled off his digits. "You not gon write it down."

"Don't need to."

"Yeah. You better use that number, girl."

Tay stuck is hands in his pockets and started walking down the street. Brandy watched him walk away. He looked back and they caught each other's glances for a split second before blushing and turning away.

"BRANDY!" Keisha yelled out of the window. "What you doin? Come upstairs, girl!"

"I'm COMING!" She walked in and up the stairs to Keisha's bedroom.

"What is *Tay* talkin bout?"

"You know him?"

"Yeah that's Daye's brother."

"For real?"

"Yeah. I don't like him though."

"Why not?"

"Cause he arrogant. He think he cute."

Brandy laughed. *He think he cute* was Keisha code for *I tried to give him some and he didn't take it.* She always said that when she liked a boy that didn't like her back. Brandy was curious to know if something happened between them. Keisha definitely tried it and lawd knew she didn't want no parts of a nigga that Keisha had been with. So she inquired.

"So you met him before?"

"No not really. He speaks to me when he walks past the house, but I haven't really talked to him. I heard he just transferred to McKinley Tech."

"Oh he must be pretty smart. I heard you need a scholarship to go there now."

"Yeah and he'll be a senior when school starts."

"You sure seem to know a lot about him."

"You know how people talk. They say he got the girls going crazy round here. But I don't see why. He's just *ok* to me. He's way too black for me."

"Keisha, you know that is messed up."

"What? You know I like my red bones with the pretty hair. I don't do no Amistad."

"You a mess."

"I'm not. You was cheesin all up in his face, though. What was up with that?"

"Whatever. I was not cheesin. If anything, *he* was cheesin."

"You gave him your number didn't you?"

"No. I did not give him my number." That was the truth. Part of it.

"Um hmm, girl."

"I didn't! I swear! Anyway. What else is going on?"

Brandy wanted to change the subject. She could tell that Keisha liked him and she had no interest in listening to her hate on him. Then she thought, *Why do I even care?* But she knew the answer to that.

She had quickly developed a little crush. For the next hour, Keisha talked and talked and talked some more...but Brandy only caught bits and pieces. She had other things on her mind...like how long would she make Tay wait before she finally gave him a call.

Give Peace A Chance

Betty had been battling with kidney disease for over ten years. Her small frame was weak and emaciated. Her appetite had long since gone away, and the medical marijuana was no longer effective. It wasn't even making her feel good anymore.

She was trying to hang on for Brenda and the kids but she was tired. Physically, mentally and emotionally spent. Her spirituality was the only place she could find solace. And peace.

The sweet sounds of her old time gospel in the mornings. The soul stirring sermons from Rev. Hendricks on Sundays and the thought provoking discussions in Tuesday night's bible study were all food for her spirit.

Having given her life to God, Betty had found a joy that she'd not had at any other point in her life. She'd found a healing spirit, and though her body slowly withered, her mind was clear and set, almost willing herself to go home and take her place with her Lord and Savior. It was time.

Her business affairs were in order. The small life insurance policy was in place and would take care of her funeral expenses. Her house was nearly paid for, so her daughters and her grandchildren would always have a place to call home. Her relationship was right and well with The Master and she'd made peace with everyone she needed to, except one. Missy.

Many years prior, they had a falling out that was never truly resolved. Missy spent years away from her and the family, but after Betty's emergency triple bypass surgery a year before, she reappeared and began dropping in to check on her from time to time. It wasn't the relationship Betty wanted, but she was just happy to have Missy back in her life in any way she could.

She went to great pains never to bother her or to ask her for anything, although there were many times that she really needed to. Instead she leaned on Brenda. Brenda was dependable. Reliable. She'd always be there.

Missy was a different story. She'd always wanted out. To get far away from everything and everyone she had known growing up, and even though Betty understood it, it still made her sad. Missy was meant for great things and she'd done amazingly well for herself. All on her own. Fueled by bitterness and a deep resentment for Betty. That's what hurt Betty the most. That Missy had every right to hate her. Based on what she thought to be true, her feelings were certainly justified.

Betty wished with all her might that she would have done things differently. But at the time, back then, she didn't feel she had a choice. And so things were what they were. She could only own it, apologize and pray that Missy would be able to forgive her. Truly forgive her, and move forward. It had to happen. While there was still time.

Brenda made the call. At Betty's insistence she invited Missy over to the house for Sunday dinner. The plan was to have the pastor, Reverend Hendricks there so that he could offer counsel to both of them. Betty knew that a heartfelt apology would fall far short of what was needed to bring them back together. They needed Jesus to fix it.

To Betty's delight, Missy agreed to come. She even said she'd bring the dessert. For the rest of the week Betty was in wonderful spirits. The "herbal" medicine was working. She was eating heartily, smiling and laughing. Brenda found it difficult to hide her aggravation but she didn't say anything. Betty thought, *Finally. I'll have my baby back.*

Missy never showed. As Brenda cleared the dinner dishes, seething over yet another no show from her dumb selfish bitch of a sister, Pastor comforted Betty and told her to be patient. She did. She waited a few days before asking Brenda to call again. As usual, Brenda protested but eventually gave in and made the call.

When the voice mail picked up, Betty took the phone. "Missy, baby, this is your mama. We missed you on Sunday. We cooked your favorite dinner, and we was waitin on that cake you was s'posed to bring. But I know you real busy baby. I understand. Can you please give me a call? I need to talk to you. It's real important, hear? I love you, baby. Call me soon as you can, ok."

Brenda grabbed the phone and hung it up.

Betty smiled and said, "She'll be calling me soon."

That pissed Brenda off even more, but as usual she kept her

thoughts to herself. When it came to Missy James, as far as Betty was concerned, anything less than a compliment fell on deaf ears. She defended Missy at all costs and to the one person who loved and took care of her for so many years, it was extremely hurtful. So as best she could, Brenda just kept her mouth shut and let it go. She thought, if Betty didn't mind being treated like shit after all these years then why should she care? But she couldn't help it. She cared.

A few weeks went by and still no call from Missy, although they'd seen her and Ray on TV promoting his new charity. *She got time for everything under the moon and the stars except her own mother and her family,* Brenda thought. A bullshit argument from over 15 years ago couldn't possibly be worth hurting her mother the way she does. Disappointing her time and time again. Gay husband or not, this was her mother, begging and pleading to hear from her. Missy was selfish and cruel. Brenda had a good mind to call her and tell her ass off again, but she decided against it. It probably wouldn't help anyway.

Thirty-four days after Missy's latest no show, Betty was back to her norm. Barely eating and sleeping most of the day. Sulking and hoping Missy would return just one of her phone calls. But she never did.

Brenda was downstairs making dinner when she heard a loud thump and breaking glass. She dropped everything and ran upstairs. The door was locked so she kicked it in. She found Betty lying on the floor in a pile of glass from the crystal lamp she'd apparently knocked over when she fell.

Twenty-three minutes later, she was wheeled into the emergency room of the Washington Hospital Center. The muscles in her face sagged, and she couldn't move her right side. She was conscious but could barely speak. When she tried to speak her words were jumbled and slurred. Brenda had never seen her so helpless.

The doctors told the family that Betty had a massive stroke and a series of smaller strokes in the days prior. They couldn't pinpoint the cause, but considering she was hypertensive and had numerous other health issues, it could have been any number of things.

Brenda stayed by her bedside for three days. Uncle Edward, Betty's older brother, had to force Brenda to leave just to shower and eat but an hour after she left she was pulling back into the hospital's parking garage. The thought of losing her mother crushed her, and she couldn't bear a single moment away while she needed her.

The medication Betty was on was so strong that she was going in and out of consciousness. Several times she had tried to speak, but it took so much out of her to try to communicate that Brenda encouraged her to stop. Truthfully and selfishly, Brenda didn't want to hear what she had to say. The reason was that the only audible word to escape Betty's lips in the last seventy-two hours was Missy's name. It was definitely an added insult to Brenda's already severely injured heart.

Uncle Edward came in to visit and to pray with his sister. Again she began to mumble and again the only audible word was her estranged daughter's name. Uncle Edward turned to Brenda. "Can I talk to you for a minute? Outside?" She smeared some Vaseline onto Betty's dry lips and then followed her uncle into the hall.

"Sweetheart, I think it's about time that you called your sister."

Brenda didn't say a word.

"Brenda. If you don't call her… I will."

"Then you go ahead and call her."

"Baby listen to me–"

"No you listen! Missy don't wanna be here! She don't want nothin to do with my mother. You know that! Why would I call her now?"

"Because your mother wants to see her, Brenda. She *needs* to see her daughter. I know you don't want to hear this out loud; hell I don't even want to say it, but baby, Betty might not be with us much longer."

He was exactly right. Hearing the words out loud gave her a sinking feeling. She leaned back against the wall for support. And the tears fell. Uncle Edwards heart broke for her but she had to hear it. There was no time to pussyfoot around the situation. Betty was dying.

"Brenda, you think she'd wanna go away from here without seeing her child? Without saying goodbye to her? You really wanna be responsible for that? For God sake she's calling the girls name."

"Ok. So now I'm supposed to be the one to take responsibility for Missy James not giving a shit about her own damn mother?"

"No, but you can take responsibility for giving your mother the last thing she asks you for."

Brenda rolled her eyes and turned her back to him. Edward turned her around and looked her in the eyes. "Brenda, you have been a great daughter. You've given her everything else. Why deny her this? Call your sister. Please."

Brenda stood there staring at her mother through the small square window of the ICU doors. She knew he was right. As much as she hated to admit it to herself, she knew it was the right thing to do. So she made the call.

A Trying Time

Tap, tap, tap.

Missy knocked at the basement door.

"Ray, can I come down?" She heard nothing. "Ray?" Still nothing so she walked down into the basement toward Ray's theater room. As she approached the door, she could hear the faint sounds of moaning. He was obviously down there indulging himself in his porn collection, the one that he didn't think she knew about since she wasn't allowed to use the theater room without his permission. She started to head back upstairs but decided this was too important to wait for him to re-emerge from his dirty little dungeon. So she screamed.

"Ray!"

There were a few seconds of silence when suddenly he snatched the door open and yelled "What!" Missy jumped back and away from him. "What the hell are you doing down here? Didn't I tell you not to come down here?"

He was holding a sniffer of cognac in one hand and smelling like he bathed in it.

"Ray I need to talk to you. I...I just got a message from..."

"What are you doing down here? And what the fuck are you crying for now? I'm not in the mood for your bullshit today Missy. And I thought I told you not to—"

"Ray! Listen! It's my mother." Her voice was shaky "Brenda left a message yesterday. She said my mom had another stroke and she's not doing well. She's on a breathing machine, and the doctors are asking for the family to come in."

"Oh. So you're leaving?"

"I was hoping you would take me, Ray."

"Take you where? Into DC? No ma'am."

"Are you serious? It's my *mother*."

"You don't even like your mother."

Missy pretended not to hear his crude and insensitive statement.

"Ray, you know my car is being serviced so I have no way to get there."

"No, I didn't know that your car was being serviced. Tell your sister to come and pick you up." With that, he turned and started to close the door on her.

In a show of uncharacteristic defiance, Missy stuck her foot in the door to prevent him from closing it. "You really want me to ask my sister to leave the hospital in DC to come to Potomac and give me a ride back to DC?"

Annoyed that she was still talking to him and interrupting his activities, Ray looked down at her foot and scowled. "I really don't give a shit what you do. Ask her, don't ask her. I said I'm not going. I have a meeting with Matt in an hour anyway. I can't miss it."

Missy stood there in disbelief. Ray didn't offer a "I'm sorry about your mother" or any semblance of empathy toward her. He barely stepped out of the room to talk to her and the audio of his porn was shamelessly blasting in the background. She knew he was an asshole but somehow thought that this time, in this particular situation, he would show her that he was at least somewhat capable of being a human being. "Fine. Can I please use your car?"

"What car?"

Visibly frustrated and trying hard to maintain her composure, she lowered her voice just above a whisper. "PICK a car, Ray?"

Noticing that she was annoyed, and not really giving a shit, Ray responded in a similarly low and deliberate tone. "Well, I'm driving the Benz to my meeting. The Shelby is my show car, the Humvee needs new tires, as you know, and you are definitely not driving my Aston Martin out on those raggedy ass DC streets. Just call a car. I'll pay for it."

With that, he slammed the door shut, leaving her standing there as if she were a Jehovah Witness that woke him out of a deep sleep on a Saturday morning. A few seconds later he yelled out, "Let me know what happens, ok?" and then the volume on his movie cranked up a few more decibels.

At that moment, any love and any compassion she had left for Ray went out the door. There was nothing left but contempt. No more pretending, no more dog and pony shows for his fans. It was over and way past time that she put an end to the bullshit. Come what may.

*****

Two hours after placing her first call, the car finally came. Ray's part-time driver and full-time coke head flunkey Mario pulled into the driveway and honked the horn.

Missy's eyes were swollen, and her head ached from all the crying she had done. In the couple hours she spent waiting for the car she had gone over her whole life in her head. From her first memories of her mother playing with her in the park to her valedictorian speech at graduation to her wedding night where her new husband, the very rich and famous football star Ray Coleman nearly knocked a tooth loose because she ruined *his* wedding.

She wondered what happened to her life. What happened to the grand plans she had for her life? How on earth did she get there? More importantly, why was she *still* there? She didn't have the answers to any of the questions rattling about in her head, but one thing she was certain of was that she had to get out. She didn't know how but she was definitely getting out…and sooner than later.

The car pulled up to the hospital's emergency room entrance, and she could hear a commotion. She jumped out of the car, and as the doors swung open she heard screams. She ran past the security guards desk in the direction of the voices and as soon as she turned the corner she saw Uncle Edward. He had Brenda wrapped in a tight bear hug to keep her from falling to the ground as her screams pierced the air.

The James family was there in numbers. Huddled together and watching helplessly as Brenda fell apart. The doctors had just delivered the news of Betty's passing.

Missy stood silent in the hallway. Listening to the cries of family she hadn't seen in years. She wasn't sure what to do. Although these were cousins and aunts and uncles she had grown up with most of her life, she felt completely out of place. They all noticed her, but no one bothered to acknowledge her. No doubt they all had their own feelings and opinions about her being there.

She waited a few minutes and then walked closer to the group that was attending to Brenda. As they backed away, Brenda stood to her feet. Before Missy could utter a word, Brenda slapped her hard across the face.

As the family pulled her away, Brenda screamed, "Where were you?! Where were you, Missy?! I called you! I left you messages. Why didn't you answer?! Why didn't you return your mother's calls?"

"Brenda I'm sorry. I didn't—"

"Shut up! Don't you say shit to me! I told you what was happening! You knew! You come in here now! Now?! Get out! Get the fuck out!"

Missy knew there was nothing she could say to make the situation better so she said nothing. She watched as half of the family tried to console Brenda and the other half just stood there staring at her in judgment. The stares seemed to burn through to her soul.

She hung her head low and sobbed, with no one there to comfort her. Part of her wanted to turn and run away, but she knew that would only make things worse. Then again, how could they possibly get any worse?

The doctor walked back over and asked if the immediate family wanted to come in and see Betty before she was taken out of the operating room and down to the morgue. Brenda answered yes, but when Missy took a step behind her, she turned around and shoved her sister back so hard she fell into the person behind her. "No! We don't need you. What the hell you need to see her for? You didn't want to come before she died, so don't try to come in here now. Leave!"

Their uncle Edward stepped in front of Missy. "Now wait a minute, Brenda. I know you upset, but you gotta be reasonable, baby. This is her mama too now."

Brenda shot daggers at Uncle Edward before she turned around and headed toward the operating room.

Missy followed slowly behind but stopped short of the double doors. She just couldn't bring herself inside. She stood outside and watched in tears as Brenda walked in, pulled back the sheet and kissed her mother's forehead.

Uncle Edward walked up behind Missy and grabbed her hand, squeezing it gently. They both stood for a few moments watching Brenda have her last moments with her mother. Gently stroking her hair and holding her hand. Talking to her through her tears. It was extremely hard to watch.

"Melissa. Your sister is just really upset right now," Uncle Edward said. "She's hurting. You have to understand where she's coming from. She's been here with your mama every day."

"I understand, and I'm not mad at her. I deserve it. I know I shouldn't be here."

"No baby. Your mother loved you. This is exactly where you

should be. Now I know you got some stuff that you gotta deal with, but right now, it's about family. That's what's most important now. Forget about all that other stuff. Brenda will come around eventually. Trust me. You two are all you got now. You got to be there for each other. And that's that. That's what Betty would want."

Uncle Edward led Missy by the hand into Betty's room. He walked over to Brenda and grabbed her hand. He laid their hands on top of each other. Then he began to pray. "Heavenly Father we come to you today…"

Oh, Brother

For Daye Mbulango, the days and nights seemed to be getting longer and harder. He was smoking dippers every day, several times a day in fact, and living more reckless than he ever had.

As hard as he tried, he couldn't put the image of Melvin's mutilated body out of his mind. Yes, he wanted him dead. But he had no idea that the Jamaican's could be *that* evil. Medieval.

Brenda was still hounding him for money that he owed Melvin. He didn't have it, or much else, because he didn't do much those days except get high. The only thing that kept him from going completely over the edge was his little brother.

His mother had called him a few weeks before to inform him that his little brother, Tay, would be coming to live with him for a while. Daye's grandmother was diagnosed with stage three pancreatic cancer, and she was still living back home in Nigeria.

A registered nurse, his mother wanted to go home to take care of her herself. With Tay going into his senior year of high school and applying for colleges, she didn't want to uproot him, so she wrote Daye a check for a few months' expenses and headed to the motherland.

Tay hadn't been to DC since Daye moved there a few years earlier, right after their father died. He was shocked to see how bad the house looked. It was a disaster. He thought his mother would have a fit if she saw her house in this condition. The grass was a mile high, the porch was falling in, and there were a couple of broken windows on the side of it. The front door was unlocked, so he walked in.

When he got inside he couldn't believe his eyes. The family house was all but destroyed. There were holes in the walls, sheets over the windows, and what seemed like an endless fog of marijuana smoke throughout the place. Daye entertained in the basement, and the weed smoke came upstairs underneath the doors and through the vents. At least Tay *thought* it was weed.

He went into to the kitchen, roaches crawled on every surface in bunches on the counters and the walls. Mice ran around boldly, playing tag with each other like the house belonged to them. The only food in the refrigerator was stuck to the insides of it and growing some weird fur. Droppings were all over the stove and in the cupboards. It was revolting, to say the least.

The bedrooms weren't any better. No sheets on the beds, soiled mattresses, ash trays half full, and empty liquor bottles everywhere. He walked down to the basement to find Daye. When he found him he was sitting on an old sofa, staring at the wall, glass eyed and sweating. A half-naked young girl was lying beside him, clearly passed out. He didn't even notice Tay standing in front of him.

Tay yelled. "Daye! What's up man?"

Through his haze, Daye managed a smile when he saw his little brother. "Oh heeeyyy. What's up bruh?" He didn't bother getting up.

"What's up? What's going on in here? What happened to the house?"

"What you mean?"

"What I mean? It looks crazy in here, man!"

Daye ignored the comment. "Come on over here and sit down next to your big brother. Aye! Get up!" He pushed the young girl onto the floor. She hit it with a thud but didn't even flinch. "You want a drink? Smoke?"

"Come on man, I'm seventeen. No I don't want a drink or a smoke. Is she ok?" Tay peered over to the young girl, looking for any sign of movement from her."

"Yeah, dat bitch aaight. She just can't handle her drink. Come on man. Come chill wit me for a minute."

"Nah I'm good. Can I get some money?"

"Money? For what?"

"So I can buy some damn groceries? Get some sheets for the beds. We need to pay somebody to exterminate and clean this house, Daye. This shit is fucked up, man. I can't live like this."

"Nah. I ain't got no money."

"What happened to the money ma gave you? Didn't she send you a check last week?"

"Oh. Yeah. Man I ain't even cash that joint yet." That was a lie. "You want a smoke?"

"Damn man. You just asked me that. No!" Talking to Daye while he was high was pointless. "Look, I'll be back. Where are your keys?"

"Why? Where you goin?"

"To the *store*. Ma gave me some money. Imma go out and get some stuff for the house. You need to get somebody in here to clean this shit up. For real. How you live like this? I'm glad ma decided not to come down here. She definitely wouldn't have let me stay here with the house lookin like this. This shit is past filthy man."

"Stop trippin, nigga. Bring me back some McDonald's. A number two. Oh and some oatmeal cookies."

Tay could hardly believe this was his brother. Since when did Daye talk to him like this? Since when did he not give a shit about how he lived, or how he looked? He had lost at least twenty pounds since he saw him last and that was only six months before, at the family reunion. He needed a shave; a haircut. Shit, he needed a bath! It was crazy to him. Was he smoking crack or what? He obviously wasn't eating.

Tay thought maybe he should call his mother, but he really didn't want to worry her. She had enough on her plate caring for granny. Still he knew there was little he could do on his own.

Before she left, his mother deposited $500 into his bank account and gave him two $100 bills to put in his pocket. It was a good thing she did because if left to Daye he would be eating McDonald's and sleeping on the floor.

Tay googled the address for the closest Super Walmart and set off to get everything he needed in one spot. Food, linens, toiletries, cleaning supplies, pest control. It was a lot. Definitely not what he expected and he wasn't sure if he was really up for it.

He had half a mind to just grab his things and get a hotel room for the night. But he was underage, so that was out. Then he thought it might be better to just drive back home to Frederick for the night, but there was really no sense in prolonging. The work had to be done and the roaches weren't going to kill themselves.

It was a real messed up situation, but he didn't have a whole lot of options so he'd just have to try to make the best of it. For now.

Truth and Consequences

It was the morning of Betty James' home going services, and there was a long day ahead for the James family. They were all meeting at Betty's house at 9 a.m. to leave for the church. The viewing was to begin at 10 a.m. followed by the funeral services at eleven, then the interment, and the repast back at Betty's house.

Missy sat at her dressing table applying her makeup for the second time. The first application didn't quite make it through her tears, despite the brand's waterproof claims.

That morning, she shed many tears. Tears of sorrow and regret. Tears of frustration and even a few tears of joy. Her relationship with her mother and family – or the lack thereof – racked her with guilt, but the last seven days with her family, particularly Brenda gave her a renewed strength and a sense of peace.

The night Betty died, Uncle Edward took Missy and Brenda back to their mother's house to talk. He wasn't going to rest until the sisters came back together. And they did.

It started out kinda rocky, but by the end of the night the sisters had a newfound understanding and were grateful for his interference. They fell asleep holding each other in Betty's bed.

The next morning, Uncle Edward invited the family over for a big breakfast. They needed to discuss Betty's arrangements, and Missy wanted to finally clear the air with everyone. She stood before them and bared her soul, apologizing for walking away and vowing to rebuild the broken relationships. They accepted her back into the fold with open arms. It was a new beginning and one of the best days of her life. She had her family back.

As she sat on the bench in her dressing room contemplating what to wear to the funeral, so many thoughts raced through her mind. She missed her mother dearly and regretted walking away from her the way she did. She regretted not getting a chance to talk to her and hold her hand before she died. To tell her that she loved her one last time.

She wanted to blame Ray but knew he wasn't the problem. Yes, he was an inconceivably cruel bastard and no he didn't want them around, but at the end of the day the decision to walk away from them was hers. She chose the lifestyle over her family. She chose to run away from her problems with Betty instead of confronting them. Now she'd never have the chance to. That's what was really breaking her heart.

Ray walked in the room. It was 8 a.m., and he was already drinking. Never a good sign. "Hey Missy. I'm not going." He loosened his tie. She heard him but didn't respond. "Did you hear what I said?"

"I heard you."

"Well don't you wanna know why?"

She sighed. Exhausted of his foolery. She asked the question, just to humor him, but after the stunt he pulled she couldn't have cared less about his *why*.

"Well. I was just thinking. I didn't even really know your mother—"

She interrupted him. "Look Ray. I CANNOT do this with you today. Please. If you don't wanna go, that's fine. Don't go! I didn't expect you to go anyway."

Ray was taken aback by her sassiness. She'd been mouthing off at him ever since her mother died, and he was about to put a stop to the bullshit right then. "You what? First of all, Miss Missy..." He stumbled over a shoe that was left in the floor and fell into the wall. "You don't tell me where to fuckin go. I go wherever the fuck I wanna go. Y-you hear me?"

Missy knew he just wanted to pick a fight with her but for her, it was definitely not the day. She decided not to even respond. But her silence only served to frustrate Ray more so he continued to pick at her.

"If I wanna go to the funeral…I'll go to the funeral. You don't tell me where to go."

She continued to dress ignoring his ridiculous commentary.

"Did you hear me Missy? HUH? Oh. So I guess you not talkin to me now." He walked over to her, reached for a handful of her hair and flipped it in the air. "Your hair is pretty." She was trying hard to ignore him but with every word he uttered she got angrier. "And I like your outfit too. What's that? Chanel?"

She walked out of her dressing room to the bed, and he followed behind her still flipping her hair, taunting her. She couldn't believe what an asshole he could be. He really wanted to pick a fight with her on the morning of her mother's funeral.

She was determined not to give him the satisfaction, so she kept dressing and trying to ignore him. She stepped into her shoes and then walked over to the mirror for one last look.

As she ran over her suit with the sticky lint remover, Ray walked up behind her and started kissing her on the back of her neck. "Can I have some of your Missy Poo? I mean your Poo Poo, Missy?" He laughed and took another swig of his drink before he sat it down on the dresser.

"Ray stop it! Dammit!"

"Stop what?" Still kissing her neck, he reached around her and started pulling up her skirt. "Can I have some poo poo, Missy? Come on baby. Let me get some of that poo poo before you go? It'll relax you. Don't you wanna be relaxed?" He grabbed her hard by the wrists and swung her around to him. Then he kissed her forcefully on the mouth.

She tried to fight him off but he overpowered her. "Ray stop! Stop it! Dammit! Let me go!"

"Stop fuckin fightin me! You know you want it!" He grabbed her hand and placed it on his crotch.

"Ray PLEASE! I gotta GO!" She shoved him off of her so hard that his back hit the dresser, and he fell on the floor. She fully expected him to get up and slap her or hit her in the face. So she braced herself.

He got up slowly and stood in front of her; staring at her with an evil drunken smirk. Then he picked up his drink off the dressing table and threw it in her face. "You go when I say you go, bitch."

With her hair and her crisp white suit soaked in cognac she walked over to the bed, buried her head in her hands and began to cry.

Ray yelled, "Now go take that shit off! I don't even wanna fuck you no more! You stink!" He started walking toward the door, no doubt satisfied that he had ruined her morning like he planned.

Missy felt like she was going outside herself. She had had enough. This was it. She just couldn't take it anymore, not for one more second. She stood and started pulling off her wet clothes. "So you don't wanna fuck me no more Ray? Because I stink, huh? No, YOU don't wanna fuck ME because I don't have a dick, you fuckin faggot."

He turned in the doorway. "What the fuck did you say to me?"

"Ohhh! You didn't hear me? I called you a faggot. You need me to say it a little louder? Huh FAGGOT?"

Ray was so confused by the comment he had nothing to say. They just stood there staring at each other in silence. Missy could see he was shaken. He was withering right in front of her, which made her feel strong, for once. Having lost the stare off, Ray turned back around and walked out of the room.

Missy was so worked up at this point the adrenaline was starting to pump. She was ready for whatever he was dishing out. She thought, *Today, somebody's truth is getting told.* She pulled her hair back into a ponytail and followed him out of the bedroom down the long hallway. She didn't even bother to get dressed first. "Ray? Raaaaayyyy. Where you going, baby? You don't wanna talk no more huh? Awww. We already know you don't wanna fuck me no more. You don't wanna talk. You don't wanna fuck. Maybe I can fuck YOU. How bout that, Ray?"

He hit the long winding staircase heading down to the foyer.

She followed close behind. "Better yet, maybe you'd like to suck *my* DICK."

He stopped in his tracks at the bottom of the stairs.

"Oh!" Missy laughed. "Guess I hit a nerve! You didn't think I knew about that did you?"

She proceeded down the stairs past him into the family room, but not before bumping him hard enough to knock him into the bannister. She walked over to the bar and poured herself a lowball full of his best Scotch, the scotch that was off limits to her, and she sat down on the sofa.

"Ray? Come on in baby. Have a seat. I got some information I think your fans might want to know. Or maybe your business partners. Oh no! Your bible-thumpin-mama. I bet she'd love to hear what her good Christian boy's been up to."

Ray walked slowly over to the couch opposite her and took a seat.

"That's a good boy. Ok, let me try to set the scene for you. Follow me now. If I start to lose you just let me know."

Ray's breathing was heavy and his nostrils flared. Missy had seen the look in his eyes a thousand times, but today she would not be intimidated. He was going to sit there and listen to every word.

"Ok, picture it. St. Valentine's Day, February, 2013. A beautiful young wife – that would be me – wanted so desperately to rekindle the flame in her loveless, sexless marriage that she decided to surprise her old, broken down, washed up, retired, has-been football star husband – *now that would be you* – by greeting him naked and gift wrapped in the boudoir of his fancy Atlanta hotel. She went all out for him, too. Spent all day traveling and getting herself dolled up just the way he said he liked her. She littered the apartment with rose petals and scented candles to set the mood. Stocked the bar and bedroom with expensive champagne and his favorite bottle of old cognac. Since it was the only ring he'd wear, she even added $20,000 in diamonds to his Super Bowl ring as a symbol of her love and a renewed commitment to their life together. Despite all he had done to her and all he had put her through, she really wanted to make it work. You see, 'til death do us part' was more than just words for her. But what did *she* know?"

Missy paused and stared into his eyes for dramatic effect. Then she sighed.

"Now realistically," Missy continued, "she suspected that her husband indulged himself in the occasional extramarital tryst. That kinda goes along with the territory when you're married to a washed up old athlete that's still trying to hold onto his glory days. But suspecting the cheating and seeing it with her own two eyes are two very different things. When she walked to the top of those stairs and saw her old husband gnawing on some woman's big, stiff titties, her heart sank into her stomach. The poor young wife wasn't sure what to do, so she decided to stay and wait to see just how far her cheating bastard of a husband would go with this woman. I know it sounds crazy, but hey, she had to know. So over the course of about twenty minutes, give or take a minute or two, she witnessed him kissing this young woman; she witnessed him undressing her and loving her so passionately. Loving her in a way that he never loves his beautiful young wife, by the way. But that's another story for another day."

Ray rolled his eyes to the back of his head. Missy acknowledged his frustration.

"Ok, ok. I know I can get a little long winded. So I'll get to it. You still listening? Ok, follow me now. Here it comes the pièce de résistance, the moment of truth, the moment that changed her beautiful young life. After hiding out in the bathroom so they wouldn't notice her as they made their way up the stairs, past the scented candles she so lovingly lit to set the mood, through the pathway of rose petals leading to the bed, the young wife stood up, wiped the tears from her eyes and mustered up the nerve for one last look into what she considered the nail in the coffin of her marriage. Then comes what she likes to call 'shock and awe.' You know, a big destructive surprise! She witnessed her husband giving this lady…" Missy leaned over and whispered for even more dramatic effect. "…a buh-low job." Then she jumped up, channeling Tasha Smith crazy, raised both arms high in the air and yelled, "Touchdown!"

Missy laughed hysterically and paced the floor in front of him as she continued to take her jabs at him. "I mean masterful, deep-throated fellatio. She could not BELIEVE it! The woman had a dick! A DICK! Now that's some freaky shit right?!"

She let out her last cackle and another big sigh before she capped up her story. "Regrettably the young wife couldn't stay for the end of the peep show. So she grabbed her belongings and crept back down the stairs, through the rose petals and past the candles, so as not to interrupt her husband's Valentine's Day festivities. Oh! I forgot one pretty important detail."

She sat on the sofa next to him, resting her elbows on her knees and clenching her hands together, attempting to mimic his posture.

"Just to make sure she wasn't seeing things that weren't really happening, she reached into her purse, grabbed her phone and snapped a few pics. You know, you'd be surprised how good the picture quality is on those new Smartphones. All you have to do is double tap the screen, and it blows the picture up SO big that you can actually see that little birthmark on the side of your face." She touched the birthmark on his face with her finger for added emphasis. "Amazing."

Satisfied that she'd sufficiently shattered his secret world, Missy stood and walked back to the other sofa. She took a dainty sip of her Scotch, leaned back, crossed her legs and stretched her arms out on the sofa. "So now what?"

Bray

In very short order, Brandy and Tay were the new neighborhood item. In the tradition of couple obsessed Hollywood, the union of two beautiful and popular people got a tag –i.e. Brangelina, Bennifer, Tomkat. Keisha started referring to them, sarcastically, as "Bray," and it caught on.

The neighborhood was all abuzz about the romance given Tay's brother was rumored to be the one who murdered Brandy's father. "Bray" was painfully aware of the rumors, but it didn't affect how they felt about each other. Love trumped rumor every time.

Outside of school, they spent all of their time together. Brandy had stopped hanging out with Keisha and her girlfriends. Tay's friends were back at home in Frederick, Daye was usually too high to even hold a conversation, and his mom was 10,000 miles away in Africa, so Brandy was his entire world.

After just a few months together, the two of them were inseparable. He drove her to school in the mornings, and since his senior year only required him to be in school for a half day, he was there waiting to pick Brandy up every afternoon.

They studied together every evening, and then he walked her home before curfew. She was to be home by eight o'clock on school nights. She protested it often, but Brenda was very adamant about the curfew. There was no way she was letting her daughter loose for the streets to raise. She knew just how powerful and all-consuming "young love" could be to a young girl, and that scared her. Brenda wanted more for her daughter, and she was definitely not trying to make teen motherhood a family tradition.

Every Saturday morning Tay knocked on the door and either Brenda or MJ kept him standing outside. Neither of them cared for him so he wasn't allowed inside the house. This infuriated Brandy because she knew for a fact that MJ entertained his girlfriend's regularly. Not just in the house, but in his bedroom.

Although Brenda wouldn't admit it, the double standard was alive and well. She felt like girls kept MJ *out* of trouble and boys would inevitably get Brandy *into* it.

While MJ's dresser was stocked with condoms, Brandy got a drawer full of pamphlets on STDs and a lecture about love and relationships. While MJ was told to make sure he protected himself, Brandy got a trip to the gynecologist to make sure she was still a virgin and didn't need birth control. Brenda didn't tell her that was the reason, but it was. Life wasn't always fair for a young girl.

Brenda was having the hardest time with "Bray." Of all the boys in school and all the boys in the neighborhood, she couldn't understand why the hell Brandy was attracted to *this* boy. As far as Brenda was concerned, Daye killed her husband, and it was way too hard to believe that Tay could be *that* different from his brother.

But as much as she hated to admit it, Brandy was happier than she'd ever seen her. She'd brought her grades up, she was helpful around the house and she'd been coming in before curfew. Tay had promised Brenda that he would make sure she got home safely before her curfew and true to his word, they were standing on her porch saying their goodbyes before eight every evening.

He seemed to be a really good influence on Brandy but she kept her eye on them just the same. She knew that the truth about her husband's murder would come out soon enough and that would put everyone in a very awkward situation. Very awkward indeed.

Back Against the Wall

Missy got up from the sofa and sat across from Ray again. She wanted to look him in the eyes. "Hey!" She snapped her fingers to bring him out of his catatonic state. "You got something you want to say to me?"

Ray sighed heavily. He started to speak, but shut down. He couldn't find his words.

"Well if you're not going to talk, I guess I will. Since the proverbial cat has finally been let out of his big pink bag, I'm done playing this game with you. This scam of a marriage is over."

He looked up at her. His expression confused. "Over?"

"Oh! So he speaks. Yes, o-VER. What, are you surprised? Ray. Sweetheart. You are GAY."

He spoke just above a whisper. "I am not gay, Missy."

"You're not gay?" She laughed. "YOU are not gay? In what world does a man get to suck another man's dick and not be gay?"

"I said I am not gay. Please stop saying that to me." He buried his head in his hands.

"Whatever Ray. Look, I've been thinking about this for a while now. Going over and over this moment in my head. Wondering when and how to confront you with this whole gay thing. I'm just glad to finally get it out of the way. It has been SO hard just looking at you the past few months. Do you realize how hard it is to get the visual of your Gay Valentine's Day out of my head?" She shuddered in disgust. "Seriously, I think I'm scarred for life. Tell me something. Who the hell did you think set the mood for you that night? Who did you think lit all those candles and chilled champagne and what not? Your little tittie baller?" She laughed at her pun. "I mean really Ray. I spent a lot of money and put a lot of work into that romantic scene. And I got NO credit for it. So disappointing. I felt like Little Richard. Wait! Little Richard?!?" She broke into hysterical laughter at the incidental reference to another "queen."

Ray looked up at her. Missy couldn't quite figure the expression on his face. It wasn't anger. Frustration? No, defeat. She continued.

"Listen, I've decided to be generous with you. I'll allow you to keep your filthy little secret under a few conditions."

He sighed again. "What would those be, Missy?"

"Well number one. We file for divorce, immediately. No stalling and no fucking around. I want this shit over with. We'll cite irreconcilable differences and disclose no details so the public will be none the wiser. No one but me, you and maybe your little she-thing will know the real story. Your superhero reputation will remain intact, and I'll be free to move on with my life... and pursuit of the man I *thought* I'd married. A real man. A man that fancies *vagina*. A man that..."

"Missy! What else?"

"Oop! Calm down, cowboy. I'm getting there. Number two, before we file divorce papers, we need to go back to your lawyer and tear up that silly prenuptial agreement. I want that nulled and voided. I never should have signed it in the first damned place. Number three. I am to remain beneficiary on your life insurance policies."

"What?"

"Oh yeah. Should your Maserati careen off a cliff in Venice or you get kidnapped by a cartel in Mexico, or contract some weird terminal virus from your little Macho Camacho, I still want in. I deserve that. "

"Missy you must be..."

She interrupted. "NUMber four and my final demand: In exchange for my complete and utter silence, I want sixty percent of all current assets and future earnings."

"Sixty!"

"Yes, my little ball muncher. Sixty. I figure, Maryland is a community property state so–"

"Maryland is NOT a community property state, Missy."

"Well I am MAKING it a community property state. As I was SAYing. If not for that silly ass prenup, I would be getting half of everything you have anyway. I want that. The other 10% is for...let's just say it's for my pain and suffering."

"Your WHAT?"

"My PAIN and my SUFFERING."

"Ok, this is getting ridiculous."

"Oh. I'm ridiculous. I'M ridiculous? So you're really gon sit here and act like you haven't been a complete monster to me during this marriage, Ray? Are you fucking serious? I have PERMANENT scars to show my pain and suffering. Care to see em?"

Ray turned his head away. Missy jumped up, leaned across the coffee table and pointed her finger directly in his face. "I *thought* not. And you fucking right you're gonna pay me. YOU are going to pay ME for ALL the shit you put me through." Just thinking about her time with Ray was upsetting. She began to cry. And then she screamed. "EVERY cut! EVERY bruise! E-VE-RY black eye! How much is my tooth worth to you, Ray? Remember? The one you knocked loose on our wedding night. Nigga, you gon pay ME for every night you treated me like a five-dollar transvestite you pulled off the fucking corner and RAPED me from behind."

Ray actually smirked at the thought.

"That shit is funny to you huh? Well we'll see how funny you think it is when I start talking to the tabloids. Better yet, I think I'll ruin your ass locally first. A Fox 5 exclusive."

Ray rolled his eyes and grunted, infuriating her even more. The more she thought about it, the angrier she became. He didn't acknowledge a word she said, let alone apologize.

"You're sitting there acting like you don't get it. Motherfucker, I'm standing here in my underwear because you just poured liquor on my HEAD. While I was trying to leave for my mother's funeral! And you have the nerve to ask me WHAT PAIN AND SUFFERING?! Nigga, FUCK YOU! FUCK YOU! I'm not scared of your ass no more!"

She ran over to the sofa and jumped on top of him. She punched him in the head and in the face screaming and cursing him to the heavens. Ray managed to get her up and off of him. Then in a fit of rage he picked her up almost above his head and threw her across the room into the bar, breaking most of the glass. Once he saw she wasn't getting up, he walked over to her and emptied several decanters of his Scotch and Cognac over her head.

She laid there, dazed as he stood over her. "No, fuck YOU, Missy. Stupid ass bitch. Jumpin on me like you crazy. I'm not giving you SHIT, and you're not going *nowhere*. How bout that? Now get the fuck up and clean this shit up. I'm going out."

He snatched his car keys off the table and headed for the door. Missy summoned the strength to pick herself up from the floor. She grabbed the heavy led crystal decanter from the bar and ran toward him screaming. Just as he reached for the door knob, she hurled it at him. It hit the front door and shattered just above his head into a thousand tiny pieces.

When he turned around, she was at his face punching and clawing. He grabbed a handful of her hair and head butted her in the mouth causing her to fall to the floor. Her lips split down the middle and blood poured from her mouth.

He reached down, grabbed her hair and dragged her across the floor. Missy kicked and screamed for her life as shards of glass tore into her flesh. She bit him on the leg, sinking her teeth in so deep he had to let go. When she broke free she ran through the living room into the kitchen, Ray gave chase. Blood seeped from her mouth and trickled from all the cuts she got being dragged half-naked through the broken glass.

She got to the kitchen and grabbed a knife from the counter. Ray was running so fast after her he nearly ran into the blade. She swung wildly, and he weaved around waiting for the opportunity to grab it. When he reached out for it, she slashed him across his forearm; a deep laceration that spat blood.

As soon as she hesitated, he was able to grab her arm, twisting it hard enough for her to loosen her grip. When the knife fell out of her hands, he cocked his right hand back and hit her hard across the jaw, knocking her to the ground. He continued to pound on her face cursing and screaming, "You stupid bitch! I should fucking kill you! Don't you ever pull a fucking knife on me!"

When he finally got up, she was barely conscious but still mumbling, lying on the floor. He got up and grabbed a kitchen towel to wrap around his arm to stop the bleeding. She continued to mumble, "Go ahead. Go ahead, you motherfucker. It's already done. It's already done." He knelt on the floor to get closer so he could hear what she was saying. When he was close enough to hear her, she smiled. Through the blood and her loosened front tooth she whispered, "Ray, you can beat me all you want. All you want. My cuts and my bruises will heal, but at the end of the day, your assss will stillll be gay." She spat in his face. "Faggot."

With that, he punched her square in the nose knocking her unconscious. After he wiped her bloody phlegm from his face, he wrapped her hair around his fist and dragged her out of the kitchen. Pulling her down the long hall like a caveman, he left a trail of her blood behind them. He opened the door to the basement and threw her down. Then he stood there watching as she tumbled down two flights of stairs like a ragdoll. He closed the door, locked it behind him and mumbled, "Crazy ass bitch".

My Sister's Keeper

So Missy bailed on the family again. No one was shocked. In fact, no one even mentioned her at the funeral. What would be the point other than to bring shame and set Brenda off. Instead they let the giant pink elephant in the church go unnoticed and mourned as if Betty's eldest daughter didn't exist. Cousin Rita read the obituary and intentionally skipped over Missy's name, something everyone noticed and Uncle Edward chastised her for later.

Brenda was incensed and she allowed that feeling to overshadow the hurt. As much as she didn't want to admit it, even to herself, she was hurt. She thought, after all they'd gone through. After all the heart to hearts and the soul searching. The tears shed and the promises to always be there for each other. This heartless bitch actually missed her own mother's funeral. It was so unbelievably fucked up she had to laugh, to keep from crying

Missy explained what her problem was with Betty. Brenda had to admit that it was awful and she did have reason to carry her grudges, but was it really enough of a reason to miss the funeral? Did it warrant not paying your last respects to your mother when you had already missed seeing her in her last moments? HELL to the, no.

There was no conceivable excuse for her blatant disregard. Not just for Betty but for the rest of the family she had just begged for forgiveness. As much as Brenda wanted to address it, she decided not to. Vowed that Missy James would never get another opportunity to hurt her and if she was so cold hearted that she could live with missing her own mother's funeral and go on with her life, then mother fuck her and she deserved whatever karma came her way. Brenda was officially, finally and irreversibly done with her ass.

The funeral came and went, as did the repast. The service was perfect, and Brenda was actually very pleasantly surprised by the turnout at the church. She didn't know Betty had so many people who loved her. With her former coworkers, church family, the neighborhood family and friends, the home church was packed.

The service was much longer than expected since everyone that knew her wanted to make a tribute. They told stories that made Brenda laugh out loud. Betty James was a character, and everyone knew it.

Brenda felt like the entire church followed them back home for the repast. There was standing room only in every part of the house. From the basement to the front yard. More food than they could eat in a month and enough brown liquor to stock a bar. The smell of burnt chicken grease made her queasy. But not as much as the troth of chitterlings one of her neighbors brought over. Stank-y.

There were endless stories and tears. Music played on the inside and outside of the house. A few people even got their two step on in the living room. Aunt Carolyn wanted to shut the party down but Brenda didn't mind. Betty always enjoyed seeing folks having a good time. Especially in her house. So Brenda let them go on as long as they wanted. It was all love.

Somewhere around the midnight hour the last of the family left while Uncle Edward hung back and helped Brenda clean the house. The girls offered to help, but she really did need some peace and quiet. She planned to clean house, have a glass of wine, a long bath, and go to sleep in her mother's bed with her children nestled in right next to her.

She locked the door, turned on some oldies and went to work on the mound of dirty dishes, half-eaten food and trash spilling from the kitchen. About an hour later, the house was clean, and the kids were asleep. Brenda was geared up for a long relaxing bubble bath and a deep semi-comatose sleep. Mixing wine with the valium she had earlier probably wasn't the best idea, but it sure felt good and she looked forward to hitting the sheets hard.

The Bob Marley station played the best Caribbean mix and Brenda felt particularly tropical as she sank into the mango-pineapple scented bubble bath. Just as she was getting into relax mode her cell phone rang. She let it go to voicemail. Another call came in. She got out of the tub, checked the number, and it wasn't one she recognized, so she ignored it. Then she set the phone on the floor within reach and got back in the tub. It rang again, same number, but this time there was a message:

"Hello. I'm trying to reach the family of Mrs. Melissa Coleman. My name is Stephanie Simmons, and I'm a nurse at Greater Potomac Medical Center. Mrs. Coleman was admitted through the emergency room this afternoon, and we only have her car registration to identify her. We're dialing the last few numbers on her cell phone and yours was the last one called. We're not at liberty to discuss her condition, but Mrs. Coleman is very badly hurt and unable to speak. If you are a relative or are able to contact one of her relatives, please give me a call on my direct line at (301) 555-8729. The hospital's main number is (301)…"

Brenda jumped out of the tub and into her bathrobe. She dialed the numbers from the message and was transferred to the hospital's directory. After being transferred five or six times, she decided to just head out to the hospital. Uncle Edward had the kids, and she didn't bother telling him what was happening. She wanted to find out what was really going on first.

When Brenda got to the hospital, she couldn't help noticing how nice it was. It looked more like a hotel than a hospital. A far cry from DC General, that was for sure. She went to the front desk and asked for Missy. The people there were so pleasant and courteous. She thought, this is what customer service is all about. You have to damn near flip the reception desk over at the DC hospital to get some help. Crazy. After she showed them her ID, they gave her a visitor's pass and escorted her to the elevator leading to the critical care unit.

She walked into Missy's room and it was all she could do not to turn around and walk back out. After the initial shock somewhat subsided, tears began to flow. Missy had been beaten so badly Brenda could hardly recognize her. Her face was severely bruised and swollen, her nose had obviously been broken and her arm was in a sling. There were also several stitches in her top lip. Brenda recognized the stitch, most likely the result of a closed fist.

They had given her some serious narcotics for the pain so she was barely coherent, but Brenda could tell that she recognized her. A lonely tear fell from Missy's swollen eye and triggered Brenda. They sat silently and cried for a while.

Brenda didn't need to ask, but she did anyway. Missy confirmed with her eyes. It was Ray. She laid there, beaten and broken in tears. Brenda's heart bled for her sister. She held Missy's hand until she fell asleep and then she went out to the nurse's station to get some answers.

"Excuse me. Ma'am?" she said. "I'm the sister of Mrs. Coleman in room 234. Is the doctor available?"

"No, I'm sorry, Dr. Shenowitz is gone for the evening. I'm her night nurse, Terry. How can I help you?"

"Terry, with all due respect, I'm standing here trying real hard to hold it together, but I really wanna put my hands on someone right now. I need you to tell me, right now, what exactly happened to my sister. And go slow."

"Mrs.–?"

"It's Brenda."

"Brenda. I understand you're very upset and–"

"No, ma'am. I don't think you do. Can you tell me how she got here?"

"Well I spoke with her day nurse, Stephanie, before she left and she told me that Mrs. Coleman arrived alone. Apparently she drove herself to the hospital. She pulled up to the emergency room and collapsed before she could make it to the front desk. She was wrapped in a blanket with just her bra and panties underneath."

"Oh my God." Brenda's eyes welled again.

"She didn't have a purse or any identification on her when she came in so we had our security check her car. We found the registration for the car and an insurance certificate. My notes indicate that she was barely able to confirm her own identity. As a formality, can you confirm that this is Melissa James-Coleman?"

"Yes. Yes, that's her. So what are we dealing with?"

"Excuse me?"

"WHAT is going on with my sister? Do you need a translator?"

"I'm sorry. Let me grab my chart." The nurse studied the chart for a few seconds and seemed to grimace when she read through it. "Ok, it says here that she has a concussion, two broken ribs, and her ring finger is fractured. Oh and a mandibular fracture. How'd I miss that?"

"Nurse Terry, I need layman's terms. What is a mandibular fracture?"

"I'm sorry, it's basically a broken jaw."

"Basically? So she can't talk?"

"Well the fracture was severe enough that the jaw needed to be wired. She can talk, but it will be difficult and likely very painful, depending on how her pain meds are working for her."

"So we don't know how it happened?"

"Most likely her injuries were the result of an attack or an assault."

"Terry, that was rhe-tor-i-cal. What medication is she on and how long will she need to be here? When can she go home?"

The nurse looked down at the chart, "We're administering her pain meds by drip right now, but it looks like that's only for the next 24 hours. Antibiotics are also being administered intravenously to reduce the swelling and to prevent infection from the cuts and lacerations. As for her recovery time, I can't tell you that. The doctor will be in around 10 o'clock tomorrow morning. You'd need to speak with him directly."

"Ok. Well she seems to be sleeping peacefully so I'll be back first thing in the morning. Nurse Terry?"

"Yes, Brenda?"

"Take care of my sister...please. "

"No worries dear." She gave Brenda a reassuring smile before she sat down and rolled her chair back over to her computer.

Brenda wiped the tear that had just escaped her eye and smiled back. "Thank you."

As she walked to the elevator, Brenda was so mad she couldn't see straight. It was almost two o'clock in the morning and she was still a little tipsy from the wine, but that wasn't stopping her from taking a ride. She set the GPS to 3330 Potomac Way.

*****

Brenda thought about calling the police and about going to pick up her girl Tina to ride shotgun, but she decided against it, for two very important reasons. The first was that she didn't want to put Missy's business in the street. If the police were called, this would definitely make Fox 5 news by morning and all the gossip rags by afternoon.

If Missy wanted to get the police involved after she recovered, she would support her 100%, but Brenda didn't feel like it was her place to make that call and make it public. The second reason was that she wanted to confront *that muthafucka* herself.

She pushed the down button on the elevator, and as it opened two police detectives – a male and a female – got off. They were plain clothed but when you grow up in the hood, you know police when you see em.

On her ride down, she wondered for a second if they were there about Missy. She'd obviously been assaulted so a call to the police had to be routine procedure. She put it out of her head. The police were the last thing she needed to deal with, at that moment anyway.

On the way to her truck, Brenda realized she left her keys, so she headed back up to look for them. When she got off the elevator the female detective was standing at the nurse's station, right next to her keys. Brenda walked over, smiled politely, picked up her keys and walked swiftly back to the elevator. Just when she thought she'd made it away the Detective yelled, "Hold that elevator please". Brenda cursed silently.

The detective hopped on the elevator and extended her hand. "Excuse me. I'm Detective Smith. Karen Smith. You're Mrs. Coleman's sister, correct?

"Uh, yes. That's correct."

"And your name is?"

Brenda answered, reluctantly. She hated talking to the police, for any reason.

The detective followed her off the elevator. Brenda stopped at the hospital's entrance. She had no intention of leading this lady out to her truck.

"Brenda, can you tell me what happened here?"

"Actually I can't. I got a call from the nurse about an hour ago and I came straight here."

"So the nurse called you?"

"Yeah. She said she got my number from Missy's phone. Apparently, mine was the last number she dialed."

"And when was the last time you spoke with her?"

"Late last night."

"What did you talk about?"

"Nothing in particular. Ma'am—"

"Detective Smith."

"Detective, I really need to get home to my kids. It's almost 2 a.m. Do you have a card or something?"

"Yes." She pulled a business card from the pocket of her blazer. "Is there a number where I can reach you? I'd like to ask you a few more questions, if that's ok."

Brenda didn't want to give her a number but she knew it would look kinda crazy if she didn't. So she did.

"I'll give you a call tomorrow?"

"That's fine."

Brenda waited for the detective to get back on the elevator

before walking out. At that moment, the very last thing she needed to deal with was the police. She'd buried her mother that morning and had just watched her sister slip into a morphine-induced coma at the hands of her creep ass husband. She'd had enough, and was plenty ready to release some pinned up frustration. As Mama Joe would say, Brenda was *fittin ta cut the fool.*

She drove up the long driveway around the motor court and parked her long black Suburban right in front of their door. Brenda banged on that door like SWAT and she had every intention of cracking Ray's fuckin head as soon as he opened the front door.

Brenda knocked and banged and kicked at it for at least fifteen minutes before it occurred to her that his cowardly ass probably left town. She walked back to her truck, thoroughly disappointed that she wouldn't be able to *lay hands* on Ray that night. She put the key in the ignition, set to get out of there when she noticed the light in the foyer switched off. That was all that was needed to get her head right again.

She jumped back out of the truck at the ready. Instead of banging on the front door again, she decided to go around to the back. Somebody was letting her in that night or some real nice custom windows was gettin smashed in. Let em call the cops, she thought. Then he could explain to them what put her in a window-smashing mood.

The kitchen was at the back of the house. There were two oversized French doors that led out to the patio. Walking up to the patio she noticed a silhouette in dim light. It appeared to be light from the refrigerator. Every other light in the house was off. Obviously whoever was creeping around didn't want to be seen.

This person was too short to be Ray. Brenda banged hard on the patio door and the noise must have startled them because she heard something crash and the light went out. Brenda was tired and aggravated. She'd had enough of the Mickey Mouse bullshit. Somebody was opening that goddamn door. So she started yelling. "HEEEYYYYY! Hey I see you, open this door."

She couldn't see or hear anything. She yelled again.

"Hey! Where's Ray? I wanna see Ray NOW!"

Still nothing.

"Ray! Bring your bitch ass out here RIGHT NOW!"

She still didn't hear or see anything and the only light she had outside was the illumination from the pool. Frustrated she grabbed the door handles, and as soon as she pulled on them, a dozen floodlights switched on and sirens started whaling like a call to war.

The noise was so terrifying that she ran back to her truck and decided to just get the fuck outta there. Getting caught with a handgun outside of a celebrity's house was not the move, she thought. And knowing Ray, he'd act like he'd never met her and press charges to the fullest extent of the law to cover up all his bullshit. So she was leaving, but she'd be back tomorrow. He could bet his saggy old ball sack on that.

Brenda jumped in her truck and fumbled with the keys for a second before getting it started. Then she shut the headlights off and peeled out. Before she could get out of the driveway, no less than six police cars came screeching to a halt in front of her. With nowhere to go, she just threw the truck in park and sat there, waiting.

"Driver! Step out of the vehicle and show us your hands!"

Seems Like You're Ready

Brandy had been hinting for the last two months that she was ready for sex. She was still a virgin but Tay had enough experience for the both of them. She could tell by the way he kissed her and by the way he touched her that making love was nothing new to him.

He told her he loved her and made her feel good. Like a woman. Brandy was ready. She was ready to finally find out what her girlfriends were always bragging about. According to them, sex was the best feeling you could ever have. According to Keisha, if you hadn't had an orgasm, you didn't know what life was all about.

Although she was young and inexperienced, she was hip to what was going on around her. She listened to the guys talk about it in school and around the hood. She'd seen it in movies and even heard her mother moaning and screaming through the bedroom door on more than several occasions so she knew what was going on. There must be something good about sex. Nobody ever had anything bad to say about it. Earlier that evening she'd overheard Tay's brother Daye telling all his boys that they had to leave because he had a "lil freak" coming over. He kept saying the freak had a white liver, whatever *that* was.

When the girl got there, in denim cut offs with her ass hanging from the bottom and a tank top with her boobs poppin out of the top, they went straight to the bedroom. They were going at it so loud that Tay got embarrassed and decided to walk her home early. Brandy thought that would be the perfect opportunity to bring it up, again.

"So, babe. Why exactly don't you want to have sex with me?"

"Well damn. Where did *that* come from?"

"Been thinkin about it. I just wanna know."

"Well who says I *don't* wanna have sex with you?"

"Obviously you don't. You push my hand away every time I try to touch you there. You stop me every time I try to pull up my skirt or put your hands down there."

"Brandy, look. You're not ready for that yet. *We're* not ready yet."

Brandy sucked her teeth and rolled her eyes. "Says who? Who says *I'm* not ready?"

"I say. Come on babe, you're only fifteen."

"And what does that mean?"

"Brandy, whyyyyy are we even talking about this?"

"Because I want to, and I'm ready. Don't you love me?"

"Stop talking crazy. Of course I love you. Don't I tell you that every day?"

"Yes you tell me, but I want you to *show* me."

Tay laughed. "Brandy. You think that's the only way I can show you I love you. That right there is the reason we shouldn't even be having this conversation."

"Why?"

"Because you don't know the difference between love and sex. That's why. You think my brother is *loving* that girl he got back there at the house?"

"Whatever. Just forget it."

"No it's not whatever. Why are you in such a rush? I'm not pressuring you. I thought you would appreciate that. You tryin to win a bet or something? Seriously, what's up?"

"Nothing is up. I love you. I want to be with you and I thought you wanted to be with me. How is it that every other nigga in the hood tryna get at me but my own boyfriend won't even touch me?"

"Number one, because I'm not every other *nigga* in the hood. Number two, because you are still underage and I'm not trying to go to jail for statutory rape just because *you're* ready to have sex. Three…"

"Tay forget it. Don't even worry about it."

"No, don't tell me not to worry about it. You brought it up so let's talk. I've already had sex, so you don't have to worry about me hounding you for it. Yes, of course I want you baby. But I'm not some horny little kid. I can control my urges."

Brandy rolled her eyes and grunted. "Hmm. So *I'm* the horny little kid?"

"What? No, that's not what I'm saying-"

"You might as well. You look at me and all you see is a little girl. You turn me down cause you've already had your fun."

"Is that what all this is about? Because I'm not a virgin?"

"Well?"

"Girl it's not even like that. You act like I'm big pimpin around here or somethin."

"You might as well be. The way them bitches be throwing it at you all the time. I hear what they be sayin about you."

Tay stopped walking and pulled her close to him. He looked into her eyes. "The only thing anybody can say about *me* is that I'm in love with my girlfriend." He kissed her gently on the lips. "Now stop acting out, little girl."

She laughed and shoved him off of her. "That's okay. If you don't want all thissssss…" Brandy took both her hands and traced her curves. "…I know *somebody* will."

"Brandy, don't play with me."

She smiled, satisfied that she had hit a nerve.

"Miss Johnson, do you know how much I love you? Look at you. So pretty and THICK. I mean damn!" He stepped back and looked her up and down. "Look at all that body. Umh. Girl, you just don't *know!*" She blushed. "Of course I want to touch you. Of course, I want to have sex with you. Are you kiddin me? How could I not want all *that?* He playfully spanked her on her butt. "I'm just saying, we don't need to rush it. Trust me. I'm not going nowhere."

Brandy sighed and grunted. "Umh hmm. You better not."

"You have two more months before your sixteenth birthday. Can we talk about it then?"

"I guess."

"Come on. Fix your face. Trust me girl. I'm gon be your first, your last and your only. Believe that."

They made it to Brandy's front door. She pecked him on the cheek. "See you in the morning. I have to be at school on time so don't be late again."

"I won't. I love you."

"Love you too."

"Brandy?"

"What!"

"What niggas been tryin to get at you?"

"Good night, Tay."

"I want names, girl!"

Brandy closed the door and smiled to herself. She had herself a good one. Tay was a good guy and he really did love her. She could wait. He was most definitely worth it.

An Unlikely Savior

Brenda sat in a holding cell at the local police precinct waiting to get her one phone call when she couldn't help noticing how clean and fresh and nice it was in there. Having been in handcuffs a couple times in her younger day, she was fully expecting a steel cot in a pissy cell with a metal toilet and no toilet paper. She was expecting to be handcuffed to some old drug addict that was nodding off and pulling at the cuffs on her wrists.

Instead, the *joint* in Potomac was granite from floor to ceiling and smelled like potpourri. There was a cushioned cot with a TV built into the wall showing a Lifetime movie. Crazy. She got so into the movie she'd forgotten about her one phone call when an officer walked over to the cell and told her she was being released.

He unlocked the cell and brought her out to the front desk to claim her property. Before she could ask a question she heard a very familiar laugh.

"Thanks Pete! I really owe you one, man."

It was Ray. As soon as he saw her he gave her the biggest hug. "Sis!" She just stood there with her arms at her sides, motionless as he had her locked in this super awkward embrace. She didn't know what the hell was going on.

"Come on here Brenda, with your crazy ass." As he ushered her toward the exit he was going on and on, talking to her like they were real family. Or at least old friends. "How many times we gotta give you that alarm code, girl? You should have just waited for us to get home if you forgot it. We'll have to change it to something you can remember so I don't have to come down here and get you again."

Brenda didn't know what to say, so she didn't say anything at all. She just followed behind him eager to get as far away from the police station as possible. Although she kinda wished he would have come after the movie ended.

They walked to his car, and he opened the door for her with a smile. "Your truck is in the lot just around the corner. Let's go over and pick it up." He closed her in. She watched him closely as he walked around the car to the driver's side. She didn't trust him.

Soon they were out of the parking lot and sitting at a stop light, about a block away from the impound lot where her car was. Ray's demeanor changed, abruptly.

"What the hell were you doing at my house Brenda?"

Brenda thought, *Um hmm, there he is.* "You really got the balls to ask me that? What the hell happened to my sister?"

He got quiet for a second. "I don't know what you're talking about."

"Really? You don't?" Brenda swung her right fist around and connected with his nose. Hard. Then she followed that up with a hard overhand left to his jaw. "Nigga that's what I'm talkin about."

Just as she unbuckled her seatbelt to really get loose on him, Ray cocked her gun and pointed it at her face. "Touch me again bitch! I dare you!" He wiped his bloody nose with the bottom of his T-shirt. "If you must know, we got into a fight. It got out of hand."

"Out of hand!"

"Look bitch. I don't have to explain myself to you or anybody else. And if you ever come back to my fuckin house again, I *will* put a bullet in your ass." He was still pointing the gun at her face. "And I advise you to keep this to yourself. I still have a few favors to call in at the precinct. We wouldn't want tonight's little incident to turn into something criminal, now would we Brenda? Dig into your life a little? Find out how you got that nice truck with no fuckin job? I'll have those little bastards of yours in foster care before you can say *projects.* We clear?"

Brenda was completely outdone. Through clenched teeth, she said, "Leave my kids the fuck outta this, Ray."

"No, *you* leave your kids the fuck outta this, Brenda. Now get your fat nasty ass outta my car before you fuck up my shocks."

As much as she wanted to bash him in the face again, she knew he wasn't joking. Ray knew just the right people to make good on his threats. So she sucked it up. Then she jumped out and slammed the door so hard the window cracked.

"Can I get my gun back?"

He pulled it back away from her, released the magazine and cocked the hammer back to release the bullet from the chamber. Then he pushed it down into his waist, laughed and peeled off, literally leaving her in his dust.

Girl, Get Over Yourself

His voicemail message sounded strangely masculine.

Hello you've reached Patrick James. I'm unavailable for your call, but if you'll leave your name and number I'll get back to you as soon as possible. Thanks.

"PJ? This is Brenda. Ion know why you tryna sound like Billy Dee Williams all of a sudden. Ugh. I need to talk to you. It is extremely important that you call me back as soon as you get this message. Hit me on my cell. You got the number. Oh and get rid of this stupid message. I almost hung up the phone on that shit. Ugh."

After the previous night's ridiculous events, Brenda was thoroughly outdone with Ray Coleman. She wasn't quite ready to call the news, but she knew that she couldn't keep it to herself much longer. Not with this crazy muthafucka loose, calling shots.

He was dangerous, and unpredictable, but he was still gon pay for what he did to her sister. Busting his big Mississippi nose was only the beginning. She knew she had to be careful, though. He had shown he could pull some strings and with a squeaky clean reputation he could definitely make things hard if she didn't watch herself.

As she pulled into the parking lot of Potomac Medical her phone rang. She didn't recognize the number but she thought with everything going on lately it was probably best to answer all calls.

"Hello?" Brenda said.

"What is so urgent that you interrupt her beauty rest?"

"Ok, first, stop speaking to me in third person and second what's with the James Earl Jones impression on your voice mail?"

"Sweetie, you called Patrick on his business line. He must be professional at all times. And if you don't want her to speak of herself in third person then you need not dial her number. Boop boop!"

Brenda couldn't help laughing. "PJ, you stupid. This is not a social call. We got some issues and drama that needs to be dealt with ASAP."

"She's listening."

"Well it's a long and ridiculous story but the gist of it is that Missy James Coleman is not living the fairy tale everybody thought she was."

"Well chile, *everybody* didn't think she was livin no fairytale."

"What?"

"Nothing, just go ahead and finish."

"Well I called you because I know you can keep shit close to your vest. I don't need this gettin around until I figure out how we gon deal with it."

"Well you called the right one. And stop giving her the mystery chile. Spit it out."

Brenda began at the beginning. She told PJ everything Missy told her that day and didn't spare any details, from Missy's wedding nightmare all the way to Ray bailing her out of jail the night before. Several times Brenda paused for reaction but oddly there was none.

"Hell-o? Are you there?"

"Umh hmm. She's here."

"So you don't have nothin to say?"

PJ let out a sigh. "Sweetie. She has known about Raymond Coleman for years now. That is no revelation."

"Uh uh PJ. Stop lyin."

"She has no reason to tell tales, darling. Everyone knows Ray Coleman is 'trade.'"

"Trade?"

"Yes darling, trade. The boys that trade sides. Ray Coleman's penchant for the chicks with the dicks is quite legendary in the A. Trust."

"No!"

"Yes chile. She's amazed he's kept it from the mainstream public *this* long. But then again, the Atlanta underworld is a pretty tight-knit bunch of derelicts."

"Well if they're that tight-knit, how you know about it?"

"She's pretending she didn't just hear that."

"Whaaaaaat? Damn. Well, why wouldn't you say anything, PJ?!"

"Say something, to whom? "

"PJ. She's your family."

"What? Please. I don't owe that bitch nothin!"

Brenda burst out laughing. "Damn! You dat mad you came right outta third."

PJ laughed. "Girl, shut up. Seriously though. I tried. She didn't wanna hear from me...so that was that."

"So you're saying you told Missy her husband was gay, and she dismissed you. I don't believe that."

"I said I *tried*. When I found out she was engaged to him, in the paper I might add, I got myself an invite to her engagement party."

"You never told me that."

"You never asked me that. But let me tell you what happened. Like I said, I pulled some strings and got an invite to her engagement party. It was at the Mandarin. My good friend Sy's boyfriend's girlfriend planned the party, and it was absolutely fabulous. I mean opulent, hunny, and Miss Missy? Oh she slayed. I mean I don't even like the bitch but she was snatched hunny! When she walked in the roooom......"

"PJ! Don't nobody need all them details. I wasn't invited to that party anyway, so I don't care. Just tell me what happened."

"Ok. Well the couple did their meeting, greeting and schmoozing, and after a long while I was finally able to get close enough to speak with her. Do you know that bitch acted like she didn't know who the fuck I was?"

Brenda giggled a bit. "Well Miss P, I'm sure you look a *lil different* from the last time she saw you?"

"Oh, I took that into consideration. So I leaned in and said, "Missy, girl it's me, PJ. Your cousin? She looked at me and gave me an ol' Nancy Regan smile, hunny. Like I was a fan. Then she said, 'Hello. It's been a long time. So good to see you.' And her eyes darted to some old white couple that was standing a few feet away from us. She was very clearly dismissing me. Hun-ty! I was pissed to the heights of pisstivity! But I bit my tongue and decided to try a little harder. So I leaned in again and said, 'Missy, I really need to speak with you privately, sweetie. It'll only take a few seconds, but it's something you really need to know. It's personal."

"Ok, so why didn't you just tell her then?"

"Because I didn't have a chance. Girlfriend waved her little assistant over to us and instructed her to get me a business card. Then she excused herself and made her way over to the old white couple she was so anxious to see."

"Oooh. No she didn't."

"Yes, yes she did. So Miss P was over her hunny. Miss P didn't give a good gay cock what Missy did with her life at that point. Boo boop!"

"Ok, well I can see how you would want to be hands off after that but come on, PJ. You should have told her. Wrote her a note or something. You can't let your blood go into something like that in the blind."

"Who was to say she was going into it blind? For one, I knew for a fact that his first wife, Tabitha, was a good Judy, and since Missy is all about the coin, she could have been, too. Secondly, I was sticking my neck all the way out by telling her in the first place and the bitch didn't even acknowledge me. And number three, fuck her."

"Really PJ?

"Really."

"Whatever. You might as well go on and sweep that little water under the bridge now because shit's changed."

"Changed how? Because of that raggedy ass apology she gave us at the house? Cause she supposed to be sorry now? Cause she supposed to love her family again, now that her husband is beatin the breaks off her? Chile please. Ain't shit changed as far as I'm concerned."

"No, cause she's your family. James girls don't treat each other like that. We stick together. Don't act like you don't know that shit."

"Umh hmm. But I ain't a girl, remember?"

"PJ."

"Ok I hear you. So she a James girl again. Yeah, yeah whatever."

"So you gon help me handle this or what?"

"Yeah I'll help you handle it, but understand that it ain't about her. Miss P has her own reasons why she wants to see Gay Coleman fall from grace. Trust. But that's another story for another time, my little petunia."

Brenda really hated it when PJ kept things from her. Plus, this sounded like it was going to be juicy. She cursed him. "Oh no bitch. You are not about to do that to me. I want the story. Gimme the story."

"Brenda, I will call you tonight. I promise you. And don't worry, we gon get that muthafucka. Now go on in there and see your sister. And tell the bitch I said hello."

They both laughed.

"Bye bitch."

"Smooches!

*****

PJ hung up the phone. He wasn't really sure how to feel. He didn't like Missy, but she was family so he knew he had to get over himself.

The best thing about this situation was that he could finally get back at Ray Coleman's ass. For the last six months, he had been racking his brain trying to figure out a way to pay Ray back, but it was impossible without breaking "the code." Now Ray had opened the door. He slipped up and got found out so the code was no longer a factor. PJ called his friend to give him the good news.

"Ritz Carlton, Georgetown, good morning."

"Biiiitch! What are you doing?"

"Where did you call. I'm working. What's up."

"I got some delicious news for you."

"Ooh. Delicious? I'm intrigued..."

"Hold on to your lacefront hunny bunches. We finally get to take a bite out of Ray Coleman's big muscular ass."

"What?"

"Yes ma'am. It's about that time."

"Don't tease me, P. For real?"

"I am so sincere. He done gone and left himself wide open. So the muzzle is about to come OFF."

"What! What's going on?"

"It's a long story but a fantastic one. My ride is waiting outside so I gotta go, but trust me when I tell you that he will pay very dearly for what he did to you sweetie. I can promise you that."

"Ugh! I hate you! You always leavin a bitch hangin!"

"Calm down dear. I'm picking you up tomorrow for brunch. Eleven o'clock. Madam's Organ. Mimosas and girl talk. I'll fill you in then. I gotta go now baby. Smooches!"

With that, Miss P hung up the phone and smiled. She would party a little harder and a little longer that night for she was about to come into a few coins; from Ray Coleman's change purse. Yaassss. Life was good and about to get a whole lot better.

*****

Brenda felt a little more at ease after talking to PJ. She really needed to get all the foolishness off her chest, and she needed to know someone had her back. Someone who could be discreet. Someone who wouldn't fly off the handle and react. Plus, she could always count on PJ for a good laugh, and she really needed that.

As she walked into the hospital lobby, she dreaded seeing Missy again. After all the excitement of the last few hours, she had managed to put the image of her sister's beaten and swollen face out of her head. Now it was coming back. Flooding her thoughts so that she was emotional again, and frustrated. Fighting back her tears was nearly impossible but she knew she had to, so she sucked them up. Missy needed her to be strong.

Her phone vibrated in her purse. She looked at it and it was that detective Smith again. The third call that morning. Brenda sent it to voicemail like the others. As she approached Missy's room she swallowed hard, stood up straight and walked in. The room was empty, pristine.

Brenda walked out to the nurse's station. "Excuse me, ma'am."

The nurse was on the phone. Clearly on a personal call and blatantly ignoring Brenda as she stood there impatiently waiting for an acknowledgement.

After about a minute Brenda interrupted her. "Ma'am, I just have a quick question." The nurse looked up at her but kept talking, so Brenda reached over the counter and pushed down the button on the base of the phone, to disconnect her call. Then she said, in a more assertive tone, "Excuse me! Where is the patient in room 234?! Melissa Coleman?

"Miss, there's no need to be rude." The young nurse rolled her eyes and reached for her patient log. "Mrs. Coleman was discharged this morning."

"What!?!"

Prince of Darkness

Missy woke suddenly and in a panic. She had been having very vivid nightmares about Ray and couldn't seem to get the vision of his cold dark eyes out of her mind. The last time she looked into them was about a second before he knocked her unconscious. That was the last thing she remembered clearly. She had no idea how she ended up in a hospital bed.

The room was way too dark; eerie. The only illumination was beams of moonlight peeking in through the mini blinds and a light coming in from under the door. She was able to lift herself up enough to reach the light string and when she pulled it down she thought for a split second that she was still dreaming. She gasped and held in her breath.

There he was, standing over her smiling. Missy started to scream, but the look in his eyes stopped her. With a wired jaw it wouldn't exactly have been a scream anyway.

"So, you're awake."

Ray knew she could barely speak and would have to lay there and listen. He also saw the fear in her eyes, so he capitalized on it immediately. "You know, I just left your sister. I guess she came to rescue you. She tried breaking into my house like the little thieving hood rat she is. Even gave me this here cut on my lip. She sure seems to love you. I bet you love her, too, don't you?"

A sudden chill went through her body. She was petrified that Ray had hurt Brenda.

"Oh don't look at me like that. I didn't touch your little sister. But that doesn't mean I *won't* touch her."

Her eyes welled, and she shook her head slowly from one side to the other. Pleading with her eyes. *Don't hurt my sister.* She was right where Ray wanted her. Afraid. He pulled up a chair close to her and took a hold of her good hand.

"You see baby, I had a little time to think over that proposal you gave me last night. Obviously that's not an option, but I have a little proposal of my own. I'll tell you more on the ride home. But first, let's get you outta here."

Bittersweet Sixteen

Brandy's sixteenth was definitely a birthday she would never forget. It started off pretty good for a Friday. She had a special birthday outfit picked out. A soft pink V neck sweater, form fitted jeans and soft pink suede Adidas Gazelles.

She'd gotten her hair done the day before. Uncle PJ convinced her to lighten her natural brown color, and he did a roller set so she had big bouncy curls that framed her face. She wasn't much for makeup, so she just put on a little eyeliner and some of Brenda's pink matte lip gloss. Tay loved her in pink.

She could smell breakfast from her bedroom. Brenda, Mandy and Uncle Larry were at the dining room table waiting and when she got to the bottom of the stairs they all broke out in a really bad rendition of Stevie Wonder's happy birthday song. Brandy played along and did a little birthday dance.

In the middle of the dining room table was a giant Cinnabon with a number sixteen candle, two more cakes in the shape of a one and a six and a bottle of chilled cider for toasting. Brenda liked to make every birthday a production.

She made a huge breakfast, and even though Brandy was running late for school, she had to indulge her mom, just a little bit. She sampled some of everything and it was all great, as usual. They had a birthday toast using Grandma Betty's good wine glasses.

Brenda sipped champagne, real champagne, and danced around the living room like she was celebrating her own birthday. Brandy didn't mind at all. She was just happy to see her mother smiling again.

She danced over to the living room closet, pulled out the gift bags and danced back into the dining room. Brandy gave her a kiss on the cheek and started digging in.

The smallest bag held a pair of gold bamboo earrings personalized with Brandy's name. Ghetto gold. Brandy squealed. She had been asking for them since last Christmas. The next bag had the perfumed gift set she wanted. Marc Jacobs Yellow Daisies. The big bottle of perfume, lotion, body wash and powder. There was even a sample sized bottle for her purse. All the girls in school wanted it but few could afford to buy the whole set.

The last and largest bag had a box in it, which had another box in it that had the Louis Vuitton Montsouris backpack she'd been begging for. And it was stuffed with bills. Brandy ran over to the other side of the table and hugged Brenda tight. "Thank you ma! You got me everything I wanted!"

Again Brandy exaggerated the birthday joy. Truth was, her gifts were nice but they were significantly less than what she was used to getting on a normal birthday, let alone her sixteenth. When she looked at the bag she could tell it was second hand. The leather was a little worn around the edges and it wasn't in the normal packaging from the Vuitton boutique. It was also filled with mostly ones, a few fives and a couple twenties. That was allowance, not birthday money. But she didn't trip. In fact, the way things were going she really didn't think she'd get as much as she did.

She knew Brenda was having a hard time. Just trying to keep things "normal" for everyone, but with Melvin gone it was impossible. His shoes were way too big to fill. Brenda hugged her baby girl and apologized for not being able to do more for her big birthday. Brandy hugged her tighter and told her it was ok. "Ma, you got me what I asked for. I'm good." She was sincere.

Ever since they had to move back into Betty's house, Brenda had been really depressed. She was so worried that she wasn't doing enough, but Brandy keep telling her that it was ok. MJ was the one with the problem. He complained all of the time. His birthday was a month after Melvin died and when he didn't get the new car Melvin promised him he had a tantrum. Brenda was so upset she gave him the truck instead of turning it back into the car dealership like she planned. Even though she couldn't afford to keep making the payments on it. MJ didn't care. As long as he got what he wanted.

So after she finished breakfast, spritzed on some of her new perfume and switched her small Louis for the bigger one she called Tay to see where he was. Before she could get a word out he said he was pulling up in front of the house. He sat on the car horn as if she was the one making *him* late. So she kissed the family goodbye, put on a fresh coat of gloss and hit the door running and yelling.

"Tay I told you not to be late today!"

She stopped in her tracks when she saw him standing at the bottom of the porch steps holding a bouquet of birthday balloons.

He looked good too. Fresh haircut, sweat suit and the new J's on his feet. She smiled. He was equally as impressed with her, standing there pretty in pink with more curve than a 16-year-old should ever be allowed.

Brandy ran down and jumped from the porch into his arms, causing him to release the balloons into the air.

"Brandy! The balloons!"

She gasped. "Oh, bae I'm sorry! I'm sorry."

She kissed him on the lips as Brenda stared out at them disapprovingly from the kitchen window. "Brandy you're late!" she yelled.

They laughed and ran to the car. Tay yelled back. "Sorry Miss Brenda! We're leaving!" They hopped into his Honda and sped away. When they got around the corner, out of Brenda's sight, Brandy gave him another peck on the lips.

"Hey boo!"

"What's up birthday girl? You looking good today! Umh. You makin me wanna throw you in that backseat and have hot nasty *sex* with you!"

"Boy, shut up."

"Ok, I'm just playin. But you look real nice today, babe. You know I'm loving that lip gloss. Can I give you another birthday kiss?"

"Yeah, later. Now hurry up and get me to school before I miss homeroom."

"Ok ok. So what you got planned today?"

"Nothing I guess. Do *you* have anything in mind?"

"Aha! You know I do. But I may not have time to pick you up this evening. You think you can get a ride home with Michelle?"

"Don't you get out of school at one o'clock? Why can't you pick me up?"

"Yes and none of your business. I got some stops to make, and I may not be back in time to pick you up. Just come straight to my house after school, ok?"

"Ok. But it better be good."

"Yeah, you better be ready." He pulled into the school parking lot. "Now give me a kiss and get outta my car."

They smooched, and she was off.

When Brandy got to school, she was almost a half-hour late, so she had to go to tardy hall until her first period class. No biggie. She didn't like her homeroom teacher anyway.

The usual latecomers were there, rowdy and out of order. Her friend Tara wished her a happy birthday, which brought the whole room over to her to give her birthday hugs and wishes. Everyone but Marsha and Raven. The gossip and the hater.

When the bell rang for first period, everyone lined up waiting to file out into the hall. Marsha and Raven stood directly behind Brandy in line. She could hear them giggling and whispering.

Marsha whispered to Raven, "Umh, that shit is cray."

Raven responded, "Yeah you gotta watch these hoes out here. Errybody that smile in your face ain't your friend."

"O-kay. If it was me, I would have fucked that bitch up. She crazy.", Marsha said.

Brandy was tired of their hot morning breath on the back of her neck so she turned around. "Hey y'all."

The girls spoke in unison. "Hey Braannndy." Then Raven, the biggest troublemaker, said, "Your hair looks cute."

Raven was never one to give out compliment so Brandy was suspicious, but she smiled and thanked her anyway. "Thanks."

"Yeah. It look like you added a few pieces in the front. It's real cute though."

Brandy smiled. "No boo, it's all mine. I don't do weaves. I don't need to." Then she ran her hand through her curls and shook them out.

Marsha laughed at the snappy rebuttal. Raven's homemade weave was always a mess. "O-kaay. I know that's right, Miss Brandy. You better work them highlights. Who did it?"

"My uncle PJ."

"Ooh Miss P?! I love your uncle, gurl. He all-ways look good. He still work at that shop uptown?"

"No he's at a shop over on H Street now."

"Oh, ok. Imma have to see him for real. Your color is bomb. He did *that*." She leaned in to get a closer look at Brandy's hair.

"Thanks. You can touch it. It's real soft."

"Can I?" Marsha pulled on a curl as Raven looked on, annoyed with Marsha's two-faceded-ness. "Yeah it is soft."

They walked out into the hall headed to class. Raven was not to be ignored. So she decided to get a little messy. "Ooh is that a new Louis? It's real cute. The straps look a little worn out, though. You got that for your birthday?"

Brandy sucked her teeth. Aggravated. She wasn't in the mood

for the cattiness or the judgment about her n-used bag. "This old bag? Girl no. I got this for Christmas, like three years ago. I just use it for luggage now. It goes with the matching set. My mother gave me a stack of bills and some jewelry for my birthday this year. Oh and the big Marc Jacobs set." Brandy held out her wrist for Raven to smell but Marsha grabbed hold of her wrist and sniffed.

"Ooh yes girl. I love that Yellow Daisy!", she said.

Brandy gushed. "I know right. It smells so good. That's all I wanted. I have the gold bamboos on…" She pulled her hair back to give them a closer look. "…but she won't let me wear my diamonds to school. You now. *Haters.*"

Marsha giggled again.

"So Brandy," Raven said, "you heard from Michelle today?"

"No. I haven't seen her since yesterday when we left school. Why?"

The girls turned to each other and whispered. "Oh, she don't know yet?"

Brandy answered. "I don't know *what* yet?"

Raven responded with much pleasure. "Michelle and Keisha was fightin yesterday."

"Fightin! When? I was with them all day yesterday."

"In the parking lot after school. Tay must have picked you up already. So you ain't talk to Keisha yesterday either? I thought that was your boo?" Both the girls started laughing.

"No, what happened?"

Marsha went all in. "Girl they got IN-TO it! Michelle whipped Keisha ass!"

"Nuh uh. Stop lyin."

Raven chimed in. "For real. Girl, it was a hot ass mess, too. Keisha's tracks was all over the ground, and she was bleedin out her nose and her mouth. Somebody called the police, and they locked Michelle up."

"Oh my God! We all walked out of the building together yesterday. Everything was cool. What the hell was they fightin for?!"

The girls looked at each other again and started whispering. Raven said, "You tell her!"

Marsha responded, "Hell no, I'm not tellin her. That shit ain't none of my business."

Brandy was getting frustrated with the girls playing with her. The second bell rang for class. She decided to let it go. For the moment. "Alright y'all. I gotta get to my class. I'll talk to y'all later."

Raven smiled. "Ok. Happy Birthday boo."

Brandy didn't even turn around. She just walked into her class confused. As soon as she sat down, she regretted ever walking in. All she wanted to do was get to her cell phone so she could call her girls and find out what was going on.

As soon as the bell rang, Brandy ran straight to her locker to get her phone. She went into the bathroom to make her calls. She dialed Keisha's cell several times. The first call was sent to voicemail and then the phone was turned off.

Brandy knew that Keisha's brother used her cell phone sometimes, so she thought maybe he had it. She called Keisha's house, and her mother answered. Keisha wasn't at home. Brandy wasn't sure what Keisha may have told her mother about her whereabouts, so she decided not to ask any more questions. She just left a message for Keisha to call her.

Brandy called Michelle's house and got an answer on the first ring.

"Hello."

"Michelle! Girl please tell me what is going on! Why the hell was you and Keisha fightin?!"

"Where you at?"

"I'm at school! Keisha not answering her phone. What's going on?"

"Can you come over here after school?"

"No I'm coming over now. I'll be there in like twenty minutes. I'll call you when I'm downstairs. Please answer your phone."

"Aight. See you in a little bit."

Before talking to Michelle, Brandy was confused, but by the time she left her house she was stunned. She couldn't believe what was happening. No wonder why Keisha wasn't answering her phone.

*****

Tay sent her a text around four o'clock telling her that he was at home and that she could come on over. She got herself together and Michelle gave her a ride to his house. She used her key to get in.

When Brandy walked through the door, she couldn't believe her eyes. The house was transformed. There were candles lit in every corner and on every surface. Dozens of them. Luther was playing softly on the stereo. The house smelled clean, and the dining room table was set nicely with real dishes and glasses.

Long-stemmed pink roses were in a large vase in the center of the table. She walked back to Tay's bedroom, and he'd done some fancy redecorating. There was a beautiful new comforter set on his bed with matching curtains and an area rug. Candles lined the dresser and there was another vase filled with white roses by the bed. A few of the petals were spread out over the bed, and there was an envelope lying on the pillow with her name on it. She opened it. Inside was a handwritten card with the picture of a globe on the front.

To Brandy. The love of my life.

You are the sweetest most beautiful person I know and you make me happier than I have ever been in my life. You are my world and that's just what I plan to give you. Happy 16th birthday babe. Let's make tonight special.

Love always,

Tay.

Brandy closed the card and sat on the bed in tears. Tay was singing loudly in the shower. Their favorite song. She walked into the bathroom and snatched the shower curtain back, startling him. When he saw her, he was surprised but pleased. He turned off the shower and stood in front of her dripping wet in all his glory.

"Hey Baby," he said. "Happy Birthday."

Brandy walked closer to him. She stared into his eyes and he returned her gaze. He reached out to touch her hand and she swung hard hitting him in the face. Tay fell down in the tub hitting his head on the faucet and causing a small cut on his forehead.

Brandy screamed. "You fucked her! You fucked Keisha! You muthafucka!" She swung at him wildly, hitting him with every blow.

Dazed and confused he called out to her. "Baby! Stop! What the fuck are you talking about?" Tay was able to get up out of the tub and shove her off of him. She hit the sink and fell on the floor. He ran over to her to help her up. "Oh my God. Baby, I'm so sorry."

"Get the fuck off me! Get OFF ME! She started slapping at him again. "How could you do this to me, Tay? How could you do this? With Keisha?!"

"Do what? Calm down! Who told you that?"

"It don't fuckin matter who told me! Did you fuck her or not?!"

"NO! NO! I didn't! Brandy, please calm down!"

Tay grabbed a towel and wrapped it around his waist. "Come talk to me baby. Please. Don't do this."

"Tay, did you fuck her? That's all I wanna know!"

"I said NO, baby!"

"Then how the FUCK did she get PREGNANT?" Brenda shoved him hard, and he fell back into the tub. "Fuck you!" She ran out of the door knocking over the candelabra sitting on the table by the window. By the time Tay got out of the tub and put the towel back around his waist, she was already out the door.

He tried to run after her but he noticed the curtains starting to catch fire so he ran over to put them out.

By the time he'd thrown the water from the vase onto the curtains to get the fire out, she was gone. Through the singed curtains he saw her hop into Michelle's car and they sped off. He could not believe what had just happened. Frustrated, he punched the wall and screamed to the top of his lungs, "SHHIIIIIITTTTTT!!!!!"

Later that evening when Daye came home, Tay was still sitting on the couch in his towel, holding the ring he had bought for Brandy. Daye could tell he'd been crying. Candles were still burning and the house smelled of potpourri and burned polyester.

Daye laughed his ass off. "What up, Romeo? What it do?"

"Bro. I'm not even in the mood for that shit right now."

"Nah, you in the mood for loooove." He fell down on the couch laughing again.

"Come on Daye. I'm serious right now. I can't do this with you, man."

"I'm just fuckin wit you. I heard what happened. That's fucked up."

"You heard? From who?"

"Nigga, that shit is all over the block. Everything from the rose petals to the butt nekkid beat down to the burnt up curtains. Niggas is clownin."

"Damn. That's all I need right now."

"One question for you. Did you fuck?"

"Brandy?"

"No nigga, Keisha."

"Well if I didn't, I wouldn't be sittin here with you lookin stupid right now would I?"

"I thought so. Damn. I *would* say just deny it, but now that she pregnant…"

"Please don't remind me. Damn! How the fuck did I get myself into *this?*"

"Yeah man. Personally, I'm appalled."

"Daye."

"Ok, ok. Let me stop playin. But I told your ass you gotta strap up with these hoes."

"That's the thing. I did man. I don't even know how this shit happened."

"That bitch Keisha be linin niggas up and knockin em down. She go hard. I thought you was so in love with your girl."

Tay sighed heavily. "It was before we starting messin with each other. Like the week before. Remember that fight party you had?"

"The Mosely fight?"

"Yeah that one. The one I didn't even fuckin wanna be at."

"Yeah you wasn't even at the party but a minute. I thought you was so tired."

"I was. Them Jell-O shots that girl made had me dizzy. I was already tired when I started taking them, so I came on upstairs and went to bed. I forgot to lock my door though. Next thing I know, Keisha was naked under the covers with me…her hands all over me…and you know the rest."

"Dayum nigga! It went down like that?"

"Yeah man. That's why I'm so blown. It happened one time, *and* I strapped up. I was a little tipsy, but I know I strapped up. I didn't even want to be with that girl. She was throwin it at me every day, and I kept turning her down. I can't even believe this shit."

"Yeah, well we know how Keisha roll. It is what it is. You just gon have to wait it out and get that test. That's fucked up you lost your girl though." Daye leaned back on the sofa and grabbed his crotch. "Brandy was aaight. She got a fat little ass. Shit now that you ain't hittin that no more, I might have to…"

Tay jumped up and grabbed his big brother by the neck. He didn't even wait for him to finish his sentence because he knew where Daye was going with it. One thing he was *not* going to do was disrespect her. Brandy deserved better than that.

"Daye, you my brother, and you know I love you, but if you ever go near my girl–"

Daye pushed his little brother off him. They both stood up. Face to face. Daye was shocked. "Damn! All this over a bitch?!"

Tay punched him in the face. The fight went on until the police came.

Carlita's Way

Missy had no idea how Ray could have convinced the doctors to discharge her, but then again he *was* Ray Coleman. Mr. DC.

When they got home he led her to the guestroom on the first floor near the kitchen. The room was all ready for her. He had a hospital bed brought in, a fully equipped entertainment center; there was a portable refrigerator and a makeshift pantry stocked with food.

After he got her settled into bed, he informed her that the maid was on vacation and he would be leaving until the next morning. Then he kissed her on the forehead and smiled. "Sleep tight beautiful."

She wasn't sure what to think but one thing was for sure; this motherfucker was crazy, and she was *really* afraid of him now. She knew he would make good on every threat against her and her family, so leaving was no longer an option. She had to let things play out his way.

The idea of it was as disgusting as it was horrifying but what choice did she have? She decided to get some rest and deal with it tomorrow. With any luck, she'd wake up in the morning and realize it was just another awful nightmare, and it would all be over when she opened her eyes.

Missy slept uncomfortably for a little over an hour. She was restless, and her mouth was as dry as sandpaper. She was craving ice in the worst way. What Ray left her in the bucket had long since melted away, and the small refrigerator didn't have an ice tray, so she decided to grab her crutches and venture into the kitchen. With one good arm and a bad ankle she knew this would be a painful undertaking, but the craving had taken over so off to the kitchen she went.

The kitchen was dark except for the light coming from the refrigerator. The door was wide open. She reached for the light switch. As soon as she flipped it on, the person in the fridge slammed it shut, obviously startled. For a second, Missy couldn't believe her eyes. It was little Miss Puerto Rico.

The woman just stood there looking like a deer caught in headlights. Wearing one of Ray's football jersey's no less. Suddenly Missy started having flashbacks of what she witnessed that night in Atlanta.

When they locked eyes Missy's blood ran cold through her veins and her chest tightened. She took a couple deep breaths in and out to try to relieve the stress. Missy tried to speak but the moment she opened her mouth a pain jolted through her entire body causing her eyes to well. Her face felt like someone had lit a match to it, but pain or no pain, she was gonna speak.

"You were with Ray in Atlanta?"

Ray's houseguest lowered her eyes and answered, "Si."

Missy scowled. "Do you speak English?"

"Si. I mean, yes. A leetle."

"Wha...what is your name?"

"Carlita."

"Do you know who I am?"

"Yes, Meesy."

Missy was beyond annoyed that this thing knew her name. But soon that would be the least of her worries.

"You're staying in my basement?"

Carlita nodded. "Si."

"With Ray?"

"Yes."

"How long have you been staying in my house?"

"Eh?"

Missy was frustrated and the pain was worsening. "I SAID...HOW LONG HAVE YOU BEEN LIVING IN MY HOUSE?"

"Um. Maybeeee seex munts now. Meesy, I am so sawdy. I no wanted to stay here in you house. Ray insist I stay with heem. He say you would be leaving soon." Carlita's eyes turned soft. She appeared to be pleading with them. "Are...are you still together with heem?"

"If you mean am I still sleeping with him, no. I haven't touched him since I saw him with you on Valentine's Day."

"You see us?"

"Yes. Long story. But I don't care about that. If he told you that we weren't together, he didn't lie. We're not."

"Then why you still here?"

Missy had to pause for a second. Not just to rest her jaw but to marvel at the audacity of this bitch to stand there in her house and question her like *she* was the unwelcomed guest. It was almost funny. She answered the question, honestly.

"That's another long story, Carlita, but believe me, it's not what I want."

Carlita's expression changed. It was strange. A mix of concern and fear. "Why did Ray do thees to you? What did you do to heem?"

Now Missy was angry. And the pain was becoming unbearable. She started scrambling around in one of the kitchen drawers and Carlita got nervous. She started to back away, but was relieved when she saw Missy pull out a pen and pad and slam it down on the counter. Missy perched herself up on a high stool and motioned for Carlita to come closer. Then Missy scribbled as best she could with her left hand. "U took me to the hospital?"

Carlita answered her, reluctantly. "Si."

Things were beginning to make so much sense. Missy started scribbling again and before they knew it the sun was coming up. They had been sitting at that kitchen counter for hours and by the end of their communication Carlita was borderline hysterical.

With tears in her eyes she packed all of her things and called a taxi. She said she was leaving Ray. Going back home. To Brazil.

✱✱✱✱✱

Ray got home around 9 a.m. Missy was so stunned by the things Carlita had told her she couldn't sleep. She was more afraid of Ray than ever. When he came in the house she could hear him walking toward the basement and down the stairs. There was a loud crash and then she heard him running up the stairs. He was heading toward her room. She pretended to be asleep.

He burst in the door causing it to hit the wall and knock over her makeshift pantry. "Where the fuck is she?!"

Missy opened her eyes slowly, feigning bewilderment. He screamed again, "Where's Carlita!? I know you know!"

She didn't speak. Just stared up at him with a confused look on her face. It must have worked because he walked out slamming the door shut behind him.

She heard him leave the house, then tires screeching as he raced down the driveway. Missy smiled and thought to herself, *I guess he's going to find his boo*. Now she could get some sleep.

Lord Help Me

Brenda finally made it home late in the afternoon, exhausted and frustrated. She wanted so badly to drive back to Ray's and see if Missy was ok, but she knew she couldn't. Ray told her never to come back to his house and she knew he meant it.

She wasn't afraid of Ray the man. Far from it. She was leery of Ray the bitch – the Ray that would have no problem getting the Feds to look into her background and make her explain how she'd been living so well with no recorded income. The Ray that would have zero problem having her kids taken away. She couldn't afford to be careless with him, but she needed to know how Missy was. This abusive asshole would kill her eventually, and she couldn't just sit back and let it happen.

Her doorbell rang. When she opened the door, there stood one of the most beautiful women she had ever seen. Behind the woman was a crowd of guys howling and hollering.

"Good afternoon. I looking for Budeenda Yames?"

"Yes, I'm Brenda James. Can I help you?"

"Si. I come for you seester. Meesy?"

"Missy! She's not here. Please come in."

"No, I sawdy. I have cab wait outside. I going to airport. I veddy late for my flight. Meesy ask me to tell you that she ok. She say you don't worry. She ask me to geev you this."

Carlita pulled an envelope from her purse and handed it over. "I have to go now." She turned and ran down the stairs to the cab.

"Wait! Miss! What's your name?"

Carlita yelled back as she's getting into the back of the cab. "Carlita!"

Brenda opened the envelope. It was a very poorly handwritten letter from Missy:

Brenda,

I needed you to know that I am ok so please try not to worry about me. I know that you came to the hospital to check on me last night. Thank you. And please know that I didn't mean to miss mama's funeral. I was on my way out the door when Ray attacked me. I would never have missed the funeral and I would never have abandoned you like that.

I love you Brenda and I miss my family. I miss my sister. I'm missing mama right now so much and I'm living with so many regrets. My life is a disaster. But I'm going to make it alright again. I don't know how I got here in this place but I'm going to get out. Please just give me some time. Please don't come for me and please don't do anything to provoke Ray.

I will contact you as soon as I can get access to a phone. Just give me a few days. I love you with my whole heart little sister. I will talk to you very soon.

Missy

Brenda cried harder than she did at the funeral. She missed her sister, too. As much as she wanted to mob up and go over to Missy's house, she knew it wasn't that easy. There was too much at stake.

She could deal with the fallout from Ray's wrath, but she couldn't jeopardize her children. Then she thought how ironic it was that Ray would be the person to make her see that she had been jeopardizing them all along.

For all the good she thought she'd done in her life, it was like she was no different than any of the other hustlers' girls in the hood.

Yes, she married her baby daddy and tried to raise her children to be decent and respectful human beings. Yes, she took care of her mother and people depended on her. No, she didn't participate in any of Melvin's dealings in the underworld and yes she badgered him constantly to go legit. All these things were true and of them she had always been quite proud, but if she wanted to keep it real with herself, it really didn't mean shit.

Knowing how Melvin made his money and accepting it for her family made her just as culpable as he was. Just as ratched as every other hood chick ridin and dyin for her man while he's out doin dirt. It was time to be real with herself and hold herself accountable for where she was, for the state her family was in.

Just thinking about her life was sobering. Her heart was heavy. Melvin was gone, mama was gone, the kids were running wild and Melvin's murderer was still walking the streets. She finally had her big sister back in her life but Missy's life was arguably more fucked up than hers. It was crazier than any story she could think of.

She thought, did other people have this kind of drama going on or was it just the James girls. God was definitely testing her faith and her will. But it was a test that she knew she would pass. If there was ever a time to draw on Mama James' strength it was now. If there were ever a time to fall to her knees and call on her God, it was now. Right now. So she did.

Brenda hadn't recited the Lord's Prayer since kiddie bible school, but the words were forever etched into her memory. She said them aloud. Repented her many sins and begged His forgiveness. His grace and His mercy. She prayed for a healing and for deliverance from what the devil had made of her life. She thanked her God for every blessing and every lesson in her life. Finally, she asked for guidance. She knew she had a job to do. A family to mend. A purpose.

You're Not Fine

"Hello."

"Bren…Brenda? It's me. I just wanted to tell you…"

The voice trailed off. Brenda yelled into the receiver. "Hello!"

Brenda looked down at her caller ID. The call was from a private number, and the voice on the other end was barely audible. Her cell signal was weak, so she walked over to the window to try to get better reception.

"Yeah. Brenda, it's Missy."

"Oh my God! Missy!" Brenda was instantly emotional "Where are you? How…how are you? What took you so long to call me, girl? It's been almost two weeks!"

"I…I'm sorry. Ray wouldn't give me a phone, and he took out all of the landlines."

"Muthafucka. Where he at?"

"I don't know. I haven't seen him in a week or so."

"Well who's there taking care of you?!"

"I'm fine. Brenda I promise. I'm fine. There's plenty of food here for me and I'm getting around ok."

"That is bullshit. You probably need to go back to the doctor by now. I could kill that muthafucka for what he did to you. You shouldn't be there alone like that Missy. I'm coming out there to get you."

"No! Please!"

"Well what am I supposed to do, just sit here and let you suffer by yourself?!"

"No, you're supposed to trust me. I'm ok Brenda. I wouldn't say it if I wasn't. And I don't want to cause you anymore trouble."

"I don't care. You're my sister." Brenda started to cry. "Please I just need to see that you're ok. I swear I feel so helpless. I'm just frustrated right now. I can't help my kids; I can't help you. And it's cuz of how I live MY life! I'm sorry sis."

"No. No baby this is my mess. All mine. I'm the one that ran off and married a fucking…maniac lunatic. Not you. So don't even think about blaming yourself for anything I have going on. I know you want to help me and I KNOW you *would* help me but I've got this. Stop crying. Stop worrying. Everything's gonna be fine."

"No, it's not fine! Nothing is fine Missy! This shit is fucked up! You don't know what you doin and—"

"Look Brenda! I am really trying to hold it together and do what I need to do to get back on my feet. It really doesn't help me to know that you're hysterical. Stop crying. You're supposed to be the strong one remember? Put your big girl drawers back on girl, damn!"

Brenda burst out laughing. She couldn't remember the last time she heard some bass in prissy Missy's voice. Oddly enough, it was calming. "I know. It's just so hard to sit back and do nothing while you're dealing with that muthafucka. And you're hurt…"

"Listen. I really have to get off this line. I borrowed the phone from the mailman while he went and delivered the mail next door."

"The mailman?"

"Yeah, I told him that my power was out and I didn't have a way to charge my cell. He didn't ask any questions. Of course, he's a Big Ray Coleman fan, so he was more than happy to help me."

"Missy, please, please don't hang up yet."

"Hey, do you have Skype?"

"Yeah I have Skype."

"Good. Ray left one of his laptops in the office downstairs. We have Internet access down there. Give me a little while to get down there and get settled and I'll Skype you. Ok? That way you can see me and everything."

"Ok, but please don't bullshit me sis. I'm giving you one hour. If I don't get Skyped in one hour, I don't give a shit what happens. I'm in my truck and on my way to Potomac. You hear me?"

"Brenda—"

"Not 72 minutes, not 63 minutes and 22 seconds. You have exactly ONE hour. Not a minute more. Kapeesh?"

Missy laughed aloud. "Capiche. As SOON as I get the laptop charged you will not only hear from me but you will see me. I'll even do the Doug E. for you. How bout that?" They both laughed. Brenda felt a little better. "Oh and I have a lot to tell you too. A LOT. But the mailman is walking back up the driveway so let me delete your number and give him his phone back."

"Ok, I love you."

"I love you too Bren-head. Bye."

"Bye. Oh! Missy wait! Who is Carlita?!"

The phone went dead. Brenda dialed the number back but it went straight to voice mail. So she waited by her computer. Just short of 45 minutes passed when she got the *ding* – a new message on Skye.

There Missy was. Looking a little thinner in the face and still wearing the sling, but all things considered she appeared to be ok – as ok as one could be after being abused and virtually held captive by her own husband. "So, how do I look?" Missy said.

"You look great."

"You liiieee. So are you officially out of panic mode?"

"I'm down to level three."

"From what number?"

"Eleven."

"Well that's good."

"You hung up the phone too quick for me to ask. Who the hell is Carlita?"

"Oh, Brenda. You're not gonna believe it when I tell you."

"What?!"

"That's mamichulo."

"What! Get the fuck outta here, Missy. That's the she thing?"

"No B.S. She's gorgeous right?"

"Oh that bitch is OVA! I wanna look like *her* when I grow up. I mean damn!"

"I told you."

"*That* is a man, Missy? I don't know if I'm buyin that. Imma need some proof."

"Getting proof is easy."

"How?"

"Next time you see her, kick her pretty ass in the nuts."

The sisters broke into hysterical laughter. And it felt real good to laugh.

"Seriously, I saw the proof. All seven point five seven inches of it…on the bone."

"That shit is beyond crazy, Missy. And he in love with that bitch? He gotta be in love with her. *I* would be in love with *her.*"

"Oh hunny. You don't know the half. He's head over heels in love with this one."

"How you know? Ok I want the details blow-by-blow. And don't leave nothin out. How did you meet her?"

"That is another MA-jor piece of this freak nasty puzzle I call my life."

"Just go slow."

"Ok. Well *Cha Cha* has been living-in-my-house."

"What!"

"In the basement."

"NO!"

"For six-fucking-months!"

"Oh, HELL NO!"

"Yes ma'am. She said she's been living in my basement for six months, and I had no idea."

"You know what. I can believe it. This is some wild shit."

"What? Why?"

"Because that night I came over looking for you, I saw her."

"You saw her?"

"Yeah but I didn't know it was her. She was rifling around in your kitchen in the dark. Standing in the refrigerator. At first I thought it was Ray hiding from me, but I could tell from the shadow that whoever it was wasn't big enough or tall enough to be Ray. So that *had* to be her."

"Well that's exactly where I found her hungry ass. In my refrigerator. Running up my electric bill. Why didn't you bust her?!"

"I told you I didn't know who the fuck it was. I was gonna find out, but as soon as I grabbed the handle to your door, the alarms sounded off and strobe lights started flashing. I had to get outta there. I got warrants, baby."

They both laughed. "You know you really are a mess."

"Missy. This is a hot ass mess, girl. How could you not know Ray had a woman living in your house all that time? You cannot be that hands-off in your own house."

"First of all, he didn't have a *woman* living in my house."

"Yeah. You got me there. But you know what I mean."

"It's because I never come down to the basement. This is Ray's dungeon. Not even the kids are allowed down here. He keeps the rooms locked."

"Missy."

"What?"

"I wish I could slap you through this damn computer screen. I know you know better than that."

"I know, I know. But I'm not exactly dealing with a sane man now am I? The truth is. He had me scared to even touch that basement door. You have no idea what I went through with this man, Brenda."

"I know. And I still can't believe it."

"Believe what?"

"That you was letting his weak ass beat on you. I just can't understand how you let that shit go Missy. Who *are* you? I mean…come on… you a James girl. You *know* better."

"Yeah I know."

"Seriously, I don't understand how women sit back and let a nigga just whoop on they ass like that. He bleed red blood just like you do. If it was me I would have…"

"Brenda! I get it. Ok? Can we just change the subject?"

"Oh. I'm sorry. That was insensitive. I didn't mean it like that."

"Yes…yes you did. But it's fine. You're right. I'm feeling a little tired. I think I'm going to go back upstairs and take a nap."

"No! Missy please don't hang up. I swear I didn't mean to offend you. I just want to talk a little longer. Please?"

"Ok. Just a little while. But I'm not kidding. I really am tired."

"I know. I'll let you go in a second. So she was there in your house all that time and you really had no idea. She didn't leave no little fingerprints or crumbs on the counter or a waft of perfume in that kitchen? You didn't notice a pair of panties in the wash or lipstick on a glass? Nothing?"

"Nope. Nothing."

"Wow. I don't know how you held it together. I would have molly-whopped that bitch!"

"Yeah, well it's a little difficult to give a molly-whop in my condition but I get what you're saying. What's crazy is that after the initial shock wore off…"

"It wore off?"

"Let me talk please. When it wore off, I began talking to her. And the more we talked, I actually started to like her a little bit."

"Missy please. Now I really wanna slap your face."

"No, seriously. She seemed very remorseful. Ray really had her fooled. Of course, Ray told her that our marriage was over, he was leaving me, we weren't having sex – the usual bullshit a married man tells a woman. I'm sure he was convincing because he was telling the truth."

"Really?"

"Hunny, after I saw what I saw in Atlanta, he and I have not so much as embraced. And he definitely didn't get to put those lips anywhere near my face. Trust."

"I hear that."

"We sat and talked for hours. Afterwards she promptly packed her bags, grabbed some of his jewelry and booked a flight home on his credit card."

"You didn't let her take his jewelry."

"Brenda, what do I care about his stupid jewelry? If I could have made it up the stairs I would have opened the safe and given her more. Besides it was worth it to hear everything she had to tell me."

"You got more?"

"Plenty more, but I'm getting the low percentage battery signal. This charger must not be working. I don't know how much time I have so I'll bullet point a few things for you. Just don't interrupt me."

"Ok. Go!"

"One, Ray is almost broke."

"What! How?!"

"I said no interruptions! He owes the IRS millions more than he has or will ever make, and he also has a serious gambling addiction that I knew nothing about. I'm sure that's the reason for all the hard drinking and the sudden money consciousness."

"Wow. Well did you check your accounts?"

"No I don't have access to Ray's money."

"No joint accounts? Investment? Retirement?"

"No. I have a debit card for our household account which is really just for groceries and incidentals, so there's never more than a couple thousand in there. Other than that no. I have my own money Ray knows nothing about."

"Smart."

"Ok, two, I think Ray was contemplating getting rid of me for insurance money so they could run off to Brazil to live together."

"What?! Nooooo Missy. Ok, I'm gettin you the fuck outta there."

"Wait Brenda! Dammit! I don't know if that's really true or not. Carlita said that he made a joke about it one day, and she didn't think anything of it initially, but when she saw how badly he beat me and left me for dead, it scared her."

"Oh my God."

"Yes and guess who took me to the hospital that night."

"Stop it."

"Yep. She said I was in the driveway struggling to get the car started when I passed out. She pulled me out and put me in the backseat. Then she grabbed a blanket from the trunk and wrapped me in it. I was still in my bra and panties."

"Yeah that's what the nurse told me."

"She pulled me out of the car and left me in front of the emergency room doors. Then she got out of there."

"Yeah, why the hell didn't she take you inside?"

"Because she'd have to be involved. I understood."

"Wow. Missy, I thought my world was crazy. This is some serious TV movie of the week shit we got going on here. When we get out of this mess we going to see Oprah or Tyler Perry or somebody!"

"Ok!"

"So you're not mad at her?"

"No, not at all. She's actually really in love…and I know he loves her back. After she left Ray came in and went ballistic when he found out she was gone. He was so upset he came in and tried to confront me."

"What did you do?!"

"The only thing I could do. I played dumb and doped up."

"Damn."

"Yeah. Maybe he went to find her. I don't know."

"But he left you for dead? Where's your housekeeper."

"He said she was on vacation, but he may have gotten rid of her. Who knows? I'm good, though. There's so much food around here, I have my TV and my music. I can hobble to the kitchen and the shower. I'm really just recuperating. When he comes back, I'll tell him I need to go to the doctor. But other than that, I'm fine."

"No Missy. You're not fine."

Brenda gasped when she saw Ray's face as he walked up behind Missy. Then the connection was lost.

To The Rescue

Brenda grabbed her keys and headed out the door. She knew she was taking a risk going to the house, but it was one she had to take. There was no telling what Ray had done to her sister by now.

She called PJ to let him know where she was going and to tell him to stay by the phone. Then she tore off into the night. Navigating through the neighborhoods of North Potomac, while in a panic was as frustrating as it was dangerous. The police were always lurking and the last thing she needed was a random D.W.B. stop. Driving While Black. The trip took twice as long as it should have, but she finally made it to the house.

Ray's car was parked right in front of the door. She didn't hear any commotion from the outside but she knew that didn't mean very much. Brenda braced herself and knocked on the door. It was open.

She walked in slowly, treading lightly. There was a door off the kitchen, and figuring it was the guest room Missy said she was holed up in, she walked over and opened it. The television was on but no one was there. She thought she heard some movement upstairs so she walked up, carefully and quietly trying to follow the sound. By the time she reached the top of the staircase, everything was quiet again.

One by one, she checked the rooms as she walked the long corridor. She figured the last one at the end with the double doors was the master bedroom. One of the doors was half open, so she eased inside, and before she could turn her head she heard a *click*.

Ray had her gun to her head. "I thought I told *you* not to come back to my fucking house." With the gun pointed at her face he backed her out of the room into the hall.

Brenda put both hands up above her head. "Listen Ray. I didn't come here for no shit with you. I came here alone and I do not have a weapon. I repeat. I DO NOT HAVE A WEAPON. I just came here to check on my sister. That's all. Now, where is she?"

"She's in the basement."

"Is she ok?"

"She's fine."

"Is it alright if I go down and see for myself?"

He lowered the gun and put it in his waist. "Knock yourself out." Then he slammed the bedroom door shut.

Brenda waited a couple seconds before she took to the stairs, leaping down them two by two in a panic. She had a horrible feeling in the pit of her stomach. Where was her sister and what the hell had he done to her! She ran around for a minute, frantically pulling on doors until she found the one leading to the basement. When she opened it and looked down the first thing that came to her mind was, *Damn, are these the steps he threw Missy down?* She called out. "Missy!"

There was no answer.

She hopped down both flights and opened the door to the theater room. "Missy!"

Startled, Missy nearly jumped out of her skin. "What?! Girl, you scared me!"

"No, you scared ME! What the hell happened? The last thing I saw was Ray walking up behind you and then the screen went blank."

"Oh, girl. The battery died on the laptop."

"The battery? Bitch! What happened? And please don't try to protect him, Missy. Tell me what *really* happened?"

"Ok, you are *way* too dramatic today. I swear to you Brenda, absolutely nothing happened."

"Well why didn't you call me back?!"

"I did. When Ray gave me my phone back, I called you and your phone went straight to voice mail. Is your phone charged?"

"Oh. No it's dead. It's on the charger in the truck."

"Ok, then don't try to lecture me on my battery life."

"Do you know that motherfucker just pulled MY gun on me?"

"He's an asshole. Don't worry about him."

"Don't worry? I could have had a fuckin heart attack, Missy! And why are you so calm? What happened when he came back? He wasn't mad? I expected to find you in here bleedin."

"Yeah, he was mad. Real mad. Mad that his little girlfriend was gone and mad that I was down in his precious little dungeon. He knew I had been in contact with Carlita because she was the only other person who had a key to this theater room."

"*Oh*, so y'all talked about Carlita?"

"Yes we did. Among other things. We have somewhat of an understanding now."

"What kind of understanding?"

"I can't go into the whole thing now…"

"Aww here we go again. What's with everybody and the fuckin mystery lately?"

"Look. I still don't trust Ray. No telling what kind of cameras he's got hidden around here watching and listening. You know he's a creep."

"True."

"There's not a whole lot to tell, really. In a nutshell, we have an arrangement that keeps my mouth shut and gets me paid. It also buys me some time."

"I thought you said he was broke, and time for what?"

"He's not *broke* broke, he's …'illiquid.' Cash poor. Not much in the bank, but he still has investments, and he has money he can get to if needed. Just not enough to get him out of the trouble he's gotten himself into. So he's rich people broke. It's different."

"Yeah I'm hip. So what's next? Are you really ok here with him Missy? Seriously."

"I wouldn't lie to you. Ray has too much to lose at this point. He won't bother me."

"You sitting here on the floor with your jaw on lock tryna tell me the muthafucka won't *bother you*? Girl, I can't with you."

"It's complicated."

"I hate when you say that."

"I know you do. But I've got it."

"I don't want to leave you here."

"Yes, I know you don't, but you have to so go. Pick up the kids. Make dinner. Do what you normally do on a weekday. I'm fine."

"So, you're staying down here? I thought this was his man cave."

"His man cave? Hmm. I'm having the locks changed first thing tomorrow and he'd better *not* bring his sorry self back down here to my woman COVE."

"Aaaah! And I know that's right!"

They slapped high fives and hugged it out.

"I love you, James girl," Brenda said.

"I love you, too, baby sis."

Brenda hit the stairs again running, eager to get home to hug her children. She imagined that day going in a whole different direction and at that moment was thrilled that Missy was still *somewhat* intact and that she wasn't in handcuffs. As soon as she opened the front door PJ was staring her in the face. Standing there with a gang of really masculine looking women behind her. They were wearing sneakers, carrying sticks and looking sour-faced.

"Wassup PJ? What you doing here?"

"We bout to nut up on that muthafucka that's what. Y'all aaight? He in 'nere?"

Brenda laughed so hard she could hardly breathe. As she leaned against one of the columns to keep herself upright, she thought *this is the ugliest bunch of bitches I have seen in my whole enTIRE life*. Nothing but big feet, big hands, bright lipstick and Adam's apples. And they were an-GRY. She couldn't wait to get back home so she could thank PJ for the best laugh she'd had in forever.

After she composed herself she assured PJ - and his gang - that everything was alright and promised him that she'd fill him in when they got back to her house.

When she got back to her truck her gun was sitting on the passenger seat. Pinky was back. It was time to get the hell outta there.

*****

PJ knocked on the door of Betty's house after all the drama. When Brenda opened the door, she could hardly contain her laughter.

"Miss P, what was up with that gang of buffarillas you was rollin with today? I'm just not understanding. I thought you was this chic and sophisticated socialite. That's how you rollin now?"

"Forget you Brenda. Them iz my gurlz. I roll with them bitches when I need to get it cranked up, cuz they go hard like that."

"You can say that shit again! HARD! Lawwwd."

"Whatever. Trust and believe they put in work. That's all that matters. And they cool so stop coming for my girls like that, before I have them come knocking on your front door."

"Shiiiit, I got Pinky locked and loaded boo boo."

"You got Pinky back? I thought Ray took it."

"He did. I got it back today."

"So what happened? What's going on with my big cousin?"

"Every fuckin thing. I swear I feel like we're all living a TV movie. I know we ain't the only people out here with drama, but the shit that's going on just seems unreal PJ. You want a drink?"

"Yes chile a stiff one. What you got?"

"I got some Kettle One and some orange juice?"

"You got any cranberry?"

"Nope."

"Ok. Screw drive me then."

Brenda poured two big goblets of screwdrivers and proceeded to fill him in. Once again, PJ was strangely unmoved by the whole situation, but Brenda thought that maybe he was just desensitized. God knew he had his own horror stories to tell.

"So now you know the whole story."

"Yeah. It's a tale. So what's next? What's her plan?"

"I don't know. She said to just wait on her to work it out...so that's what I'm doing. I don't like it. But that's what she wants, so we'll see. But right now, we gon get into what your issue is with Ray? I know you didn't gather up all those buffies just to rescue Missy. Ya'll wanted a piece of his ass. WHAT'S the beef?"

PJ sighed and looked away. Brenda could tell he was about to get really melodramatic. She didn't mind. "Miss P" was pure entertainment. And she wanted to the get the story, so she took a sip of her drink and settled in.

"Ok sweetie, I *really* hate talking about it because it always makes me emotional. So bear with me girl." PJ fanned his face with his both hands and took a deep breath. "Do you remember my friend Wendell?"

"Yeah, of course. The little red guy you used to hang with. The one with all them fine ass brothers? "

"That's him. *She* actually goes by Wendy now. Here's a good picture of her." PJ took out his phone and pulled up an album. Brenda scrolled through.

"Oh my God! He looks so much different now! Look at that body."

"She's fancy right? That's my baby. Lots of work done. Anyway, she moved down to Atlanta last year to be close to her boyfriend. He plays for the Falcons."

"Really? Who?"

"Never mind who he is. Just listen to the story. With your nosey ass. She took a job working as a concierge at the Ritz."

"I hear that place is really nice."

"It is. She used to put me up there whenever I visited. The place is fabulous. Well, about a week after Valentine's Day I got a call from Wendy's mother telling me she was in the hospital. She asked me if I would fly down to Atlanta with her to see her. When we got there, Wendy was in the ICU, barely clinging to life." PJ teared up. "Ugh. I'm sorry, girl."

Brenda took his hand to comfort him, as he fanned away his imaginary tears with a takeout menu.

"She was found in her apartment beaten and left for dead. The police didn't have any information and they didn't seem to care. The detectives that were working the case were clearly homophobic. As far as they both were concerned, this was just another fag that probably got what he asked for.

After a week, Wendy was still comatose, so all we could do was sit and wait – wait for her to come to so that maybe she could tell us something. I tried to do my own digging, but like I told you before, they are a really close-knit little society down there in Atlanta. If you don't have an 'in,' you're definitely outside of it all. I couldn't get anywhere.

I was finally able to get in contact with her boyfriend, but I couldn't get anything out of him either. He was way more concerned with protecting his identity than finding her attacker."

"How did you know it wasn't him?"

"I really didn't. But he seemed genuinely affected by what happened. I could tell he loved her. I just felt in my gut that it wasn't him."

"Well if he loved her so much why didn't he try to help you?"

"I just told you he wanted to protect himself...his wife...his kids...he's a football player."

"I see."

"Anyway, after two surgeries and a couple of weeks waiting by her bedside Wendy came out of the coma, but she still wasn't able to speak very well. She suffered a skull fracture that caused a hematoma on her brain. The doctors didn't think the effects of her head trauma were permanent, but she would need extensive and very expensive rehabilitation before she would walk and talk normally. It was devastating to see her like that. She had tubes coming out of everywhere and was having random seizures. It was the scariest thing I'd ever seen, and believe me, this girl has seen a lot.

Even though he never made it to the hospital, the boyfriend stepped up and foot the bill for all of it. I made sure of that. After a few weeks Wendy's mother had to get back to work so I promised her I would stay down there and take care of her. I wasn't leaving until my friend was better and until I found out exactly what happened to her. So I spent my days at the hospital and my nights trying to dig up anything I could on her attacker. I was there for almost a month before I got a single lead."

"So Ray was the one that beat her up?"

"You know what Brenda, you are a te-rri-ble listener. I've always told you that. Why can't you just listen!"

"Ok, ok. I know. I'm sorry. Go ahead."

"No, that's ok. You know everything. Why don't you tell *me* what happened next?"

"PJ! I said ok. I'm listening." Brenda made her dramatic hand gestures. "Look, I'm zipping my lips, lockin em' up, throwin away the key. See?"

He rolled his eyes. "Anyway. To make a very long story short, I did some more digging and was eventually told by a friend of a friend that it was Ray. I was able to confirm through the security cameras that Ray was in her building the night she was beaten."

"Well, why did he do it?"

He glared at Brenda, frustrated. "I don't know. Some bullshit about Wendy setting him up to get robbed. Apparently his apartment was broken into…and some jewelry and cash was stolen."

Brenda raised her hand as if she were sitting in a third grade classroom. "Umm, can I ask you a question?"

He sighed. "Why not?"

"Did she set him up?"

"YES! But that's not the fuckin point!"

Brenda burst out laughing. "Ok! Sorry, sorry, sorry. Go ahead."

"You laugh, but do you know how long it took that girl to get back? MONTHS of physical therapy, speech therapy, hell, psychotherapy! To this DAY, she slurs her speech and can't remember what happened to her. It's probably a good thing she doesn't remember what that muthafucka did to her." PJ stood and grabbed his purse. "Alright Brenda. I gotta get outta here."

"No! No, PJ. I'm sorry. I really didn't mean to be insensitive about your friend. Please don't go."

"No, it's fine. I have to go anyway. I have a date with the boyfriend, so I need to go get myself snatched and pulled together tightly before he gets home. I'll call you tomorrow." PJ leaned in and air kissed Brenda on either cheek.

"Ok, promise me you're not leaving because you're mad. I really am sorry about your friend."

"No. Never mad. Love you baby, bye bye."

With that, Miss P tossed her cashmere Burberry pashmina over her shoulder, placed her oversized sunglasses over her eyes and ever so dramatically flung open the porch door, catching the attention of the girls and boys on the outside. Her heels clicked and clacked loudly on the pavement. Brenda could see the red bottoms of her shoes with each exaggerated step she took back to her custom Range Rover, which was parked just far enough from the house for her to do a runway walk for the haters. She walked tall and proud and just swiftly enough to generate a breeze to blow through her mane.

Brenda couldn't help thinking how fabulous her cousin really was....and how vain. Miss P was a real live reality show. And she loved every minute of it.

I'm In Brazil Bitch!

Missy was in the kitchen making her lunch when she heard the doorbell. She hobbled over to see who it was.

A stern looking woman in an ill-fitted navy pantsuit stood in the doorway. "Good afternoon, Mrs. Coleman?"

"Yes, I'm Mrs. Coleman."

The woman flashed a badge. "I'm detective Karen Smith. Do you have a moment to talk?"

"Uh…Sure. Please, come in."

"Thank you." Detective Smith surveyed the house. "You have a beautiful home."

"Thank you so much. I'll pass along the compliment to the decorator. My husband."

"Really?"

"Yeah, all him. Most everything was like this when I got here."

"That's interesting. Not many women would give up *that* kind of control."

"Well, not many women are married to a man like Ray Coleman. So how can I help you, Detective…?"

"Smith."

"I'm sorry. I'm really terrible with names. Detective Smith, please have a seat."

"No worries. I'm here about your incident. Looks like you're recovering quite well by the way."

"I am, actually. Thank you."

"Yes ma'am. I've been out here a couple times before. But this is the first time I got an answer."

"Oh. Well we spend a lot of time in the basement. Sometimes it's hard to hear the bell down there."

The detective pulled out a notepad and began jotting. "I was able to catch up with your husband earlier today at his office. We spoke briefly."

"Oh? What did he have to say?"

"Not as much as I hoped he would. That's why I'm back here.

It seems crazy that it's taken us weeks to get in contact with you all. Why did you leave the hospital so soon?"

The question had Missy unnerved. She wasn't sure what to say which caused her to stammer over her answer. "W…Well…my husband thought – I mean, *we* thought – it would be better for me…to be here…at home."

"You both thought it would be better to leave the hospital to recover? One day after surgery?"

"Uh…yeah. We had a nurse here. It was fine. Just fine."

Detective Smith began to write in her pad again. "Mrs. Coleman, we need to talk about your attack."

"There's nothing to talk about. I'm sure my husband already told you that I don't remember what happened."

"Actually, he didn't tell me that. What he said was…" She flipped a page on her notebook, "…and I quote, 'You police are a fucking joke. I guess I'll have to find my wife's attacker myself.' Then he asked me to leave. That's why I'm here. Mrs. Coleman, we're not the enemy, and we can't help you unless you help us."

"Detective…?"

"Smith."

"Like my husband said, we can handle this ourselves."

"I don't think you understand. This is not something for *you* to handle. The minute you walked into that hospital, it became a police matter. Now whether or not you decide to cooperate with the investigation, Mrs. Coleman, that's your choice, but I will continue to investigate this matter until my superiors instruct me to do otherwise. Now, can you tell me anything about your attack? Your attacker? Anything at all?"

"Like I said Detective *Smith*." Missy got up from the sofa. "*I don't remember.*"

The detective stood, reached in her breast pocket and took out a card. "Well, if something should happen to jog your memory, because that tends to happen sometimes in cases like *these*…" The detective gave Missy a knowing glance. "…just give me a call. In fact, if you should find yourself in trouble, of *any* kind…"

Missy took the card. She didn't know if the lady was trying to help her on hit on her. "Good afternoon, Detective Smith."

"Good afternoon, ma'am."

The detective walked back to her car and set off down the driveway. Missy's hands were shaking. She sat back down on the sofa to gather her thoughts. What the fuck did she mean by *these* cases? Maybe she knew. Missy didn't appreciate being accused of hiding something…but then again she *was* hiding something. And where the hell was Ray? She was instantly agitated at the thought of him. His absence. He couldn't bother to call her and tell her that he spoke with the police. She had a good mind to call the detective and tell her what happened. But that wasn't the deal she made. It wasn't part of the plan.

As soon as the detective was out of her sight, she picked up the phone. There was half a ring and then she was sent to voicemail. She called again, and again she was sent to voicemail. She left a message.

"Ray, I don't know why you're not taking my calls, but I need to talk to you immediately. Not now, but right now. Dammit CALL ME BACK!"

Ten minutes later her phone rang.

"You raaang?"

"That's cute. A detective came by the house today."

"That Detective Smith?"

"Yes, that Detective Smith. What the hell did you say to her?"

"I didn't say shit to her. Why?"

"You told her *you* were going to find my attacker?"

"Oh, yeah. That's what I told her."

Missy could hear an intercom in the distance. "Ray, where are you?"

"What?"

"WHERE ARE you?"

"I'm at the airport."

"The airport? Going where?"

"Brazil."

"Oh. No! You mean I'm sitting here getting grilled by the police, trying to protect YOUR sorry ass, and you're on your way to Brazil to see your BITCH?"

"Come on, Missy. You know you don't give shit what I do."

"Wrong. I don't give a shit who you *fuck*. But you and I have an agreement, Ray. If you want me to keep doing my part, playing happy homemaker, then you need to stick to it and bring your happy ass home!

"You are really overreacting."

"You know what? I don't know *why* I'm doing this shit. It's not worth it. *You* are not worth it. Hello? Hello? Ray!?"

The call was dropped. She wondered if he had heard anything she said. Ray was half right. She really didn't give a shit what he did, but she'd be damned if she was going to continue to live a miserable lie while he was out sunbathing with his little she-man in Brazil. She wasn't trying to complicate her life any further by seeing someone else, but she was lonely. She needed a friend. Someone to talk to.

Someone that cared.

Hey Stranger

He picked up on the first ring.

"Hey Stranger. It's been a long time."

"Hooole up. Wait-a-min-nit. Is that my boo, Missy?"

"Yes Chucky. It's me. How have you been?"

"Miserable every day without you."

She laughed. "Will you stop it?"

"Alright, alright. I'm actually doing pretty good these days. Just got word that the network picked up my show for another season. You know I'm executive producer now, too."

"I know. I saw it on the credits. Congratulations. You deserve every good thing you're getting. You know that?"

"Thanks baby girl. That means a lot coming from you. So what made you dial my number? It's been a long time since you called *me*."

"It was an accident."

"An *accident*. Hmm."

The line went dead. Missy waited a couple minutes and called him again.

He picked up on the third ring. "I knew you loved me, girl."

"You're an asshole."

"And you're in denial."

"About what?"

"You want me don't you? Don't be shy. You might as well admit it. Shiiiit, if I was you, I'd want me too. I'm a handsome muufucka."

"Shut up. Act-u-al-ly, I just got a new phone and was transferring my contacts when your number popped up. So I decided to call and check up on you."

"Stop lyin. You know you miss a nigga. You want me to come over dere. Rock dat ass for old time's sake? You can say it. I won't talk bad about you."

Missy burst out laughing. "Chucky, you still play way too much. I'm really just checking up on you."

"Well, whatever the reason, I'm just glad to hear your voice again pretty girl. So how are you, really?"

"I'm good. Things are fine."

"Then why don't I believe you?"

"I don't know. You tell me since you got all the answers."

"Nah. Imma leave it alone...for now. So I hear you're a stepmom now. How's that going?"

"Good. I mean, I only get to see them a few times a month. But they're sweet kids. It's fine."

"There you go with that word again."

"What word?"

"*Fine.* Everything's *fine.* Usually when people use that word too much, things ain't really fine. So what's the deal?"

"Damn! What's with you? Everything in my life is good, Chucky. Can't I just call a friend without getting interrogated?"

"Calm down, girl. Yes, you can. I was just messin with you."

"Ok."

"Missy I have to take a conference call in a few minutes. Do you think we can meet for lunch this week?"

"Um...no."

"Why not?!"

"Because I'm *married.*"

"Come on girl. Since when can't an attractive woman and a handsome, funny, rich, successful, extremely well-endowed black man, have a platonic lunch together. Now if we happen to end up back at my house, butt nekkid on my living room floor, you know. That's just a bonus."

"You never quit, do you? Ok, yes. Lunch, Wednesday at one o'clock. Meet me at Loriel Plaza and do not be late."

"Looking forward to it, pretty lady."

"See you soon."

Missy hung up the phone and smiled. She was really looking forward to seeing her old boo. Having a little outlet. A familiar face. Some fresh conversation. A fucking laugh. But the most important question in her mind. What was she going to wear?

For The Good Times

Brenda was in a pretty good mood. She had a lot going on and a lot coming up. MJ was at home and in good spirits. Brandy, thank goodness, had just broken up with her little boyfriend that she was getting *way* too serious with. Mandy wasn't whining for a change, and Aunt Pat was coming home in two days, just in time for Thanksgiving.

She would be staying in a halfway house for a few months then coming to Betty's house to live. Brenda was really looking forward to finally getting to know her aunt. She was also looking forward to having another adult in the house to talk to since uncle Larry barely left the basement.

The family was finally coming together, and it was happening without Melvin and Betty. Very bittersweet. Brenda really missed her husband and her mother. Losing them just a few months apart was devastating, but there was so much other drama going on she hardly had time to grieve.

Thanksgiving was just days away. The first holiday without them. She knew it would be hard, but she also knew that she could get through it as long as she had her family around her. And as long as nobody let Aunt Bessie bless the food again this year.

The last Thanksgiving, Betty's crazy baby sister gave a 20-minute blessing that ended with her catching the Holy Ghost and speaking in tongues. All while holding a lowball full of Crown Royal. She jumped up and down and not a drop spilled on the floor. Brenda thought she would definitely have to remember to get Uncle Edward to do the prayer this year.

Missy had agreed to come to dinner. It would be her first time being back home for Thanksgiving since she went away for college. That was also a bittersweet thought because she knew it was the thing that would have made Betty the happiest. But there was no sense in dwelling on that. Things were the way they were and everyone would have to figure out a way to deal with them, as they were.

Missy seemed to be dealing pretty well lately. She seemed happy. Apparently whatever plan she and Ray had concocted was well underway and she was good with it. She and Ray were in the media pretty regularly. They were photographed together at the Skin's games, charity events, red carpet events. They even did a short segment together on Fox 5 morning news promoting Ray's foundation for underprivileged kids in sports. Missy was ever the doting and supporting wife. They *looked* happy.

All things considered, whatever Ray promised her must have really been something big because she was earning it for sure. Brenda was dying to know what it was, but she promised not to pry. Missy said she knew what she was doing so that was that.

Thanksgiving was interesting, to say the least. Brenda set up a banquet table in the basement since it was the only space that would accommodate all 18 guests.

There was Brenda and her three children. Brenda was drinking Kettle One martinis like water, Mandy was whining, MJ had the munchies so he was complaining that dinner was late and Brandy was sitting quietly in a corner, looking sad. Uncle Edward and Aunt Carolyn were arguing about nothing as usual, and Uncle Larry was on his second bumper of Schlitz Malt Liquor, so it was only a matter of time before he started to show out.

Aunt Bessie came with her hands-y old husband Floyd who got drunk on every possible occasion and felt somebody up. Then you had Aunt Pat who walked in fresh off a 23-year prison bid looking like a grown ass man. Sitting across from her, but not speaking to her, was her only son PJ, aka "Miss P," who was hopped up on a mix of ecstasy and estrogen, more beautiful than any girl in the room.

Each of the Pats were accompanied by their significant other – a pleasantly plump Mexican mamacita named Consuela and a tall potbellied Persian man named Ahmed in custom Armani, a Rolex Presidential and the pocket mark dots of a tragic hair plug experiment that PJ talked him into.

Next there was August and September James, Brenda's 25-year-old ghetto fabulous cousins from the Westside of Baltimore who showed up to Thanksgiving dinner without so much as a phone call. They were identical twins born a minute apart as August turned into September. Both strippers and professional boosters so they came to dinner with a trunk full of hot merchandise to sell just in time for Black Friday. One never did anything without the other and neither of them did anything good to speak of.

They brought a burned-out looking young girl with them that was obviously one of their coworkers from the looks of her outfit. A 20-inch blonde weave, 6-inch platforms with a clear heel, and a velour bodysuit with cutouts that revealed she was missing her undergarments. Her name was Precious. She walked across the room like she was working for tips and the men were trying their level best not to stare at her ass as it jumped, wiggled and jiggled from the north to the south. Uncle Floyd could barely keep his hands to himself and Aunt Bessie was trying hard to bite her tongue. The tension was mounting.

Aunt Carolyn's eyes darted back and forth from Precious' ass to what she thought was Uncle Edward's sneaky peripheral peeking. It didn't take a rocket scientist to figure out she was going to blow at some point during the evening. Most likely after she finished the whiskey swirling around the glass in her hand. Brenda kept a close eye on her.

Last and very late, but not least, there was Missy who showed up just as Aunt Bessie caught the Holy Ghost over the fried turkey. Lagging a few steps behind her was a very handsome and very famous young man whose last name *wasn't* Coleman. It was her ex and one of the funniest men on TV, Chucky Wilson.

Brenda thought, *so this is why Missy has been smiling so much lately.* She couldn't wait to corner her after dinner and find out what was really going on. But for now she was focused on keeping the tension down in the room. Aunt Carolyn was eyeballing Precious, and she wasn't being the least bit discreet about it.

A few sarcastic comments from Aunt Carolyn and a few off-color jokes from Chucky aside, dinner went pretty well. Everyone enjoyed the food, and there weren't any major arguments. She'd planned perfectly and the food was ready on time-ish. Brenda's first solo Thanksgiving was a win.

While most of the women stayed downstairs to wrap up food, nibble and chat, the guys went upstairs to watch the football game.

The James girls laughed and talked for hours. They had the best time reminiscing about old times. Missy was fitting right back into the fold, and Brenda couldn't have been happier. She was still itching to catch Missy alone to talk, but the family time was way more important...for the moment.

Aunt Carolyn excused herself to go upstairs and check on the men and two minutes later all hell broke loose. They heard a crash, and screaming. All of the ladies went running upstairs to see what the commotion was.

When they got upstairs, Aunt Carolyn had Precious by her hair punching her in the face while the rest of the family tried desperately to pull her off the girl. Once they got them apart, and gave Precious back her hair, Aunt Carolyn calmed down enough to tell what happened.

Apparently when she got upstairs, the football game was off and the stereo was playing while Precious was giving out lap dances. According to Aunt Carolyn, Uncle Edward was waiting his turn and according to him he was doing "no-such-a-thing". He just kept saying, "Carolyn I can't control what other folks is doin now." To that she replied, "Edward you know you was sittin there waitin for that little girl to sit on yo lap! I saw it in yo *FACE*! And Floyd, you know you oughtta be *SHAMED* at what you was doin! All y'all mens need to be shamed a yoself!"

Brenda knew she had to do something to diffuse the situation. She walked around picking up the dollar bills scattered around the living room and she moved the tables out of the way. Then she put her iPod on the dock. She had a special Thanksgiving day playlist that she knew would get the family together.

When those familiar horns from the intro to Frank Beverly and Maze's "Before I Let Go" blasted through the speakers she grabbed Uncle Larry by the hand and attempted to get the party started. The guitar from Al Green's "Love and Happiness" got Aunt Bessie and Uncle Floyd going, and the sweet percussion from Marvin Gaye's "Got to Give It Up" got everybody up on their feet.

Aunt Carolyn was in the kitchen putting the food away, still cursing about the little stripper girl. Brenda walked in and pulled her out of the kitchen by her arms. "Come on Aunt Carolyn, you knoooow this is our song." Carolyn resisted initially, but Marvin could always win her over.

The soul train line was taking formation and the James family was having a good ol' time. For the first time in a long time Brenda had forgotten about her problems and everybody else's. She was happy. It was a good day indeed.

*****

Brenda called Missy first thing the next morning. "Rise and

shine, big sis!'"

Missy peered over at her alarm clock, through blurry hangover eyes. "Brenda why are you calling me so early in the morning? It's four o'clock."

"Cause I'm about to go out and do my Black Friday shopping. I just couldn't wait to talk to you. Sooooo what's up with you and Chucky? You didn't tell me you were bringing a *date* to Thanksgiving dinner."

"Oh, it was last minute, and Chucky is not a *date*, Brenda, he's a friend."

"Not the way you used to talk about him. I was way too young for you to be telling me this, but I distinctly remember you calling him a donkey dick? You said he was the best thing you ever had. So tell me, is it still good to you gurrrl?"

Missy laughed at the donkey reference. "I did say that didn't I. Well he *is* blessed, that's for sure, but unlike my husband, I do not cheat, so I wouldn't know what it's like now."

"Swear on ma."

"I'm not doing that. But seriously, Chucky is sweet and he loves me to death but we really are just friends. He's helping me get through my mess of a life right now. I appreciate him for that."

"Yeah. I bet you do."

"Brenda."

"Well, it's very obvious how he feels about you. Just be careful. Don't hurt him, Missy."

"That's the last thing I would do. He knows where we stand."

"So I see you've been gallivanting about town with your husband. Is that part of your little *agreement?*"

"Something like that."

"I would ask how you're doing but you seem really happy. Chucky really cracks you up, huh?"

"Oh yes. If nothing else, that man can make me laugh."

"Well they say laughter is the quickest way to a girl's heart. Or is it the *D?* I forget."

"You have dirty mind."

"Let me ask you this. Could you see yourself with him?"

"Brenda...I told you..."

"No, I don't mean right now. In general. Like later on down the line. Could you see yourself with him?"

"Well...I don't know...maybe. Under the right circumstances, I guess."

"You mean being divorced from your gay husband?" Brenda laughed.

"Too soon Brenda."

"I know. Sorry. Couldn't resist. Well I don't wanna keep you up sissy, and I gotta pick up Carolyn and Bessie so we can get to this damn mall."

"Black Friday indeed. I have never wanted anything bad enough to wait in line at the crack of dawn in the cold. You all have fun."

"Yeah well us po folk gotta do what we gotta do. Times is tough. But you'on know nuttin bout dat do you punkin. *You* rich"

"Goodbye Brenda."

"Bye."

After cursing the existence of Black Friday, Missy replaced the satin sleep mask over her eyes and pulled the covers back up to her neck. She was sleepy as hell.

Facepaging Blues

Brandy was in pure agony over her breakup with Tay. It had been almost two months since she walked out on him, and she missed him every second of every day. She wanted to call him so bad. Just to hear the sound of his voice. But when she thought about him and Keisha together, those urges dissipated.

She could never go back to him. Even if Keisha's baby wasn't his, he had humiliated her, slept with her best friend, and been stupid enough to do it unprotected KNOWING what a ho she was. It was crazy. She thought she knew him.

Brandy had so many questions in her head. When did it happen, where did it happen and how many times? Was it before they got together, was it after, or both? Who knew about it? Were people smiling in her face knowing it was going on the whole time?

As for Keisha, after everything that happened she had no remorse. They'd been friends since they played in the sandbox together, and she hadn't offered an explanation or apology for her betrayal. In fact, she was hard at work throwing salt on Brandy's open wounds.

She spread a ton of false rumors trying to get their friends to pick sides. Told everyone that Tay was hers first and Brandy was the one who tried to take him from her first. Things had gotten so bad that Brandy stopped using social media. She couldn't handle seeing one more picture of a sonogram, or one more play by play account of Keisha's doctor's visits. The baby shower talk on Facepage, the hinting at the sex of the baby on Instapic. It was all too much.

Michelle was ever the supportive friend, responding to every one of Keisha's posts with a threat of bodily harm. She publicly declared that she was going to beat Keisha's ass again as soon as her baby dropped. Probation or not. And she meant it. As far as Brandy was concerned, Keisha Thomas wasn't worth the trouble.

As many questions as she had, Brandy never gave Tay the opportunity to explain himself. He tried by voice mail dozens of times after the incident, but she never returned his calls. Once he admitted that he'd slept with *her*, everything else was irrelevant. Or so she told him. He had betrayed her trust, and that was that.

Eventually, he just stopped calling. Well, after Brenda cursed him out and MJ threatened to kill him if he ever knocked on their door again. He got the message because ten days, seven hours and thirty or forty minutes had passed since she'd heard anything from him (by her last count). The very last message he left said that his grandmother died and his mother was back home, so he was going back to Frederick to spend Thanksgiving with her. He said he wouldn't be back until after the New Year and he wished her a happy holiday.

Brandy told herself that she didn't care, but that was a lie. She was still hurting, and didn't know how to deal with it. She needed *something* to make her feel better. Someone. Anything.

The day after Thanksgiving, she saw Keisha for the first time since the day she found out about the "cheatation". Brandy was with her mother and great aunts in Walmart. Keisha was there in the baby section with two of her skanky cousins from the south side.

From what the gossips were saying, Keisha was about six months pregnant. She was definitely showing. When she saw Brandy, Keisha and her girls started laughing loudly and talking about the baby. Taunting her.

Brandy really wanted to walk over and punch her in the face, but she decided not to even feed into the drama. She didn't want to give the bitch the satisfaction and definitely didn't want to give the gossips more to talk about. So she asked her mother for the keys and went to sit in the car for a while. Seeing Keisha was just too much to handle and she needed to get away before she was provoked.

When she got to the car and turned on the radio, the Christmas carols were in full swing. Sleigh bells ringin and mommy's kissin on santa. Happy music that made her incredibly sad. She flipped the station away from the holidays and caught the tail end of "Spend My Life With You." It was her and Tay's song. She couldn't bring herself to change the station, so she listened. And then she cried.

What was it about Keisha that he just had to have? All that time she thought Tay was a good guy, but he wasn't. That's what he pretended to be. He was just like the rest of them. No good. Just trying to get some ass. There was a light bulb moment. She thought, *that's why he was holding out. He was probably fucking Keisha the whole damn time.*

Brandy felt like her whole relationship was a lie and that made her cry even harder; so loudly that a passerby came over to check on her. "Young lady, are you alright?" She assured the old man that everything was ok and tried her best to compose herself.

Over an hour later she was still waiting on her mother and aunts to re-emerge from their Black Friday frenzy. Bored and desperate to get her mind off the drama, she decided to log back onto Facepage and see what her friends were up to. She'd intended to delete Keisha and anyone who was friends with her so she wouldn't see anything from her ever again, but her curiosity got the best of her. She went to Keisha's page.

The profile picture had just been changed to a picture of her holding up a teeny tiny pair of denim coveralls with a matching baseball cap. The caption read, "It's a boy!" She had clearly just taken the picture in Walmart and posted it.

A glutton for punishment, Brandy couldn't resist the urge to flip through Keisha's photo albums once more before deleting her. Going through her photos was torturous. One album was titled "My Little Family" and there were at least a dozen photos of her baby bump. Every outfit was two sizes too small to accentuate it.

The sonogram was prominently featured, and there was also a picture of Tay sitting in what appeared to be the waiting room of a doctor's office. Apparently, he had gone to the doctor with her. It was hard to tell, but it didn't seem like he was aware the picture was being taken. The caption read, "That's just my baby daddy." Typical.

It made Brandy wonder what was really up with the two of them. Could they really be together? Of course Keisha would love for her to believe that, but she would need proof before she'd believe. Sex is one thing, but would Tay really *be* with a girl like Keisha? Claim her as his girlfriend? Not the Tay she knew, but then again, the Tay she *thought* she knew would never have touched Keisha's ratchet ass in the first place.

As she scrolled through the rest of the pictures, growing more emotional with each intentionally hurtful caption, she heard familiar voices. It was Keisha and her cousins coming out of the store. They were loud and animated as usual. Pushing a cart filled with tons of baby junk.

Brandy slunk down low in the back seat. The last thing she needed was for them to see her swollen eyes and red face. They passed the car and then their voices started to trail off. Thankfully they weren't parked close by. When she felt they were far enough away not to notice her, she lifted her head. She couldn't believe what she saw.

They were getting into Tay's car. The car that was his prize possession. The same car that he washed every week and kept a cover on. The car that he wouldn't even allow his own brother to drive. She watched them speed recklessly through the parking lot with the music on full blast. Still laughing at her no doubt. So there she had it. They were really together. Brandy thought she couldn't be more hurt than the day she found out the truth. But she was wrong.

She was quiet on the ride home. Brenda noticed her through the rear view, trying to hide her face with her scarf.

"Brandy what's wrong with you?"

"Huh? Nothing ma."

Brenda knew exactly what the problem was. The aunts were also in the loop. Aunt Carolyn chimed in.

"Baby. You young. There's gon be plenty more boys to cry for. Trust me. So don't let that lil boy worry you like that. You a purdy girl and you smart. You gon be ok. Hear?"

Brandy managed a half smile, but she wished everyone would just leave her the hell alone. When she got home, she went straight to her room and cried. Then she tore out every page of her diary that had Tay's name on it. He didn't deserve to be in there.

Trying to get her mind off her drama, and avoid Brenda asking anymore questions, she decided to sit in her window and people watch for a little while, just until she got herself together. There was always something interesting happening on the block. An argument, a scuffle, some tall tales being told. It was as good as any other way to pass the time.

Two of her classmates were sitting on crates not far from her bedroom window with one of the older corner boys. He was telling big lies, and they were eating it all up. After a while, they walked off, and some older guys sat down and lit up a blunt. Brandy hated the smell. She wanted to close her window, but the conversation was getting interesting.

One of them mentioned a big fight party that was happening that night. She listened a little closer and discovered that the party was going to be at Tay's house. She thought that would be just the thing to get her through her drama. What better way to show folks that she didn't give a good goddamn about Tay and his baby mama than to show up at his house while he wasn't there and chill with the big boys?

The more she thought about it, the better the plan sounded in her head. She'd walk in looking pretty hot and tempting. The boys would fight their way over to her. She'd dance a little, flirt a little. Take a few pics and pass out her number. Daye would report every dirty detail to Tay, and it would drive his ass crazy.

Even better, it would get back to Keisha that she was there and that would definitely drive her ass crazy wondering if there was something still going on with Tay. Brandy smiled to herself. That was it. That was the plan.

So she went through her closet looking for just the right outfit to give that bitch a good stomach pang. She would have no problem getting Michelle to tag her in a photo on Facepage the next day. She thought, *Tonight is going to be fun!*

Cards On The Table

Missy and Ray had been getting along remarkably well, under the circumstances. Mostly because he spent so much time away from the house. In a few short months, they'd come to a very comfortable place in their relationship. Not quite a friendship but a comfortable place just the same.

At that point, their marriage was all about the PR. Missy played the role of the good wife, and Ray worked hard to bolster his family man image, hoping to land himself the gig of a lifetime – a gig that would put him back on the map and get him out of financial trouble.

This was all part of their arrangement. Ray had agreed to give her pretty much everything she originally tried to extort from him, on the condition that she would do everything in her power to help get him back on financial footing.

Between his spending habits, gambling and tax debt, Ray was seriously in the red. In fact, he faced the possibility of tax evasion charges if his upcoming audit didn't go the right way. Knowing what he knew, chances were it wouldn't go the right way and when it didn't he needed to make sure he had enough cash on hand to repay the government and pay his bills.

Missy had no idea that Ray was in any financial trouble before Carlita dropped that little tidbit on her. Hearing it for the first time was jarring, to say the least. She confronted Ray on it directly because with everything else she had to put up with in their shitty sham of a union, broke-ness was an absolute deal breaker. She thought, no money, no mas. Simple as that.

During her confinement to the house, Missy had a whole lot of time to reflect on her life and how it had gotten to the horrible point it was; on how and why she was behaving like such a coward. After all, he was just a man. A big man, yes, but like Brenda said, he bled red blood just like errybody else.

Missy decided that she'd put up with his abuse for the last damn time, and the next time he raised a fist or even cursed her he would regret it. She'd make sure of it.

The day he came back from his little hiatus and caught her on his laptop skyping Brenda, he tried it. His usual scare tactics. Standing over her, staring her in the face making threats. When she didn't respond to him in the manner he was accustomed, he raised his hand. Before he could get it halfway down, he swallowed the entire contents of a key chain-sized container of mace.

As he coughed, gagged, screamed and squirmed around on the ground, Missy covered her face with a bath cloth and hobbled out of the office, locking the door behind her. Ray cursed her for a good ten minutes, and when it seemed that he had calmed down she thought it was time to address her issues.

She yelled them through the door. "So, you ready to talk now or what?"

"Bitch! I swear to God, when I get my fucking hands on you–"

"Ray please. Save that shit for somebody else. I already called the police, and they'll be here any minute. Now that I know your ass is BROKE, I really don't give a shit. I'm sending your broke ass to jail."

There was dead silence on the other side of the door.

"So how's your little girlfriend, Carlita?" she said.

She waited a moment, unlocked the door and opened it. He ran out of the office and into the bathroom to splash some water on his face. When he finally came out he asked, between coughs. "Did you really call the police?"

"No, but I did call my sister, and if I don't call her back in the next fifteen minutes to let her know I'm ok, the police *will* be here." That was a lie.

"Did you really have to spray me with fucking mace?"

She looked down at her arm in the sling and then back at Ray. "Do you really have to ask me that?"

Ray was still hacking and coughing. The mace was still burning like someone had set his face on fire.

Missy hobbled back into the office and sat down at the desk. "Come on in here and have a seat. We have a lot to discuss."

Ray coughed, "Damn! You mind if I go and take a shower. Wash this fuckin fire off my face?!"

Missy grunted. "If you must. I'll be down here when you're done. Waiting."

That night they talked for hours. So many tears shed, so much wine consumed. Virtually every emotion that could be felt or expressed by a human being had been displayed that night. There were major confessions, brutal truths, shocking revelations.

By the end of their talk, Ray had admitted that he married her on the advice of his agent, Matt, and Missy admitted that she didn't really love him when she married him. Ray couldn't risk the public knowing about his tranny love, and for Missy, Ray was a good look. Basically, they both fit the other's proverbial bill.

Ray admitted that he was already deeply in love with Carlita when they married, and Missy admitted that she almost backed out of the wedding after seeing Chucky the night of her bachelorette party. Ray admitted Carlita was in St. Maarten the week of their wedding and he spent the night before the wedding with her. Missy threw her goblet of red wine in his face.

Missy relived her abuse for him. The battery, the verbal abuse, the cruel way he reminded her that she couldn't bear children. She needed him to know how much he had hurt her, and she wanted to know why. After talking to him for a while she figured it out.

Ray Coleman was a consummate asshole, that much was true, however Missy understood that she was nothing more than collateral damage in his war with his own sexual identity. No matter how beautifully adorned she was, at the end of the day her husband was hopelessly in love with another man and trying desperately not to identify with his homosexuality. Separating himself from other gay men because he didn't consider Carlita a man. Yet he couldn't love her in the open. He was a tortured soul.

It wasn't long before Missy began to empathize with him. He was deeply in love with someone that he wasn't supposed to love. Engaging in activities that he believed to be perverse before all this Carlita business happened. Ray was essentially a homophobic homosexual, and he didn't know how to deal with those thoughts and feelings, so he took them out on the closest person to him - her. She got that. She didn't appreciate it, but she got it.

In response to her strong assertion that a man could not be with another man and not be gay, Ray opened up to Missy like he had never done. With anyone. He let it all loose. His feelings and all of his insecurities were laid out on the stained glassed coffee table with the decanter of vintage red they conversed over.

That night, Ray swore that he had never ever had a relationship with a man before meeting Carlita. He reiterated, tearfully, that he was not a gay man. He was just in love with a woman who hadn't had the change.

Of course, Missy needed a more in depth explanation, or rationalization, justification, summation, and any other "ation" that would make some sense of the bullshit that was coming out of his mouth. She knew very well that it would be as difficult for her to hear as it would be for him to say, but she had to know, and in detail. So they uncorked another bottle of their finest Bordeaux from the cellar, and he began at the very beginning.

Fight Night

Brandy knocked on the door. There was no answer, but she could hear people inside. Obviously, they couldn't hear her so she started kicking it. A few minutes later Daye flung the door open.

"Damn Brandy! What the fuck you kickin on my door like that for!"

"Oh, my bad."

"Tay ain't here. He outta town."

"I know. I gotta be here for Tay? I came here to chill like everybody else. Watch the fight."

Daye looked at her. He had never seen her dressed like this before. Her white down coat was wide open and underneath she was wearing a midriff sweater and low rise jeans. Her red thong popping out of the top.

She was smiling and batting her little lashes. He couldn't tell if she was trying to flirt or not, but the fight had just started, so he wasn't about to stand there and try to figure it out. He walked off leaving her standing in the doorway.

Brandy let herself in and closed the door behind her as Daye ran back down to the basement. She hung back a bit. Everything looked as it did the last time she was there. They hadn't even changed the curtains. The padlock on Tay's door was secured but she still had the combination. So she let herself inside.

Not much had changed there either. His space was neat as usual. The comforter set he bought for her birthday was still on his bed. His shoes were neatly lined up by the window, and his collection of designer colognes were arranged according to height on his dresser. She stopped in her tracks.

There on his dresser sat a copy of a sonogram. The same one from Facepage. She felt a lump in her throat and wanted to cry but she fought back the tears as hard as she could. Brandy refused to waste anymore of her tears. The relationship was over anyway. She thought, *fuck him and her. As a matter of fact, fuck that baby, too.* She was done.

For a second, she contemplated just going back home, but the more she thought about it, the angrier she got and the more she wanted to piss *him* off. It was *his* turn to be upset. To wonder what's going on with *her*. So she headed on toward the basement, intent on turnin up and memorializing her good time for the Facepagers. It would be her final *fuck you* to her bff, and Brandy planned on making it a good one.

She walked downstairs and could barely see the steps in front of her for the thick cloud of smoke that filled the room. The basement was packed like a sardine can and hot as hellfire. She took off her coat and threw it on the bed in the spare room. Then she went in the bathroom to check herself out before joining the party.

Brandy couldn't help admiring herself in the mirror. Her hair was tight, and her nails were freshly done. Just enough eyeliner, just enough mascara and a whole lotta her mama's glossy pink Mac lip glass. There was just enough of her red thong peeking from the top of her low-rise Seven jeans to make the boys wonder. The faux belly button ring was on display, attached to a belly chain so it was impossible to miss. She was perfect. Sexy. Ready to party.

She stepped back out into the smoke-filled room. All eyes were on the big screen TV. There were mostly guys there, maybe ten, or so. She immediately recognized one of the girls, who wasn't exactly a girl. It was the Chinese lady Miss Kim that used to work in the convenient store by the elementary school. She was sitting on Daye's lap, and they were passing a blunt back and forth. Weird.

There were a couple other girls that she had never seen in the neighborhood. They were older, and kinda skanky lookin. Not being a big boxing fan, Brandy stood in a corner and observed. She was really just waiting for a good opportunity for a photo op. Then maybe she'd leave. The smoke was getting to her and nobody was talking to her anyway.

One of the old girls went into a refrigerator in the corner and pulled out a punch bowl with a lime green concoction. She sat it on the table next to Brandy, dipped a plastic red cup in and took a taste. "Umh." Then she went back into the refrigerator, pulled out a big glass bottle and poured the entire contents into the punch bowl. She winced at the second taste. "Uhm! Yaaasss. You want some?"

Brandy looked around to see who she was speaking to. "Who me? No, I don't drink."

The girl said, "For real? Ok, then I got somethin for you. Hold on." She walked over to a cooler in a corner and pulled out a tray with a bunch of little colorful cups on it.

"Here try one of these."

"What's that?"

"It's Jell-O. Just try it. It's real good. It's like nothin is even in it."

Brandy didn't quite understand what she was saying, but she didn't see anything wrong with having some Jell-O. "Do you have a spoon?"

The old girl laughed. "No girl, just throw it in your mouth. Like this." She tilted her head back and squeezed the little plastic cup until the Jell-O fell down her throat.

Brandy grabbed one of the cups and followed suit. She thought, *This isn't too bad. A little bitter, but pretty good Jell-O.*

Seven or eight little cups later, she was getting dizzy. The smoke was in her throat and she coughed until the old girl handed her something to drink. Brandy thought, *Dang that stuff's good too. And so pretty.*

Everybody seemed to be having so much fun and despite the mild dizziness, she was having a pretty good time herself. Just people watching.

She'd heard some of the funniest conversations. One of the girls kept talking about how good the punch was and how it tasted like Jolly Ranchers candy. Brandy thought, *that's what it tastes like. Jolly Ranchers.* She dipped the big red plastic cup back inside and took a sip. It was SO good to her and damned if it didn't taste just like apple Jolly Ranchers. Nothing like the stuff she and Keisha drank when they snuck into grandma Betty's liquor cabinet. She filled up her cup one more time and finished watching the people that were watching the fight.

After the fight, the after party was in full effect. They turned the music up and the lights off. The only light in the room was a strobe light that flickered annoyingly. Brandy was feeling good but still a little dizzy. Someone offered her a pull on a blunt. She was still coherent enough to decline. Barely. "Nooooo, no, I don't smoke."

The guy passed the blunt to someone else then he grabbed her hand and started to dance with her. A few seconds later, he and his friend had her in a sandwich humping her to the rhythm of the latest Lil Wayne.

Her head was beginning to spin, but she was still on her feet trying to move to the music. Wannabe rappers screamed the lyrics to every rap song as if they were front row at a concert. She blacked out momentarily and when she came to, she was lying on the couch. Her eyes closed again and when she came to she was in a bed. She could feel hands on her, pulling at her clothes, but she was helpless to stop it. She screamed, or at least she thought she screamed, but then again she wasn't sure if it was just in her head. She heard voices, laughter. And then she blacked out again.

When Brandy woke up again, it was morning. A ray of sunlight shone through the small window of the basement level bedroom. She was wearing a bra and nothing else. Her head was pounding, and her mouth was as dry as sand. She tried to lift herself off the bare mattress, but it was hard because she had slept on her arm and it had fallen totally asleep. Her body ached all over and there was blood dried on the inside of her legs. She didn't remember what happened, but she knew exactly what happened.

She folded her legs to her chest and started to cry. The cries were loud and desperate, and her whole body shuddered. She thought, *How could I let this happen? Why would I ever put myself in this position?* Her mind flashed back to her getting dressed for the party then to her dancing with a drink in her hand. She wasn't sure, but she thought she remembered smoking something at some point during the night.

The house was eerily quiet. Realizing that she was the only person in the basement, she finally eased out of the bed. Her jeans were lying in the corner on the floor, but her shirt and panties were nowhere to be found. Then she started to panic thinking her mother would be walking the streets looking for her. She'd probably called the police by then.

Brandy didn't know what to do. Her purse and her cell phone were gone. She had no idea what time it was. She pulled on her pants, as painful as that was, and searched around the filthy basement for her shirt and coat. She never found them.

She walked upstairs and looked around. The house seemed empty. Daye's door was closed, but when she walked past his room she could hear someone inside. Brandy didn't want to see him, or anyone. So she moved as quietly as she could toward Tay's room.

She went into his room thinking she could grab a sweatshirt from his closet. As soon as she walked in she saw the sonogram, still sitting there on top of the dresser, mocking her. She screamed and threw everything off of the dresser onto the floor. Then she fell onto the floor and started to cry again.

The sonogram landed on the floor right beside her. She picked it up and studied it for a second. Then she tore it into tiny pieces and threw it back on the floor. Sitting on the edge of the bed, consumed with grief and heartache, haunted by Tay's essence that was still so prominent in the room, she thought, *Tay and this baby is ruining my fuckin life!*

Over The Edge

Brenda knocked on the bedroom door.

"Brandy?"

"Yes!"

"Can you open the door please?"

"Ma, I told you I don't feel good."

"Girl, if you don't open this damn door! This is not just your room. Your sister wants to go to bed."

Brandy got up, opened the door and slumped back into the bed. "Why can't she sleep in your bed?"

"Cause she can't. That's why. What's going on with you? You've been in this room for a whole week. You not eatin, you not talkin. What's wrong? That lil boy still got you upset?"

"No ma. I just don't feel good."

"Every day for a week? Don't bullshit me, Brandy. What's wrong? Talk to me."

"I just told you! Nothing! Now can I please be left alone? *Please?*"

"I know you better watch your tone with me. You lucky I got someplace to be. Do you have my lip gloss?"

"What lip gloss?"

"The pink Mac gloss I just bought."

With the mention of that damned lip gloss, Brandy's mind went instantly back to the fight night. "No, I don't have it." It was the truth. Whoever stole her purse had it now.

"Ok, well look out for your sister. I'll be back in a few hours. Call my cell if y'all need anything, but Aunt Pat'll be here in a little while."

"Ok." Brandy turned over and pulled the covers back over her head.

Brenda was on her way out for drinks with her girlfriend Tina. She was looking good and feeling even better. Things were finally calming down. No one was sending out any distress calls, and at the moment no one needed her for anything.

Things weren't perfect, far from it, but she felt like she could exhale a little and enjoy a night out with her girl to catch up. Maybe talk about somebody else's drama for a change.

She checked herself out in the full-length mirror one last time. Five foot seven with smooth cocoa brown skin, incredible full lips and big beautiful brown eyes that sparkled amber in the right light. She wore an ample triple D brassiere and had a full forty-four-inch booty to match. All natural beauty in a time where women were literally risking life and limb on operating tables and in secret hotel rooms to replicate her curves.

There had been so much going on in the last few months she'd lost her appetite and a subsequent sixteen pounds. It suited her well, as did the uncharacteristically sexy body conscious dress she donned for the evening. Black, sleeveless and low-cut, the dress hugged every curve just right and for the first time in her life she was completely comfortable with herself. Confident in all her glorious curviness. Owning it unabashedly. She thought, tonight they will stare, and this time I will let them.

She grabbed her purse and hit the stairs. "Bye Brandy!" When she opened the front door Aunt Pat was standing there with her key in hand.

"Hey hey hey! What's poppin Auntie?"

"Well well. Don't *you* look good?"

"Yeah I know, right?" She couldn't help giggling at her own conceited response. "I'm bout to go out and get my drink on and I'm late so I will see y'all la-ta."

Brenda set off smiling when Aunt Pat grabbed her by the hand. "Wait. Baby, I need to talk to you. Come back inside for a minute."

"Can it wait? I just finished lying to Tina telling her I was already on my way."

"No it can't wait. Come here. Where's Brandy?" She had a very serious look on her face.

"She's upstairs in bed. Why? Why you lookin so serious?"

"I have something…I think you need to see."

Aunt Pat walked over to the TV and pulled an unmarked DVD from her back pocket. She put it in the player.

The first images were of a party. Brenda saw thick clouds of smoke. The music was loud, people were dancing. The camera was being passed around. It panned to Daye. The sight of him made Brenda twitch. He was making smoke circles from a blunt and then he took a long pull and blew the smoke into some girl's mouth. The girl looked familiar to her.

As the camera panned in closer, she saw that it was Kim, from the gun store. Brenda thought, *Why would she sit there and tell me all that shit about Daye but still be messin with him?* There went that trust. She made a mental note to go back down to the gun shop to holler at her about it. One thing Brenda hated was a fake ass female, and she didn't have any problem calling one out. Especially one that was pretending to have her back. She would see her later. Definitely. She turned back to Aunt Pat, confused.

"What is this about? Why are we watching–"

"Shhh. Wait a minute, Brenda. Just watch it."

The video went on for a while with people passing a blunt back and forth, spouting rap lyrics and other nonsense into the camera. Then she saw something she never thought she would. It was her baby girl. Brandy was taking a pull off a blunt from one hand and holding a red cup in the other. Brenda jumped up off the couch and screamed, "Brandy!" She turned to Aunt Pat. "I can't believe her! I'm so glad you brought me this. Her little ass is mine. Brandy!"

Aunt Pat pulled her back down onto the sofa and hushed her. "No! Don't call her down yet. I need you to see the rest."

Brenda's head was so hot she felt like steam was coming out of her ears. She sat back down and watched Brandy take a swallow from the red cup, look into the camera and go on a rant about Keisha and her ex. Cursing and screaming *fuck this* and *fuck that. Fuck your ugly ass baby.* Brenda couldn't believe this was her daughter. At one point she turned to a guy and put her tongue in his mouth, just for the camera. Brenda jumped up from the sofa. She'd seen enough.

"When the hell was this!"

"Last Saturday night. She was at a fight party around the corner. Keep watchin. And sit down."

They continued to pass the camera around recording more random nonsense. Aunt Pat hit the fast forward button, and when Brandy came back on the screen she slowed it down again. She was in the middle of two guys that were dancing on her, putting their hands inside her top and down her pants. One was pulling at her underwear, which were obviously intentionally being worn outside of her clothes.

Brenda felt like screaming, but she continued watching, breathing heavily, trying to remain calm. Aunt Pat hit the fast forward button again.

Her baby girl was in a room on a bed surrounded by a group of guys. Two of them were undressing her, as the rest of the guys cheered them on. The person holding the camera turned it around to their face and laughed into the camera while saying something about a young bitch. Brenda thought she recognized the face. She knew she'd seen him in the neighborhood before.

The camera was all over the place. It panned over to Brandy on the bed. At that point, they had taken everything off of her except her bra. A guy was standing over her unbuckling his belt. Brenda's tears were flowing at that point. She couldn't watch anymore. She tried to grab the remote from Aunt Pat's hand. "Turn it off!"

Aunt Pat held it firmly in her grasp and pulled it to her opposite side, out of Brenda's reach. "No, you need to watch this."

Brenda jumped up again and stood over her "I said turn it OFF! You think I wanna see this! What the fuck is wrong with you!"

Aunt Pat hit the pause button on the remote, stood slowly and yelled in a booming voice. "I said SIT YO ASS DOWN!"

They stood in each other's faces for a moment before Brenda flopped back down on the sofa. Aunt Pat sat back down slowly, staring her down with one of those don't-you-ever-in-your-fuckin-life looks on her face.

She hit play again. The camera got shaky again, and then there was some commotion in the room. Someone came in and pulled the guy off of Brandy. Both guys started tousling. There was a lot of screaming and cursing, but the music was too loud to hear what was being said. The only clear thing was one guy telling everyone to get the fuck out.

The person holding the camera walked to the far side of the room and sat it down on a table so the picture was turned sideways and slightly out of focus but Brandy could still be seen lying motionless on the bed. People were filing out of the room, and there was a lot of commotion going on outside.

Minutes later, the music stopped, and it got very quiet. Aunt Pat hit the fast forward button again. She slowed it down when a guy came back in the room. He hovered over Brandy, and then he started to kiss her on the mouth and neck. Brenda braced herself as tears streamed down, meeting at her chin.

Brandy wasn't moving at all. He got up off of her, and when he came back into view his shirt was off. He started kissing her again and whispering something in her ear. Brandy never moved. He must have noticed the light on the camera or something because he got up and walked over to it.

You could see that he was completely naked. He picked up the camera and began to toy with it. It was going in and out of focus for a few seconds until it finally stopped moving and the focus became clear. The man holding the camera was Daye. The screen went blank. Aunt Pat hit the power button, and Brenda screamed to the Gods.

*****

She laid there on the floor crying. Gut wrenching sobs that caused her chest to heave. Aunt Pat pulled her up and held her close. "Brenda, come on baby. You gotta pull yourself together now. We gotta go get that baby and take her to the hospital. Right now. Come on."

Brenda wiped her eyes and sat back down on the sofa. "I can't even believe this shit is happening. This is so fucked up. SO FUCKED UP!"

Aunt Pat sat down next to her. Feeling just as helpless. The situation was fucked up indeed. There was nothing she could say. Nothing she could really do to console her. So she sat there and listened. Let her get everything off her chest.

Brenda yelled. "Lord, what more can I TAKE? What do you want from me?" She walked over to the TV. Then she threw it to the ground and cried out. "This is MY fault! It's MINE! I did this to my family! I let this shit happen! God what can I do! What can I do! Oh my God. My baby. My baby girl!" She sat back down again and sobbed. Aunt Pat held her close to her chest and comforted her as much as she knew how.

"Naw, this ain't on you baby. You can't blame yourself for this."

Brenda pulled away and composed herself. Suddenly serious, she looked Aunt Pat directly in the eye. "I need this muthafucka dead. I want him dead. Dead. You hear what I'm saying? I'm not fuckin around with this shit no more."

She jumped up from the sofa and started to pace the floor. "I shoulda killed him myself. I should have killed this muthafucka myself! Fuck!" She picked up the lamp from the side table and threw it against the wall. It crashed, loudly.

Brandy came running downstairs holding Mandy in her arms. "Ma! What's wrong?"

Brenda looked into her baby girl's eyes and broke down again. She fell to the floor.

Brandy was confused and panicky. She'd never seen her mother cry. Ever. She put Mandy down and ran over to her. Brenda grabbed Brandy and held her tightly in her arms, repeatedly crying out, "I'm sorry! I'm so sorry!" Brandy was getting scared. She looked up at Aunt Pat with tears in her eyes, looking for answers.

"What's wrong with her? What's wrong with my mother!"

Aunt Pat knelt down in front of them and put her hand on Brandy's shoulder. "Baby, we need to talk.

"O…Ok, but can you *please* tell me what is going on! Why is she crying like this!"

"It's about what happened to you. Last Saturday night."

Strange Love

Ray encountered Carlita Amado six years earlier. At the time she was waitressing at a high end seafood spot in Atlanta that he and his friends frequented whenever they were in town playing the Falcons.

He was taken in from the moment he laid eyes on her. She was an exquisite beauty, yes but he was more drawn in by her demeanor. She was so cool and professional. Personable and friendly without being flirtatious in the slightest. She was serving a table of some of the most famous and influential men in the world and was completely unfazed. A couple of them made advances and she took care to put them in their place without putting them off. Ray was impressed, and turned on. This girl would be a challenge. And he was up for it.

He went back to the restaurant the next night alone and asked to be seated in her section. Ray hadn't met a woman he couldn't pull with a single flash of his pearly white veneers. Add a compliment and she was virtually at his disposal. But Carlita was different. She barely acknowledged his toothy Colgate smile and his compliments were accepted with an obligatory thank you just before she asked another waitress to trade stations with her. She thought Ray was creepy.

When her replacement informed him that she was working another section Ray's ego was completely smashed. This woman really didn't like him.

Not one to give up easily he paid the check, left a ridiculously generous tip and waited in his car until the restaurant closed. When he saw her leaving he got out and followed her to her car. She realized she was being followed so she picked up her pace. Ray Followed suit.

"Miss! Wait a second!"

When Ray was within arms-length and reached for her arm Carlita turned and hit him with the hardest closed fist punch of his life. He fell backward and blood spurted from his nose. "God Damn!"

She fumbled in her purse for her keys. Ray laid on the ground moaning. Trying to stop the blood flow with the bottom of his shirt.

"Ahhhh shit. I think you broke my nose."

She found her keys, got in and locked the doors. Then she started it up and rolled down the window. Ray was still rolling on the ground. She grabbed a pack of tissues from the glove compartment and threw them out to him. "Addr you ok."

"No. No I'm not. Why'd you have to hit me like that?"

"Why you follow me?"

"Geez. I just wanted to introduce myself. Apologize for coming on so strong earlier. I wasn't trying to hurt you. Ahhh." Blood was still seeping from his nose.

"Peench eet."

"What?"

"Hol you head back and peench eet."

She turned the car off and got out. Then she grabbed a few of the tissues and knelt down in front of him. "Here. Hold you head back and peench you noss. Eet'll stop the bleed." She pinched it.

"Oww!"

"Si. Ees buddoken."

Carlita accompanied Ray to Peidmont Hospital's emergency room and from that night on the two of them were inseparable. Ray spent most of his off time in Alanta. During the season he flew her up to DC and out to be with him wherever he was on the road. He needed her in his space.

They dated for almost eight months before she would allow him to get anywhere close to second base. She was an old fashioned girl and said that she needed to be in a serious relationship before she could even think about having sex. Ray thought it was charming and a nice change of pace. Aside from the occasional cold shower, he was fine with it.

Carlita was a modest girl despite her beauty, and that attracted Ray more than anything. She wore very little makeup, and her thick, black, waist-length hair was usually tied back in a ponytail. Everything she wore was buttoned up to here and hanging down to there, but try as she might, she could never fully conceal that bodacious body of hers. Even in sweats Ray could see she was a knockout. He had to have her.

As frustrating as it was to make out with her, to sleep next to her with a barrier between them, to be constantly pushed away, it was the very first time in his adulthood that he had to chase a woman, and he loved that. Appreciated it even. He'd respect her terms for as long as she asked him to because Carlita Amado was a keeper and whatever it took, he planned to do just that.

About a year into their courtship, Ray took her back home to Mississippi to meet his family. The Colemans loved her, and she fit right in. He was thrilled. He knew he had made the right decision. A week later, they flew to Brazil to meet her family, and the Amados loved Ray even more. Everything was going as well as he could hope.

On the big night, the women in Carlita's family were busy in the kitchen preparing a huge traditional Brazilian feast while the men were in the backyard enjoying a spirited (drunken) game of bocce ball. Ray's parents were on the way from the airport, and "Operation Ball and Chain" was in full effect.

Dinner was going wonderfully. The families ate heartily on churrasco, large skewers of beef and lamb, Arroz de coco and Brazilian collard greens. They sipped Sauvignon wine and Sao Paulo lime and vodka until the entire room echoed with laughter.

Everyone knew what was in store except Carlita, who was behaving quite strangely. Ray found out later it was because she suspected the proposal was coming.

Just before dessert, Ray summoned the nerve to kick things off. He stood and tapped his glass with his fork to get everyone's attention. After thanking his parents for coming all the way to Brazil and thanking Carlita's family for being such gracious hosts, Ray took Carlita's hand and walked her to the center of the room.

Both families tried to suppress their excitement as Ray got down on one knee and pulled out that old familiar red and gold box. Inside of it was one of the most exquisite diamonds Cartier had to offer. A perfect emerald cut 5 carat diamond set in a platinum band.

He asked for her hand and she accepted amidst the eruption of cheers from the family. It was the happiest moment of Ray's life. Sure he'd been married twice before and yes he'd had children, but this day was different. In his mind it was truly the first day of the rest of his life. A defining moment. A game changer. He wasn't wrong.

After she said "yes," all Ray could think about was finally getting his hands on his wife to be, finally being able to make love to her. He was praying she didn't start that "not until our wedding night" foolishness.

The concierge staff had already set up the ambiance in his hotel suite and Ray planned to make the night special.

At the end of the evening, Carlita asked Ray to go ahead of her and take his parents to the hotel so that she'd have a few moments to spend alone with her family. He happily agreed, figuring that would give him time to freshen up and make sure the room was perfect.

When he walked in, he was pleased. The entire suite was candle lit and littered with trails of soft pink rose petals. From the front door to the bed and over to the bath. Votive candles were arranged neatly into the shape of a heart around the sunken bathtub. Alongside the bath was a silver tray with an assortment of Brigadeiro, a bottle of Carlita's favorite Spanish wine and his and hers crystal wine goblets that Ray had engraved for their engagement. The bath was drawn with scented oils and so many petals you could scarcely see the water beneath.

He made a mental note to give the concierge an extra tip for his troubles and then he gave Carlita a call to get her ETA. There was no answer.

Several hours later, the bath was cold, the candles were blown out and Ray sat on the edge of the bed with a near empty wine bottle. Waiting for her. His excitement had turned to worry. She wasn't answering her cell. He'd called her parents' house twice, and they informed him that she was long gone.

Just as he was about to call the Sao Paolo Police, there was a knock at the door. When he opened it Carlita stood there red faced, her eyes wet with tears.

Before he could speak she grabbed him, pulled him close to her and kissed him like she never had. Full of passion and wanton desire. This excited him beyond anything he had ever felt. The time had finally come. The wait was over.

He threw her down on the bed, eager to make passionate love, ready to show her everything she'd been missing. But she had her own plans. She rolled him over onto his back, freeing him from the confines of the black satin lounging pajama pants he was wearing just for her. Ray was mildly disappointed that she didn't react to his manhood in its full and erect glory, but he quickly put that out of his head, because it was about to go down.

She made a trail of soft wet kisses from his neck to his navel. Then she took him in her mouth and gave him a pleasure he never thought he could experience. It was the best head he'd had by far, and that was saying quite a bit for Ray Coleman, the superstar who had gotten his knob polished in every corner of the globe.

The uncharacteristically premature orgasm, which was a mix of anticipation and raw, intense emotion, was confirmation of Carlita's prowess. It actually drew tears from his eyes.

When he looked at her, he saw an angel. His angel, and he couldn't wait to walk down that aisle, to say the vows. Almost instantly he was ready for her again. Ready to return her the pleasure that she had just gifted him.

He pulled her from her knees and on top of his chest. Then he took her face in his hands and kissed her softly and lovingly, tasting the sweetness of her tongue. He rolled over on top of her and began to unbutton her blouse. Her breasts were perfect. Just like he knew they would be. After making love to them, he slid his hand under her skirt and reached between her legs.

She jumped up from the bed. "Ray. I cannot do thees."

Ray reached out to her for her hand and whispered. "Sure you can. It's alright. Come here. Just let me love you baby. I don't think he can wait any longer. He smiled and looked down at his penis, stiff and throbbing. Aching for her warmth. Then he took her by the hand, put her forefinger into his mouth and sucked it gently.

She snatched it away. "No! I say I can't."

Ray stopped. He thought, the tone of her voice was weird and there was a wild look in her eyes. Something was off. He knew it wasn't about waiting until marriage. So he looked her in the eye and asked, reluctantly. "You can't do what?"

She looked away. "I lub you beddy much. But I cannot do thees. I cannot marry you. That ees what I came here to tell you." She began to pull the engagement ring from her finger.

The site of her attempting to remove the ring completely freaked him out. He leaped from the bed and grabbed her hand before she was able to wriggle it off. "No, wait! Babe, come on. What's going on here? What's wrong?"

"I…I just cannot do it." She wiped away a tear. "Ees not you, is me. I lub you but I…"

He interrupted. "Ok. Ok, let me get you some water or something. Can you just sit down for a second? Please. Let's just talk."

He poured a glass of water and handed it to her. She sipped and sipped until it was gone. The words didn't come easy. For a long while she paced the floor, and cried and paced some more. She professed her love several times. Ray sat quietly but nervously. Trying to brace himself for some not so good news. Was it another man? Had he done something wrong? He hadn't so much as looked at another woman since they started dating so it couldn't have been that.

Ray wanted answers but he was also afraid of them. Afraid of anything with potential to break them apart.

Finally, Carlita pulled herself together and said the words. "Ray. I...how do I say? Um. Ees no easy way to say to you, so I just say." She paused and took a deep breath. Then she spoke as clearly as she knew how. "I was no born a wooman."

Ray's eyes nearly bulged out of his head. He heard what she said, but it wasn't exactly registering. He shook his head from one side to the other, opening and closing his eyes. He needed to refocus. And wind it back. "Wait. What did you just say to me?" His expression was stern.

"I'm no...how do you say...a *natural* wooman. I'm so sawdy, Ray. I want to tell you many times but–"

Suddenly he grabbed her by the neck and slammed her up against the wall. Then he reached under her skirt, pulled her leg to the side and found what he was hoping to Christ wasn't there. The second his hand touched flaccid penis and scrotum, he screamed. Then he fell to his knees and cried like an infant. He started beating himself in the head with both fists and calling out to his God. She knelt down in front of him in an attempt to console him and he grabbed her by the neck again. He blacked out.

When the room came back into focus, his hands were around her neck, and he was squeezing with force. Her muffled screams were fading. Somehow he was able to snap himself out of it, in the nick of time. She fell to the floor, and he stood there bewildered, as she coughed and gasped for air. His mind was still reeling from what she'd said, not to mention what he'd just felt. He thought, *what the fuck is happening to my life!*

The events of earlier in the evening replayed in his mind. The love and the laughter. The moment she said yes. Sliding the ring onto her finger, as she smiled and the family cheered. The happiest moments of his life. Now his heart was breaking and the pain was so real he felt like his heart would burst out of his chest.

Rage. Loss. Nausea.

"Oh my God," he said, "oh my God. Why the fuck would you do this to me?"

Barely able to speak, she whispered and hung her head, low. "I know. I so sawdy. I reely want to tell you. I deed."

"All this time. ALL THIS TIME! I just *proposed* to you, Carlita. In front of my fuckin PARENTS!"

Through his tears, Ray began to laugh hysterically, which had Carlita more than a little scared. He let out a huge sigh and wiped his face. Took a second to compose himself. Then he walked over to where she was sitting on the floor; still and afraid to move or speak. He leaned down to her and grabbed her by the hair. His words were careful and very deliberate. "Carlita Amada. I need you, your *dick* and both of your fuckin *balls* to get the fuck out of my hotel room, right fuckin now. And listen to me clearly: If I ever see your face again, if I EVER hear about this from *anyone*, I *will* kill you. Do you understand me? Dead."

Silent tears fell from her chin. It was over. She pulled herself from the floor and lifted her purse from the dresser. "Si." Then she turned around and left.

Ray cried longer and harder that night than he had his entire life. Tears of anger, frustration and extreme sadness. Somehow, some way, he had fallen madly in love with a tranny, and as much as he wanted to he couldn't hate her. Love just doesn't disappear because the person we thought we knew turned out to be someone or in his case, some*thing* else. It wasn't that simple.

*****

In the beginning, the sex was very awkward. He flinched every time he felt her erection, and it threw things off. He could only have sex with her from behind so that he couldn't see her genitalia. If he saw it or if it touched him in any way, it threw things off. Eventually, she loosened him up.

One night after many tequila shots, she gave him a strip tease. She undressed slowly and seductively revealing her entire naked body to him for the very first time. She showed him her penis fully erect. She had him look at it first then she took his hand and began to stroke it with him. He acted like a child being forced to eat brussel sprouts.

She told him how much she loved him and that it was just as important for her to be pleasured as it was for him. In fairly short order, they were making love full on. He really would have done anything in his power to please her. After that experience, Ray was more in love with Carlita than he'd ever been and that's something he didn't think was possible.

Best Laid Plans

Aunt Pat called a family meeting. Not the whole family, just those who would be able to handle what was going on at the moment. Brenda, PJ and Pat's best friend Jean sat around the living room trying to figure out what to do about Brandy's situation.

Earlier that day, Brenda and Aunt Pat took Brandy to the doctor and had her tested for everything known to man, including pregnancy and HIV. The doctor said it would be a few days before the results would come in and the wait was excruciating.

As awful as Brenda felt for what happened to her child, she wanted to wring Brandy's neck for putting herself in that situation. It was so out of her character, so unlike something she would ever do. Brandy was always so responsible and sensible, yet she left the house dressed like an A-town stripper and acting like a reject from the Bad Girls Club. Drinking and smoking in a dark basement full of guys. Something was bound to happen to the girl.

As angry as she was, Brenda didn't want to do anything to make Brandy feel any worse than she already did, so she bit her tongue and directed her rage at the person most deserving of it – Daye.

She knew that if she could get her hands on Daye she could have killed him. Dead. This man was taking her family apart piece by piece, and maybe if she'd done something to him sooner, her daughter would have been spared. She couldn't get that thought out of her head.

As Aunt Pat was going through her list of reasons why the police shouldn't be involved, Missy walked in with a shit-eatin grin on her face. "Hey! I was in the neighborhood so I thought I would stop by. Why is everyone looking so serious?"

Brenda answered, dryly, "What are you doing here, Missy?"

"Well damn. Thanks for the warm welcome. Chucky's around the corner visiting his grandmother, and I thought I'd drop by to check on you. I didn't realize I needed an invitation." Everyone in the room was quiet. "So what's going on?"

"Family problems."

"Oh. Ok, well I'm family." Missy sat down on the sofa next to Aunt Pat. "So what's going on?"

Aunt Pat looked to Brenda for the ok. She got the nod and proceeded to fill Missy in. Three minutes into the story, Missy lost it. "Oh my God! Where's Brandy? Is she ok? Has she been to the hospital?"

Pat answered her questions and continued explaining, finally going into her spiel as to why the police shouldn't get involved.

Then Missy really freaked out. "So you didn't call the police! Are you serious?"

Brenda responded, "Missy please. Calm down and stop actin like you not from Ridgewood."

"And what the hell is that supposed to mean? You're just gonna let this fucking animal walk the streets? Because you don't want to be a *snitch*! Really Brenda?"

In an attempt to diffuse the situation Aunt Pat interjected, "Missy. We got this handled, baby. Don't worry about it. Everything gon be alright."

"Excuse me? Handled? I don't believe this. Where is Brandy? I'll take her to the police station my damned self."

Brenda yelled out, "No! You not takin her no fuckin where! Didn't you just hear? I got this!"

"You *got this*? How?" Missy folded her arms and asked, facetiously. "What are you gonna do? Go over there and shoot him yourself? Get somebody else to do it for you?"

Brenda's response to that was a blank stare. The rest of the room was silent.

Missy looked around the room, in disbelief. "I can't believe this. So, I guess everybody's a gangster now. Do you all realize that you're holding evidence of a crime? You're obstructing justice, as we speak! Do you understand that?! Does anyone here have any sense?"

Brenda decided it was time to shut it down and send Missy's overly reactive ass on her way. "Look Missy! When *you* have a daughter and she comes home crying after some nigga raped and left her for dead in a filthy basement, then *you* can tell me what I'm supposed to do. Until then, I really don't wanna hear shit *you* got to say. This is MY child so umma handle this MY way. Now if you don't mind…"

Missy felt like she had just gotten punched in the gut. Brenda knew full well how badly she wanted children and that her infertility was a sore spot. She understood that the situation was upsetting to everyone, but she certainly didn't deserve to be treated like this. "Ok, well you go ahead and set it off then *Cleo*. And when your ass ends up behind bars, don't even think -"

Brenda interrupted. "Bye Missy!"

Missy snatched her purse and walked out slamming the door behind her.

Brenda turned back to the group. "Now that the fuckin *DA* is gone…" That comment evoked a giggle. Aunt Pat stood to address the group once again. "Now this ain't gon be easy, girls. But trust me, it'll work." She looked at Brenda. "We just gotta be a little patient."

"Aunt Pat, I ain't got no more patience for this muthufucka. You already know how I wanna carry it."

"Yeah, well you better fuckin find some. Shiiit, you wanna go to jail…or you wanna go home?"

Brenda rolled her eyes before taking another swallow of her neat Ciroc.

Aunt Pat continued. "Now, as I was saying…"

Got To Give It Up

Purging themselves of all the pain, secrets and the lies was hardly easy but it was very necessary. It needed to be done for them to establish some trust between them, and to cultivate this new alliance they so desperately needed to make their plan work.

"Operation Get Back" was in full effect. Matt advised Ray to get as much exposure as possible so in just a few months' time they'd crisscrossed the states attending every social function they could. Everything from political fundraisers, charity events, celebrity events. Ray even did a guest appearance at wrestling mania. For 200 grand, he sacrificed himself, getting thrown from the top of a 12-foot steel cage into a crowd of angry fans. It took almost a week for Ray and the angry fans to rehearse it.

Every photo op was seized upon and they were both twittling, Facepaging and instan-piccing nonstop. The extra exposure had gotten Ray a guest spot on a national morning talk show and an offer to sit on the board of directors of a national charity for young underprivileged athletes.

There was an offer for his own cable TV sports show on the table and several offers to coach football at the collegiate level. He'd even been encouraged to run for mayor of his small city. All of those things were wonderful in and of themselves, but none of them paid the kind of money or offered the kind of security Ray needed to pay his debts.

The IRS debt was looming and the bills were piling up left and right. He just stopped opening the mail. Worst of all his social engagements were keeping him from Carlita, the only thing he really cared about.

All Ray wanted to do was make enough money to pay Missy off and stockpile enough cash so that he and Carlita could live their happily ever after in some remote part of Europe, as far away from the public eye as possible. Considering she refused to have a sex change, she'd never become a woman and would therefore never *truly* be his wife. Their relationship would remain his dirty little secret. Ray learned to live with that. He would have lived with just about anything as long as he could be with her.

As strange as it sounded, Missy wanted him to have everything he wanted. Carlita seemed to make him happy and everyone, including her mixed up husband deserved happiness. She didn't want him anyway and Chucky was doing his part to keep her smiling from ear to ear lately. So it was all good.

As time flew by, she saw less and less of Ray. They weren't doing any engagements and their once foolproof plan seemed to be falling way off track. He'd stopped answering her phone calls and she was now intercepting calls from the IRS. Missy was getting worried. She wasn't about to go looking for his ass but she needed to see him. She remembered that she had Carlita's email so she decided to send her a message:

Carlita, this is Missy. I'm looking for Ray. He hasn't been answering my calls and he has some very important business to attend to here in Maryland. If he's there with you, will you please relay that message and tell him to call me as soon as possible? I would very much appreciate it. I hope all is well.

Within minutes she received a reply:

Hi Missy! I talked to Ray and he will be back in Maryland tomorrow afternoon. Everything is good here. I wish you could come out and visit sometime. Anytime you want. Just let us know.

Missy thought, "us." Carlita was trippin. But at least she'd gotten Ray to bring his dumb ass home. He was jeopardizing everything they were working so hard for, and if he didn't get his shit together, his precious Carlita would be traveling back to the states to visit his ass in jail.

She also did not appreciate him wasting her time and energy so he could lay up with his "mister-ess." Yes, she was empathetic to his little situation, but she had her limits. When he got home, she would have one final talk with him, and if he couldn't keep his end of the bargain, she was going to cut her losses and move on with her life. She'd already gotten him to revise the prenup giving her half of all his current assets and future earnings, so whatever happened from that point on, she knew she'd be fine.

Missy just wanted to be happy. Finally, be happy. She wanted to date and travel, to spend time with her family. She wanted to hang out with her old girlfriends and cut up a little. Just live.

During the two short, miserable years she was with Ray, he'd systematically sabotaged every relationship she'd had outside of their marriage. Family, friends and most associates that he thought were getting too close to her. All gone. She vowed to never give anyone else that much power over her life EVER again.

That evening when Ray's cab pulled up to the house, she greeted him at the door with a snifter of Cognac. She knew he was going to need one. "Well look who the wind finally blew in. How was Brazil?"

"Missy, I'm tired. It was a long bumpy flight, and I just want to take a shower and lay down."

"Oh no sir. You can rest when you're dead. We gotta talk so put your bag down and come cop a squat with me."

Ray sighed and followed her into the living room. He plopped down on the sofa and took a swallow of the smooth brown potion. "So what's up?"

"What's up? Really? Ray, why do I have to email your *lover* to get you to come home and take care of your business? *You* asked *me* to play this game. I could be out of here in a condo and living my life the way I want to. You think I need this?"

"Come on, Missy. Let's not pretend this is all for me. You do get a little sumthin out of the deal."

"Yeah, something I deserved anyway. I already worked for my half. I'm helping *you* out."

"So I guess you called me halfway across the world to bust my balls?"

"No, I called you home because you have business here. I'm fielding calls for you all day. Matt, your business partners. That detective keeps calling. Ray, a couple of really serious looking guys stopped by the house last night looking for you and…"

"Wait. What guys? What did they look like? A big black guy?"

"Yeah and a greasy little white guy. Italian. Kinda reminds you of Joe Pesci."

"Shit! Rob and Giovanni."

"Yeah I heard the black guy call the little one Giovanni."

Ray stood up and paced the floor. "Well what did they say?!"

"Not a whole lot. Just that you needed to get in touch with him. The little guy."

"Fuck. I'm so fucked." Ray pulled a pack of cigarettes from his jacket pocket.

It was the first time she'd ever seen him smoke anything. He was tapping his feet nervously and taking way too many pulls from the stinkin cigarette. She ignored it. "So you owe them money?"

Ray answered, sarcastically. "How'd you guess?"

"Don't get all smart ass with me. I'm just trying to help you. How much do you owe anyway?"

He took another pull. "You don't even want to know."

"Whatever Ray. I've been trying to get you all day because my debit card didn't go through at the grocery store this morning. I called the bank, and they told me that the account was frozen. By the IRS."

"What!"

"Yes. They wouldn't give me any more information. Just a toll free number for the IRS. The number's on the fridge."

Ray hopped off the sofa. "Fuck! Where's the mail?"

"Where it always is."

He walked over to the credenza and sorted through the mountain of unopened mail. There were four IRS notices, the last notifying him that since he didn't respond to the audit requests, they determined that he owed more than $17 million dollars including penalties and interest. A bank levy would be enacted within five business days. The letter was dated over a week earlier. And it was Saturday. "Fuck! Fuck! Why didn't you tell me about this Missy! You didn't even open the fuckin mail!"

"Look, I'm not your fuckin secretary! You should have been home to check your own mail! I left you messages telling you that you had mail from the IRS, and you never returned any of my calls. If you would have called and *asked* me to open your mail, I would have opened it. Didn't you get a call from the auditor?"

"No, I didn't. Damn. I thought we were supposed to be a team, Missy. This affects you, too, you know. You sittin there acting like you don't even give a shit!"

"You know what? You are really fucking amazing. NOW we're a team? You go away for weeks at a time, and *I'm* the one that doesn't give a shit? And do you see my name on any of these envelopes?" She flipped through the mail and one by one threw the envelopes on the floor. "No, you were so busy trying to keep me from your money. We don't file joint returns. This is *your* fuckin problem."

"You're still my wife, so you're still partly responsible."

"Really? I'll tell you what. I'm outta here. You can deal with this bullshit yourself from now on. Let them sue me. I don't even give a shit anymore. I have things to do." Missy got up from the sofa and grabbed her purse. She walked toward the front door.

Ray ran after her and grabbed her by the arm. "No!" he yelled. She looked down at her arm and back up at him. He let her go immediately and apologized. "I…I'm sorry. I didn't mean to grab you like that. Please don't leave now. You're the only chance we got."

She glared at him again. "We?"

"I mean, you're the only chance *I* got to get through this. "You know I can't do this without you, Missy. Please."

She dropped her purse and keys on the foyer table. "Ok, let's get this shit straight once and for all. Missy does not *need* to do this. Missy will be just fine on her own. Understand that."

"Yes, I do. You're right."

"Missy is helping *you*."

"Yes she is, and I appreciate it very much. Now please come sit down and talk to me."

She pointed her finger at his face. "No more fuckin trips to Brazil. You hear me? You are gonna have to put your little bromance on hold until you get shit straightened out at home."

"Absolutely. You got it. No more trips."

"Ok. So what's the next step?"

"Sweetheart, I really don't know. But I'll figure something out."

He did all of his figuring at the new Maryland casino. Figuring himself deeper into a whole he'd never climb out of.

Doing it My Way

Brenda laid on the floor, staring at the ceiling, thinking *Fuck my life*. She thought it until she began to speak it, then spoke it until she started to scream it.

As painful as the memories were, the tears were long gone. Dried up. She'd cried enough over the last six months, and since crying had gotten her five miles past nowhere, she decided to do something.

Waiting on Aunt Pat's slow-ass plan to work out wasn't an option. Brenda was sick to death of sitting and waiting while her life and the lives of everyone she loved crumbled before her like stale bread.

She couldn't help thinking if she had done something earlier maybe her life wouldn't be in such shambles. If she would have put her foot down about Daye from the beginning maybe Melvin would still be alive. If she'd dealt with Daye like she wanted to, maybe her daughter wouldn't have been violated and deflowered by her father's murderer. What the fuck.

Her precious baby girl's first sexual experience was a drunken rape scene, most of which was caught on video. The thought of it made her eyes well, but she refused to cry. No more crying. Tears were her unproductive enemy, but action was about to become a very close friend.

Brenda had been up all night. At nearly 5 a.m., she was still wide open. Emotional, excitable, ready. Fifteen minutes prior, she'd watched the video, for the third time. Prior to that she'd flipped through her wedding album and a family photo album with Melvin's obituary neatly displayed behind the cellophane. It was just the motivation she needed to do what she knew she had to do.

She wiped away the one tear that managed to escape the corner of her eye and ran for the stairs. Underestimating the influence of three quarters of a fifth of Ciroc vodka, she tripped up the stairs and fell on her face. She got up and brushed herself off, trying desperately to focus and ward off the dizzies, which seemed to be creeping slowly upon her.

Holding the rail every step of the way, she walked slowly up the stairs to her bedroom. Once inside, she locked the door and pulled the heavy gray metal box from beneath her bed. The box that held Pinky.

She changed into her sneakers and grabbed her coat on the way out of the front door. Since MJ was long gone with her truck, Brenda decided to walk. When she opened the front door the cold smacked her in the face. She zipped her coat up to the chin. There was a light mist of rain and a slight pre-dawn fog. Brenda flipped the hood up on her ski coat and started walking.

Stumbling and swerving, she thought she'd never get there. The five blocks felt like miles. A couple blocks and the rain picked up. Cold winds assaulted her face and hands but the inside of the Northface Arctic Parka felt more like a sauna. Finally, she made it to Daye's front door.

His car was parked in the front of the house, and the basement light was on so she knew he was there. Brenda was nervous. Her stomach was bubbling but the cold air had cleared her mind a bit. She knew exactly what she was doing, however nervous she was at the thought.

She knocked on the door with her hand clasping Pinky in her coat pocket. Half hoping he wouldn't answer, she waited a couple minutes before knocking again. Standing there in the cold morning air, images of her family flashed in her mind. Her daughter lying on that dirty mattress unconscious and unaware that she was about to be violated. Her baby waking up naked and afraid, realizing what had happened to her. Melvin's mutilated body lying cold on a gurney in the DC morgue. Melvin lying in his casket at the funeral home. Barely recognizable after the embalming and heavy handed makeup.

In her head, she could still hear the sounds of his mother and sister screaming out as his casket was lowered into the ground. Holding back her tears put a massive lump in her throat, that was impossible to swallow. So she threw it up. All over the porch. Suddenly she felt better. Ready.

She banged on the door so hard the old windows on the front porch rattled. She waited and waited, yet there was no answer. Something told her to try the handle before walking away. It was unlocked. She opened the door slowly and walked in.

The house was dark but she could hear music coming from the

F.J. Stevens

basement. By this time, Pinky was out, and she was holding her firmly with both hands at the ready, just like Melvin taught her. Just like she'd seen her girl Olivia do it on Law and Order SVU.

Stepping quietly down the stairs, she thought, *This is really fuckin happening.* She knew there was no turning back.

When she got to the bottom of the stairs she brought her weapon up to her chest ready to aim and fire at the first thing moving. Leaning against the wall of the stairway, she peeked inside the basement. She immediately recognized the space from the video.

The brown shag carpet was old and musty. There were two badly worn mismatched sofas against either wall and a big screen television at the far end of the wall ahead of her. Music blared from the television at a high decibel.

To her immediate left was a small bathroom with the door slightly ajar. The light was on and she could hear the exhaust fan going. To her right, about 10 feet down a small hallway was a spare room. That door was wide open but the room was dark. She eased over to her left and tapped the bathroom door with her foot. It opened slowly. She raised the gun prepared to take a shot. There was no one there.

She walked toward the room at the end of the hall. Slowly and carefully with her gun raised and at the ready. When she entered the room she could barely see in front of her. She thought she heard a noise but the television was so loud in the other room it was hard to tell. So she slid along the wall and over to a bedside table near the window.

Brenda took one hand off the gun and reached for the lamp on the table. When she pulled the chain and the light came on, there was a loud moan from across the room – so loud that it startled her causing the gun to discharge. The force from the gun knocked her back into the wall and onto the floor. She pulled herself up off the floor, and with her gun repositioned she walked over to the other side of the bed.

Lying on the floor in the fetal position, clearly afraid and trying to hide. It was like deja vu. She'd seen this moment in her mind a thousand times. Standing over him, gun in hand. Making him beg for his life. She'd rehearsed her speech over and over again.

"Daye! Get your ass up!" She pointed the gun at his face and kicked him hard in the leg. "Get the fuck up!" His moans stopped but his breathing was labored. She reached down and pulled him over onto his back. His white T-shirt was soaked with blood and torn apart. She looked closer and realized that the shirt wasn't just torn, it was bullet-ridden.

There was blood seeping from several holes in his chest and stomach. She moved closer and saw that his face was badly beaten. His left eye was swollen shut. Blood trickled from his nose and lip. Someone had been there just before her. Someone that wanted him dead. Good for them.

She decided to get out of there. But not before telling him what was on her mind. She'd waited too damn long for it.

The music was loud so she leaned in to make sure he heard every word she had to say. With her gun pointed squarely at his nose, she purged.

"I want you to know that I came here to empty this muthafucka into your evil ass, but I see somebody beat me to it. I'm disappointed now cause I really wanted to do it myself. For my husband that you murdered." Daye began to shake his head from side to side. "Yes…yes I know you had Melvin killed, muthafucka." She took a deep breath in as the image of him hovering over Brandy's half naked body flooded her mind. She looked over at the bed. The same bed. The thought choked her up. "And you *raped* my daughter." Brenda couldn't stop the tears from escaping her eyes. She wanted to put a bullet in him then and there.

Daye was still shaking his head but fighting for every breath. His chest heaving up and down.

"You have done everything you could to destroy my family. But what I won't do is let you destroy my life. You're not worth it." She hocked up everything in her chest and spat it in his face. She was done.

Brenda put the gun back into her coat pocket and turned for the door. She noticed a cordless phone charging on the nightstand so she picked it up and dialed 911. "Operator, I need to report a shooting at 1212 2nd St NE. A man has been shot. Please send an ambulance right away." When the operator began to speak, she hung up. Then she threw the phone on the floor and walked out. She thought whatever happened she'd done her part. The rest was up to God.

Can This Be Love

This day, Missy was happier than she'd ever been in her life. She hadn't heard from Ray in over a month, and to be honest, she'd really given up on that whole charade they had going. It wasn't working anyway.

Nothing was panning out the way they had hoped, and they'd spent way more money in travel, wardrobe, and charitable contributions than they brought in. They were just getting further and further into the red. So Missy was over it and moving on. Ray could clean up his own mess.

Things with Chucky were going superbly. They hadn't been intimate, yet, but she had a very strong suspicion that was about to change. Even though she'd opened up and shared the real truth about Ray and her marriage, Chucky told her that he could never make love to another man's wife. Apparently he meant it.

She tried seducing him every which way she could think of, but he wouldn't take the bait. The harder she threw it at him the more adamant he was that he would not have her. He'd even threatened to stop seeing her if she didn't ease up. For the first time in her life she'd made advances on a man and been rejected.

Although she understood why he was fending her off, her ego was still bruised. She thought for sure that he would have given in. As infuriating as Chucky was, she had to admit the turn downs were a complete turn on. Missy wanted him bad and could not wait to get out of her farce of a marriage and get her hands on him. Her man. A real man.

Chucky had become everything she had ever thought he would be. Everything she wanted him to be. Everything she needed in a man. But timing was a motherfucker. She couldn't help thinking what her life would have been like if she'd just stayed in L.A. with him.

The day she kissed him goodbye for the last time at LAX was a pivotal moment in her life. Thinking she was trading up, she walked away from the best man – not to mention the best sex – she'd ever known to be with a yuppie politician with erectile dysfunction and then later ended up with an abusive, sadistic pervert. Karma had turned out to be a big, fat, angry bitch.

She didn't have any of the answers about life she needed, but one thing was for sure – some good "D" would take her mind off it all. She hadn't had sex in almost a year, and there was only so much she could expect out of her poor little white rabbit or her blue dolphin with the rotating head, or her new massaging shower head. It was time to retire the gadgets and lay her hands on some flesh and warm pulsating blood; to feel the weight of a strong sexy man on top of her again.

Missy could remember the last time she and Chucky had made love, out on the terrace of his penthouse suite in L.A. It was the night before she left him to come back to DC, and he was trying his best to convince her to stay. She enjoyed every second of it, but her mind was already made up. She was on to bigger and better things, or so she thought.

All she could think about was Chucky's hands touching her body. Since they'd rekindled their friendship, they'd shared a few sweet kisses. When they embraced the sexual tension was undeniable, and when Chucky's body responded through his trousers, he quickly retreated and bid her goodnight in a most gentlemanly fashion. That shit was killing her.

Hollywood had grown him up and into a distinguished gentleman, but at that moment she would have given anything for one night with the old immature Chucky with the raging hormones and the perpetual hard on for her. The one that convinced her that sex was better while watching big ghetto booty porn or listening to the disgustingly misogynistic soundtracks of 2 Short or the 2 Live Crew. She even re-enacted the music videos for him. He really had a way of bringing out her inner "heaux".

Missy wanted the guy that liked to squeeze baby oil on her ass and make it jiggle before he mounted her from behind, wrapped her long mane around his fists and rode her like a stallion. She had to cross her legs real tight when she thought about it.

That's what she was missing in her life. One good unadulterated, uninterrupted night of "Chuck Nasty." And she had every intention of getting it…sooner than later.

They had a movie date on a Friday night, and she called him to cancel. One of her designer friends was doing a trunk show at the new W Hotel downtown and she'd promised to help her out. Missy asked Chucky if he would mind picking her up afterward and taking her home since she'd likely be drinking.

Thinking nothing of the small favor. He agreed. When that was settled, she took a trip into Georgetown to the Pleasure Chest and Whole Foods for some sweet treats.

That Friday night when Chucky called for her to come downstairs, she asked him to come up to the room to help her carry bags from the purchases she supposedly made. Ever the gentleman, he pulled his car to the side, flashed his hazards, and ran up to meet her.

When he got to the room, the door was held open by the latch. He pushed his way inside and found it dark and empty. He walked over to the bedroom, and when he opened the door his bottom jaw nearly dropped to the floor.

There stood Missy in front of an open terrace in a black, crotch less fishnet bodysuit and 6 inch come-fuck-me heels. She was wearing a super long black wig, mile long lashes, and cherry red lips that were glossed to shine. He stood there speechless with a pulsating bulge in his pants. She had his full attention.

He swallowed hard before he spoke. "Missy – what are you doing?"

She didn't speak. Instead she trailed an exposed nipple with a finger until it was erect. He pleaded with his eyes for her not to force him. She tweaked and teased the other nipple until they were both at their peak, begging for his attention. Then she slowly began to tear at the front of the body stocking until both breasts were fully exposed. She reached over to the table and grabbed a bottle of Johnson's baby oil, like they used back in the day. He loved her body that much more when it was wet. She poured it over her nipples and began to massage it in.

Chucky stood there silently in the doorway, drinking it all in.

Missy reached down between her legs and pulled the stocking at the crotch, tearing it slowly away from her body. She stepped out of it completely, giving him full frontal – a flawless hourglass figure with a small waist, sensuously curvy hips, and perfectly toned legs that were a mile long in her stilettos.

She stood there in front of him naked and wanton. He didn't speak or move. He just stared, intensely waiting for her next move, trying to contain himself.

She slowly turned her back to him, pulled her waist-length mane to the side and seductively peered at him over her shoulder. Then she began to squeeze the bottle of oil. It trailed down her back, over and into her round ass, down her legs.

When she looked up at him again, he was rubbing his crotch. Missy knew she had him. She could see Chucky Nasty coming to life before her very eyes.

He licked his lips and broke his silence. "Make that ass clap for me baby."

She was happy to oblige.

He was happy to see her sexy as in motion. Shiny and wet. Begging for him. Just like old times. "Uhm hmm. That's right baby. Now turn back around and let me see that sexy body."

She turned to face him. He was undressing.

"You sure you ready for this Missy?"

With an impeccable French accent, she responded. "Missy? You must have me mistaken, monsieur. Mon nom est, Michelle."

Role play. She was *really* turning him on.

Chucky undressed down to his platinum chain and his pearly whites. At full arousal and in full swing, he walked toward her. Missy's body tingled with anticipation as he came closer. It had been many months since she felt a man's hands on her body. He stopped directly in front of her, so close she could feel his breath on her neck.

He reached up and ran a finger over her nipple and with the other hand he parted her legs. The moment he touched her, Missy's whole body shuddered.

He backed her into the patio door and knelt in front of her. Then he buried his face inside her to take in her scent. He missed her smell. He missed tasting her, almost as much as she missed his long and superbly talented tongue. The tongue that had never failed to bring her quickly to orgasm. Sometimes to tears. He pushed her legs further apart and proceeded to satisfy his craving until her soft moans turned to screams.

He could feel her legs weaken, so he pulled himself back up and pressed his naked body against hers, pinning her against the glass and kissing her gently on the the left side of her neck. He remembered the spot.

She whispered sweet French nothings in his ear which was only turning him on more. "Embrasse moi, me toucher. Je veux que vous l'interieur de moi. Me faire l'amoure. Me faire l'amoure."

Chucky grabbed her hand and placed it around him allowing her to feel the full power of his erection. He nibbled on her earlobe before he whispered. "Michelle. I'm about to fuck the shit outta you."

He lifted and carried her over to the bed. Then he threw her down and gave her everything she had been wanting and waiting for. They made love until the sun rose, and by the time they left the W, they both knew that they would spend the rest of their lives together.

No Worries

Brenda was jarred awake by the banging at the front door. Feeling the effects of the vodka binge, she yelled for Brandy to get the door. The banging continued on for longer than her head could take so she threw on her robe and walked downstairs. Pissed. She snatched the door open ready to curse somebody's rude ass out.

"Dang Aunt Pat, you bangin on the door like the po po. What happened to your keys?"

"I dunno. I must have left them at Jean's. You heard the news yet?"

"What news?"

"Somebody killed our boy last night."

"Oh. For real?" Brenda turned and walked into the kitchen to get a Goody powder and a cold soda.

"Did you hear what I just said?"

"I heard you."

"That's all you got to say?"

"Yeah, basically. What do you want me to say?"

"Bren-da?"

"Aunt Pat?"

Aunt Pat walked into the kitchen and took the soda out of Brenda's hand. "You got something you wanna tell me?"

Brenda snatched the soda back from her hand. "No. I don't."

"Don't fuck with me, girl. If you know something, you better damn well tell me right now."

"Listen! If you're asking me did I have something to do wit it, the answer is no."

"Then what the FUCK were you doing on 2nd Street this morning?"

Brenda stood there wide eyed and completely caught off guard, thinking *how the fuck does she know everything*. Trying to think of a good answer she stalled. "Can I get my kids out the door first? It *is* a school day."

"Yeah go ahead. I'll be sitting right here. Waitin."

Brenda went upstairs to wake Brandy and to get Mandy ready for daycare. She opened the door to their room, no one was there. She ran downstairs and grabbed her cell phone.

Just as she was dialing her cell, Brandy walked through the door. "Hey Aunt Pat. Hey ma."

"Hey? Where the hell you been? Where's Mandy?"

"Dang, calm down. We were at Uncle Edward's."

"Where?"

"Remember, you sent us over there so y'all could talk last night?"

"Oh yeah, I did."

"Get it together, ma. I already dropped Mandy off at daycare. I just came back in to grab my books for school. I'll see you later." She walked over to Brenda and gave her a kiss on the cheek.

"Ok, bye baby. Try to have a good day today ok? I love you."

"I will. Love you too. Bye Aunt Pat."

"See you later, baby."

Aunt Pat sat at the kitchen counter with her arms folded. Waiting for an answer. Losing her patience by the second. As soon as the front door was shut she was back on it. "Now then, I repeat. What was you doing on 2nd Street early this morning, Brenda?"

Still trying to think of a good explanation, Brenda said the first thing that came to mind. "You want some coffee? I could use some right now."

She put on a fresh pot and proceeded to tell Aunt Pat everything that happened.

"So…I got exactly what I wanted and I didn't have to wait half a year *or* use my gun to get it."

"Brenda, that shit you pulled was reckless, and it was stupid. I don't know why you refuse to listen to what the hell I tell you! It's like I'm talkin to a fuckin child when I…"

"Look! Aunt Pat, I love you and you know I respect you and everything, but I couldn't just keep sittin around waitin for karma to take care of my problems. Sittin around is the whole reason I'm in this mess. I don't expect you to understand, but it's ok. It's over now, so we can move on with our lives."

"Is that so? You got it all figured out huh? You got all the answers, huh baby girl?"

"Pretty much."

"Ok, well, let me ask you something. Did you remember to wipe your fingerprints off his phone? How about the doorknobs? Do you remember if you touched anything else in the house while you was there? Where did your bullet go?"

Did you think to pick up the shell casing before you ran outta there? Do you remember passing anyone on the street coming or going? How do you think I knew you were on the block this morning, Brenda? The streets don't sleep baby. This ain't no game you playin!"

Brenda's facial expression had quickly changed from a smug, self-assured smirk to that of a child who'd just realized that she'd picked the wrong multiple choice answer on her math test. Every question Aunt Pat posed was a valid one, and she didn't have a good answer for any one of them.

"Oh you quiet now? Witcha dumb ass. Girl, GO get me your gun!"

Brenda jumped at the sound of Pat's booming voice. "For what?"

"Because I *asked* you for it."

"No. I'm not giving you my gun."

"Brenda."

"No. You act like I'm holdin the murder weapon or something. I didn't kill him so I don't really have nothin to hide. I'm not worried about it."

Aunt Pat let out an exasperated sigh. "Well. Since you seem to know every fuckin thing, I guess my services ain't appreciated around here. I'll be at Jean's if anybody need me."

"You don't want no coffee? I got that good Starbucks."

"No I don't want no coffee. I'll catch up with you later."

Now that the kill joy was gone Brenda was free to enjoy the rest of her day. She proceeded to make herself a breakfast fit for a queen. All her favorite hangover foods. Cheesy eggs, honey wheat toast, fried potatoes and onions, and more bacon than her doctor would ever recommend eating in one sitting. It was a victory breakfast of sorts. The bane of her existence was floating around somewhere in purgatory. Her daughter was safe and her husband could finally rest peacefully. She could officially close that chapter and move on with her life.

She sat down in front of the TV with her food tray and flipped channels. Two hours of paternity-revealing talk shows later, Brenda had succumbed to what black folks call "the it-is." With a full belly she was fast asleep, snoring and immersed in a recurring dream about her nemesis, pre mortem.

Brenda had killed Daye a dozen different ways in her dreams, but that day she found herself replaying the morning's events, slinking down the stairs into his basement with Pinky firmly in hand.

Everything happened just as it did earlier that morning, but when she turned on the lamp, Daye grabbed her arm and threw her on that dirty mattress. The gun fell to the floor. He pinned her down with his knees on both her arms, and she couldn't move. His eyes were bloodshot, and there was a disgusting white foam in the corners of his mouth.

When he reached down to pull down his shorts, she was able to free an arm and pounded on his face. As hard as she tried, none of the blows seemed to faze him. Like she had weights on her arms. She managed an effective groin kick, and he let up enough for her to roll to the floor and pick up the gun. He took a step toward her and with her back on the floor she squeezed the trigger until there were no more shots to take.

Every bullet hit him in the chest before he hit the bed and bounced off of it to the floor. Brenda got up off the floor. Still holding the gun, she walked over to where Daye was lying, bleeding and moaning.

Out of the corner of her eye, she saw a man at the window and it startled her. He started banging furiously on the window. Brenda woke up to loud banging at her own front door. "Police! Open up!"

A New Beginning

When Missy opened her eyes, Chucky was coming in for a good morning kiss, and a little more lovin for the road. It was almost checkout time, and her head was still spinning, not from all the champagne they drank the night before but from finally consummating their new relationship. The right relationship. The one she deserved.

He kissed her softly on her neck, her shoulder; glided his tongue down to her chest. He pushed her full breasts together and sucked them gently. Her nipples hardened under the flicker of his tongue. Missy's body was screaming to be opened. She pulled her legs up and apart, resting her feet on the bed and arching her back. Chucky took the cue. He kissed his way down until he reached the spot she was silently begging him to attend to. Then he pushed both of her legs back further, reached one hand under her bottom for leverage and used a combination of his tongue, lips and all five fingers on his free hand to bring Missy to an orgasm with screams so loud they brought housekeeping to the door.

Once Missy composed herself, and stopped the kicking, Chucky climbed up and rested his head on her stomach. They laid quietly for a while. Just enjoying each other. She stroked his head and ran her fingers through his short curly hair. They were finally making it happen and the thought really blew Missy's mind. Not only was Chucky wealthy and successful, he was a good man and he loved her. Genuinely and wholeheartedly he loved her. Cared about her thoughts and feelings. He didn't just want to see her happy he wanted to make her happy. And that he did. In every conceivable way. She couldn't have asked for anything more.

After the second call from the front desk, they got dressed and headed out. When they got downstairs, Chucky was informed that his car had been towed. He had completely forgotten that he left the car double parked at the entrance to the hotel. He had only gone up to help Missy with her packages when he got blindsided with her seduction routine. It was well worth the tow.

The front desk had called every room trying to find out who the beautiful black Porsche Cayenne truck belonged to, but by the time the call came to their room the happy couple was so deep in the throes of new love the sound of a ringing phone was nothing more than background noise. They could not be disturbed.

The hotel manager apologized so profusely that Chucky had to calm him down. The manager insisted that they take the hotel's corporate limousine until they retrieved his truck from impound. Just then, Missy remembered that her car was in the garage, but Chucky was already sold on the idea of driving a limo for the first time, so he requested the keys.

The manager was a bit confused. "Oh, no sir, we have a driver that will take you anywhere you want to go. He's at your disposal for as long as you need him. We'll call you as soon as your car is returned to the hotel."

"Nah, I don't like being driven around. I can take the wheel. Just toss me the key."

"Very well, sir."

Chucky grabbed the keys and tossed his black card on the counter. "For incidentals."

He opened the door to the backseat and ushered Missy inside. "My lady."

As he closed the door, she grabbed the handle, and motioned for him to come inside. "What's your rush?" she said. "You have someplace to be?"

He took the hint. They spent another hour in the parking garage, steaming up the windows and causing a stir with the nosey parking attendants. Missy wanted to return the gift he'd given her that morning. And that she did. She removed his shoes, unbuckled his belt, pulled his jeans down to his ankles and over his feet. He asked her why he needed to take his pants all the way off. She told him that she wanted him to get completely comfortable for what she was about to do.

Chucky laid back on the leather seat and Missy did things to him with her tongue that she never had. Courtesy of "The Art of Fellatio", an instructional video she'd downloaded and studied especially for the occasion. She brought him to his peak several times and pulled back before finally allowing him to release in her mouth. She'd never done that for him.

Chucky screamed, shuddered, then stomped the floor of the car until the tingling stopped. Then he pulled Missy up to him and held her so tight she could hardly breath. He kissed her all over her face and neck whispering "I love you" over and again. She knew she did good.

In just a couple minutes he was ready for her. Really ready. He reached for her down there and begged to be inside her again. "Missy please. Just let me put it in real quick. I need to feel you baby." He wanted desperately to return the favor. To hear her screaming out for him. But she wouldn't let him. Instead she kissed him on the forehead and climbed into the front seat. "Come on we gotta go! We have plenty of time for that, right?"

Chucky dressed himself, pouting, and then he got out and stepped into the front seat. He kissed her hard on the lips. "Girl, when I get your ass home...umh! You know you gon get it right?"

She laughed "Promises, promises."

They took the scenic route to Potomac, through Rock Creek Park. The sun shone brightly through the trees, nearly causing them to collide with a family of deer crossing from one side of the forest to the other. Chucky screeched to a halt as several oblivious fawns trailed a mother doe across the two-laned road. Missy smiled as the little ones crossed. It made her think of babies. Then the reality of what was about to take place set in.

"Chucky?"

"Yes, my little CUM-quat." He gyrated in his seat.

She giggled. "You sir, have sex on the brain."

"You madam, are to blame for that. And when'd you learn to speak French? That shit was HOT!"

"Oh really? Well that's just a taste. I have many, *many* tricks and treats up my sleeve, Mr. Wilson. You'll see."

He bucked his eyes wide like a cartoon character. "Got dammit girl, don't you threaten me wit a good time."

They laughed. Missy loved how he made her laugh. Chucky was a nonstop good time, but sometimes he didn't know when to quit. "Can we be serious for a minute?"

"Sure. What's on your mind, baby?"

"I need to know. Are we really doing this? I mean for real. Me and you?"

"You serious?"

"Yes. I'm serious."

"Missy If I hadn't been so stupid...so damned immature I

wouldn't have let you leave me in L.A. I've regretted it all these years, and now that you're giving me a second chance. Hell yes, we doin this! It's me and you from here on out, baby. That's it. Why, you havin second thoughts?"

Missy blushed all over herself. She was as excited as she had ever been. Things were finally, *finally* going her way. "No second thoughts."

They drove along in silence for a while, just enjoying being in each other's company. Chucky smiled to himself and grunted. "Umh."

"Umh what? What you smiling about over there?"

"You."

"What about me?"

"Degenerate little cretin."

"I beg your pardon?"

Chucky laughed. "That's what you called me when I met you. You said you would never go out with a degenerate little cretin like me. Remember that?"

"Yes! I did say that! You didn't know what a cretin was did you?"

"No, but I knew it wasn't nothin good." They both laughed.

"Yo, I have never been cursed out so eloquently in my life. I didn't even know how to take it. I had to go home and get a dictionary just to understand how offended I *should* be."

Missy laughed so hard she spat out a little of her water. "Well, luckily I changed my mind about you."

"Yeah, after how many years of me chasin you?"

Missy grabbed hold of his free hand and clasped her fingers inside his. "Well the chase is over, Mr. Wilson."

"And I thank you, Mrs. Wilson."

"Wowwwww. *Mrs. Wilson.* That actually sounds nice."

"Yes, it does. We can go to Tiffany's right now if you want."

"Whoa…slow down cowboy. I've got a little paperwork I have to get out the way first. But you know I'm going to hold you to that, right?

"I hope so."

"My God. Chucky! I cannot believe I'm finally leaving that house. That house is bad. So bad. Nothing but bad things have happened there."

"Well, we gon get to work on making some good memories.

New good memories. I got big plans for you, pretty lady."

They were getting closer. "Oh babe, take 39A to 190 off the beltway."

"Cool. I don't know why you gotta go back there at all. I can get you whatever you need."

"Don't be silly. I really just need to pack a couple suitcases. Some important documents. He can keep the rest of that shit. I'm leaving my wedding ring right on the kitchen counter. As of today I am D-O-N-E."

Chucky snapped a finger and waved an arm in the air. "Yassss! I hear you, sister gurl!"

She laughed and pushed his arm down. "You play too much. I swear after today I never want to see Potomac Maryland again."

"Yeah, I hate Potomac. It's too fuckin far from the city for me. Too quiet."

"Well once upon a time I thought quiet was what I needed."

"I know what's not quiet, that phone. It's been buzzin non-stop since this morning. You know you can answer it."

She kissed his hand. "Nah. Everything important to me is sitting right here next to me."

"Awww, baby. You so sweet." He kissed her hand. "But seriously that could be anybody. I ain't goin nowhere girl. Answer your phone."

She sighed. "If I must." She pulled her phone from her purse. There were dozens of missed calls and several text messages. Several calls from Carmen, a few unknown numbers and several calls from Ray. Missy thought, *now he wants to contact me. Hmm.* She sorted through the texts first. Carmen's first text read:

I understand if you need some time. I know we haven't talked in a while but please know that I love you very much and I'm here for you whenever you need. Please call me as soon as you're able to talk. I love you Missy. Call me.

The one above that read:

OMG Girl this shit is so fuckin crazy! Where are you? Are you ok? You're not answering your phone. PLEASE call me as soon as you can. I'm worried!!

The next six texts were from Ray. She realized she needed to start at the top to read them in order. The first was at 1:18 am. At that particular time, she and Chucky were busy rediscovering their love for each other so the ringer on her phone was intentionally switched to silent mode.

Hey :o) I need to talk to you. It's important. Call me asap!

The next text was at 2:37 am. There were three missed calls within five minutes of that text.

Missy! I'm calling you! Pick up! What the fuck are you doing? Answer the phone!

The next message was lengthy and littered with misspellings so Missy imagined he was pretty drunk by then. It was 3:51 am:

Bae I know you're mad that I haven't not been in touch, and I'm so sorry about. I just needed to get away and clear my mind for a while. Just so you know, Carlita and I are done. That bitch is CRZY and I need to have my head my fucking head examined for ever starting with her. It's a long story but the shit is really hitting the fast right now and I have talk to you. Call me back!

At 4:13 a.m.:

I don't have any place else to turn Missy. I can't even believe this shit happening. I can't even turn on the fuckin TV. If you ever losed me you'll pick up the phone. I really need you babe. Please.

5:16 a.m.:

Really Missy? Really? Fuck you then bitch!

The final text was at 7:03 a.m.:

Yeah. I knew you didn't give a fuck about me. But it's cool. You just remember I ain't the only one with something to lose here. So fuck you and whoever the fuck you with that won't let you answer my call. You all have a nice life. - RC

Missy laughed to herself. It didn't take a rocket scientist to figure out somebody finally got himself exposed. She thought, *Oh well, that's no longer my problem.*

Chucky inquired. "What's up, babe? Everything ok?"

"I'm pretty sure it's not. But it's nothing I can't handle."

She checked her voice messages, and it was confirmed. The game was officially over. There was a message from Matt, Ray's agent telling her that "it" was all over the news and that they needed to do some damage control immediately. He asked her to call him right away so that they could set up a conference call with Ray.

Missy thought she could give a shit about damage control right now and even less of a shit about Ray. He was the one with the problem. Her life was about to take on a new direction, and when the dust finally settled, she would have everything she ever wanted. And it was about time.

She flipped on the radio, caught the end of Russ Parr's morning radio show. Ray Coleman was breaking news. They were recapping the story and already making dirty jokes about it. America's superhero was in a relationship with a transvestite, and there were explicit photos to prove it. They already had Carlita's full name and some of her background. It was all over every social media outlet, the TV and radio.

Chucky was visibly pissed. "Damn! This is some bullshit! Now look at the shit you gotta deal with behind his *punk ass.*"

"Yeah, tell me about it." Missy was quiet for the next few minutes, staring out to the window, trying desperately not to let Chucky see the water welling in her eyes. They were getting close to their exit.

"Is this my exit?" Chucky said.

"No. I need you to turn around. I need you to drive me back to my car."

"What? Why?"

"You know why." They missed the exit.

"No, I don't know why." He pulled the car over onto the median. "Missy…baby, look at me when I'm talking to you."

She turned her head. Her face was wet with tears. "Chucky. Just take me back to my car."

"I'm not takin you nowhere but back to that house to get your shit. You ain't gotta deal with this shit no more, Missy! You let him deal with that faggoty shit on his own."

"You know that's not how it works. He's still my husband,

Chucky."

He pulled off the median, nearly side swiping another car. He whipped a U-turn and ran a red light in the process. He began to speed.

"Damn! Slow down, Ricky Bobby! You trying to kill us or what?!"

"Nah. I'm just tryna get you back to your ride, that's all."

Missy took his free hand in hers. "Baby. Listen to me. Nothing between you and I has changed. I meant it when I said everything I care about was sitting right here with me. But this is something I've gotta deal with on my own. You can understand that right?"

"Umh hmm."

"You know I didn't plan for this to happen. Especially not today. Babe, this has been the happiest day of my life. Please believe me when I tell you that. But I have to deal with the situation, and this is not exactly the time to announce to the world that I'm head over heels in love with a man that's *not* my husband. No matter what he's doing."

He kissed her hand. "I know. I'm just so tired of waitin. I been waitin for you for years, girl. You hear me? YEARS. Now *this* bullshit. Can I get my turn?"

Missy laughed and wiped her eyes. "Your turn? What am I, a ride at the amusement park now?"

"Actually yeah. Imma start callin you the Whirl-a-girl. Cause you be spinning me, baby."

"Ok, now *that* was corny."

They both managed a giggle.

"I'm serious, Chucky. This doesn't change anything. You said you weren't going anywhere, right?"

"Right."

"And before this, you were all ready to wait out my divorce and just be my friend. Right?"

"Right, but that was before you greased that *thang* up and put it on me." He shuddered and grabbed his crotch for emphasis.

She pushed him into the door and laughed. "Will you stop playing! Can you be serious for one minute?"

"Yes. I get what you saying. I know you gotta deal with this. I'm just anxious to be with you. That's all. But I'll let you handle your business. I just hate to see you going through this. You sure you ready?"

"No, but it's not like I have a lot of choices. It'll work out. You'll see. Before long, it'll all blow over."

W.T.F.

Brenda's worst nightmare was coming true. The police were escorting her out of her home in handcuffs, as her children and the entire neighborhood looked on.

She was in a haze. Everything around her was going in slow motion, and the sounds of chatter around her were faint. She was shaking her head and body as if she could somehow wake herself from the horrible dream.

In the distance she could hear Brandy screaming and Mandy whaling at a higher decibel than usual. There was a lot of commentary from onlookers. Some were yelling at the cops while others were asking her what happened and who they should call. Brenda snapped out of her haze long enough to yell for Brandy to call Aunt Pat.

When they reached the squad car, an overzealous female officer who looked vaguely familiar shoved her head inside, causing her to fall onto her side. The handcuffs were way too tight and digging into her flesh. She couldn't sit up straight, and the car was going so fast that it was throwing her around the backseat.

The seats were hard plastic, and the car smelled of urine. Brenda felt sick. The officers were laughing, as she was thrown to and fro. The lady yelled into the backseat, "You alright back there, killer?" and then burst into laughter when her partner made a sharp turn that caused her head to hit the window. Her life was in shambles. Hood gossip and fodder for the officer's amusement. What. The. Fuck.

Her head was spinning and she was nauseous. Between the motion and the stench, she couldn't take it anymore. She threw up. All over herself. She was in hell.

Brenda prided herself in being strong, but this day she was anything but. She cried like a baby, as they waltzed her into the station, humiliated and stinking of vomit. She was scared and confused, embarrassed for her children.

Before the police handcuffed her and read her rights, they informed her that she was being charged with "the murder of Fridaye

Mbungalo." The police turned her house upside down and the overzealous female came rushing down the stairs, cradling Pinky high above her head. She screamed, with the excitement of a lottery winner, "I got it!"

Brenda stood watching as they took the clip from the gun revealing that it was empty. She knew that she always kept the gun fully loaded, and if her memory served her correctly she had only let off one shot – a shot that never even hit him. *If* she remembered correctly. The truth was, she wasn't a hundred percent sure of anything, but she was pretty sure. She thought.

This certainly wasn't the first time she had been cuffed and brought to a police station. Actually it had only been a few months since the Potomac incident so she remembered the process quite well. But this day was different. She wasn't coming in on a misdemeanor charge for possession of half a joint or for a fight with some neighborhood chic that was trying to push up on her husband. She was being booked on murder one. Premeditated. Life sentencing.

As much as she wanted to talk, to tell the truth about what happened, she had seen enough episodes of The First 48 to know that whenever possible, keep your cool and ask for your lawyer. The police had a way of twisting your words, and since she was already confused on a few points, she thought it best to keep her mouth shut until she had a chance to speak with a lawyer.

As soon as they led her into the interrogation room, she asked for her lawyer. Her request was ignored. The two high-strung detectives paced the floor all around her, yelling and whispering, threatening and reasoning, pulling the all too familiar, and hopelessly cliché good cop/bad cop routine. As if she didn't own a television. Brenda didn't budge, not even when they illustrated what would happen to her children once she was convicted of murder. She sat there stone faced and when it seemed they were exhausted of their shenanigans she politely repeated herself, I'd like to call my lawyer.

Their last ditch effort before allowing her to use a phone was sending in that overzealous female cop.

As soon as she walked in, Brenda remembered where she knew her from. "I thought I was supposed to be gettin my phone call."

"Long time no see huh. How's life?"

"Look, I don't have time to play around with you, and I'm not gon say it again. I'm not talking to nobody BUT my lawyer!"

"Calm down girl. We gon get you your lawyer."

"Then do it."

"Can I get you something? Your lips look a little dry, babe. You need some water."

Brenda ignored the comment. The bitch was trying to provoke her.

"You know something," the cop said. "I'm not even supposed to be in here. I'm not a detective, I'm a patrol officer. But I told them I knew you and that maybe I could help."

"I don't know what you did that for. I already said everything I had to say. Ph-one call. Law-Yer."

"You know, I could've had you locked up, right? All those years ago."

"LaWann, I hope you don't think I owe you somethin. The only reason you didn't press charges on me is cause you knew I would whoop your ass again. *And* because you know your ass started it. Running your fuckin mouth. Playing games with my husband. You should have kept me and my man's name outta your mouth, and I wouldn't have had to beat your ass like I did."

LaWann laughed. "You still don't get it. Do you realize how much shit you in right now? That temper ain't done nothin for you but brought your ass back to the 5th District precinct in handcuffs, this time for the long ride. I can't say I blame you, though. If I found the asshole who killed my husband and raped my daughter, I probably would have done the same thing. But we ain't talking about me. We talking about you. I'm just here to help."

Brenda was shocked to hear that she knew about Brandy. Daye setting Melvin up to be killed was all over the streets, but how did the police already know what happened to Brandy? "I don't know what the fuck you talkin bout, but what you can do to *help* me right now is loosen up these cuffs. You can see, they cuttin into my wrists."

LaWann walked over and grabbed her cuffs. "You know I *will* taze you if you try anything right?"

"I'm not gon try anything. I just want the circulation back in my hands. I might need to use again one day."

"Well, seems like you know how to use them pretty well. You damned near emptied that clip in your boy. You a good shot too. Oh and that's a real pretty pink gat you got. Where'd you get it?"

Brenda leaned back in her chair and folded her arms, determined not to say another word.

"Ok, well if you not gon talk, just listen. Two things you should know here. Number one. We already have a witness that saw you leaving Daye's house around the time he was killed, so we know you did it. And two. We have the DVD, so we know what happened to your daughter. That gives us opportunity and a clear cut motive. They sent the gun to ballistics. Tell me, where in the hell did you get pink bullets? Why would someone ever want to shoot someone with a pink bullet?" She laughed. "That was *super* stupid. Girl. Well, you can sit tight. Looks like you'll be with us a while. I'll go get you that phone now." She laughed again, "Ahhhhhhh! Super stupid."

LaWann's little update sent Brenda's head spinning. Things were getting more confusing by the minute. Was she being set up? Obviously it was her gun. She couldn't believe that she still had those stupid ass pink bullets Kim gave her in the gun.

And Someone had to have used it and put it back in its box, under her bed. But who? She remembered that MJ came in and out of the house that night but then again; so did Brandy and so did Aunt Pat.

Brenda used her phone call to reach Joshua Cohen. He was Melvin's lawyer and good buddy. He'd gotten Melvin out of many a jam and had a reputation for winning. Melvin bragged about Mr. Cohen's win loss ratio all the time. He rarely lost a case taken to trial. The guy was expensive, but worth every penny, and although he was getting up in age he was still as sharp as a razor. She knew if anyone could help her he could.

His receptionist, Martha took the call. She informed Brenda that Mr. Cohen had passed away a few months prior and that his son David took over the practice. Bummer.

Brenda remembered David. They'd been introduced once at the office and she remembered him to be a bit strange. Grungy. He had passed the bar but didn't seem to have much interest in following in his father's footsteps. Mr. Cohen complained about him a lot. But since he was her only option, she asked to speak with him.

About an hour later, he was led into the interrogation room. He looked just as Brenda remembered. Grungy. His hair was way too long and unkempt, as was his beard. He looked like a reject from ZZ Top. David wore khakis and a black polo shirt, both of which looked like they could use a good wash and iron. It was terribly unbecoming of an attorney, let alone one that was conducting business outside his office. His father would be ashamed. He also smelled of alcohol. Brenda had a bad feeling about him, but unfortunately for her, Dirty

David was her only option.

She had little money, and she knew he'd be flexible on fees because they had somewhat of a history. Besides, she wasn't about to put her life in the hands of a public defender. So she pushed back her reservations and proceeded to spill her guts.

Brenda told him everything she remembered about that night, leaving out no detail. After a few hhm's and ha's he agreed to take her case for whatever money she had, considering this would be his very first murder case. That little revelation made her beyond uneasy…but again, what choice did she have?

He informed her that his investigator would be in touch with her and her family within the next day. And that was that.

As she sat in her cell, all she could do was worry. She worried about her kids. Where were they, and what were they thinking? Which one of them committed this crime? It absolutely *had* to be one of them. Who else could it be?

She had to admit that some of the events of the night in question were a bit of a blur, but she knew without question that she didn't kill the man. As much as the evidence pointed in her direction, the fact was that she didn't fire the bullet that killed him, but it troubled her that proving her innocence just might send one of her children to prison. Her best hope was that this lawyer would be able to get her off on circumstantial evidence or some other legal loophole, and then she could figure out the next step.

The first step was the one that gave her the most pause. Her lawyer was a drunken imbecile who probably couldn't litigate his way out of a wet paper bag, yet he was the only person she could depend on. Besides, he had to be pretty smart to pass the bar, didn't he? Surely some of his father's skills rubbed off on him. He was at the office or in court with him all the time.

She rationalized her way out of her panic and decided to hang her hat on the fact that she was innocent. The events as they occurred seemed unbelievable, but they were what they were and prayerfully Dirty David could make a jury see it.

Meanwhile, she needed to get in contact with Aunt Pat. If anyone could find out what *really* happened, it was her.

*****

Two days passed, and she was informed that she had a visitor. Patricia James. Wonderful. She walked out to the visitor's hall and picked up a receiver.

"Hey Aunt Pat."

"Pink bullets? Really Brenda? Come on."

"Please don't start. Yes, yes, yes I know it was dumb. Kim gave me those bullets with the gun. I thought they were cute; I was supposed to let em all go the next time I went to the range; I just never got around to it. So, that's that. I mean...it ain't shit I can do about it now so..."

Aunt Pat shook her head, and sighed. "Well, anyway. How you holdin up in here?"

"I'm holdin."

"I got word into some of my people in here. You'll be aaiht."

"Thanks. I appreciate it. So what's the word on the street?"

Aunt Pat pursed her lips and shook her head again. "Girl...I'm so PISSED with you right now? You know that right?"

"Please Aunt Pat. I asked you not to start wit me—"

She leaned into the partition. "Start what? Telling you that if you would have just done what the fuck I asked you, you wouldn't be in here right now?"

Brenda disregarded the comment. "You know; I think my boy did this."

"Yeah, he did."

"Seriously?"

"You know I don't like talking on these phones—"

"What the hell difference does it make now."

"Right. Fat Jean saw him comin outta the house. He said he heard the gunshots and a few minutes later he saw him run back out to the alley and pull off in your truck."

"Damn. Ion really know if it's true, but LaWann said they got a witness. You think it's Jean?"

"Hell nah. Jean ain't talkin. He a stand up dude. Plus he know better."

"Then I wonder who it is."

"It could be nobody. Maybe she was just fuckin with you. But I'll look into it."

"Have you talk to him?"

"Who?"

"My boy."

"No, nobody has. He missin. He ain't in southeast, he ain't around the way or with any of the little girls he fools with. I got my people out looking for him."

"Shit. Well we know he had to come back to the house to put my gun back."

"Yeah, then he left in your truck and ain't nobody seen his dumb ass since. You know umma fuck him up when I see him, right?"

Brenda shrugged. "What's done is already done Aunt Pat. I just need you to get me up outta here."

Pat scowled and pursed her lips, angrily. She spoke just above a whisper. "That's just it. This ain't no fuckin parkin ticket, Brenda. And I ain't no damn Jeannie; I can't just make this shit go away!"

"I know. Calm down. I'm just thinking out loud, I guess. We'll figure somethin out. How are my girls doin?"

"Brandy won't leave the house. She's takin care of Mandy, and you know Mandy don't ever stop cryin. I'm givin Brandy a little time to herself before I make her go back to school. I know she ain't looking forward to answerin all them questions. I'm tired of folks comin to me, so I know she gon get attacked with the bullshit soon as she set foot out the front door."

"I know. That's what's killin me. I let them down." Brenda teared. "I keep lettin 'em down."

"Well, like you said, what's done is done. We just gotta figure out how we gon fix it. And we will."

"Right. I remember when they told me mama died. I screamed out loud, 'God what else could happen to me?'"

"Yeah well some shit you just shouldn't put out in the atmosphere."

"Ain't *that* the truth?"

"Let me ask you somethin. Let's say we can't get you outta here. All this evidence is pointin to you and the onliest way we can get you home is to tell them everything we know. You willin to do his time?"

Brenda paused. She felt almost guilty for needing to mull it over. She'd kill for her children, without a doubt, but would she be willing to do hard time in their place?

"A guard yelled out, "Times up! Visiting hours are over, ladies."

"Well I guess that's me," Aunt Pat said.

"Yeah." Brenda answered. Grateful to the guard for the interruption. She didn't know how to answer that last question. "My lawyer has an investigator comin by the house tomorrow. Can you give him some help?"

"I got you covered, baby girl. We gon figure this out. You stay strong, you hear?"

"I will. Love you. Kiss my girls for me. Tell em I love em."

"You know I will. Love you, too, baby."

Going back to her cell was like walking the green mile. Hearing Aunt Pat say, "What if we can't get you out of here" was jarring. The shit had gone way past serious, and as of that moment she could no longer take solace in that whole, "the truth shall set you free" thing.

The cards were stacked way too high against her, and as far as the police were concerned they had the truth, a motive, the murder weapon and apparently a witness. The universe had a crazy way of playing things out sometimes. She did everything *but* kill da nigga, and now she was facing spending the rest of her life in jail.

As much as she wanted to believe that she would do anything for her children, *this* anything wasn't that damn simple. What she knew for certain was that her son wouldn't last five minutes behind anybody's bars. He may have gotten up the nerve to pull a trigger, but that was the easy part for half the little boys in the hood. A life in prison was something different, something he could never handle.

MJ wasn't nearly as strong as Brandy was. He'd fold like an envelope under any kind of pressure. He always did, even as a small child. All you had to do was yell at him and he confessed to shit he didn't even do.

She shuddered to think what his life would be like if the truth came out. On the other hand, letting him get away with taking a life, no matter how despicable that life was, couldn't be the right thing. Could it? What kind of message would that send?

Considering she walked the same street to Daye's house holding the same gun with the same intent; what could she possibly say to him without sounding like a hypocrite? Brenda was faced with the hardest decision of her life and before too long she'd have to make it….one way or the other.

The Money Shot

When they got back to the hotel garage Missy and Chucky shared a passionate kiss and an embrace that seemed to last for hours. Chucky didn't want to let her go, mainly because he didn't know when he'd be able to see her again. So much had changed in the last 24 hours. So many changes were about to come. Finally, he let go, and she went on her way.

On the ride home, Missy was strangely excited. The real game was about to begin. If she played her cards exactly right this would be the best thing that could ever happen to her.

Ever since the day she found out about Ray's little secret, she contemplated how she'd handle it, if and when it was ever exposed. What happens in the dark inevitably comes to light, so she knew that at some point she had to be prepared to deal with it. And as the poor unsuspecting wife, she could really milk it.

She thought, Cookie Johnson recovered from her scandal and her family was on their way to billionaire status. Hillary Clinton was on her road to the White House. And their husbands weren't even gay! If she played her cards right, Ray's tranny love would make her famous and she'd be rubbing elbows with Oprah again in no time.

The scandal would go down in history, and like every other one it would be old news soon enough, but it was all about how she handled it. She could let it ruin her or she could use it to her best advantage.

Having spent the better part of a decade in advertising and marketing, Missy James knew full well how to make pink lemonade out of a nasty rotten lemon. And that's just what she intended to do.

As she drove along the beltway, she imagined who'd play her onscreen. There were lots of beautiful mulattos in Hollywood. The Mawry sisters, Persia White, Rashida or Kidada Jones. Sydney Poitier's daughter was definitely a good contender. Alicia Keys had been acting more lately so she could probably pull off the part. They were all good choices.

Missy had gotten so carried away with her fantasizing that she almost ran into the back of a van that was double parked at the end of her street. As she pulled around it, she noticed it was a news van. There were news trucks lining the street and hungry paparazzi milling bout. Lying in wait. For her.

She pulled into the long driveway causing a frenzy. News anchors, cameramen and paparazzi were all vying for position. She stopped the car midway up the driveway, reached into her purse and pulled out her sunglasses. It was show time.

*****

The sound of dozens of reporters yelling at her, the shutters and the flash bulbs from the cameras were in stereo. At least a dozen reporters yelled for her attention. "Mrs. Coleman!" "Mrs. Coleman!" "Did you know?!" "How do you feel knowing your husband is gay?!" "Are you getting a divorce?!" "Have you spoken with your husband?" "Where's Ray?!"

The barrage of the attention was exhilarating. It was all she could do not to turn around and smile for the cameras. But she knew she had to stay in character. She was the victim. Should she cry? No, that would be too much. Maybe later.

Her eyes danced behind the darkness of her oversized Chanel sunglasses as she pursed her lips, desperately trying to save a smile from forming.

Feigning extreme emotional distress, she pushed her way through to her front door. She fumbled needlessly with her keys as cameras flashed behind her like showers of lightning bolts in a storm. One of the paparazzi came eagerly to her aid.

"Mrs. Coleman, please allow me."

She let out an exasperated sigh. "Thank you. This is all just too much." She handed him her keys and turned to address the cameras. "Please, everyone please. My family is going through enough. I'm sure you can understand this is a very difficult time for us. And we ask that you please, please respect our privacy. Thank you all so much."

The photog opened the door wide and handed her the key. As soon as she crossed the threshold, Missy let out a blood curdling scream, and then she slammed the door shut behind her, but not before Mr. Helpful snapped a photo that would pay enough to send him into early retirement.

I Got You

The arraignment was scheduled for the day after Brenda's arrest. D.C. Superior Court at 9 a.m. She was nervous, but David assured her that it was just routine. He said he'd make a request for bail but they would probably deny it, which was pretty standard on a murder charge.

All she needed to do was enter her plea and then another hearing would be set. "Piece of cake," he said before patting her shoulder and walking out of the room, back to his freedom.

The next morning, at eight o'clock she was retrieved by two U.S. Marshal's. They escorted her from the jail to the courthouse. The older of the two was a real sleaze. On the trip over he introduced himself as Percy Davis. She thought, *ew*. Even his name skeeved her out. He was middle age, with a slight belly pouch and balding, badly.

As they waited outside the courtroom he stood over her, undressing her with his pervy old yellow eyes. Asking too many damn questions. Personal ones like what was her bra size. Fed up, that was the only question she responded to. "A thirty-eight triple SHUT THE FUCK UP!" The younger marshal nearly fell over in a fit of laughter as Percy rolled his eyes and sucked his teeth.

Brenda just wanted to hurry up and get the court shit over with before the idiot caused her to get into even more trouble. She closed her eyes and tried to tune "Pervy Davis" out, but he kept at her. Grating on her nerves. When she opened her eyes, ready to curse his dumb ass up and down the hall she caught a glimpse of something sweet.

There was a long, tall, handsome vanilla latte walking down the hall toward them. When he came closer to, and better into focus she could hardly believe her eyes. It was David. The new and improved version. The clean shaven one. The one dressed like he was headed for the boardroom at a Fortune 500 company. David 2.0.

All eyes were on him as he walked the long corridor with his expensive leather briefcase and all the swagger of a natural born winner. She thought, *Damn he's fine*. He even smelled good. He sat down on the bench beside her, and when he spoke Brenda was so taken by him that for a minute she could only see his lips moving.

Sensing that she wasn't quite receiving what he was saying to her, he snapped a finger in front of her to pull her out of her gaze. "Brenda. Are you listening to me?"

"Yeah, yeah I'm listening."

"Then what do I need you to do?"

"Oh. Just sit and listen. Stand when I'm asked to, and when he asks me how do I plea, I say not guilty."

"That's it. He's gonna tell you what the charge is but don't let that freak you out. You're innocent right?"

"Right."

"So the rest doesn't matter right?"

"Right."

"Now gimme some." He put his fist up for a bump. She didn't know whether to be amused or offended. She hated when white people tried to be down. But she bumped him anyway. Why not.

"That's my girl. After this is all over. I'll take you down to Joe's for some crabs."

She laughed. "How'd you know I like crabs?"

David smiled, flirtatiously. "You'd be surprised what I know."

"Whatever. All black people like crabs."

"Well ion know bout all that, but I know *you* like crabs, and you like crabs from Joe's and when I bust you outta here that's the first stop we make."

She smiled. "Yeah, well imma hold you to it?"

Dave leaned in to her, smiled and whispered. "Hold me tight."

Brenda thought, *wait, is he really flirting with me? For real?* "You know you clean up pretty well, counselor."

He adjusted the knot on his tie and brushed his lapel. "Well thank you. I went out and bought this suit just for you."

She blushed. "Whatever."

"I'm serious. I saw how you looked at me yesterday. Broke my heart, too. A brutha had to step his game up today."

Brenda had to put her hand over her mouth to stifle her laugh. She thought, *oh lawd he's a wigga*. "Ok, stop it."

"Fine. It's time to go in now anyway. Let's get in here and get this over with. The sooner we get this nonsense behind us, the sooner we can get us some crabs, right?"

"Right. Dave."

"Yeah."

"I'm nervous. I mean *really* nervous."

"I know, but you'll be fine. Trust me." He smiled again and placed his hand on top of hers, for reassurance. Dave had a great smile. Bright and sincere. She was totally taken in. She followed him into the courtroom like a lovesick puppy as Percy mumbled insults under his breath. "Cracka ass muthafucka. What the fuck he gon do with her." Brenda turned to him and said, "A-ny-thing-he-wants."

The young guard stifled another laugh. "Come on Percy, leave that lady alone before you get us in trouble."

Just as Dave said, the hearing was routine and took only a few minutes for the judge to recite the charge, ask for her plea and set a trial date. Hearing that she was being charged with first degree murder and the maximum sentence it carried was not at all a piece of cake, but David had prepared her. She was doing better than she expected.

Before the marshal's led her out of the courtroom, Dave told her not to worry and that she'd be fine. His last words to her were, "I got you." They were the second best three words she'd ever heard. Melvin used to say it to her whenever she worried about something.

She thought, *Brenda, girl you are in way too much trouble to be crushin on this white boy. He's here to do a job. Get your mind right.* Then she smiled to herself as the melody to Jungle Fever played in her head.

The Aftermath

Ray Coleman's suicide was the biggest media sensation DC had seen since the president jizzed on that chubby intern's blue dress.

First the superstar football hero's tranny love is exposed and then his wife finds him hanging from two stories up in their foyer. The foyer of the home that was scheduled to be foreclosed upon within 30 days. They even published a copy of the foreclosure notice in the tabloids. Everything was being exposed at once:

"…upon further investigation, FMZ discovered that Ray Coleman was virtually penniless and under investigation for tax evasion when he died. He reportedly owed the government more than $17 million in back taxes and according to our sources, a close personal friend of the family, he was in huge amounts of gambling debt with several Las Vegas bookies with ties to the mob…"

There were endless gay rumors. Trannies were coming out of the woodwork claiming to have been with Ray. Missy didn't know who or what to believe. Normally when an athlete died, the most the wife had to deal with was a paternity test…or two. The Coleman family was dealing with grief and humiliation of epic proportion.

Missy thought she had prepared herself for the fallout that would inevitably come when Ray's lifestyle was exposed, but the situation at hand was utterly unfathomable.

Some of the rumors were beyond ridiculous. According to the rags, Ray was a crossdresser, he was secretly planning to have a sex change operation, his first wife was really a man and his children were adopted on the black market.

One tabloid wrote that Missy herself was a man and that Ray met her while trolling for trannies in downtown DC. It was amazing what people would do and say and dream up for a dollar.

The latest story was that Missy was aware of and even supported Ray's lifestyle and relationship. She suspected that one came from Carlita. Since it was true.

And where *was* Carlita? Missy was very surprised she hadn't tried to contact her since Ray's death. She didn't show up for the funeral, which was a good thing, but she had to be grieving, somewhere. She loved Ray as much as he loved her. That was fact, not an act.

Then again, she could have been the one to expose the whole situation. Maybe to get back at him for something he did; he was a world-class asshole after all. Maybe it was to finally expose him so she could be with him in the open. Who knew? The story got leaked somehow, and the pictures of them that were leaked were very personal. At any rate, Matt had warned that contact with Carlita was off limits, so it would probably remain a mystery. At least for the time being.

Given how he treated her, she didn't feel much sympathy for Ray, but she did love him once so she felt she owed it to him to at least try to minimize the damage the rumors were doing to his family.

His parents were really suffering. She couldn't understand why he would take his life the way he did. He didn't leave a clue or a note so there was no closure. No understanding. Was it just to punish her? He knew that she'd be the one to find him hanging there so that *had* to be it. He made a distress call, and she didn't answer it so he was going to show her. But instead of feeling guilty, she was angry. Furious even.

Of course, the man had to be in a lot of pain to take his life in such a manner, but it really was the meanest, most selfish thing he'd ever done – not just to her but to his family, to his children. Missy thought, if he expected to ruin her life with his final fuck you, he was sadly mistaken.

She'd taken all the grief from him she was going to in life *and* in death so after the appropriate amount of public mourning, and maybe a few more sessions with Dr. Cartwright, she would do her level best to put all things Ray Coleman far behind her. But first things first, she thought. I have bury the man.

*****

Ray's service was short and solemn with mostly his family and close friends in attendance. Despite the wonderfully written funeral program and the elegant speeches made by his former teammates and coaches, the service was painfully awkward.

Instead of a fond remembrance, it was as if the Good Rev. Dr. Kenneth Abernathy was eager to get Ray and his scandal the hell out of his church, which was pretty ironic considering his eldest son

Darien, who was standing tall beside him directing the church choir, was a flamer.

According to Ray's mother, Darien's "preference" was the worst kept secret in town. For that reason, in the confines of the pastor's study, Mrs. Coleman dared Kenny or his uppity first lady, and former "shake dancer" Mirna to deny her son a proper service in his home church.

She was prepared to go to whatever lengths necessary to honor her son and she made that known. The pastors obliged. But they didn't like it. As far as Mrs. Coleman was concerned, they didn't have to.

After saying what she knew would be her last goodbyes to the sweet country Coleman's, Missy headed back to Potomac to take care of business. There was much to resolve.

A couple of days after Ray's death, Missy discovered that her idiot husband no longer had life insurance. When she called the company to file a claim they informed her that his policy had recently been cancelled. Apparently he'd cashed out all of the value and stopped paying the premium.

Missy was astounded by his selfishness and the lack of regard for the welfare of his children. She knew he could care less if she got a dime from his death, but to cheat his kids out of their security was so much worse than she ever thought him capable of. She paid the funeral costs from her personal account but certainly didn't have enough to pay off his debt, so some hard and fast decisions needed to be made.

First thing the next morning, she allowed an agent with Elite Motors access to their garage. Ray had defaulted on loans for several of his vehicles and when they got the news of his death they decided to inquire into the estate's ability to bring his loans current. He had been keeping them at bay with his charm and his good name, but since they were no more, it was time to settle up.

One by one the Bentley, the Humvee, and his precious Aston Martin were hitched to a tow truck, taken down the driveway and off the property. She couldn't wait to see that damn Aston Martin go. It had been his newest obsession, and several times she had to suppress the urge to put a key to its body.

The house was to be sold at auction in a matter of weeks and with the IRS debt looming Missy knew that everything else they shared of any value would be taken and sold – the jewelry, furniture, his Heisman and MVP trophies, his '68 Shelby Green Hornet and the classic 1950 Ferrari Testarossa that he had sitting in storage. Even the land and property that he had been meaning to sign over to his children, but never got around to, had to be sold.

Missy had never driven any of his cars, so seeing them roll away was hardly a loss for her, but it was definitely a very public shame. Still, as bad as everything was, it was nothing she couldn't handle.

With a little time and a lot of good PR, she'd not only get through it, she'd be able to start over, standing firmly on her own two Christian Dior clad feet.

For the next phase, she reached out to some high-level contacts and sold enough of her assets to pay off a considerable amount of Ray's debts. She was able to reach a more reasonable settlement with the IRS, and the sales from his vintage cars paid off the balance of their mortgages after the short sales.

When all was said and done, she had taken care of all his obligations, and she still had a considerable amount left for the kid's trust fund and to give to his parents.

Missy didn't want a dime of Ray's money. Once the Coleman Estate was debt free and distributed to his family, Missy was officially loosed of his stronghold, and from that point on she intended to profit from her pain. She deserved it, and she was going all in.

*****

In an effort to keep some family affairs private, Missy enlisted Matt's help in getting her message out. She gave an exclusive interview on the Fox 5 Morning News show and later, after much demand, she did a couple of interviews on major network morning shows up in New York.

She and Matt agreed that putting their own story out to the public was better than allowing the rumors to continue to grow wings. So they did. Ray was the villain and she the victim. There was really no other way to play it. And it wasn't exactly an untruth. By the end of that PR run, Missy had won over the sympathetic hearts of many and she planned to swipe that sympathy card until the name rubbed off.

According to her television interviews, she was just as shocked as everyone else to find out about her husband's secret lifestyle; but after much soul searching and counsel with her pastor, she had forgiven him.

According to an excerpt from her first in depth interview with Ebony Magazine, at first she hated him when she found out, but when you loved a man as much as she loved Ray Coleman, how could you ever really hate him? He was a good man, and she felt sorry for him because it must have been very hard for him to live a lie for so long, to not be able to love who he wanted to love.

When Robin Roberts asked if there were any "signs" in her marriage, Missy's reply was after taking a long hard look at her marriage, there were many things that she ignored but she would not be specific because that would dishonor her husband and family. That vagueness left the door open for variety of strategic maneuvers in potential crisis management. Matt was all over it.

With his help, the offers were pouring in. Interviews and photo ops were plentiful. There were speaking engagements and invitations to sit on boards of various women's groups. At every opportunity, she rattled off her educational and professional background, what her plans were for the future, and how she wanted her experience to help other women.

She professed her love, forgiveness and understanding of her dearly departed and profoundly misunderstood late husband. She was empathetic to his plight but careful not to actually *say* that she supported or agreed with his lifestyle choice.

Per Matt's direction, she straddled that fence just enough to gain the public's sympathetic support but not to offend folks on either side of the spectrum of sexual orientation. Politics 101.

In interviews she shamelessly plugged her new nonprofit for young wayward teens "James Girls," reciting her carefully crafted mission statement for prospective clients and donors in her target market. Marketing 202.

That PR run was the thing all great campaigns were made of. She thought, she should definitely get into politics after conquering the business world.

Matt planted and Missy confirmed the allegations of spousal abuse. She quickly became an advocate for battered and abused women. She shared how her controlling husband left her in financial ruins and how her business acumen helped her to quickly get her family back on financial footing. She 'd won over the LGBT community by forgiving her husband and empathizing with "anyone who wasn't allowed to love who they wanted to love."

At the end of the cycle, she'd given enough phony insight into herself and her marriage to make the idea that she'd been supremely duped a feasible one. She was the victim. The poor wife. The last to know. It was brilliant. She capitalized on every available opportunity and she had a supremely fat bank account to show for it. It felt great!

As she sat in her private room at the Red Door Spa, immersed in a warm peppermint-scented mud bath and sipping a glass of Veuve champagne, Missy never felt more like a winner. She raised her glass to the sky and yelled out, "Got DAMN I'm good!"

The Great Escape

Brenda was definitely tiring of the jail thing, but much to her amazement, other than missing her kids, she was getting along pretty well. She listened to her iPod, kept herself busy with school. Read books that she would have never picked up on the streets – Hemingway, Shakespeare, Baldwin. She was just about halfway through the Holy Bible and planned to tackle the Holy Koran next.

Her cellmate was a radical Muslim, full of ridiculous opinions and disrespect for Jesus Christ. Brenda was tired of hearing her interpretation of the Bible and Koran, so she wanted to see for herself if the crap Amina Shabazz, fka Tracey Norwood, was spouting was anything close to the truth.

Brenda's existence inside was relatively peaceful. She learned early to trade on the James name so she got everything she needed. Aunt Pat's name carried weight inside, so nobody fucked with her.

That was better than any of the other poor inmates could wish for. There was some tough shit going on around her – drugs, gangs, prostitution. The bullying was brutal, and if you didn't stand up for yourself, you could hang it up. V for victim would be stamped on your forehead, and your life would be pure hell.

Women were women in or out of society, so the cliques and the cattiness were par for the course, but in jail, it was to another level. When you belonged to a clique, you *belonged*, and straying wasn't an option. Not if you wanted peace behind those cement walls.

One visiting day, Aunt Pat was supposed to come down and give her a family update. Brenda had been looking forward to it all week. She couldn't get to the visiting hall fast enough. Other than the occasional visit from Dave, which she loved, those weekly visits from Aunt Pat were all she had to connect her to the outside world and to her family.

Brenda smiled wide when she saw Aunt Pat pimp over to the phones. In her signature flannel button up and super timberlands. She was the coolest dude Brenda knew.

"Hey baby girl," Aunt Pat said. "How you holdin up in here?

They takin care of you?"

"Yeah I'm ok. Things have been ok. Well…I mean…as ok as they *can* be up in here."

"I hear you. I put a word in to my girls and the CO's. Nobody is to fuck with you. You shouldn't have no problems here. On the off chance that a bitch comes at you, just let my girl Angel know. I told her to come see you today. Introduce herself."

"Ok, I got it. So what you got for me?"

"I think we found MJ."

"Oh God! Thank the Lord. Where?"

"He's been staying with some girl in the projects in southwest. You know a Cassandra?"

"No I haven't heard anything about a Cassandra. Is he ok? Did you get to talk to him?"

"Nah, every time I go by there he's not there. And I hear he's gettin high."

"Shit. He's smokin again."

"Yeah but it ain't weed."

"Then what?"

"Dippers."

"What?!"

"Yeah. That's what I said."

"Lord MJ's little pea brain can't handle no PCP. That's shit'll kill him."

"Well that ain't all. Monte said he think MJ snortin, too."

"Coke?"

"No. H. He sellin and usin it."

"Oh my God." Brenda put her head down and closed her eyes. "My baby. MJ ain't built for that life, Aunt Pat. Them southwest niggas'll eat his ass up. He can't survive in them streets like he think he can. I gotta get the fuck outta here."

"I know. I just had to run down on some dudes drivin your truck. They said MJ owed em money. I got the truck back, and I'm keepin the keys. They sayin he gone on it, Brenda. You can't trust him no more."

"Gone?" Brenda started to cry. "You sure?"

"I'm sure."

"I can't even believe this. What have I done to my family? This is all my fault. All this shit is my fault. I'm the reason my son don't know how to cope. I put that gun in his hand. I put that dope in his nose."

"Baby, you can't blame yourself for the choices your kids make."

"Yes I can. And I do. I pretended the life I was living was ok. And it wasn't. None of it was. Look where it got us." Tears streamed from her eyes. "Melvin's gone. Killed like a fuckin animal. MJ is out of his mind. Brandy's tryin to cope with being fuckin violated. Aunt Carolyn said Mandy's not developing, and I can't even help her because I'm in here. I feel Iike I'm being punished sometimes. I deserve everything I get but not my kids. They deserve better than this."

"What you want me to do?"

"We need to get MJ home. Get him some help. Send him down to Blue Falls or something. Maybe Uncle Jim can take him in. I don't know. But he gotta get away from DC. Now."

"Brenda, it ain't simple as that. You know you can't reason with him if he on that stuff. He ain't gon just come with me cause I ask him."

"Then make him. Do whatever you have to do. Just get my baby home."

"Whatever? You sure?"

"I mean whatever."

*****

The next morning, two of Aunt Pat's goons kicked open Cassandra's back door and dragged MJ out by the hood of his sweatshirt. He was in mid nod, with fresh residue still on his nose when they snatched him up and threw him into a van. They brought him to the basement entrance of Pat's bar, shoved him inside and padlocked the door from the outside, per her instruction.

She had him locked in that basement for four days with nothing but peanut butter crackers, bottled water and a detox cocktail of Tagamet pills, Maalox and Imodium AD. The same method she used to kick her habit back in the day.

She didn't know how bad his habit had gotten but she left everything he needed in the small bathroom, including instructions on what to take and when.

The detox was a painful process to say the least. He'd be nauseated, dehydrated, weak, probably have diarrhea the first couple of days. He'd get the chills and the shakes. Probably want to die. But he'd get through it.

Pat had every intention of detoxing MJ herself. They needed answers, and the only real chance of getting any was if MJ had a sober mind.

There were cameras in the basement with monitors upstairs in her office. For 72 hours, she watched as MJ screamed and cried and kicked at the doors of the desolate dungeon, which was stripped of all its contents for his stay.

The furniture had been removed and replaced with one pillow and one blanket. Lying in a corner with that one pillow and that one blanket, MJ went cold turkey.

He mostly cried and slept. It was difficult to watch but a necessary exercise to get somewhere close to some truth out of him.

At the end of the fourth day, she went down to let him know why he was there. She unlocked the door, and the stench caused her to gag.

There was a corner of the room that the cameras didn't capture. That was the corner he decided to relieve himself in. Number one and number two. Vomit and waste everywhere but inside the bathroom, inside the toilet. The soap, towels, toothbrush and fresh clothes she left him were still stacked neatly in the spot she left them in. She walked over to the far end of the room where he was huddled up, scratching and shaking.

She thumped him on the top of his head. "MJ! Get yo nasty ass up!"

He jumped at her touch. "Aunt...Aunt Pat?" There was foam in the corners of his mouth, and his lips were so dry they were nearly cracked.

"Yeah it's me. Sit up when I'm talkin to you, boy."

"Where am I?"

"Don't worry bout where you at."

"So *you* got me here?"

"Look boy. I ain't got time for all them damn questions. You know where your mama is right now?"

"No. Can I get somethin to drink? My mouth is dry."

"Yeah, I'll get you somethin in a minute. You know why I brought you here?"

"No."

"Cause I need some answers from you, and I ain't gon get em

while you high. That's why. Boy, what the fuck you out here doin to yourself? I know you know better than this! I mean…baby, I know y'all done been through a lot this past year…but you better than this. You ain't gotta do this. This shit ain't for you."

His head fell to his chest. He didn't want to cry, but he couldn't stop the tears from flowing if he tried. "Ion know, Aunt Pat. It's just hard. I miss my dad, man. I miss grandma. Shit is just fucked up. I fucked up so bad."

"Yeah you right. You fucked up. Your mother is in jail right now MJ. For some reason, they think *she* killed Daye. Now you got somethin you wanna tell me boy?"

He pulled his knees to his chest and laid there on the cold floor crying in the fetal position. Pat let him have a moment to get it out before she shook him back to their reality.

With somewhat of a clear mind he confessed to everything. It wasn't anything Pat didn't already know, but she really needed to get it straight from his face.

After they talked, he seemed to calm down a bit, relieved to have gotten everything off his chest, but he was clearly devastated at the thought of his mother being behind bars.

Pat gave him nourishment and the most comfort she had ever been capable of giving another human being, before telling him that she was taking him to see Brenda the next morning. He nodded, knowing it was something he had to do.

The next morning, she came down with some breakfast and clean clothes. The tiny crawlspace window in the bathroom was broken. MJ was gone.

Out Of Touch

Missy smiled, sitting across from Carrie Bradshaw at Bed, the newest hottest nightclub in the city. The party was really poppin. A hot DJ, beautiful people, casual celebrity sightings. And Missy was oddly at ease being in the company of her number one style icon. They sat with both well-heeled feet up on the bed, talking as though they had known each other their whole lives.

Just as they toasted and were about to take a sip from two perfectly chilled cosmo's, Missy opened her eyes and her ears to the theme music from Sex and the City. It was the ringtone on her cell phone, which had been ringing for some time.

She removed the satin sleep mask from her eyes and grabbed the phone from the nightstand. She didn't recognize the number so she silenced the ringer.

It was early on a Tuesday morning. She'd only been asleep for a couple hours, after a very long night of schmoozing. First happy hour at The National Press Club for the Positive Black Women Coalition and then a dinner at the Occidental honoring the new president of the National Council for Colored Women.

She'd been asked to join both organizations, and NCCW was attempting to woo her into an executive post in their marketing division. Offers were coming left and right, and she was so busy she rarely had any time to herself. On that day, she planned to sleep in.

She managed to doze off into another fantasy when her phone vibrated again. Annoyed that someone was so insistent on disturbing her rest she snatched the sleep mask from her eyes. "Hello?"

"Hey."

She was still half asleep. "Who's this?"

"Who is this? You forgot me that quick?"

"Oh, no. Hey Chucky. I'm sorry. I'm just waking up. What time is it?"

"It's almost one o'clock in the afternoon."

"Wow." She sat up in the bed. "I didn't get in until this morning."

"Hmm."

"Babe, can I call you back? I need to get up and get myself together."

"No."

"Excuse me?"

"No you cannot call me back. I'll call you." Chucky hung up the phone. Missy looked at the receiver in disbelief. She dialed his number. He answered, dryly, on the third ring. "Hello."

"Ok, what was *that* about? Is everything ok with you?"

"Everything is fine with me. How about yourself, Missy?"

"I'm detecting a little attitude."

"Yeah? Well good for you, detective."

Missy sighed and looked up at the ceiling. It was all she could do not to hang up on him. "Look, I'm way too tired for this right now. What is your *problem*?"

"What's *my* problem? You really got the nerve to ask me that? Missy, I haven't spoken to you in over a month! Every time I call you I get your voicemail or your little assistant tells me you're not available. And why the hell do you have an assistant anyway? You don't even have a damn job!"

"First of all, I have an assistant to help me handle my business. Matt and I are starting a marketing and consulting firm."

"Well congratulations. At least I know I'm getting pushed aside for a good cause."

"Chucky please. You know I've been going through a lot. I could use a little support."

"Support! What the hell you think I've been tryin to do! You tell me not to show up to the funeral. Ok, I understand that. But I can't get as much as a phone call after that. You're all over the TV and in the papers. Seems like you got time for everything and everybody else *but* me. I don't even know where the fuck you live! How am I supposed to feel about that, Missy?"

"Ray! I. mean...Chu..." When Missy realized her slip she paused then there was a very awkward silence.

"Missy. Do you love me?"

"Yes of course I do–"

"DO-YOU-LOVE-ME?!"

"Yes! Yes! I love you...I–"

"Then stop pushing me aside! *Please*. I'm tryin real hard to be patient with you."

"I'm not pushing you aside, Chucky. I told you that I needed time to work some things out."

"Work out what? Huh? What things? Gettin famous? Makin a name for yourself? Missy I'm not blind. I see exactly what you're doing. I watch the interviews. I see the pictures. And to be honest, I think it's kinda low. Did you enjoy the party at the mayor's house last night? I'm sure it was nice seeing your old boyfriend again."

"So you're checking up on me now."

"No, it's on Instapic. And Facepage. And your Tweeter page. And your blog. You don't think it looks a little odd to people that you're out schmoozing and partying six weeks after you supposedly had the most 'traumatic experience of your life'? You out and about doin all that shit, and I'm supposed to believe you worried about how it looks that you and I are *friends*? Come on. Get the fuck outta here with that shit, Missy."

"Ok, I think you need to calm down just a little bit. I told you it's not like that. As soon as I can get things worked out we can pick up right where we left off. Nothing's changed about that. I just need you to be a little more patient."

"Oh I'm calm. And I know what you told me." He yelled. "Both times!"

"Babe. Please. Stop it." She softened her voice in an attempt to diffuse the situation. Chucky was getting a little too emotional. "Can we talk about this later? Over dinner?"

Another awkward silence. "Nah, I have plans tonight. You know...*business*. But I'll have my people call your people. See if we can't coordinate our schedules. Maybe we can "*do lunch*.""

Missy was really tiring of his sarcasm. "Ok. Whatever Chucky."

"Yeah, it's whatever."

"Yeah."

"Seriously though. When you ready. And I mean *really* ready, Melissa, you give me a call. Until then...take it easy."

Missy laughed. "Really? Take it easy? That's how it is?"

"That's exactly how it is, *friend*. Oh and while you at it, you might wanna check in with your family. I hear your sister not doin too well these days."

"My sister? What does she...hello?" He had ended the call.

Missy was still so tired. She didn't have the energy to deal with Chucky's little tantrum. He'd get over it eventually...and if he didn't, well, that's what happens when you're on your way to the top. People can't deal with it.

She also didn't feel like dealing with her family and their dumb ghetto drama, but she knew she couldn't ignore them forever. It had taken a lot to get back in their good graces, and she didn't want to ruin that again, but she was still upset with Brenda for the way she was treated the last time they saw each other. Missy placed her satin mask back over her eyes. She'd give Brenda a call. Tomorrow.

Never Give Up

A guard banged his club against the cell bars waking Brenda from a peaceful nap.

"Hey! James! You got a visit."

She had almost slept past visiting hours. She hurried and brushed her teeth and hair before running to the visiting hall. Seeing Aunt Pat every week was the only thing she had to look forward to those days. When she got there, she was pleasantly surprised.

"Your hair is positively dreadful, hunny," PJ said. "Don't they have a salon in here?"

"PJ, who the hell am I tryin to look good for up in here? Now stop playin. I thought Aunt Pat was coming today."

"She was. She said something came up so I came down to check on you. How you doin?"

"I'm in jail."

"Ok, I guess I had that coming. I meant how are you holding up?"

"Honestly, better than I was yesterday, and the day before that. It gets a little bit better every day I think. Especially now that I've got something occupying my mind. I don't know what I would do in here without school."

"I can dig that. Do you need anything?"

"Not really. Aunt Pat got me hooked up in here. Plenty of money on my books. I'm good for now. How are my girls doing?"

"They're holding up ok. But Brandy really wants to see you."

"No. No, PJ. My babies will not be coming to a jail for any reason to see anyone. Not even me. *Especially* not me. This ain't no place for my girls."

"Ok, but I think it might make her feel better. Can you at least call and let them hear your voice?"

"I guess. I just hate for her to even hear the announcement that the call is coming from a correctional facility. PJ, I fucked up. I fucked up so bad. I thought what I was doing was what I had to do. It's like...it's like I don't even know who I am anymore. I got so much time to think in here. Time to just…go over my life. Everything I've done. Everything I should have done. Sometimes I think this is the best place for me. I have a clear head in here. I'm in school now–"

"Brenda, girl knock it off. I can't even believe you sayin this. *This* is not where you need to be. You have not committed a crime. It's not like you killed the nigga. He got just what the fuck he deserved, but *you* didn't do it. The truth will come out soon. Just hold on."

"Yeah and then what? I trade places with my child? It's not like I haven't already fucked his life up enough. Y'all know MJ can't handle *this*!" Brenda was tired of crying, but she was exhausted and it was the only emotion that made sense. "You know, sometimes I think I should just fuckin confess and get it over with. I've been in here for months, just waiting on whatever to happen. Every day that goes by I think about how I fucked up my life. How I've ruined my kid's lives. They're probably better off without me."

"I'm sorry, sweetie. I know this is hard for you, but you gotta remember that your children love you and they need you. The sooner we get you out of here, the better. Come on now, stop crying. This will all be over sooner than you think. We've got your lawyer paid up. We're handling things out here. Just sit tight. Keep takin your classes and stay outta trouble. Keep ya nose clean." PJ leaned in closer to the glass and whispered into the phone. "And keep ya booty clean…"

Brenda broke into laughter. "You are a mess. Trust me, I'm good on that. It's strictly dickly over here sweetie. That ain't gon change."

"Uhmm hmmm. That's what your aunt said."

"Boy don't play wit me. Seriously, I'm alright in here. It's just the idle time. Too much time to think. You know."

"Yeah, well I'm sure they have things in here to help you with that darling."

"I'm drug free PJ. But on another note, have you heard anything else about Missy's situation?"

"Girl, fuck Missy. She hasn't even called to check on you. I know she knows you're in here by now. No offer to help with your legal bills. No offer to come and help with the kids. As far as I'm concerned, that selfish bitch is dead to us…again."

"Don't be like that, PJ. She's still family. She got her own shit to deal with right now."

"What shit! She knew that nigga was gay!"

"Yes she knew but can you imagine her situation. She dealt with a lot of shit before she even found out who he really was."

"Really? Like what?"

"Look, that's her business. All I'm saying is that she didn't have it as easy as everyone might think. All the stuff with her and ma. Not knowing her father. I had my father in my life every day until he died. I'm sure she feels some type of way about that too. I know if affected her. Shit, she found her husband hanging from the fuckin ceiling in her house. You don't think that fucked her up, PJ? You don't think that's affecting her?"

"Ok she found her husband. Yes, I'm sure that affected her in some way, but at the same time, she on TV pretendin to be shocked and awed by his 'alternative lifestyle.' Then two weeks after she finds him, she's like already over it. On a soapbox even. Hosting benefits for her new charity and rubbin elbows with politicians. She's a fuckin fraud. You know it, and I know it. And don't give me that she's a James girl bullshit either. She ain't never been no fuckin James girl. Blonde hair, blue eyes. She a whatever her damn daddy's last name is girl. She got more of that peckerwood blood in her anyway."

"Yeah well your eyes ain't exactly charcoal, buddy."

"Yeah, well that's cause I got *Indian* in my family."

Brenda giggled. "You are so dumb. Can you at least get me an address for her? She already left the house in Potomac right?"

"What, you wanna write her a love letter now?"

"PJ."

"She's living in some apartment in Adams Morgan, ok? I'll send you the address."

"Thank you."

The security guard called out. "Ok, visiting hours are over in 5 minutes, ladies! Let's wrap it up."

Brenda backed her chair from under the table. "I guess that's us cuz. Oh, before I go, how is everything going with you and your mom?"

"Everything like what?"

"Like your relationship, PJ. She told me y'all still not really talkin. She said it's tense."

"Why wouldn't it be tense? She been in jail like my whole life. I barely know her. And she damned sure don't know me."

"It's not like it has to be that way. You have the power to

change that. Don't just give up on her. She's the only mother you got. I'd kill to have my mother right now."

"Yeah I'd kill her to have your mother right now, too."

They broke out laughing. "Now you know that's not what I said. Seriously. Family is too important to just throw it away like that. Like it or not. We all we got."

"Apparently. That's why you chasing after Missy's tired ass."

"I'm not chasing her. Just trying to give her a chance. One thing about family, you can't pick em and you ain't gotta like em, but you do have to love them. That's just how it is. I didn't make the rules."

"I guess."

A buzzer sounded. "That's my bell. I gotta get back. Just promise me you'll think about it."

"I will. Hey. I love you, Brenda. You be good."

"Love you, too, baby."

When Brenda got back to her cell, she sat with a pencil and pad. It took her two hours, but in the end, and on the front and back of four legal-size pages, everything that ever needed to be said was memorialized on paper. She just hoped Missy would listen. She had to.

Mama's Boy

After a few days of pondering, PJ decided to finally pay his mother a visit. The conversation with Brenda had a pretty profound effect. There was so much that was left unsaid, and he knew that he couldn't continue to smile while so much pain was still festering inside of him.

He needed to address it. He needed to purge it and lay it at the feet of the one who caused it. It wouldn't be pretty, but he really needed his mother to know how her choices affected his life.

Since she'd come home there had been nothing but criticism from her. The few times they were forced to be in each other's presence the tension was palpable between them. He desperately wanted that to change.

He decided to surprise her at her bar. When he got there, her business partner Rocky, a tall lanky woman of a particular age, was holding court with a group of interesting looking ladies.

"Hey Rocky," PJ said. "Have you seen Pat?"

"Hey baby. Yeah she's in the back. Go on back there. How you been? You look….interesting."

PJ laughed. "Thanks. I think."

He walked back into the office to find his mother in a heated exchange with one of the bar girls. It seemed personal.

"I'm sorry," PJ said. "Am I interrupting?"

"Not at all." Pat waved him in. "Ki Ki, let me holla at my son for a minute. I'll come get you when I'm done."

The young girl stormed out of the room slamming the door behind her.

"Wow, she looks mad," PJ said.

"She'll be aight. So what's with the outfit?"

"Outfit? It's a sweatshirt and jeans."

"…and Timbs. I didn't know you dressed like that anymore."

"Like what?"

"Like a dude. I thought you were *so fabulous* now."

"Well, there's a lot you don't know about me. As you can

imagine, a lot has changed since you been gone. I didn't think you'd come home with a Caesar haircut and some lady's name tattooed across your neck. But hey, to each *his* own right?"

Pat didn't appreciate the sarcasm. "What did you come here for Patrick?"

"Well damn. Can't I just come to see my mother?"

"You can do what you want. But I know you ain't come way over northeast for a free drink. So what's really up?"

PJ sat quiet for a second. Debating what to say. How much to let go of. Finally, he said, "What's really up is we need to talk."

"Then talk."

"No ma. I mean *really* talk."

"Ma? You ain't called me ma since you was a kid. I guess you do wanna talk."

"I really do."

And talk they did. For hours on end. PJ opened up in a way that he never had. He completely let his guard down. He thought, *If you can't tell it to your mother, then who can you tell it to?*

He replayed his life from the day that he was torn away from her in that courtroom to the day she came home from jail. He recounted the abuse. The emotional, physical and sexual. How it started. When it finally ended. How it affected him even to that day.

Pat's heart bled for him. She felt helpless. She was too angry to cry but took care to wipe her son's tears as she vowed silently to have a very private, very serious conversation with her father-in-law. He was now 73 years old, and from what she'd heard bedridden with onset Alzheimer's. But that was hardly a reason to forego the conversation. She had every intention of jogging his memory, if only for a little while.

Things got a little contentious when PJ shared his feelings about Missy – and the fact that he was the one who leaked the photos of Ray and Carlita to the press.

"Patrick! Why the fuck did you do that?"

"Wow. I didn't expect that reaction."

"Why wouldn't you?! That is your family, boy! Now I heard about the bullshit goin on between y'all, and it's stupid. You really that mad cuz she didn't speak to your ass at a party? Really?"

"Look ma, I did what I did. I didn't expect for it to go down like it did, and trust me, I wasn't tryin to hurt Missy. I was just tryin to make sure Ray got what he deserved. How was I supposed to know his weak ass was gon go and kill hisself?"

"Yeah I have to admit; I didn't see that comin from him either."

"Right! That shit ain't my fault. Missy don't seem that hurt either…if you ask me. I probably did her a favor."

"Now you sound stupid. You can't go fuckin with people's lives like that, boy."

"You really telling *me* that? If that ain't the pot tellin the kettle, I don't know what is."

"Yeah. Well, I hope it was worth it to you."

"On my life I didn't get a dime for the pictures. That's not what it was about. And I'm about tired of everybody taking up for Missy fake ass. Fuck her. Family or not. Brenda keep runnin off that *she's a James girl* bullshit. That bitch ain't no James girl for real."

"Yeah, well neither are *you.*"

"And I guess *you* are?"

They both smiled at his snappy comeback. Aunt Pat raised her glass to him. "Touché my dear, Patrick. Touché."

That night, Pat "squared" laughed and cried together. They caught up on years of family gossip and hood drama. They drank Cognac and ate Chinese takeout as they poured out their souls to each other, neither wanting to leave the other after so many painful thoughts and feelings, secrets and memories had been shared.

It was a tender yet vulnerable place for the both of them to be. A bonding experience that they were both grateful for. Most importantly, it was a starting point. A new beginning. As soon as he could, PJ planned to thank Brenda for that.

Small(ish) Favors

The letter was four pages of handwritten emotion. It was as concise as Brenda could make it with everything she had to say and to ask of her sister.

As she read, Missy went through a range of her own emotions. She laughed. She cried. She worried. Brenda was really in jail. It wasn't just some bullshit angry talk they were having that day at the house. She really shot that guy. This was just too crazy for words.

Missy tried calling around to get some answers but nobody picked up the phone. Not Uncle Edward, not Aunt Pat, not Brandy. She even called Chucky. Since he clued her in, he must have some answers or at least some gossip. He'd changed his number, though.

The following day was visiting day. Brenda was expecting her. Missy was dreading it. She'd never seen the outside of a jail let alone the inside, but she knew she had to go and see about her sister.

When Missy walked through the doors of the CTF, she was disgusted but also saddened. The waiting area was filled with mostly women. Mothers there to support their wayward kids; desperate old women in flimsy dresses and bright red lipstick; young girls with babies in their bellies or perched on their hips, or both.

After waiting over an hour to be admitted, she was told she had to walk three blocks back to her car because she couldn't bring her purse inside the facility and the guest lockers were all full. When she returned, the guard that sent her to her car had left for lunch so she was forced to go back to the end of the line and wait again.

Waiting in line, she witnessed a belligerent visitor getting thrown out by a guard and two girls fist fighting after realizing they were there to see the same guy. Both of them had children, and apparently neither of them new about the other. It was a soap opera.

They cursed and fought right in front of the children. The other visitors and most of the guards were completely unbothered by what was obviously a normal occurrence in the waiting room. It was terrible. She wished she could do something about it.

Two hours after her arrival, she was finally led through two metal detectors and three heavy steel security doors to the visiting room. She sat on a low stool in front of a Plexiglas window with telephone receivers on either side.

Eventually Brenda walked out wearing two French braids and an orange jumpsuit. Her hands were cuffed in front of her until she got to the table and a guard removed them. Missy couldn't help thinking how impossibly fresh her sister looked. She'd obviously lost some weight, but it wasn't in that "lost-it-too-quick-and-now-you-look-sick" kind of way. She looked healthy. Her skin glowed and she looked well rested. Almost happy.

"Hey big sis."

"Brenda. I have to say this. You *really* look good."

"Well I guess that's what a few months of detox and rest will do for you. So I see you read my letter."

"I did."

"Have you thought about it?"

"I've thought about nothing but."

"That's all I ask right now. For you to think about it. I mean seriously think about it."

"I have, but Brenda, why me?"

"Because you're the only one I can trust. You don't have to answer me now. Just give it some more thought, alright?"

"Yes, I will."

"Good. How are you holding up? I heard about Ray. I'm so sorry that happened. I didn't have your number to call or anything."

Missy sat quietly for a few seconds. "It's alright. I mean. What can you do but keep moving right? Keep living."

"Yeah, but you seemed to be doing ok. I caught you on the news last week. Looks like you got a lot going on lately."

"I do. But I didn't come here to talk about that Brenda. I'm here for you. What's happening with your case?"

"Just go ahead and ask me."

"Ask you what?"

"What you really want to ask me. You don't have to beat around the bush."

"Well…I mean. If you wanna tell me."

"Um hmm. I can't really go into too much detail right here…" Brenda's eyes darted toward the guard standing within earshot. "…but the short of it is that I didn't do this."

"Ok."

"No, I'm serious Missy. I…did…not…do…this."

"Well what about the night—"

"Missy! Listen to me. I didn't do it. I was at the scene and my gun was used in the crime, but I didn't kill him. I swear. I didn't kill him."

Missy gave Brenda a suspicious side eye. "Then how the hell did you get in here, Brenda?"

Brenda shrugged. "Like you always say, it's complicated. "

Missy blurted out. "Complicated!"

Her voice echoed in the hall and she drew stares from the guard and a few other visitors. Brenda shushed her and spoke just above a whisper. Through clenched teeth. "Yes, it's fuckin complicated. Just listen. I know who did it."

"What?"

She whispered again. "I know who did this."

"Then tell! Are you crazy?"

"I can't!"

"Who the hell are you protecting?"

"My child, Missy."

Missy rolled her eyes. "Aww shit. Seriously?"

"Seriously."

"Dammit. Ok, well you didn't do it, so obviously they can't convict *you*."

"My thoughts exactly. But I don't know if it's gonna be that easy."

"Well it can be. Who's your attorney? I'm sure I can get someone—"

"No! No, I don't need you to do that. I already have an attorney."

"You have an attorney? Who? And how good could he be? How are you paying for him?"

Brenda was mildly offended. "Don't worry about how I'm paying for him. I have an attorney, and he's good. I don't need your help."

"Brenda! Are you kidding me?! This is not the time to be proud. This is a murder charge! Do you understand that?!"

"You don't think I know what it is?"

"Then how can you be so fucking calm?"

"Because I have to be. What, you think it would help if I fell apart? Oh fuck. Missy, please don't start crying. I can't take it right now."

Missy started balling. "I can't help it. I don't want this for you."

The guard made his announcement. "Look, they're calling for me. I gotta go."

"Ok, can I do anything for you. Do you need anything? Anything at all?"

"I just need you to think about what I asked you? That's it."

"I don't have to think about it anymore Brenda. The answer is yes."

Brenda was nearly overcome with emotion. She held her hand up to the glass partition. "Thank you. I love you, big sis."

Missy touched her hand to the glass. "I love you, too."

They placed the receivers back on the hooks and Missy watched tearfully as Brenda was cuffed and taken back through the heavy steel door.

She wasn't sure what she was about to get herself into, but one thing she was sure of was that she loved her little sister and would do anything to help her out of this horrible situation. Her pride be damned. Brenda was all she had and Missy had no intention of losing her ever again. Especially not like this.

It's Just Me Against The State

Day one of her trial. The State vs. Brenda Elaine James-Johnson. She was dressed demurely in a silk floral dress and sensible heels that Dave carefully selected for her from Macy's department store the night before. It was a replacement for the Valentino pantsuit and stilettos that PJ brought her the day before that.

Dave had a hard time explaining to him that Brenda's extravagant lifestyle, with no recordable income, would come into question during the trial, so an eight-hundred-dollar suit and $1200 hooker heels weren't exactly the image they wanted to project. After some protest, Miss P digressed, and Brenda trusted Dave to handle it for her.

He prepared her well for what was to happen. The jury selection went as well as he could have hoped. They had a healthy mix of backgrounds in the jurors' box, with a few that looked like they'd be appropriately sympathetic to his client's dilemma.

His experts were some of the best in the business. Despite the mounds of circumstantial evidence, he thought he had more than enough in his arsenal to invoke a reasonable doubt in the mind of at least one of the jurors. He felt good about their chances, and although he was careful not to make any promises, Dave made sure that he kept her optimistic that she'd get through it.

Truth be told, Dave had developed a major crush on Brenda. She was so different from any woman he had ever dated or even socialized with for that matter. She was beautiful, intelligent and her sharp wit was disarming. He had never laughed as hard and as often as he had with Brenda James. Her big brown eyes were soulful and sincere. Her voluptuous hourglass frame was sensual and womanly. He loved her natural hair in its big beautiful uniqueness. She was certainly one of a kind, and he kinda thought that maybe she could be the one.

He sensed that there was a mutual attraction, but was very

careful never to cross any lines. As hard as that was, he had a job to do and could only do that with a clear head and heart. One thing was for sure, he was bringing her home, whatever it took. Then maybe he could think about, maybe, possibly, approaching their friendship in a different way. If it suited her, of course.

The prosecutor, Tyrone Pettis, a.k.a. "Petty Ty," was a world class ass, an ultra-conservative black Republican with a superiority complex and a personal vendetta against anyone that *he* felt brought disgrace to his race.

Petty was born and raised in one of the roughest housing projects in Southeast DC to two crack addicts. His childhood was impossible, but he worked hard to get out from under and become everything his parents weren't. With a Harvard law degree and a budding career in the U.S. Attorney's Office for the District of Columbia, he'd accomplished far more than he ever imagined. And he never let anyone forget it.

Pulling himself up so far by his own bootstraps robbed him of any tolerance and any empathy for black folk who, according to him, "made a conscious choice to be nothing" – people cheating the system and poisoning their own communities, lying back and bleeding the taxpayers.

His perpetual disgust with his own people made him wish he could wash the color from his dark skin. But since that wasn't an option in this life, he decided it was his personal responsibility to fix all the ones that needed fixing, to punish the ones that needed punishing, to do his small part to make things right.

After reading her jacket and hearing the stories, his investigators told of her lavish ill-gotten lifestyle, Petty couldn't wait to sink his teeth into Mrs. Brenda James-Johnson, to expose her for the despicable woman she really was. For on top of the blatant discrimination against his own people, he was an extreme chauvinist that believed women were ultimately the cause of most men's downfall – a belief born of the knowledge that his junky mother introduced his father to the narcotic and ultimately ruined their family.

His opening statement was concise but seemingly effective. He assured the jury that they were about to hear an open and shut case that ended with a drug kingpin's wife getting revenge on the man that was allegedly responsible for murdering her husband and evidently responsible for raping her young daughter.

He painted Daye, the victim, as a despicable character that deserved to be punished for crimes both known and unknown, but stressed that vigilante justice inflicted by a woman that was just as much a part of "the game" as he, was not to be condoned.

From the look on the juror's faces, the case had already been decided. Dave knew he had his work cut out for him but he was definitely up to the task. He wasn't about to lose his first big case and more importantly, he was bringing his girl home.

He'd been rehearsing his opening statement for over a week. Fully prepared to rebut the character assassination that was surely to come early on in the case, he went to work.

"Ladies and gentleman of the jury, the prosecution would have you believe that the defendant, Brenda James-Johnson, is a vengeful, cold-blooded murderer...But the truth is, Brenda James is a devoted mother of three children, a devout Christian, a law-abiding citizen, and an upstanding member of her community. Right now, this courtroom is filled with people who can and will attest to that. But ultimately, this case isn't about who Brenda James is or is not. Not really. It's about what she did or did not do. And Brenda James did not commit this crime. During the course of this trial..."

Judge Mark P. Heinrich presided over the case. He was tough but fair. He was also the longtime friend of Dave's dad. Not that Dave expected any preferential treatment but quite the opposite. When Heinrich became aware that Dave was on the case, he called him into his chambers to let him know just that. There would be absolutely no special treatment. He would judge this case just as he would any other.

Dave had no issues with the judges' assertion. In fact, he was counting on it.

Heinrich was a far left-winged liberal that marched with Dr. King and generally empathized with the disadvantaged. A former acid-dropping, grass-smoking hippie himself, he supported the legalization of drugs and was therefore softer on his drug cases than most. He was a strong supporter of women's rights, civil rights, gay rights and all other rights that allowed people to be who they were and do what they wanted as long as they weren't hurting anyone else.

What he had no tolerance for was bigotry, which is why he had a perpetual hard-on for Tyrone Pettis, who ironically was viewed by Heinrich to be the disgrace to his race. Since he couldn't exactly share that opinion openly, Heinrich used his robe and gavel to make

Pettis earn every single victory. It was *his* small part to make things right.

Heinrich usually gave the defense a little more leeway when he could empathize with the accused but more important to his case, the victim was a scumbag rapist, and the judge already despised the prosecutor. Dave thought, if nothing else, he'd be granted enough leeway to make his points to the jury.

Over the course of the trial, Petty Ty detailed every bit of the Johnson family's lavish lives from the luxury cars, to the fancy vacations to the carats in baby Mandy's ears. He went so far as to ask that the video of Brandy's violation be brought into evidence to establish motive for the murder. Moreover, he asked that it be played in open court. That nearly caused a fist fight in the judge's chambers.

Dave voiced his disgust at the lengths the prosecution would go. He cursed Petty for trying to destroy a child's life for a win and when Petty mouthed *Looks like Mrs. Johnson already did that.* Dave lost it and lunged at him. He grabbed Petty by the lapels and nearly lifted him off his feet before the judge pushed them apart. Heinrich shouted.

"Do I have to put you two assholes in lockup for the night? Now sit down!" They took their seats. Judge Heinrich walked back around to his desk and took his. "Now Ty I'm not letting you play that tape in open court." Ty lifted up and started to speak but the Judge interrupted him. "But I will allow it into evidence."

Dave sprang from his seat in protest. "Judge! With all due respect! I…"

The Judge raised his hand. "Dave I will absolutely have you jailed, tonight, if you interrupt me once more. As I said, I will allow the video into evidence but the jurors will view it privately."

Petty stood back up and straightened his lapels. "Fair enough." He looked over at Dave. "I'll see you back in court counselor." Then walked out. Dave stood and headed toward the door. Judge Heinrich called out to him.

"Dave. Come here a sec."

Dave doubled back. "Yes sir."

"I don't know what just happened here. I don't know if it's the pressure of your first case or if it's the little girl, but you seem…a little too invested in this. Are you alright to continue?"

"Yeah…yeah Judge I'm fine."

"Alright then. If you say you're fine, then I believe it. You know you have a fight on your hands. Petty won't hold back. Bring your best son."

"Oh I will. I will"

Problem Child

Brenda was notified of a visit. When she got to the visiting hall, LaWann was sitting there waiting. She picked up the receiver. "Look LaWann, you know I don't like you, and you don't like me either, so whatever it is you need to say to me, just get to it."

"Well hello to you, too, Brenda."

"You have two minutes...and counting."

"Ok then I'll get right to it. I know your son murdered Daye."

Brenda's posture was suddenly stiff, and her voiced lowered to a whisper. "You don't know *shit* about my son."

"No? I know he got picked up on the south side last night. I know he's in Central Cell Block right now awaiting a bail hearing. I also know that he used your gun before you tried to, and now *you're* on trial for *his* crime. I'm sure you love your son, but are you really willing to do his time?"

Brenda acted as if she didn't hear the last comment. "He was picked up, for what?"

"Possession with the intent to distribute. They caught him riding around with cases of stolen cigarettes and a couple gallons of embalming fluid in the back of your truck. He had about a pound of weed stuffed in the glove compartment and a few bags of powder in his pocket. They arrested two more guys that were in the car with him and both of them are saying everything was MJ's. He could do some real time Brenda. Which pretty much means...you got yourself in here for nothing."

Defeated, Brenda laid her head down on the counter. She took a minute to digest the information before putting the receiver back up to her ear. "How'd you know what he did?"

"The streets is always watchin and talkin. You know that."

"Any chance you'll tell me what they saying?"

"Well I would. Except I think my two minutes are up. You have a good one." LaWann stood up and signaled for the guard.

Brenda banged the glass with the receiver. "LaWann! LaWann wait. Please. This is my child!"

She waved off the guard and put the receiver back up to her ear. "I don't have a lot of time so I'll give you the short version. There's a camera in the alley behind Daye's house, and it has MJ going in the back door. The neighborhood watch put it up last summer, after a few houses were broken into. It has motion sensors, so anytime someone comes through the alley after dark, a floodlight comes on, and the camera starts recording.

From what I hear, there's a time stamp and everything. Not only did the camera get him going in and coming out, but you can hear the shots and see the flashes of light coming from the basement window minutes before he ran out the back door. From what I hear, he'd definitely get convicted if the video came out."

"From what you heard? So you haven't seen it?"

"No I haven't seen it, but trust me, it's out there. And it's only a matter of time before the police get a hold of it."

"Well where is it now?"

"I don't know exactly. The video was taken from the camera in Mrs. Hung's yard. The police already went to her asking about the disc. It was gone, along with the surveillance equipment and her computer."

"Then how did it get out?"

"Her niece. Kim Lee."

"Fuck!" Brenda hit the partition so hard with her fist she thought she broke a bone.

"One more thing. You remember Day's cousin, Ju Ju?"

"The big dude they call Amistad?"

"Yeah that's him. He's at the jail and talking a lot of shit about what he's gon do to MJ when he comes in. He got a whole crew of crazy dope heads in there and I hear they're pretty vicious."

"Ok LaWann. Why are you telling me all this?"

"Just thought you might wanna know."

"It's not like I don't appreciate it, but it's kinda hard for me to believe you doin this out of sheer kindness. I'm just sayin. Ain't you police? Don't you have some type of obligation to report this?"

LaWann shrugged. "Yeah I would, but like you said, I don't know shit about your son. Take care, Brenda."

She stood and walked over to the exit to wait for the guard, leaving Brenda sitting there stunned and a little bewildered. Brenda couldn't figure out why LaWann would help her. It just didn't make sense.

After the beating she took Brenda was amazed LaWann was talking to her at all, let alone helping her. She thought, maybe LaWann had a beef with Kim or with the police but whatever the reason, it didn't really matter at that moment. MJ was in distress. She had to move fast.

As soon as she got back to her pod, she made a call to Aunt Pat. She told her everything Lawann said, and pleaded with her to go to the courthouse first thing in the morning and make MJ's bail. The minute he was out she was to put him on a bus. A one-way ticket to Blue Falls, North Carolina.

Down there he could get detoxed and get his life in order. There was plenty of family there to make sure he was taken care of. He'd be safe. It wasn't ideal but jumping bail for possession was nothing compared to murder one. She had to get him the fuck out of D.C. and fast.

Plan B

Kim stepped out of the shower feeling particularly festive on a Friday morning. She had a date with a new piece that was easy on the eyes and even easier with his wallet. Her newest "enhancements" had settled enough for her to have relations, so after a long dry month she could finally get her some. Everything was good.

She wiped the steam from the mirror and stood there for a moment admiring her new curves. All $20,000 worth. She pouted her freshly plumped lips and recited her morning affirmation, "Mirra mirra on the wall, who's the baddest bitch of all? Me dats who. Owwwww!"

Plastic surgery was Kim's latest addiction. After all the attention she received from her first, a boob job two years prior, she couldn't stop goin under the knife. She indulged in many things but seeing herself unveiled was a rush that compared to no other. New boobs, new abs, new booty. In a couple years Kim had gone from rail thin and awkward to an exotical beauty with a body that easily rivaled Kim K. Full breasts, thin waist and an ass way too bodacious for an Asian. But the boys loooved it and that's really all that mattered to her.

Her iPod blasted through her new Bose compact stereo. Pandora's Jukebox was set to Drake radio, and she was rapping along, lyric for lyric, while twerking her new booty to the floor and watching its reflection in the mirror on the wall.

She took a pull from her joint and walked into the kitchen to grab a cold soda, the only thing to hydrate her when she was on a hangover.

Out of the corner of her eye she noticed some movement in the living room. She turned around, so startled, she dropped the can on the floor spraying the dark sudsy liquid all over her feet and her new beige carpet.

"Good morning Kim."

"Ms. Pat? How…how did you get in my house?"

"I said *good morning* Kim."

"Um, I'm sorry. Good morning. How are you?"

"I'm fine, and I don't have a whole lot of time. Come on over here and have a seat. There's somethin I want you to see."

"Um, okay…you mind if I grab a towel?"

"You're fine. Come over here and have a seat."

Slowly and very reluctantly, Kim walked over and sat down on the edge of an armchair, next to the sofa, next to Aunt Pat. She pulled a couple pillows up to her chest to cover herself. The video was already cued up. They watched it in it's entirely, in silence.

When the camera panned to Kim, Aunt Pat turned to look at her. Kim avoided her gaze. When it was over, Kim hung her head. "Ms. Pat, I'm so sorry this happened. I swear I was so high that night I didn't even realize that was Brandy."

"Really? That's why you called her by her name before you offered her the joint?"

"Ms. Pat—"

"It's Pat."

"Pat—"

"Don't say shit to me. I really don't wanna hear shit you gotta say to me right now. All I want you to do right now is go put some clothes on. We goin for a ride."

Kim's throat was suddenly dry and her body hot, but she sat there frozen. She had heard the stories about Ms. Pat. Her reputation preceded her, and it was nothing good to speak of. Kim's eyes watered and then she stammered. "I…I have to go to work today. They'll be expecting me to open up the store and…Oh please Ms. Pat…"

Aunt Pat's face was expressionless. Emotionless. "Girl, calm down. Ain't nobody tryna hurt you, but we got some business to take care of, so please. Go put on some fuckin clothes…and don't keep me waitin out here either."

"Oh…ok."

Kim went back into her bedroom. She thought about calling the police but decided against it. She thought if Pat really wanted to do something to her, she would have done it already. Still, she had no idea where they were going. She dressed in a hurry and headed back to the living room.

"I need to call my brother and ask him to open the store today."

"You can do that in the car. You got ID?"

"Yeah." She pulled her driver's license from her wallet.

"No, I mean "*ID*, id.""

"Oh. No. All I have is my real ID."

"Don't worry about it. We'll get you one on the way."

Kim grabbed her jacket and her keys. "Where are we going...If you don't mind me asking?"

Aunt Pat ignored the question as she followed Kim out to her car. "We're taking my truck." Kim got in the passenger side of the old red pickup truck, not knowing where she was going and when she'd be coming back, and since questions were clearly out of the question she just said a silent prayer of protection and buckled her seatbelt.

They made a stop in an industrial area of northeast to get Kim's new identification card. She was now Myung Hye Hong. There could be no trace of a visit from Kim Lee Davis. But Brenda had to see her. Face to face. Aunt Pat made a call and then they headed over to the C.T.F.

Brenda picked up the receiver. "Hello Kim."

"Hi Brenda."

There was a long awkward silence. Just seeing Kim's face shook Brenda. She thought, *Where do I even start with this fuckin girl?* "Do you know I have literally been dreaming about what I would say to you when I saw you? I've been going over it in my head. I had this whole speech planned...but I swear, I can't."

"Listen, Brenda I understand how you feel but–"

Aunt Pat gave Kim a knowing glare that completely shut her down.

"Oh, you understand how I feel? Ok, then tell me."

"What?"

"Tell me how I'm feeling right now. Tell me how you would feel *right now*, if you were sitting directly across from the bitch that sat back and let your daughter get raped."

"No, no. That's not what happened–"

Brenda came closer to the glass partition. "Bitch, you put a *blunt* up to my daughter's lips. You sat there watchin while two grown men put their hands up her shirt and down her pants. She's sixteen!"

Kim hung her head low as Brenda unleashed on her.

"You watched them take my baby into that room."

Kim began to cry. "No, I–"

"Yes. Yes, you did. You sat there laughin and smokin and

drinkin with the *same nigga* you had just told me killed my husband. *Her* father. And then you watched him walk into that room and rape my child. You let him rape my child."

By then Kim's face was wet and her throat was burning. Hearing it aloud somehow made it all real. Seeing the hurt in Brenda's face made it very real. There was absolutely nothing she could say.

"You got anything to say to me?"

"I'm sorry."

"Oh you're sorry." Brenda laughed. "I bet you are sorry. You sorry about all that shit you been talkin too huh?"

"Huh."

"Yeah *huh*. You really need to watch who you talkin to. DC is way too fuckin small to run your mouth and think shit won't get back to the people you talkin bout. I heard you said my daughter was a young ho, just like her mother was? You said she's pregnant, and she don't know who the father is? What else…oh yeah, my baby girl is slow because I was still smoking weed and drinking when I was pregnant with her. My son is a crackhead, and I'm sittin in jail because I know he's too much of a *bitch* to do his own time. Did I get all that right?"

"Oh my Goooooodddd! Brenda. Who told you that shit? I swear to—"

"Uh uh. Kim. Let me stop you right there, boo. That shit was rhetorical. I don't really wanna hear nothin you got to say to me right now, and I don't need you swearing to whoever it is you serve. I know you said it. I know it for a fact. So stop tryna bullshit me."

Kim looked away. No defense. Guilty as charged.

Brenda continued. "See, I already knew you was a cruddy bitch. And understand, I *never* considered you a friend of mine. You, sweetheart, are a friend to no one. You sat and told me the intimate personal details of the lives of every one of your close personal friends *and* some of your family when you hadn't seen me since elementary school. You told me shit that would break up marriages and ruin friendships, get people killed or locked up for the rest of their lives. And all for the sake of some fuckin gossip? You sat there and told me that the man you pretended to hate, but were still *fuckin*, set my husband up to be murdered. I didn't ask you that shit, you volunteered it. And as far as I'm concerned, that's not the worst of it. Once you told me how you sold your brother and father out to the police to save your own ass, I was already done with you." Brenda pointed her finger at Kim, just touching the glass. "Bitch, you low and you dirty. I would never trust your ass. But what I didn't expect was for you to sit and watch and basically contribute to my daughter gettin raped. That was probably the last thing I expected from you. Especially since you said I was your *friend*."

Kim didn't know what to say. There wasn't much she could say. She was getting smacked in the face with her truth and it was sobering.

Brenda continued. "At first I thought, I can't blame Kim for everything that happened. It's not like she brought Brandy to that party. But the more I thought about it, the more I understood that if you would have been any kind of *friend* that night, any kind of *human being*, you would have sent my child home or at least called me and told me to come and get her. And then we wouldn't be here right now. Would we?"

Kim wiped the tears from her face and tried to compose herself. "Brenda I'm sorry. I'm so, so sorry. You have to believe me. I swear if there was anything I could do–"

"There is."

There was another long and uncomfortable silence.

"As much as I want to come through this glass and put my hands around your fuckin throat, bash you in your fuckin face over and over until I can't see you anymore, let my aunt have her way with you…"

Kim looked over at Aunt Pat who was gazing at her with the slightest smirk on her face.

"…I know that wouldn't change anything. I'd still be in here and you'd still be out there runnin your fuckin mouth. So, I figured out a way you can make this right."

Kim looked back at Brenda, pleading with her eyes. "Brenda, I swear, I'll do anything."

"Oh yes…yes you will."

Brenda made her proposal. It wasn't a bad proposal at all and certainly not what Kim expected. She fully expected to get her neck rung and her face bashed in. But this was harmless. Ultimately, it was no skin off her back, and if all went well she could help her father out if his situation too. So this was a win for everyone involved. A no-brainer. She happily agreed.

As she and Aunt Pat were led out of the visiting room, she

breathed a sigh of relief. She even cracked a smile because in her mind she'd escaped yet another one. A beatdown that is.

She waited in line to collect her personal effects from the locker while Aunt Pat went ahead to pull the truck around to the front. When she opened the locker, it was empty. Her purse, keys and cell phone were gone. In the distance, she heard the old pickup pass by the jailhouse.

Two hours later, Kim got home to find her house completely torn apart and Aunt Pat sitting in the same spot on her sofa. This time, she was with a friend. A very tall, very masculine looking woman with excessive facial hair, multiple piercings and tattoos covering her entire upper body, up to her chin. The woman was six five if she was an inch, and she looked like she lived for pain, and a weight bench.

The most imposing accessory was the bull ring hanging from her nose. Aunt Pat looked like a Disney princess compared to this lady. Kim didn't dare ask where her purse was or why she was left at the jailhouse.

"Um, hi Ms. Pat.

"Pat."

"Um…Pat. Did you forget something?"

"Where's the disc?"

Kim removed her heels and sat at the dining room table to rest her feet. They were swollen and blistered at both heels. She tried rubbing them, but they hurt to the touch. She was also stalling, trying to think of something to say. She went with the obvious. "Um. What disc?"

Pat glared at her for a second before she rose up from the sofa. Before she could even stand up straight, Kim was already crying.

"OK, ok. I don't have it. But…but I know where it is. We can go get it right now–"

"Is it more than one?"

"No. there's just one. And we can go get it right now."

"Then let's go."

"Ok. But do you mind if I go and change my–"

Aunt Pat's friend stood and shouted, "Let's GO!"

Startled, Kim jumped up and skipped out the door with her heels in her hands. The ladies were trailing close behind as they headed down the walkway toward the truck. Kim was already on edge, and the commentary between Pat and her giant lady friend wasn't helping.

"I told you she was sexy didn't I?" Pat said.

"Hell yeah! I'm still trying to figure out how a Chinese girl got all dat ass. And titties, too? Damn. Imma enjoy dat. Umh um um. Rice cakes."

As they slapped five, Kim's legs buckled and she nearly fell to the ground. The ladies snickered at each other. Stuffed in the front seat of the pick up between the two manly women, the truck peeled away from the curb, and Kim started to pray again.

Bad Timing

The trial was nearing its end when Dave paid Brenda a visit. He had some very important information he needed to relay to her. And he was only too happy to have a reason to see her outside of the courtroom. The attorney client meeting room was semi private. Quiet. He was looking forward to it.

When Brenda was summoned for the impromptu meeting with her legal counsel, she was oddly excited. Normally she didn't take as much care with her hair for a visit. But this day she had just enough time to get to the bootleg beauty salon to get a quick fix up. She dabbed a little Vaseline on her lips, and hydrated herself with the homemade mango shea butter her cellmate lent her for the occasion. Then she sat and smiled and waited for the guard to fetch her.

Brenda's affections had surpassed a mere crush and were well on their way to being "feelings." Unbeknownst to her, those "feelings" were mutual.

When she reached the meeting room, Dave was already there. He stood as she entered the room and pulled her chair as soon as she was un-cuffed. Always the gentleman. The CO took note of the interaction, staying a little closer to the door to make sure nothing inappropriate occurred on her watch.

"Brenda."

"Hey you." Brenda was nearly blushing. Dave noticed and immediately felt at ease. She could be a little hard to read. But he was feeling good rhythms. He had to squelch the urge to take her hand. Especially with the guard peering in on them.

"So, how are you holding up?"

"I'm holding up."

"Well you look like you're holding up pretty well."

"I'll take that as a compliment."

"As well you should."

They were both smiling like Cheshire cats.

"I have some news for you."

"Good or bad?"

"Depends on how you look at it, I guess. They're offering you a plea deal. Reducing the charge from first degree to manslaughter. Ten years, parole in seven."

"Well, what do *you* think?"

"I think we should tell them to shove it up their asses. Cause we're gonna win this case."

"You sound pretty confident."

"Yeah, actually I am. We have more than enough for reasonable doubt. Petty knows it. That's why he's backpedaling. I could get them down even farther than that if I wanted. But it's not necessary. Cause we're gonna win this case. And then we're going out for crabs."

"You promise?"

"Brenda, I like you."

"Wow. Where did that come from?"

"You know where it came from. Why don't we stop pretending?"

"Dave–"

He held a hand up. Effectively shushing her. Then he began to scribble on his legal pad. He tore the sheet off, folded it in half and pushed it in front of her. She picked up the note and opened it. Then she broke into laughter before picking up the pen and marking her response. The note read:

Brenda Elaine James, will you go out with me?

Yes ___ No ___ Maybe when I get out of jail ___

X marked the maybe. Dave smiled from ear to ear. And then he touched her hand, CO be damned.

"Now that we've gotten *that* out of the way," he said, "let's get you home."

*****

The day before summations, the court was made aware of a new witness for the prosecution. Dave vehemently objected. He hadn't been notified of the witness and was therefore unprepared to cross examine. Judge Heinrich overruled the objection and allowed the witness' testimony, giving Dave less than 24 hours to prepare his cross. This was even more a surprise considering every motion since the confrontation in Heinrich's chambers had miraculously gone his way. Dave had no idea who this witness could be or what they'd have say. But when he found out he was more confused than ever.

The next day, Kim Lee Davis took the stand and told everything she knew, up to and including seeing the shooter enter and exit the house. When asked to identify the person she saw entering and leaving Mr. Mbungalo's home, she pointed at Brenda.

Dave threw everything he could at her, which wasn't much considering he had so little time to prepare. He brought her character into question. Her criminal background. Insinuated that she was giving her testimony in exchange for felony gun charges being dropped on her father. The prosecution objected as Dave went on even after the judge had sustained the objection. He was warned, and the jury was instructed to disregard most of what he exclaimed.

Summations went as they typically do, with the prosecution painting the defendant a vengeful monster, while the defense argued the opposite. The jury received their instructions and court was adjourned.

Dave went back to the holding area to speak with Brenda one last time before the jury came back with their verdict. He walked in seething and slammed his briefcase down on the table. "What the fuck was that? Can somebody please tell me what's going on here? Because I'm lost you know."

Brenda was stone faced. Curiously calm. "Dave. I think its best that you don't know. But it'll work out."

"What the hell does that mean and who is this girl? I thought you said you trusted me, Brenda?"

"I do. I trust you. Believe me I trust you, but it's not just me I'm thinking about here. It's not just about my life. I wish it were but it's not."

"I still don't get it." He lowered his voice to a whisper. "Did you do this?"

She sighed. "I've had a lot of time to think. I've gone over this in my mind a thousand times. This is the only way I can make sure that everyone gets what they want. Well, what they need, which is more important. My son is sick. Maybe I can't fix that, but I can make sure he doesn't spend the rest of his life in jail. It's what I have to do."

Brenda went on to explain her plan. It was a complete longshot, but if it worked everyone would be all right...eventually.

Dave leaned back in the chair. He took a few minutes. Trying to figure how this could possibly work. Looking at it from every possible angle. He just didn't see it happening. He shook his head at her. "No. You're taking a risk, Brenda. A huge risk. Not to mention obstructing justice. I wouldn't be doing my job if I didn't tell you that. As a matter of fact, I shouldn't even be listening to this."

"I know."

"What if this doesn't turn out the way you think? What if it all blows up in your face? Are you prepared to deal with it?"

Brenda was getting sick of defending her plan. The ball was already rolling on it and there was no turning back so she didn't need to hear no more naysaying. She'd already had enough of it from Aunt Pat. "Yes. Yes, I am. So stop badgering me. You'll get paid either way, so don't worry about it."

Dave glared at her in disgust. "Are you kidding me? Is that why you think I'm doing this?"

"Well, isn't it?" Brenda regretted the comment as soon as it came out of her mouth.

"Wow. Ok, then." He stood and grabbed his briefcase. "Since you've got it all figured out, I guess there's nothing more for me to do here. Good luck to you Mrs. Johnson." He motioned to the guard and left without looking back.

Judgement Day

Three days came and went with no word from the court. Nothing from Dave. After the word got out about Kim's testimony, a dozen people had come down to the jail to see Brenda. She refused every one of them. Even Aunt Pat.

Brenda wasn't sure about what she had done after all. It seemed like a good idea. It seemed like the best option at the time. This way everyone would ultimately win. But would they? If it backfired how much time would she really have to do? Should she have just taken the plea? There would be jail time either way. She tried to put it out of her mind. The decision had already been made and there was no turning back so there was no point in second and third guessing it. She would have given her left tit for a bottle of Grey Goose right about then.

Two more days went by before she heard from the court. The verdict came in on a Friday afternoon. The first warm day of spring, which brought the spectators out of the woodwork. Aunt Pat rounded everyone up to show support. And everyone came.

The courtroom was full, to capacity. Tay and his mother sat directly behind the prosecution. When Brenda was escorted in she noticed Keisha walking into the courtroom holding her baby. Keisha settled in beside Tay and handed him the baby. Brenda wondered how Brandy was handling that.

Missy, Brandy, Mandy and both Pat's sat on the first row behind Brenda. Behind them were Uncle Edward and Aunt Carolyn, Uncle Floyd and Aunt Bessie. The cousins from the Southside. The twins came with their crew from Baltimore. Brenda's friends were behind them and then there was the rest of Ridgewood Terrace.

Dave sat beside Brenda, trying to focus on everything but her. He shuffled papers needlessly, engaged in some meaningless chatter with Petty Ty and scribbled notes on his legal pad here and there.

The bailiff instructed the courtroom to come to its feet. "All rise for the honorable Judge Mark P. Heinrich." The judge strolled out of chambers and took his place behind the bench. He leaned down to speak with the clerk for a moment and then motioned to the bailiff.

The Bailiff instructed the courtroom to come to its feet once again. "Please rise for the jurors." The jurors filed in and took their seats in the box to the left of the room. Brenda looked them over. With the exception of a sour faced elderly gentlemen who clearly didn't want to be there and a twenty something young woman who looked like she'd done a little too much partying the night before, most of the jurors were expressionless. No doubt ready to get to business so they could be excused for the weekend.

The courtroom was asked to take their seats and Judge Heinrich started the proceedings.

The clerk read from her docket sheet. "Case number 12-52075, the District of Columbia vs. Brenda Elaine James-Johnson."

The judge asked for counsel's introduction for the record. Both counsel stood and stated their names with the parties represented. When they were seated Judge Heinrich continued.

"I have been informed that the jury has reached a verdict. But before that verdict is read I'm going to take this opportunity, as I do in every case, to ask, respectfully that the courtroom remain quiet after the reading. Cases of this nature can be very emotionally charged and though the proceedings have remained fairly civil to this point, I feel it is necessary to iterate the importance of allowing the proceedings to move forward without disruption. That said, if there is anyone present who does not feel that they can adhere to this request, I ask that you take this moment to step outside of the courtroom." He allowed a few seconds pass. "Ok, no takers. Then I'll assume that everyone understands. After the verdict is read, the clerk will poll the jury. Alright then. Will the defendant please rise?"

Brenda, David and his part time paralegal Andrew stood facing the jury. The judge continued. "You may proceed at this time madam clerk."

The clerk summoned the foreperson. "At this time will the foreperson please rise and state your number for the record."

A very stern looking forty something woman in a smart gray skirt suit stood from her seat and responded "Number 12."

"Thank you, madam foreperson. How do you find the defendant, Brenda Elaine James-Johnson as to count one, first degree premeditated murder as to Fridaye Mbungalo?"

There was a brief pause as the woman turned and looked directly at Brenda. "As to count one, we the jury find the defendant, guilty as charged."

Aunt Carolyn screamed at the top of her lungs, "Noooooo!!!!!!" which frightened Mandy, causing her to wail and then the rest of the family completely broke down.

Missy held Brandy, who held Mandy as they cried together. Aunt Pat held a distraught PJ in her arms, a place he hadn't been in many years. Uncle Edward prayed aloud and not to be outdone, Aunt Bessie summoned the ghost from Thanksgiving and fainted in the aisle.

The clerk continued on, speaking louder, above the noise. "How do you find the defendant, Brenda Elaine James-Johnson as to count two, possession of a firearm in the commission of a felony."

"As to count two, we the jury find the defendant, guilty as charged."

"How do you find the defendant, Brenda Elaine James-Johnson as to count three assault with intent to murder?"

"As to count three, we the jury find the defendant, guilty as charged."

By the time the reading was done the courtroom was in total chaos. The James family cried out while the rest of Ridgewood Terrace cursed the court for its decision. The consensus from the Terrace, that resonated throughout the courtroom was "This is some BULLSHIT!"

Daye's mother was the only one still seated as her head was still bowed in silent prayer. Tay helped her to her feet and led his little family out of the courtroom before it got too crazy. They stepped over Aunt Bessie and out of the courtroom.

Judge Heinrich banged his gavel until it nearly broke and ordered the courtroom cleared so that the jury could be polled and the proceedings concluded.

The scene was worse than any nightmare Brenda had ever dreamed. Her face was stoic, but her heart broke for her daughters, as she heard them yelling out for her. She couldn't bear to look back at them. The noise and the confusion and the screaming and the crying was getting to her. With help from one of the marshal's, the bailiff ushered the emotional crowd out of the courtroom but the cries and protesting could still be heard long after the heavy mahogany doors closed behind them.

Brenda held herself together amazingly well until she turned around and caught a glimpse of a teary eyed Brandy pulling Mandy out of the room. Mandy was still screaming and reaching back for her. Suddenly she thought of how long it would be before she'd get to see her baby girls again. MJ came to mind. Her baby boy. It took the wind out of her. The tears fell. She mouthed, *Lord what have I done.*

Though David anticipated the worst, his heart still sank when the guilty verdict was read. He would have given anything to bring Brenda home that day. He could see that Brenda was now afraid and unsure. Gone was the criminal mastermind from the jail house just days before. The one who had everything under control. He was staring at the woman, the mother afraid of what would become of her life and the lives of her children. Without regard for Judge Heinrich, Petty or any of the courtroom officials, he touched her chin, gently nudging her to face him and he mouthed, *I got you.*

Petty Ty didn't bother to conceal his smirk; mentally patting himself on the back for a job well done. He cleared the table of his paperwork, fastened his briefcase and thought, *Good. One less murderous nigger on the streets of DC.*

Nothing got past Judge Heinrich. The smirk cost Petty his next two cases.

Once the courtroom was cleared, and quieted, the clerk polled the jury. One by one they affirmed the guilty verdicts and each affirmation chipped away at Brenda's confidence in the plan. She stood on shaky legs as the judge thanked the jury for their service and excused them. Calendars were checked and sentencing was set for six weeks from that day. The young marshal walked over to Brenda with handcuffs and she knew it was real. It was official. It was over. For now.

Epilogue

Labor pains were coming fast and furiously. She was more than ready. The doctor's orders were followed to the tee. Prenatal pills, a healthy diet, proper exercise. Missy didn't miss one Lamaze class. Still she wasn't prepared for what was happening. The doctor gave the instruction to push. Beads of sweat had formed on her brow. It was time.

The first push brought the bundle of joy to crowning. She breathed, focused and the second push was so strong the baby nearly slid out of the doctor's hands onto the floor. It was beautiful. Missy insisted on cutting the cord. She couldn't stop the tears from flowing if she wanted to.

She laid the beautiful chocolaty baby girl down on Brandy's chest.

"Well sweetheart. Looks like we got us another James Girl. Have you thought about a name?"

"I really wanted to name her after you Aunt Missy."

"Oh, God no. Give this child her own identity. One Melissa in the family is plenty. Besides, I always hated that name."

"Ok, then I like Misa. What about Misa?"

"Hmmm. Misa. Misa James. That doesn't sound bad at all. What about her middle name? Wouldn't you like to include your moth…"

Brandy snapped. "No! I wouldn't."

Missy didn't bother to inquire into Brandy's attitude. "Well ok then. Misa James it is." She picked up her beautiful grandniece and held her close. Missy was as happy as she'd ever been. She kissed her on the forehead and thought to herself, this one's gonna be different. This one's gonna be a superstar. I'm gonna make sure of it.

Lost in her thoughts, she didn't even hear the child's mother calling. "Aunt Missy. Can I hold my baby now? Hello. Aunt Missy…"

*****

The ride to Blue Falls seemed to take days instead of hours.

Time always seemed to drag when you wanted to get high and couldn't. An hour after posting bail, Aunt Pat put MJ on a Greyhound. A one-way ride to the south.

Eleven hours after its departure from D.C., the bus pulled into a terminal that seemed to be in the middle of nowheresville. He was the last passenger on the bus, and the Brown clan stood outside waiting for him. They didn't wait for him to step off the bus, they all walked on.

"Where ya bags at boy?"

MJ didn't know what to think. He'd never seen these little men before in his life. They was supposed to be his cousins, but these wasn't no cousins of his. The stocky looking one yelled at him, "Where ya bag at nigga?"

He pointed at the big black duffel bag in the overhead. "It's right there."

The little dude picked up the bag and carried it off the bus while two other little ones grabbed the back of his shirt and pushed him off the bus.

"You getting high, boy?!" Yet another little man grabbed him by the back of the neck. "Nah he ain't getting high. Brown men don't get high. Right boy?"

MJ was terrified. He felt like he was on an episode of scared straight, but unlike half of the boys on the show he was really scared. Who were these people? Was this really his family? He was about to find out. They threw him in the back of the pickup with the duffel and took off down a dirt road.

*****

The custody hearing went without a hitch. Brenda signed over her rights to the girls after her conviction and Missy happily welcomed her beautiful nieces/daughters into her home. Once they were settled she enrolled Brandy into the private school that she attended in Georgetown. Mandy was bussed to Chevy Chase to a school for children with special needs. She was diagnosed with Pervasive Development Disorder, a mild form of autism. Just three months of therapy and she was communicating better than ever, making great progress. Missy hired a nanny for Misa and worked part time from home so she could spend more time with her girls.

She'd heard that Chucky moved back to L.A. and was engaged to a neo-soul singer from Philly. It didn't matter. She'd just been blessed with the best gift she could have ever asked for – motherhood. And that was all that mattered in her world.

*****

Aunt Pat made the long drive to Ohio alone. PJ didn't need to know about it. When she finally reached her destination, she sat in the parking lot watching the residents as they enjoyed their daily outdoor activities. The weather was nice out that day. A sunny 83 degrees. They'd probably be outside all day.

She walked past the front desk undetected. The reception area was empty. Most of the nurses and apparently the receptionist was outside enjoying the early summer. She walked down the hallways searching for room number 312.

The number system seemed a little out of order, but it wasn't long before she reached him. She opened the door, and there he was, lying back watching an old episode of *Sanford and Son* and sipping on ice water.

"Hello Ronnie. Long time no see." When he saw Pat, his eyes bucked and he choked as a jagged piece of ice lodged itself in his throat. He reached out to Pat but she just stood there. His face turned purple and shortly after his body went limp. Ronnie Holmes closed his eyes for the very last time.

Aunt Pat resisted the urge to put hands on him anyway. There was no need. This time good karma beat sweet revenge to the finish line. It was time to go home.

*****

The appeal took 26 months. About that length of time for Kim to come out of "hiding" and write a letter to the police recanting her testimony. At least that was the story being told. For her honesty, she received a 13-month sentence for perjury, a Louis bag filled with three hundred $100 bills, and a promise of protection while she was inside. Too bad nobody told her about the second part of the plan.

*****

Dave was waiting for Brenda at the gate. They shared a tender kiss. The first *real* one from the outside of a state correctional facility.

The drive from the Fluvanna Correctional Center for Women in Troy, Virginia to Upper Marlboro, Maryland took them just under four hours. The top was down on the convertible and the happy couple held hands until they reached the steps of the courthouse. No pomp and circumstance, no sappy vows or teary eyes peering dreamily from behind a veil. Just two people taking care of the business that cemented their love in the eyes of the law for a lifetime.

The backseat of the convertible brimmed with gifts. Brenda was on her way to see her babies. To give them the wonderful news and bring them home. Their new home. A palatial estate in the wealthy suburbs of McClean, Virginia.

Mama had done quite well for herself this time. She'd struggled and sacrificed and compromised her whole life and now it was *her* time. Brenda was ready to live. A good, right life with a good man, free of all the drama and lookin over her shoulder. She'd been through hell and back and finally, everything would be perfect. But she'd learn soon enough. Things aren't always what they seem.

About The Author

F.J. Stevens is a creative writer, a native Washingtonian with an immense love for her city and a wildly vivid imagination.

She spent the better part of the last 20 years in corporate America, until the day that a corporate merger (and a fairly generous severance package) sent her home to her sofa, where she was able to exhale, put up her feet for a while and pen her first novel, the first in a series of gritty urban family sagas, "James Girls".

F.J. loves to hear from readers so please, visit her website www.fjstevens.com, email her at info@fjstevens.com and connect on social media for more info on the James Girls, upcoming projects, promotions and events.

https://www.facebook.com/F.J.Steven.books